THE SONG THE
OGRE SANG

THE SONG THE OGRE SANG
Copyright © 2018 by Peter Fane

Published by Silver Goat Media, LLC, Fargo, ND 58108. This publication is protected by copyright, and permission should be obtained from the publisher prior to any reproduction, storage in a retrieval system, or transmission in any form or by any means, electronic, mechanical, photocopying, recording, or likewise. SGM books are available at discounts, regardless of quantity, for K-12 schools, churches, non-profits, or other educational institutions. To obtain permission(s) to use material from this work, or to order in bulk, please submit a written request to Silver Goat Media, LLC, PO Box 2336, Fargo, ND 58108, or contact SGM directly at: info@silvergoatmedia.com.

This book was designed and produced by Silver Goat Media, LLC. Fargo, ND U.S.A. www.silvergoatmedia.com
SGM and the SGM goat are trademarks of Silver Goat Media, LLC.

Cover art: Kan Liu and Lucia Xiang, *The War Singers* © 2018 SGM
Cover design: Travis Klath © 2018 SGM
Author Photo: Tamara Weets © 2016 SGM

This book was typeset in Perpetua Silver by Cady Ann Rutter.

ISBN-10: 0-9858212-0-5
ISBN-13: (Silver Goat Media) 978-0-9858212-0-3

A portion of the annual proceeds from the sale of this book is donated to the Longspur Prairie Fund.
www.longspurprairie.org

Started by

Peter Fane is on Facebook, Twitter, and Instagram. Let's talk dragons!

First SGM printing – December 2018, Fargo, ND. 1.0 – 011218
Printed and bound in the United States of America.

The Song the Ogre Sang

A Tale from the Canon of Tarn

Peter Fane

SGM

This story is for Daniel—
true of heart.

The Kingdom of Remain spans all space and memory.

It is the Eternal Kingdom, the Silver Kingdom, an ancient sphere born of our love and our sorrow, our blood and our joy.

The Kingdom of Remain encompasses countless stars and minds. It has served our people for millennia. And we have served it in return.

The Kingdom of Remain is our place. It is our home.

The Kingdom of Remain is our legacy. It is our story.

It is the only tale we have worth telling.

The following events take place in the Twenty-Eighth Year of Dorómy III, Founding Year 12,040.

Cast of Characters

The following characters are family members, soldiers, or henchmen loyal to Bellános Dallanar. This side of the Remain's High House resides in the Tarn, the High Keep of the Duchy of Kon.

Coat of Arms — Acasius's Star in silver on a field of high blue.

High Lord Bellános Dallanar, Duke of Kon and Ward of the Tarn. Also known as "The Silver Fox," or – in loyalist circles – as "the High King," or simply as "the King," the younger brother of Dorómy Dallanar with whom he disputes claim to the Silver Throne.

High Lady Adara Dallanar, Bellános's wife and queen, the Mistress of the Tarn; also known as "Adara the Good."

Lord Tomas Dallanar, Lady Adara's firstborn; assassinated in F.Y. 12,039.

Lady Eíra Dallanar, the Duchess of Aradan Primu and Lord Tomas's wife; assassinated in F.Y. 12,039.

Princess Kyla Dallanar, Lady Eíra's firstborn, a girl of fourteen years.

Bruno, a cloud mastiff, Lady Kyla's protector and friend.

Lily, a cloud mastiff, Bruno's mother, protector and friend of High Lady Adara.

Prince Tarlen Dallanar, Lady Eíra's second-born, a boy of eleven years.

Ponj, an ogre of Jallow, son of Colj, and the sworn shield of Lord Tomas's children, Tarlen's protector and friend.

Princess Susan Dallanar, Lady Eíra's third-born, a girl of seven years.

LORD MICHAEL DALLANAR, Lady Adara's second-born, the Dark Lord of Kon, the High General of the Tarn, and the wielder of the Vordan, a warrior of legendary ferocity.

STEPHEN YATES, Captain of the Lord Michael's High Guard.

LORD DOLDON DALLANAR, Lady Adara's third-born, Master and Defender of the Tarn's Kitchens, Wards, and Armories, a feaster and lover of life and day.

CELINE QUAY, Captain of Lord Doldon's Guard.

GART PYLON, the Chief Steward of the Tarn, one of Bellános's oldest friends.

MASTER FALMON D' JYRE, Weapons Master of the Tarn.

CORDEN SHUM, co-janitor of the Fourth Gallery of Cannon.

TELLY CROOT, co-janitor of the Fourth Gallery of Cannon.

TENDAL "CHIEF" YOP, BENJY DALTER, JUDER LOWN, MATEO ZOUDER, CRAZY BILL FEMP, VALERI PENANCE, ROST GON-NERDUN, STEF TORN, JASS XI-SWOL, GILDA BORNWINDER, KAN ZEBBER, LITTLE DAN EADLE, cannon cleaners of various ages.

GEORGE CADENS, Second Steward of the Tarn.

ERIKA CADENS, George's daughter, a girl of six years.

LORD GAREN DALLANAR, Lady Adara's fourth-born, the Lord Librarian of Remain, Master of Spies, and Finder of Secrets, a scholar and mind unmatched in the Realm.

BRADLEY DURN, Captain of Lord Garen's High Guard.

KELTON TOLLER, Lord Garen's Chief Huntsman, Master of Beasts, Raptors, and Scouts; killed during the first year of the Siege of the Tarn, F.Y. 12,038.

GEORGIA TOLLER, Kelton Toller's widow.

FILIP TOLLER, Kelton Toller's firstborn, a scout and herald of fifteen years.

Jordun Sledder, Delen Quine, and Brode Tellerman, the scouts of Filip Toller's squad.

Nordo Ness, Lord Garen's Chief Librarian, an ancient man from the Void.

Lord James Dallanar, Lady Adara's fifth-born, a twin; called "The Executioner" by his brother, Michael.

Derek Pylon, Captain of Lord James's Guard, also son of Gart Pylon.

Lord Jeremy Dallanar, Lady Adara's sixth-born, a twin; drowned in the Sea of Ice at the age of eight, F.Y.12,029.

Lady Katherine Dallanar, Lady Adara's seventh-born; recently returned to the Tarn from Paráden and parts unknown.

Captain Fellen Colj, an ogre of Jallow, Chief of the Tarn's Watch, new Captain of Lady Katherine's Guard.

Vudj, Khadj, Rudj, Doj, and others, Captain Colj's ogres.

The Davanórian Contingent, Loyal to Bellános Dallanar

Captain Anna Dyer, a renowned dragon rider of Dávanor, a girl of seventeen years; beloved by Michael Dallanar.

Moondagger, a war dragon of Dávanor, Anna's mount, pure white, blind, 22 paces long, three years old.

Master Roger Khondus, Master of Dragons of House Dradón, a Davanórian veteran.

Master Bengamon Zar, Master of Arms, an Anorian veteran.

Gregory, a messenger dragon of Dávanor, Master Zar's pet and friend, 11 palms long, four hundred and seven years old.

THE FOLLOWING CHARACTERS ARE FAMILY MEMBERS, SOLDIERS, OR HENCHMEN LOYAL TO DORÓMY DALLANAR. THIS SIDE OF THE REMAIN'S HIGH HOUSE RESIDES IN THE KÁLADAR, THE HIGH KEEP OF PARÁDEN.

COAT OF ARMS — Acasius's Star in gold on a field of creamy white.

HIGH LORD DORÓMY DALLANAR, Duke of Paráden and Ward of the Káladar. Also known as "the Iron Lion," or — in loyalist circles — as "the Pretender," or simply "the Traitor," the older brother of Bellános Dallanar with whom he disputes claim to the Silver Throne.

HIGH GENERAL VYMON RUGE, Duke of Rigel, Lord of the Siege of the Tarn, one of Bellános's and Dorómy's oldest friends.

LORD JANNON RUGE, General Ruge's firstborn, a wastrel and libertine.

LORD JARED RUGE, General Ruge's second-born, a shy and gentle soul.

LORD JON RUGE, General Ruge's third-born, Duke of Kesst, a schemer and narcissist.

HIGH GENERAL JAMES TAVERLY, Count of Nordán, Underlord of the Siege of the Tarn, one of Bellános's and Dorómy's oldest friends.

LADY JANE TAVERLY, Lady of Rigel, General Taverly's first born.

HIGH GENERAL CORLEN LESSIP, Duke of Peléa, Underlord of the Siege of the Tarn, Dorómy's spy master and torturer.

HIGH GENERAL ANTHONY CAROLE, Count of Nordán, Underlord of the Siege of the Tarn, one of Bellános's and Dorómy's oldest friends.

HIGH GENERAL ADJOA SERÁN, Countess of Ebavia, Underlady of the Siege of the Tarn, one of Bellános's and Dorómy's oldest friends.

HIGH GENERAL BAO SHU, Count of Ferragias, Underlord of the Siege of the Tarn, one of Bellános's and Dorómy's oldest friends.

HIGH GENERAL KRODAN, Duke of Yor, Underlord of the Siege of the Tarn, a man without mercy.

CAPTAIN MARDEN JULANE, Captain of the Guard of the High House of Gelánen and High Lady Eleanor Julane's uncle, a man out of his depth.

"Many Princes have asked: 'What makes the perfect Soldier? Is it Courage? Is it Ferocity? Is it Discipline? Is it Loyalty?' All will make for a great Warrior — but they are nothing without Heart. Without Heart, a courageous Soldier is a Contradiction. Without Heart, a fierce Soldier is a Savage. Without Heart, a disciplined Soldier is a Slave. Without Heart, a loyal Soldier is a Zealot. A Warrior's Heart is the Source of a most sacred Power, binding all Strands together, yet standing wholly on its own. For this Reason, I say: 'Give me but one Soldier, true of Heart, and I will give you a World.'"

— Katherine II, *The Canon of Tarn*, "Prolegomena to Imperial Tactics and Diplomacies." F.Y. 189

PROLOGUE

"YOU ARE CERTAIN? You have no doubt?"

"It is he, my Lady. Without question. The one for whom we have waited. And he found us, as was foretold."

"Does he require our protection?"

"No, my Lady. He is a perfect warrior, a living weapon, and they love him for it. He shall soon command all the Kingdom's loyal hosts; the Realm shall tremble."

"Do they know what he is?"

"Some suspect. But they are quick to forget — and easily misled."

"Does he know what he is?"

"He feels our song within him, but understands not what it means, nor whence it comes."

"And what of the child queen?"

"She is a threat, my Lady. Especially to him. She is cunning, she is strong, and she does not fear him. But she is young — and entirely alone."

"Is she vulnerable?"

"Perhaps. The coming three days hold many opportunities."

"The work must be protected."

"The promise must be kept."

THE FIRST DAY

1

"WHAT'S A MATTER, big fella?" Little Dan Eadle asked Storm-hammer.

Stormhammer — an enormous battle cannon — didn't answer.

Little Dan frowned, tucked his cleaning rag into his belt, and rubbed his hands together. It was freezing down here! Cold and dark, the stone walls wet and shiny like they always were, but *real* cold tonight, a nasty cold that got down in your bones, froze your toes into little frozen beans.

"Frozen beans!" Dan hollered, kind of singsong. "That's what I mean! Frozen beans!"

Little Dan nodded to himself, stepped off his toolbox, and picked up his clay lamp. Then he stamped his feet to get blood flowing to the beans and walked around Stormhammer head to tail, running the little lamp's flame along the cannon's huge side. He was looking for smears or smudges. Those things could make the big fella upset. And even though Stormy didn't have any beans to freeze, Dan was pretty darn sure the big boy didn't like the cold none, either.

"I miss somethin', Stormy?" Dan shivered. The lamp shook. The orange flame wobbled and smoked. "That why you upset? I do it bad somewheres?"

He cocked his ear toward the cannon, listening.

Stormhammer didn't answer.

Dan nodded and gave the gun a pat. Stormhammer's huge muzzle looked exactly like the mouth of a big, roaring dragon: lips pulled back from big dragon fangs, dragon eyes squeezed shut like he was getting ready to breathe fire.

A draft flickered Dan's lamp. He cupped the little flame to protect it. A drip of water plinked somewhere in the dark. The air was so cold, you could see your own breath.

"Dunno what you're worried for, Stormy." Dan scratched

his head. "No, sir. You're lookin' good. *Real* good. You're a fine lookin' dragon. For truth!"

But there *was* something off.

Little Dan was only eight years old, but he'd been cleaning the Tarn's battle cannon since he turned six. The Chief and the others were always saying that Dan didn't know his head from a hole in the ground. That might be true. But Dan did know this: He knew when there was something wrong with one of his guns.

2

IT WAS THREE bells before dawn. Little Dan had been working in the Tarn's lower armory most of the night. The armory was a huge room, about a hundred paces long, its walls made of big, grey stones. Here and there, iron clamps and hooks for torches and lanterns and whatnot stuck out of the joints, but none of that stuff was lit, so it was dark, so dark you could barely see one side of the place to the other. A drip of water kept drip-dripping somewhere. And it was cold. Cold and dark like a cave.

Now, some folks might think that working your tail off in a

butt-freezing dungeon in the dead-middle of night was tough — or at least not so much fun.

But not Little Dan.

"No, sir. It's *good*. The best job there is. Yes, sir. For truth!"

The best time of the day, the best place to work, the best everything. The cannon masters and war adepts and all the others had left a few bells past, and the rest of the cleaning crews had long since crawled off to their bunks.

So it was dark, and it was cold, but it was good.

"They might have the smarts, but they dunno *that* secret." Dan patted Stormy's side.

The secret was this: Little Dan loved being down here in the cold, cleaning the big guns. He loved listening to the cannon's old songs in the middle of night. And — more than anything — he *loved* being a soldier.

"Yes, sir!" Dan walked along Stormy's side, holding his lamp up, looking into every nook and cranny. "Good soldier I be! One, two, three! Yes, am, me! One, two, three!"

And he was always trying to get better.

"That's right, boy." Little Dan stopped in his tracks and

growled, making his voice all rough, talking to himself in Master Falmon's rough voice. "Every day's a day to do better. Every day." Now Master Falmon, *he* had the smarts. Yes, sir. Every day, do better. One of the rules. And Dan was pretty sure that Master Falmon never felt the cold none, either. No, sir.

"Do the best and make it right, every day before the fight!" Dan sang to the dark.

It really was perfect. No pals to play with, nobody to mess with, nobody to get in the way of the work. Just him, a dozen giant battle cannon, and his best friend in the whole world: Stormhammer.

Just how Little Dan liked it.

3

AND THEN DAN saw the spot.

It was just a little thing, right there behind Stormy's eye. Not a big spot, hardly a spot at all, about half the size of a coin.

"Missed a little thing there, Stormy." Dan touched the big gun's side. "Easy fix. Yes, sir. Easy as pie. Sorry 'bout that.

Nothing to worry for."

Little Dan set down his lamp and dragged his toolbox over. He draped his rag over his index finger and squeezed the rag so it pulled tight on his fingertip. Then he spit on his finger, stepped onto his box, and cleaned the spot with his fingertip, polished until the scale shone like buffed silver.

"See, Stormy?" Dan picked up his lamp, squinted at the scale. "Told ya. Nothin' to worry for. No, sir! Real sorry 'bout that. Just a little thing—."

Behind him in the dark, a gloomy reflection lurched in the cannon's side, a hunched beast with hooked wings, hissing fangs.

"Who's there?!" Dan yelped and spun around, banged his elbow on Stormy's side, almost dropped his lamp, nearly tripped off his box.

"Who's there?!" He squeaked again at the dark, lifting his lamp, staring wide-eyed into the shadows, his elbow all sore now. The lamp's orange glow made the cannon shadow dance.

Nobody.

"'Course nobody," Dan muttered to himself.

Sometimes, the big guns just showed you scary stuff like that, right there in their skins. Dan's knees shook, and his teeth chattered. He sat on his box, set his lamp away from him so he wouldn't knock it over, and rubbed his sore elbow.

"Ouch."

His shoulder was hurting a little, too. And his legs were cold; freezing.

"Darn pants, you ain't no good." He rubbed his shins up and down, sitting on his box, trying to get warm. "Gotta get back to it, soldier. Can't take breaks." Not how the work got done. Every soldier knew that. Breaks were how you got cold.

"You must be a crazy, sittin' in the cold like that," he said to himself, tapping the center of his own forehead. Then he changed his voice so that it sounded all mellow like Chief Tendal's. "You a *crazy*, Little Dan? A stupid, little *crazy*? Ain't you? *Ain't* you? *Crazy* little *crazy*."

"I might not have the smarts!" Dan answered in his own voice, rubbing his elbow. "Sisters know I'm sorry for it! But I ain't no crazy, Chief! No, sir! I'm a good soldier!"

"You sure, Dan?" Dan asked himself in the Chief's voice.

"You sure you ain't a stupid *and* a crazy?"

"Not a crazy," Dan hollered. "Sisters' truth! No crazies down here! Is there, Stormy?"

Stormhammer didn't answer.

"See?" Dan nodded. "No crazies."

Dan stepped back onto his box and gave Stormy a big hug. Stormy was cold, but Dan hugged him anyway, sharing a bit of his own warmth. He knew it wasn't how a proper soldier would do it, but this was one thing where he really didn't care. And Stormy didn't mind, either. In fact, Dan was pretty sure the big boy liked it.

"Gotta finish up, Stormy." Dan's teeth chattered. "Gotta make sure you're shiny, top to bottom. No dust, no dirt, no nothing."

He got back to wiping the cannon down, going over everything one last time. "No time to waste. And *you*, sir." He patted the big gun. "*You* gotta settle down. No more showing that scary stuff. They'll be countin' on ya, Stormy. High Lords comin' down right soon. Master Falmon said so. Day after 'morrow. High Lords called you up to fight——."

Dan stopped mid-stroke and straightened up.

"Is *that* what's got you all worked up?" He cocked his ear to the big gun's dragon mouth, listened carefully, and then patted Stormy's side. "Shoulda known! You're just *excited*, Stormy. That's all. You're lookin' fine. Real fine. You'll do great. Nobody holds a candle to you, Stormy! Now, how 'bout those chops? Big mutton head."

Little Dan got off his box, scooted it around to the cannon's front, and shook out his rag. He folded it twice, stepped back on the box, and starting on the bottom of Stormy's jaw. Dan thought that the old master from olden times who had made Stormy had done a real good job. Stormy wasn't just a cannon that looked like a dragon. He *was* a dragon. Stormy's pal, Oblivion, was made in the same way, but he looked like a huge, roaring lion. All the other big guns down here were like that. Dawnshatter was a howling wolf. Hakon's Fist and Aaryn's Might were a pair of bellowing bulls. Nightbliss was a screaming gargoyle. Fel's Bane and Rattlin' Jimmy, those two new guns that had just come down a couple months past, they were a couple hissing snakes.

Dan patted Stormhammer's cheek. "But dragons are the best. Ain't that right, Stormy?"

Again, Stormhammer didn't answer.

Stormy might not be talking now, but it was still true. Dragons *were* the best. And sometimes, if nobody was around, if you were real nice to him, you could put your hand on him and you could hear his dragon song. Yes, sir. Just whispers at first, then a kind of warm hum up your fingers, up your hands, through your arms, all the way to your heart.

Little Dan nodded.

An olden song from the olden times.

"A song of silver and blood," he whispered respectfully.

Stormhammer's song.

Little Dan stopped polishing and glanced around. Then he scooted his toolbox away from Stormy's muzzle, back to the side of Stormy's head, and stepped onto his box. There, he pressed his chest against Stormy's cheek, spread his arms wide and listened.

He knew it'd be cold at the beginning, but he wanted to hear it. There was always something, if you waited long enough. You had to be patient. You had to be nice to Stormy. And you had to wait super quiet, like a little mouse . . . .

Dan closed his eyes and pressed his ear against Stormy's

freezing scales, the silver smooth and hard against his cheek. He stretched out his arms, resting his chest against the cannon's cold curve, letting some of his own warmth move into the big gun . . . .

There!

Soft at first. Real soft. Right there, where you almost couldn't hear it. A kind of low beat, a kind of low thump. A bit of warmth coming into your fingers. A warm tingle. A warm hum, right on the edge of your hearing, like you could just barely hear it. Then a beat, a kind of cry, like those birds up in the sky, warmer now, warming your chest up, the thumping coming up and down, up and down. It felt good, it felt warm, like a coming summer storm, a distant cry, far away, not forever, not today. Like a thing that *wanted* to come closer, wanted to come out — but got pushed back, closer and back, closer and back . . . .

"That's right, Stormy," Little Dan whispered. "That's right." He hummed his own little song back to the big cannon, his eyes shut tight. He was getting nice and toasty now, Stormy's silver warming up. The song was still far away, but close enough to get you warm. One day it would be here, Dan knew that; one day the song would come all the way out. But not today. And that didn't matter, because he was warm now, so warm.

"Feels good," Dan muttered. Then he laughed, holding onto Stormy's warm side. "*You* the crazy one, Stormy." Dan nuzzled the big gun. "Yes, sir! You the one! Ha-ha!"

Little Dan smiled and shook his head.

How could *he* be a crazy?

He was warm, wasn't he?

And if Stormy's song made him warm, then how could he be a crazy?

"You got the *best* song, Stormy," Dan whispered, pushing his chest against Stormhammer's warm scales. "Dragons *so* good——."

"What you doin' huggin' that gun, Eadle?" a rough voice growled behind him.

Everything vanished at once.

Stormy's song, his music, his warmth – bang and gone just like that. The icy cold rushed back like silent dark.

"Master Falmon, sir!" Little Dan yelped, jumped, spun, banged his sore elbow again, nearly fell off his box as he tried to salute. "Sorry, sir! Master Falmon, sir! I – I was just—. I – I'm sorry, sir!"

Dan wobbled, steadied himself on his box, stood tall, saluted, fist across his chest, spat on his rag, and started polishing Stormy like mad, even though he'd just cleaned that same spot not two moments ago.

Master Falmon grunted and walked up to Stormhammer. He carried an iron lantern. He looked Dan over with his one good eye. Master Falmon's other eye was covered by a patch of old leather. A tattoo of a six-pointed sun, the Tarn's symbol, marked the Master's temple. The rest of the Master's face was a mess, his nose smashed flat, his right nostril nothing but a slit. His good eye was mostly closed by another big scar that ran from the top of his head to his jaw. His white hair was shaved short. His hands were twisted and bent, his knuckles busted by a thousand fights. Crazy Bill, one of Little Dan's pals, sometimes made fun of Master Falmon when the Master wasn't around. But not Little Dan. No, sir! That wasn't a good game, and Dan knew better. One of the most important rules: Never make fun of another soldier.

Master Falmon hung his lantern from an iron hook, gave

Stormhammer a pat — and stopped short, keeping his palm on the cannon for a long moment.

Then he looked down at Dan.

"What you been doin' down here, boy?"

"Cleaning, sir!" Dan yelled as he cleaned, not looking up. "Working! Soldier's duty! Every day, that's the way! Sorry, sir! Clean, clean, clean — makes our guns mean, mean, mean!"

Master Falmon didn't say anything, but he kept his hand on Stormy's side for a while. When Dan glanced up, Master Falmon was looking at him, a weird look on his face.

"Cleaning?" Master Falmon asked.

"Cleaning! Yes, sir!" Dan swallowed and nodded. "Every day, sir! Best way, sir! Cleaning! That's what Little Dan does! Yes, sir! Master Falmon, sir!"

"Hmm." Master Falmon said. He didn't say anything for a bit. Then he nodded. "The cannon masters and war adepts'll need him at six bells. Some tests this morning. He gonna be ready? Big day, day after tomorrow."

Little Dan turned, stood straight on his box, and hollered at the top of his lungs, "Yes, sir! Master Falmon, sir!" Then he saluted again, remembered that he'd already saluted not a moment before, blinked, and turned back to his cleaning. One good thing about Master Falmon was that the Master was *fair*. He could be hard, but he was fair, too. If you did a good job for Master Falmon, then you were good.

"You finish Oblivion?" Master Falmon asked.

"Yes, sir! Master Falmon, sir!" Dan shouted as he cleaned, not looking up. The light from Master Falmon's lantern made Oblivion's lion shadow wobble.

"Very well," Master Falmon said. "Keep to it."

Little Dan nodded and kept polishing. You can do it, soldier. The good part was that he wasn't cold anymore, not a bit. The bad part was that his elbow was *real* sore where he'd banged it, and his shoulder had been ouchy already—.

Master Falmon turned and said, "Lord Michael, Lord Doldon, they're ready."

Little Dan's hair stood on end.

The High Lords of the Tarn!

Dan took a breath, swallowed, looked up a moment, then remembered to keep his head down, to keep working.

He hadn't heard them come in.

But now, right there in Stormy's side, he could see their reflections.

The Lords of the Tarn.

Lord Michael and Lord Doldon.

You knew it was Lord Michael because of his black clothes. He was the best fighter in the Kingdom, he always wore black, and he could kill you just by looking at you. Sisters' truth. Lord Doldon, he was Lord Michael's brother. He was a little taller and a little bigger, but he wasn't as good a fighter. Lord Doldon was the one in charge of the Tarn's walls, and towers, and guns, other stuff like that. He was always down here.

Dan risked another peek over his shoulder and saw that the High Lords weren't alone. Behind Lord Michael was a black-haired lady in silver armor with a silver sword hanging from her belt. Dan had never seen her before. Beside the black-haired lady, there was a bald, purple dwarf. The Tarn's six-pointed sun was tattooed in white on the dwarf's forehead and a little blue dragon sat on his shoulder. On the other side of the black-haired lady, there was another lady, but this lady had blond hair and wore it in a ponytail.

The blond lady carried a long case like a rifleman would, and a big, grey dog sat next to her, the biggest dog Dan had ever seen. Behind that lady was big Captain Colj. Dan didn't know those ladies and that dwarf, but he *did* know Captain Colj. Yes, sir! Captain Colj was one of the Tarn's Captains of the Guard. He was an ogre, of course, so he was about twice as tall as Lord Doldon, twice as wide, and thick, like a tree. Captain Colj wore a giant suit of ogre-sized armor and carried a huge iron lantern. Everyone knew Captain Colj.

"Guns are looking good," Lord Doldon said. He stepped toward Stormy. His voice was deep and friendly. Then he stepped closer, right beside Dan, and patted Stormy on the nose. "Very good."

Master Falmon grunted.

"What's wrong, Falmon?" Lord Doldon chuckled. He patted Stormy again. "Come on. Look at him shine. He's perfect. Don't think big fella's ever looked better. Even you've got to admit that."

Dan's ears went warm. He tried to work harder. Every day's a day to do better! Yes, sir! But he was polishing so hard, it felt like his arm was gonna fall off, and his darn elbow was killing him. So he bit his lip, blinked, and kept polishing.

"It's not that," Master Falmon muttered.

It went quiet.

Nobody said anything.

Then Lord Michael said, "It always seems wrong to bring these great weapons to bear against our own. Is that not so, Falmon?"

Little Dan didn't really understand what Lord Michael meant, but he could *feel* something inside his words. Lord Michael's voice was way softer than Lord Doldon's, but it filled up the whole room, like magic. Without thinking, Dan stopped polishing and looked at Lord Michael. He couldn't help himself. Lord Michael seemed real sad and real tired, but also real angry. There was something in his eyes, too, something Dan could see but couldn't quite understand, like falling into a dark hole. The little blue dragon squeaked. The purple dwarf fed it a scrap of meat, then wiped his fingers on a napkin tucked into his belt.

Then Dan noticed Captain Colj looking at him. There was a strange look on Captain Colj's big ogre face. Dan knew he should be working. But he'd never seen the Tarn's Lords this close before. And he'd probably never see them like this again. And with Lord Michael's voice, you just *had* to listen. Little Dan couldn't have stopped listening, even if he wanted to.

Lord Michael gestured again at Stormy. "Does it not seem wrong to bring this living fire against our own?"

"As you say," Master Falmon grunted. "They're our men, my Lord." He glanced at the black-haired lady in the silver armor. "No matter what some may say."

The black-haired lady frowned. "You make no distinction between a man who remains loyal to your Lord and King, Master Falmon, and a man who betrays him?" Her voice was hard. Dan didn't understand what she meant exactly, but there was something scary in her voice. "You see no difference between a man who fights for the Realm and a man who fights against it? You surprise me."

"Don't lecture me on loyalty, Captain Dyer," Master Falmon growled. "I've spent as much time on Dávanor as you have, quite a bit more, in fact. And, again, I say: Those are *our* men out there. All of 'em. Whether they serve Dorómy or Bellános, Lion or Fox, each man, each death, is *our* loss.

That's been true of every civil war there's ever been. No different here."

The black-haired lady — Captain Dyer, Master Falmon called her — made like she was going to say something else, but Lord Michael raised his hand and stopped her.

"Agreed, old friend," Lord Michael said. "Agreed. But Ruge and his sons, the others — Serán, Carole, Shu, Taverly, all of them — they're more than our men. They're our comrades, our brothers-in-arms. For this reason we fight: 'Not against our friends or enemies — but for the truth that is the Silver Kingdom, for the truths that are the Kingdom's High Laws, for the truth that is Remain.' And day after tomorrow, Great Sisters protect us, we'll end this fighting for a time, give ourselves pause to bring friends back to the fold. Give a chance, perhaps, for lasting peace."

"Speak my own teachings back to me, eh?" Master Falmon said.

"They're all I know," Lord Michael said. He looked so tired. "In any case, the cannon look excellent. Pass our thanks to your teams. How're our adepts?"

"Exhausted," Master Falmon said. "Can't ask much more

of 'em, my Lord. Some have got a couple days left, some a couple weeks – and that's with the limited fire they're giving now. They need proper rest." The Master glanced at Stormy and Oblivion. "And if the big guns see action during parley, Great Sisters forbid . . . ."

"How're your shifts running now?" the purple dwarf asked. Dan knew that the war adepts sang with the big guns in "shifts," just like cleaners worked in shifts, but he also knew that the adepts didn't sing as much as they used to, because they were so tired. The big guns were tired, too.

"Fair question, Zar." Master Falmon adjusted his eye patch and touched the scar on his forehead. "We had adepts moving through every six bells up until two weeks ago, but we didn't have the manpower to keep up the pace – especially with Ruge throwing everything he has at us day and night. So, we moved them to a four-bell rotation a week ago. Hasn't helped. In fact, made it worse." He shook his head. "It's not the time on the guns that's the issue. It's that there's no time off. And even if we had fresh adepts, the guns themselves are exhausted. It's a mess. Stormhammer and Oblivion have plenty left, but we need to save them, should something real come up."

"Can we bring fresh guns through from Anor or Espónyo?" the purple dwarf, Zar, asked. "What of Dávanor?" He fed his little dragon another scrap of meat.

Master Falmon nodded. "Lord Nor and Lady Dontaigne sent everything they could a year ago. They're under siege themselves; Dontaigne is pressed with force. And Khon-dus sent us everything Dávanor could spare two months back." Master Falmon cocked his head at Captain Dyer. Then he looked at Lord Michael. "We're out-manned and out-gunned. We're driving our adepts to their graves." He gestured at Stormy and Oblivion. "We've got these two left, my Lords. That's it. We must have peace."

Lord Michael looked from Master Falmon to Lord Doldon.

"Hard to disagree, Michael." Lord Doldon frowned. "Not sure what the plan is, but I do know we can't keep this up. Two years since the siege began. Don't know if we need peace, but we do need time. Time to recover."

Captain Colj listened to all of this very carefully, like he was paying special attention to all the words. Captain Dyer frowned. The blond lady with the rifleman's case shivered and crossed her arms, like she was trying to stay warm. The big grey dog lay his big head on top of her boot.

"If parley doesn't work," Master Falmon continued, "if we can't reach an understanding, then we've got near nothing left. And without our great cannon, it'll just be Garen's trees. And when they go, Ruge can storm the Long Bridge whenever he wills. We won't hold. The Tarn will fall."

"The Tarn will *never* fall," Captain Dyer said. Her voice chilled Dan to the bone. "Not while we're here."

Master Falmon made to speak, but Lord Doldon was there first. He wasn't smiling anymore. "I agree with the sentiment, Anna. And I applaud you and Dagger and your squads. But the mathematics — they're real. Dorómy's forces outnumber us ten to one. That ratio changes daily and not in our favor. If we knew that Lord Jor was in-bound with his army, as he promised, then we might be able to wait, to hold, but where is he?" Lord Doldon looked at Lord Michael. "Dorómy moves in earnest, Michael. We now face his very best. At least two battalions of the Silver Guard were spotted a week ago, on their way in. Those boys know how to fight, and they're not afraid to die——."

"And they're fanatically loyal to Dorómy," the blond lady with the ponytail added. It was the first time Dan had heard her voice. It was soft and beautiful.

Captain Colj nodded slowly.

Master Falmon said, "That's right, Lady Kyla." He looked at Lord Michael. "We just heard that parts of the Fourth, Ninth, and Twentieth Legions were moving up. They might be here already."

"I heard that, too." Lord Doldon nodded. "But moving up from *where?*"

"Still looking." Master Falmon shrugged. Then he glanced at Lord Michael and Lord Doldon. "Maybe time to get James back, send him out to see. Any news from him?

Lord Doldon shook his head. "James is the one brother who truly marches to his own drummer."

"Truth." Master Falmon nodded. He looked at Lord Michael. "Might be time to consider alternatives, my Lord."

"Such as?" Captain Dyer asked.

"Not my place to say, Captain." Master Falmon looked at her. "But I can tell you this: Sometimes you can't kill your way out of a problem."

"You sure about that?" Captain Dyer asked.

Beside her, the blond lady, Lady Kyla, closed her eyes.

"I'm sure," Master Falmon growled. "And you'd be sure, too, if—."

"Enough," Lord Michael said softly. His tired eyes were dark, but something moved in the air when he spoke. "Save that talk until after our next days' efforts. My father has given orders. Preparations for parley will continue. The command of the High King will be followed – to the letter."

Captain Dyer and Master Falmon bowed. Lord Michael nodded at Captain Colj. The group started walking away from the cannon, out of the armory, back the way they'd come. The big grey dog snorted, snuffled to his feet, and padded after them.

"Master Falmon," Lord Michael said as they walked away. "I understood you wanted to show me something in the lower vaults."

"Yes, my Lord," Master Falmon answered. "For Colj. For parley."

"So Colj will serve as Garen's honor guard?" the blond lady, Lady Kyla, asked.

"Yes, Ky," Lord Michael answered.

Zar said, "Sensible choice." The little dragon squeaked from his shoulder.

"You know, Falmon," Lord Doldon said as they walked out the door. "Couldn't you have taught Garen a bit more about — I don't know — *fighting*? Isn't that what weapon masters do?"

Master Falmon grunted. "Boy always liked his books and beakers better than honest bullets and blades."

Lord Doldon laughed.

Nobody else did.

Dan watched as they left.

When they were gone, he turned back to his work — and started polishing as hard as he could. His elbow was sore, his shoulder hurt, and it was gonna be worse in the morning, but he couldn't stop.

"Not now," he whispered to himself.

How could he stop?

Never in his whole life had his work been more important.

Master Falmon was counting on him.

The High Lords were counting on him.

The High King was counting on him.

And they were all counting on Stormy, too.

"We *gotta* do good for 'em, Stormy," Dan said, polishing harder than ever, his elbow really hurting now. "We can do it. Gotta do right by 'em. You hear me, Stormy? *Gotta* do good. You hear me?!"

Dan realized that he was yelling at Stormy and stopped.

A big step came from behind him. The orange glow of lantern light.

Dan turned.

It was Captain Colj.

The big ogre captain was standing there, looking down at him, holding his big lantern, a strange look in his deep ogre eyes. He was enormous. One of his ogre hands was bigger than Little Dan's whole chest. His ears were slightly pointed. His big head was almost as big as Little Dan's whole body. The light from his lantern shone in his silver armor and made a giant ogre shadow behind him.

Dan swallowed, bowed his head, and closed his eyes.

He was just so *tired*.

"Should've gone to bed, stupid," he whispered to himself.

He hadn't meant to yell at Stormy.

Stormy was his best friend. For truth.

"I'm sorry, Captain Colj, sir," Dan said, keeping his head down. "Forgive me, sir. I – I know my work, sir. I—. Please. I'm a good soldier. I'm not a . . . well, it won't happen no more like that, sir. I won't yell like that no more. I work harder. I work *way* harder from now on. Please, sir."

And then, not sure what he was doing, Little Dan turned back to his job and started polishing again, waiting for the punishment to come. He didn't look up. He didn't know how giant ogre captains punished bad workers, but he was scared out of his wits to find out.

"You just take it, soldier," Dan whispered as he polished. "You take it, boy."

But Captain Colj didn't do anything or say anything.

Dan kept polishing.

After for a long time, Captain Colj said, "There is an ancient story we tell on Jallow. It was a favorite of my son, Saj. Before death found him. It cannot be told in your tongue. But I will share it, all the same."

Dan didn't look up. He didn't understand what Captain

Colj meant, but he did know that he had to keep going, that he had to show Captain Colj he was a good soldier. Dan was tired, sure. But everyone got tired. Soldier's life. One of the rules.

"Every day's a day to do better," he whispered. "Every day, like today. Every day, there's a way." Besides, if he didn't understand Captain Colj's words, then he might as well just shut his stupid mouth and work.

Then Captain Colj started talking.

But he was talking like Dan had never heard before.

Dan didn't know *any* of these ogre words. Not one. The sound was like rocks crunching together in some old gorge. But it was nice, too, Dan realized.

And as Dan listened, it seemed to him like the grumbling words also had a kind of music inside them, like an ogre song all their own.

Captain Colj talked for a while, and as he talked, Dan kept his head down and worked.

Then Captain Colj finished talking. He waited for a moment, then he took off one of his huge armored gloves, put his big hand on Stormy's side, and closed his eyes.

And then Captain Colj started to hum. It was real low and rumbly, a big sound from his big ogre chest.

Dan looked up and stared.

Captain Colj kept on humming, not opening his eyes.

Dan stood there, blinking.

Then he reached out, put his hand on Stormy's side, bowed his head, and listened to the ogre's deep song.

Dan had never heard anything like it before.

But, no.

That wasn't true.

There *was* something in the ogre's song that Dan *did* know. Something Little Dan could *almost* understand——.

And then Captain Colj stopped humming.

Dan opened his eyes, blinked, and looked up.

Captain Colj was looking down at him.

After a moment, Captain Colj said, "Well done."

His ogre voice was so deep.

Dan swallowed, then nodded. He didn't know what to say, or if he should say anything at all. And his elbow was killing him, so he just nodded again.

"Finish your work," Captain Colj said. "Get some sleep."

Captain Colj looked at Stormy. "In two days, you will face battle together."

Little Dan stared, then blinked.

What did it mean?

Captain Colj looked down at Dan for another long moment. "I will see to it. You will be tested. You will face battle together. You have my word, little soldier."

Then the ogre turned and left, his armored footsteps slow and strong and deep.

Little Dan watched him go.

Then he yawned, gave Stormy one last wipe, and packed his box, made sure everything was just so.

"Goodnight, Stormy." Dan patted Stormy's side. "I go to bed now. You be good down here. See you tomorrow."

Stormhammer didn't answer.

But his great dragon eye followed Little Dan all the way to the door.

4

ABOUT A BELL earlier, in one of the Tarn's underground firing ranges — a long storage cavern that only recently had been converted to training space on account of the siege — fourteen-year-old Kyla Dallanar adjusted the coon skin muffs at her ears, sighted down the barrel of her carbine, and did her best to ignore the sloppy snorts and snuffles of Bruno, her cloud mastiff, who snored on the ground beside her. Kyla was envious. The giant war dog could sleep like the dead.

"All right." She pushed a lock of blond hair from her face and snugged her carbine into her shoulder. "Let's try for perfection."

Kyla's shooting posture was a classic one, that of a standing marksman. In terms of accuracy, it was the most challenging rifleman's stance: leather boots shoulder-width apart, weight on the balls of your feet, back slightly bent, stomach muscles tight. Unlike a prone or kneeling firing position, a standing posture demanded that all stability come from the soldier herself. There was nothing to lean against; you were entirely on your own.

At the center of her carbine's sight, Kyla held her target: a cracked clay jug at the far end of the range, a little over one hundred paces distant. The jug rested on a wooden beam set against an earthen berm, lit by a pair of oil lamps. Filip Toller had helped Kyla set up the range a couple of months ago. It'd been his idea to use the damaged vessels for target practice. Kyla smiled. Filip was practical like that, the son of Kelton Toller, one of the Tarn's most experienced woodsmen, not prone to waste or embellishment. "Might as well get another use out of it." Filip had shrugged in that simple way of his. When he spoke, he looked at her directly, his honest eyes the color of winter sky.

Filip didn't know it — and Kyla would never tell him, *could* never tell him — but his eyes had become quite important to her as of late, lights in the dark. More and more often, especially when he was gone on a mission or out on patrol, Kyla found herself thinking of Filip, his eyes, the rightness she saw therein. "You're a better shot than me," Filip had said last week as they'd practiced down here, the day before Kyla's uncle, Garen, had sent Filip's squad out yet again. "If Lord Garen asked me for our best sharpshooter, I'd tell him it was you." And that was the thing about Filip. He didn't say these things to compliment or to flatter. Kyla would have known it instantly. He said these things because they were true. And it was a relief to talk with someone — to be with someone —

where you didn't have to pretend, where you could just be who you were.

Kyla took a deep breath, finger resting on trigger guard, the carbine's contoured stock snug against her shoulder. "Shooting is an exercise in reason," Master Falmon would always say. "An exercise in science." Kyla agreed entirely. Her finger wouldn't move until she was ready to destroy her mark. Her focus was pure, her trained awareness tunneling into absolute clarity of vision. The clay jug was all she could see, the center of everything, perfectly aligned. She would not miss.

"Goodbye." She let out her breath.

Her finger moved smoothly on the trigger, and she fired.

CRACK!

The jug exploded.

A perfect hit.

And then – without warning, entirely of their own accord – her eyes filled with tears and her fingers went icy cold.

And then, as usual, the anger came.

Her hands trembled.

Immediately, despite herself, Kyla imagined Garen – the

young, brilliant, perfect scholar — standing there behind her, concerned, polishing his silver spectacles, worrying about his sensitive niece. And then, in the same vision, before she could stop it, Michael stepped up — the young, brilliant, perfect warrior — shaking his head, vexed by her shaking hands, troubled about her faculties as a soldier.

Kyla frowned, set her carbine down on the firing table, and blinked the image away before the rest of the family could pile in. She rubbed her hands together. She was a better shot than any of them. And she had a cooler head, too.

But none of that mattered.

What mattered was that she had been at the range for almost a full bell now, that she had hit every target she'd set up — but that she *still* couldn't get rid of the shakes. From his place on the floor, Bruno snuffled, looked up at the ceiling, yawned, and shook his big mastiff head, grey jowls and slobber flapping. A trained war dog, he hadn't even twitched at the gun's discharge. Now he stretched his muscly grey legs in front of him, stumpy tail moving slowly as he rolled onto his side and gave a deep, snuffling snore. Kyla massaged her frozen fingers, tried to push some warmth into them.

What would Filip say if he was there? Would he take her cold hands in his? Warm them with his own? In her daydreams, his hands were always warm.

And what would the family say about that? Kyla wondered. What would Michael say? What would Grandpa say? What would Nana say?

Kyla already knew.

"The Tollers are good people," Nana had nodded kindly a couple months ago. "The most loyal of servants." Key emphasis on "servants."

And that was the end of it.

Filip might be "good people," but he wasn't good enough for her.

Kyla shook her head and tried to push the thought away. Was it strange that she valued Filip's company more than that of her own family? Not really, she realized. Filip never made her feel useless, never made her feel weak. When he was around, she just felt *good*.

Maybe they could run away together? Leave this stupid siege, this pointless war behind. Flee for another duchy, one not wholly consumed by violence. Or maybe renounce her name and title altogether? Such a thing was not unprecedented. Take Filip to Gelánen, some other beautiful world, get married, leave the Tarn and its pressures and powers and responsibilities behind? Oh Sisters, wouldn't it be wonderful? On the stone floor, Bruno snorted and gave another deep snore, his tail quivering in the midst of some pleasant dream.

Kyla smiled.

Because they *were* dreams. Sweet, but childish. Kyla knew her duty, she knew her place, and she knew her purpose. She was a High Lady of Remain. A Dallanar princess, the firstborn daughter of Tomas and Eíra Dallanar, first grandchild of High King and Queen Bellános and Adara Dallanar, a representative of the High Family of the Tarn, and potential heir to the Silver Throne. There were expectations. She'd been trained to meet them. And she *did* meet them. And she would *continue* to meet them. Regardless of where her foolish heart might look in the deep of the night.

She wiped her carbine down with a soft cloth. There were many reasons she came down to the range so late, it wasn't just that she couldn't sleep – she hadn't slept well in a year. One of the reasons was that she knew what was wrong. She knew why her hands went cold, why despite all her training they trembled and shook. She knew why she found herself blinking back tears that came for no reason. Garen, Michael, Doldon, Nana, Grandpa, even James — the rest of them — they all knew what was wrong, too.

My family is killing itself.

The truth. Plain and simple.

But they were horrible at talking about it.

And everybody knew that the High Family was perfect anyway, so what was there to talk about, really? How could there be a problem with perfection? What was there to talk about when everything and everybody was always "excellent?"

Never mind the fact that her perfect family also happened to have led the Realm into civil war, a war that had consumed the Silver Kingdom for over five years now. The irony would have been comical, if it weren't for the horror of it all, the ceaseless death.

But down here at the range, none of that seemed to matter. Mother, Father, and Master Falmon had taught her to shoot; they'd taught her the science of it, the tranquility of it. And even though Mother and Father were gone — Great Sisters sing their praises — target practice always made her feel closer to them, as strange as that sounded. Indeed, the high silver carbine with which she now practiced had been a gift from her parents a year ago, on her thirteenth birthday. "Nana and Garen did some extra work on its pedigree." Father had winked at her as she'd unwrapped the gun's polished case. "It was originally carried by Katherine the Second. Ancient, very special." Mother had nodded, smiled, and taken up the thread. "Nana carried this very gun during her own rites of passage. Just like you will carry it, Ky. A weapon of storied lore. Use it well." Regardless of the identity of its original owner, the carbine was a priceless gift. A gift fit for a queen. Ancient, indestructible, deadly — and worth more than a hardworking woodsman might make in ten lifetimes. The kind of gift given to someone of whom much is expected. The kind of gift that demanded something of the receiver. The kind of gift that was hard to live up to.

And then, Mother and Father were gone.

Just like that.

Assassinated by Grandpa's brother, Kyla's great uncle,

Dorómy Dallanar.

Killed by the "Iron Lion."

Slain as they slept by cutthroats' blades.

Murdered by family.

Her hands seemed to go colder still, the trembling worse than ever. She closed her eyes, concentrated on her breathing, on her trained awareness, allowed a lifetime of teaching to drop like a grid over her emotions. "You conquer the world when you conquer yourself," Nana always said.

A nice idea.

But once again, the conclusion provided by Kyla's clarity of mind was simple and absolute.

My family is killing itself.

So, yes.

She knew what was wrong.

Her family *was* perfect – perfect at tearing itself apart. The real mystery was how everyone else seemed to get on. Sometimes, it was almost like nothing had happened, like nothing *was* happening. Sometimes, when the family was together, especially at dinner, it was like her parents had never lived. Her father, High Lord Tomas Dallanar, firstborn son of

Bellános Dallanar, High King of Remain, and rightful heir to the Silver Throne. Her mother, High Lady Eíra Dallanar, Duchess of Aradan Primu, a scholar and soldier of unmatched skill. Both slain as they slept by her Uncle Dorómy.

Kyla closed her eyes, seeing the dinner scene at table. Even during the worst of the siege, Nana always insisted they make time to eat together. So they'd sit and they'd eat and they'd discuss the day's action, the latest intelligence, the week's logistics – and all Kyla wanted to do was to stand up, slam her goblet to the floor, and scream, "Don't you people *see*! They're *gone*! Who's next? When will this thrice-cursed insanity *end*?" Even Tarlen and Susan, Kyla's younger brother and sister, seemed to be moving on.

It didn't seem possible.

Yet, there it was.

Kyla frowned. It had been the same when her aunt, Kate, had left two years ago. Father and her uncle Michael had both been furious at first, near out of their minds at the rumors that their little sister had gone over to Dorómy, that the brilliant, young Lady Katherine Dallanar had betrayed them, that she had betrayed the Tarn, that she had betrayed family for family. Kyla herself had never believed it of Kate. But it hadn't mattered, because – just like that – Kate's leaving had passed, as if nothing had happened. Just another loss to the Great War. And everyone had just moved along, kept working, kept fighting, like perfect soldiers – as if Kate had never lived. Everyone except Nana, of course. Nana, as always, had just smiled and had folded Kyla into one of her big Nana-bear hugs. (While it was not common knowledge to her subjects, High Queen Adara Dallanar gave the most incredible hugs.) "Kate's the best we have, dearest," Nana had said. "Wherever she is, you can be sure she's got good reason, that she acts for us and our well-being." And for some reason, even though there'd been no real information in Nana's words, the words had been enough.

And now Kate had returned.

Just like that. Kate was back as quickly as she had left. Kyla hadn't seen her yet, but she couldn't wait to talk to her, to hear everything.

Kyla rubbed her hands together, took a deep breath, lifted her carbine again, sighted down range.

Another little jug sat there, held once again by her sights.

But now her hands *really* shook — jittery and off-target. And her breath was all wrong, too. She couldn't seem to center, to find her balance.

She took a deep breath, allowed training and muscle memory to take over. Then she aimed, let her breath out. "Goodbye."

CRACK!

And destroyed her target.

"Nice shot." A clear voice came from behind her.

Bruno snorted, eyes snapping open, his foggy grey fur shimmering like lightning in cloud, and then he quietly vanished from his place on the ground at Kyla's feet with a puff of cave dust — PFT! — the sound like a pearl dropped on a pillow.

Kyla didn't turn at the voice.

There was a reason why cloud mastiffs were so highly prized as guard dogs. Bruno's mother, dear Lily, was no different; that old girl was just as loyal to Nana as Bruno was to Kyla — and just as deadly to any would-be assailant.

Besides, Kyla already knew who it was. So instead of turning around, she took a deep breath, raised her carbine effortlessly to her shoulder, and fired again — CRACK!

Another little jug exploded into dust.

Kyla smiled.

When she was performing for others, she could do anything.

Oh, yes.

Indeed, "performance" was as much a part of her training as anything else. The duties of a Dallanar highborn were many, but one of the most important was sustaining the image of honor, of power, of perfection. Any fourteen-year-old girl could play and dream, could try and fail, but a Dallanar princess could never miss — ever.

Especially in front of an audience.

Kyla cleared and checked the chamber of her weapon, set her gun down on the firing table, and acted as if she hadn't heard the voice, as if her furry earmuffs had blocked the words. Then she pretended to blow her nose, wiped her face and eyes with a handkerchief, pulled her blond ponytail tight. Only then, when she'd done everything that she could do to get herself together, did she turn around.

Anna Dyer — Captain of the Sundaggers, leader of the most famous squad of dragon riders in the Realm — stood behind

Kyla in full battle gear, running her hands through Bruno's fur. Anna's hair was dark, and she wore it loose, falling streams of black mane over gleaming silver shoulders. When Anna looked up at Kyla, her eyes were clear and bright. *Merciless*. The first word that came to Kyla's mind – and the most correct. A deep scar ran along the bottom of Anna's jaw, down her neck, disappearing below her blue riding scarf. Large circles of untanned skin ringed Anna's eyes, weather marks from her flight goggles. You could always recognize a dragon rider by those telltale signs. Anna wore a revolver of high silver strapped beneath her left armpit, its handle worn with use. Kyla took a breath, focused on her training, on the inner workings of her mind and spirit, and willed herself calm.

On the outside, she knew it worked perfectly.

And she was glad.

Because her insides still shook. And because Anna was standing there with that kind of relaxed easiness, that kind of measured stillness that Kyla had always admired and envied. You could see it everywhere, in all the Tarn's elite fighters. A kind of economy of movement, a kind of clarity of position.

Nothing wasted, always ready. The stance of a professional soldier. And Anna fit the part – perfectly. Her armor was of the finest high silver, flawlessly fitted, worn with a kind of nonchalance that was entirely unstudied, exactly the kind of attitude that the Dallanar appreciated and honored. Indeed, both Anna's armor and sword had been gifts, on two separate occasions, from Kyla's grandfather, Bellános Dallanar. Rewards well-earned from the hand of the High King.

Of course, Kyla knew why Anna was there.

And Kyla knew who'd sent her.

Michael.

Checking up on her, yet again.

"Captain Dyer," Kyla nodded. It was a very particular gesture, respectful but curt, yet completely appropriate between a warrior knight and a High Lady of the House to whom that knight gave allegiance. Like everyone else, Kyla stood in awe of Anna, in awe of her dragon, Moondagger, in awe of her entire squad. And the Sundaggers *were* legends, there could be no doubt about that. At the same time, Kyla recently had begun to wonder if Anna and her ruthless Davanórians weren't part of the larger problem, this perpetual war, this endless killing.

Kyla shook her head. That she could have such a thought while practicing with one of the deadliest weapons in the Silver Kingdom — the irony of it — was not lost on her.

"Lady Kyla." Anna Dyer bowed, the gesture filled with absolute deference. "Lord Michael and Lord Doldon will be down shortly to inspect the great cannon and to peruse arms for Colj and his squad. Lord Michael asked me to check in on you — that's to say . . . to see if you and Bruno would care to join us, my Lady." Anna thumped Bruno's side. The big cloud mastiff leaned into her, his grey fur shimmering like living fog. Then Anna looked up, like she was remembering herself, and bowed politely again.

Always perfect obedience. Always perfect decorum. Everything they said about her was true: Anna was indeed the perfect soldier.

"I think I will join you, yes." Kyla nodded. "My thanks." She turned back to the firing table, took up her carbine, and pointed it down range, one eye squinted shut, checking the breech out of habit.

But Anna didn't turn toward the exit, and Kyla could feel

the dragon rider's dark eyes on her. It was not a new feeling. Something had changed in the last week, something that Kyla couldn't put her finger on. Since Mother and Father had been killed a year ago, many things had been strange. But then, about a week ago, something *else* had shifted. Things had been feeling like they might someday get back to normal and then – *snap!* – everything was odd again. The hidden looks, the eyes hastily averted, covert glances passed between family members when she walked into the room. As if she wouldn't notice. Kyla scoffed. Like all Dallanar highborn, her early training had centered on both fundamental awareness and on mental resilience, in both combat and elsewhere. And in these skills, she was a true master. The only person who *didn't* act like there was something to hide was Nana, but now that she thought on it, Kyla hadn't seen her grandmother in several days either; she could use one of her big Nana-hugs right now.

Kyla snapped the carbine's breech shut and began wiping down the weapon. "Did Lord Michael give you other instructions, Captain?"

Behind her, Anna took a breath, as if to speak, but then said nothing. Bruno snorted and shook his big head, jowls and slobber flapping.

Kyla turned back to the dragon rider, cradling the gun proficiently in her elbow. Kyla had to admit it, Anna was a gorgeous young woman. Her perfectly fitted armor revealed a form that was well worth noting. Especially that luxurious black hair, always loose, even on the battlefield – black hair streaming behind her as she and Moondagger dove against their foes again and again, sowing fire and carnage, destroying the enemies of the High House of Remain.

Oh yes, Kyla understood Michael's feelings about Anna.

What was not to love?

Anna was courageous. Anna was fierce. Anna was disciplined. Anna was loyal. And useful. Don't forget utility. A flawless match, really. Kyla knew that if Anna had come from a House of even slightly higher standing, Michael would've married her immediately after her second triumph over Dorómy's forces on Dávanor, just two years past. "But they're waiting," the silly gossips said. "True love can always wait." Waiting until Anna came of legal age. Eighteen years old. One more year. The age of womanhood. Waiting, also – and perhaps more importantly – for Anna to achieve further triumphs, to garner more glory. After all, the honor of the High House must be upheld. Despite Anna's loyalty, skill, and ferocity, consistent victory in battle was the only currency that could outweigh the potential value of a political alliance through marriage between Michael and some other powerful woman of another High Family. With each successive victory, Anna's descent from a powerful but simple merchant House on Dávanor became less and less important. Because in war, winning was more important than lineage.

In war, winning became lineage.

Not that Kyla could disagree with Michael's choice, of course. Just the opposite, in fact. Kyla truly admired Anna, as everyone did. It mattered not from what step on the ladder she came. And, as far as Kyla was concerned, anyone who served her family with such devotion would be more than welcome to join it, no matter what the snots in court might say. More to the point: Anna made Michael happy. Could anything be more valuable? Besides, wasn't Kyla herself overly concerned with the honest eyes of a plainspoken son of a woodsman? In that sense, Michael's regard for Anna helped Kyla's own cause, too.

Kyla smiled, then raised an eyebrow at Anna's silence. "Speak freely, Captain. Did Lord Michael give you any other instructions? Don't stand on ceremony, please. Your words are valuable – especially to me."

Anna looked back at Kyla, patted Bruno one more time, then smoothed a lock of dark hair behind her ear. "Lord Michael asked me to see if you were well, my Lady. That's all. He said you've been up late hours. He knows you shoot down here." She gestured downrange.

Kyla returned Anna's gaze. "And what will you tell Lord Michael, when you report on my status?"

"That you're quite well, my Lady." Anna looked her in the eye, then she grinned and cocked her head at the destroyed jugs. "And that you need more targets down here."

It was another thing that Kyla appreciated about Anna: her wits, her cleverness. And it was a warrior's cunning, too, a keen eye for detail – and weakness. It's why Michael had sent Anna to check on her in the first place.

"Thank you, Captain," Kyla said.

Anna inclined her head. With his wet mastiff nose, Bruno

nudged at Anna's hand, looking for more attention.

Anna scratched Bruno behind his ear. The cloud mastiff closed his eyes, savoring the pleasure. "I understand that your aunt, Lady Katherine, has just returned," Anna said.

Kyla appreciated Anna's pivot in the conversation and nodded. "I am glad for it. I've missed Kate. She's been too long gone."

Anna said nothing, but a slight frown touched her lips. Kyla knew that Anna had never met Kate in the flesh. Kyla also knew that Anna's initial opinion of Kate had been governed by Michael's rage at Kate's departure two years ago. Their meeting would make for an interesting moment.

"You two have much in common," Kyla said. "You're almost the same age, only a year apart."

Anna raised an eyebrow.

"And you're both brave, fierce, and true." Kyla looked at her sincerely. "I admire you both."

"Thank you, my Lady." Anna inclined her head. "You shoot down here often with Bruno?"

Again, Kyla appreciated Anna's ability to guide their banter.

"Yes." Kyla patted her thigh, summoning the big mastiff. "He stays with me." She thumped Bruno's meaty side, then touched her high silver carbine. "My parents gave this to me last year, before they were killed. It was Nana's – the High Queen's – before it came to me. I come down here to shoot – and to think."

Anna nodded. "I understand, my Lady. I'm the same way. Dagger and I go out sometimes at night, hunt boulders or treetops by moonlight. Just testing our aim. Or maybe just flying. We like the time alone. We need it."

"Moondagger must enjoy that, too."

Anna grinned at her dragon's name, inclined her head. "He likes the peace, too. The stillness. Especially these days. Lots of fighting. Nice to have the solitude, sometimes."

Kyla nodded. It was the closest thing to a complaint she'd ever heard from the dragon rider.

"Do the riders of Dávanor prepare for the coming parley, Captain?" Kyla moved to the other side of the firing table so that she could look at Anna while she finished. She picked up her kit, opened her carbine's case, started cleaning up.

"Yes," Anna said flatly. When Kyla looked up, she saw that

the dragon rider's gaze was dark, the barest hint of criticism in her eyes.

"You don't approve?" Kyla asked, careful to frame the tone of the question as an honest invitation.

Anna shook her head. "Not my place to approve or not, my Lady. The High King has ordered and agreed to parley. We'll see it done."

"It *is* rather sudden." Kyla nodded. "Surely something to do with Kate's return. If nothing else, it's a striking coincidence. Kate's gone for two years, she's back for a day, and parley is commanded moments thereafter? I haven't yet spoken to her. Have you heard anything?"

"The High King has commanded parley," Anna repeated.

Kyla looked at her directly. "You think Michael should contest my grandfather's decision?"

The dragon rider's eyes flashed, then it was gone. For a long moment, Anna looked at Kyla without a word. Kyla returned her gaze, allowing honest curiosity to show on her face, using all her skill to communicate a combination of strength and candid openness.

But Anna didn't take the bait. "Lord Michael would never

challenge the High King's command. Not even in private. Nor would I."

"Of course." Kyla inclined her head. "But surely Michael sees value in a chance for peace? Or even a respite, perhaps?"

"I can't speak for him, my Lady. He'll always obey the High King's orders."

Kyla nodded, placed her carbine in its case, and continued packing the rest of her gear, taking her time. "I know that Doldon favors parley, to a certain extent at least. Can't say about James, of course. He's been out for a week now on some mission for Michael. I haven't seen Kate yet, and I'm not sure she understands everything that's happened in her absence. I'm sure Nana supports the idea — I suspect parley might be her idea to begin with. Or maybe it was Garen's—."

"Lord Garen's not a soldier, my Lady," Anna said bluntly. "And the High Queen is—." The dragon rider stopped suddenly, looked strangely at Kyla, then shook her head.

"The High Queen is what, Captain?" Kyla's eyebrow arched. Then, not waiting for an answer, she continued pleasantly. "And you're quite right: Garen isn't a soldier. Certainly not as skilled in killing as Michael, Doldon, and

James are — or even as my father was. But on the issue of parley and peace? I wonder. What would a soldier recommend?"

Anna lifted her chin. "A soldier will do as she's commanded, my Lady. Always."

"Come, Captain," Kyla said charmingly. "I don't test you. I ask only for your honest judgement. Surely you can give it without fear?"

Anna looked at her directly. When she did, Kyla realized that the dragon rider fully understood the veiled challenge in her words.

A different approach, then.

"Please, Captain." Kyla cleared her throat. She cocked her head at the high silver carbine lying open in its case and rubbed the wrinkly grey fur on Bruno's head. "We're both trained in arts of war. We're both loyal. I ask only for your opinion. I have my own ideas, of course, which I'm happy to give. I find these days that I listen to my own thoughts far too much. I would hear yours, if you will share them."

Anna looked at her for a long moment, as if weighing Kyla's request.

Kyla kept quiet, not dropping her gaze, allowing her own authority to fill the space between them. It felt slightly wrong, to assert herself like this, almost ordering the dragon rider to speak on the matter.

But she wanted to know.

In two days – suddenly and for reasons Kyla didn't yet fully understand – Garen would meet in ceremonial parley with High Commander Vymon Ruge, the Lord of the Siege, her great uncle Dorómy's most respected field commander. It would be the first formal ceasefire in nearly two years of siege. And even though it had seemingly come from nowhere, even though Kyla was certain it had something to do with Kate's mysterious departure and return, Kyla could sense Garen's and Nana's careful machinations behind it all. Which meant that Michael wouldn't like it, almost by default. But what of Anna? Did their best warrior approve?

"Very well." Anna nodded and looked Kyla in the eye, almost as if reading her mind. "My opinion is that placing Lord Garen at the end of the Long Bridge in front of those treacherous dogs for the sake of 'peace' is a waste of time and an indefensible risk. It's a trick. Lord Garen will be fired upon. He could be killed. And the war will continue just as it has these last five years, but with one important difference: Our most knowledgeable scholar and healer, a High Lord whose understanding remains unmatched in the entire Kingdom, one of our most valuable tactical assets, will be dead." She touched two fingers to her temple. "A traitor's bullet in his skull."

"Michael won't let that happen," Kyla said automatically. But her blood ran to ice. She tried to say the words with confidence, but they sounded strange in her own ears, and she felt her carefully constructed posture begin to buckle. Once again, as if on cue, her hands began to shake. She breathed it out, tried to let her training come to the fore. "Michael would never let that happen," she repeated, rubbing her cold hands in Bruno's fur.

Anna smiled, a glimmer in a knife's edge. "Lord Michael is a force of nature, no doubt. But he can't fight enemies he can't see. And he can't protect Lord Garen when the High Laws demand a protocol that'll keep him behind the walls, three hundred paces distant from where death strikes."

"You won't let that happen," Kyla said.

"I'm honored by your faith, my Lady." Anna inclined her head. "We will be there, ready to serve."

Kyla nodded. "And you won't be alone. If I understand correctly, Michael has given you another ten squads and that Master Khondus comes through tomorrow with five more. A mighty force of dragons, the likes of which has not been seen in recent memory."

Anna nodded. "Nearly all of Dávanor's best will be committed."

"See?" Kyla interrupted her with a smile, trying to keep her cold hands from shaking. "*You* will protect him. Vymon Ruge and Dorómy don't have dragons."

But the smile didn't work.

Anna was looking at Kyla's hands.

In fact, the entire conversation felt like it was no longer under Kyla's control. Kyla had asked Anna Dyer for her honest opinion – her soldier's opinion – and she'd received it.

A sudden vision flashed in Kyla's mind: Garen dying on the Long Bridge, bright blood spattering white marble pavers, snow swirling, the slow pump of a mortal wound, his silver spectacles hanging cock-eyed, one lens cracked, soulful eyes staring vacant at Kon's winter sky, a bullet hole in his throat, a tiny tunnel burrowed by the black worm of war. One more beloved slain by her great uncle's treachery.

Your family is killing itself.

Kyla tried to blink the vision away – and failed.

Her hands felt like ice.

"The enemy doesn't have war dragons, that's true." Anna nodded. "But you know well that Ruge has recruited other airborne forces which can provide good cover for their ground troops. More importantly, his field artillery outnumbers ours ten to one. And that's just his big iron, traditional guns forged here on Kon. He has yet to bring his ancient great cannon to bear – we don't know why he waits or how many he has." Anna gestured at the cave's wall. "The Tarn is entirely surrounded, my Lady. Vymon Ruge is one of the most experienced field commanders in the Realm. He and your grandfather, the High King, might once have been close, but Vymon is Dorómy's man now. We're cut off from our allies. The Pretender's local riders and infantry have almost entirely isolated us from the rest of the duchy. Yes, Lord Jor now rides to our relief, but he's overdue. If Jor was here, if Jor approached *now*, then we might have a chance to push out, to break the enemy's lines as they wheel to face Jor's column, but where is he? Nowhere to be found, not even a messenger in the last two weeks. And what if the Tarn's High Gate is breached by the Pretender's adepts, what then——?"

And then Anna stopped short.

It was as if she'd suddenly remembered what she was saying, how she was saying it, and to whom she spoke. Anna shook her head, stood tall, and looked at Kyla. "I'd gladly spend my life and the life of my dragon to protect Lord Garen, my Lady. Indeed, we'd gladly die to protect all of you, to protect the Tarn, from those thrice-cursed traitors out there." She gestured at the wall. "But as to your original question, I can say only this: Parley is a *risk*. I don't know why it's been called now, what's changed. Perhaps it does have something to do with Lady Katherine's return, as you say. I know not. But I do know that parley is dangerous. If something happens, if something goes wrong, many will die. Lord Garen will be at the front of it all, one scholar with a handful of ogres against the Pretender King's entire army."

"Then it's settled," Kyla said. She cleared her throat, tucked the last of her shells into a side pocket, and clicked the case closed. "We must make peace." She slung the case over her shoulder. Bruno nudged at her thigh.

Anna stared at her; the dragon rider's eyes were bright.

"What is it, Captain?" Kyla asked. "Yes. I said it. *'Peace.'* That dirty word. And you have provided overwhelming evidence for the conclusion. By your own words, we are outnumbered, outflanked, and outgunned. Even with its superior quality, our air power has been matched – if not countered – by Vymon Ruge. For years, Dorómy and his agents have worked hard to turn local populations against us, and they've succeeded in many instances, especially this 'Mountain King' and his guerillas around Aaryn's Cry. And I can tell you firsthand, from my own work with Doldon in the storerooms: We are running out of everything. We are in the middle of a logistical nightmare. Why am I here, using this storage magazine as a firing range? Because there's nothing to store, Captain. The only things keeping us alive are our High Gate, our last great cannon, and Garen's 'star trees,' entities which no one fully understands. How long can those trees last, Captain? Do you know? I most certainly do not. More to the point, neither does Garen. Our entire defense thus rests upon the strength and, dare I say, the 'good will' of ancient entities with whom we can barely communicate. So, what else can we do? Fight 'til there's nothing left? The Tarn protects far more than men and guns and swords. It is more than a 'fortress,' as the High Queen says. And she's entirely correct. There are the collections to consider, the artifacts, the other treasures of the Tarn's repositories. To say nothing of the lives of the unarmed highborn nobility and the thousands of loyal men, women, children, and orphans we received when Tarntown fell during Vymon Ruge's initial offensive. If we can't win – and by both our reckonings, we are very hard-pressed – are we to die here? To take all the Tarn's treasures, innocents, all of it with us into the void? Fight until there is nothing left?"

And then Kyla saw Anna's face clear, the dragon rider nodding, as if with sudden understanding. And at that same moment, Kyla realized that she herself had said too much and worse – that she'd revealed what she truly felt.

And now Anna thought her afraid.

Or weak.

Or worthless.

Or perhaps all the above.

But that wasn't true. Kyla wasn't afraid of fighting. Nor was she opposed to war on moral grounds – that would be absurd. Rather, she truly felt that there had to be another way. A way besides these two great armies' constant, bloody flailing across the whole of the Kingdom, a way besides her family gnawing off its own limbs.

Yes, parley was a risk.

Obviously.

But a risk greater than this perpetual war?

Of course, Kyla hated Dorómy. More precisely, she hated what her great uncle had done to them, to her, to the Realm, to her family. But her hate was born of what had once been love. Far more importantly, her hate was a luxury that she could not afford, an emotional indulgence best left to amateurs and children. "The closer a person's mind is to calm, the closer she is to strength," Nana always said.

Kyla lifted her chin.

She didn't want peace because she was weak.

She wanted peace because she was smart.

"Very good, my Lady," Anna said formally. "I thank you for this discussion. Lord Michael and Lord Doldon will be down in moments. Shall we join them?"

"Anna——," Kyla started.

Anna said nothing, she just stared at Kyla unflinchingly, her posture almost at attention, almost as if she needed her military discipline to contain herself. Kyla felt her face warm even as her hands once again threatened to tremble.

"What would be your plan, Anna?" Kyla asked simply. "If we could do anything, if *you* could do anything, what would it be?"

The dragon rider's cold decorum was palpable. She said nothing.

Kyla looked Anna in the eye. "If Michael had his way, what would we do?"

Anna looked at her for a moment. Then she nodded. "Very simple: We would attack. And then we would attack again. Without mercy. Without end. This madman in the hinterlands, this 'Mountain King,' and his traitor guerrillas who've isolated us these last months, cut the Tarn off from support here on Kon? We send assassins. We execute him. This traitor, Vymon Ruge? We take my dragon squads, we drop under cover of darkness behind the siege lines, we burn the enemy's command tent to ash. We follow Lord Jor's superb plan, we re-open the Trange, the Great Road between Tarntown and mighty Konordun, to the other side of Aaryn's Cry and the loyal cities of the south. We discover the Pretender's Gate, discover how the traitor brings his forces to bear—."

"Surely you can't—."

"Even Lord Garen agrees," Anna continued. "If we control Kon's only gate, from whence do the Pretender's armies come? What other answer can there be? The sailors of Póntokos have remained entirely neutral throughout all this — and even if Dorómy has won them over, there'd be no way for him to pay or support the kind of deployments we've seen. That's the key, my Lady — the key to it all. We find the Pretender's Gate, we attack, we destroy it, and then we kill every traitor on Konish soil. Then we kill every traitor in the Realm. Proper intelligence, lightning strikes, followed by further strikes. Advance and attack. Advance and attack. Lord Michael is right — he has been right for years: We can't do anything just sitting here. We must attack. We must attack without end, without mercy."

"Why don't we act as you suggest?" Kyla asked carefully, already knowing the answer.

"The High King and——." Anna shook her head, dark eyes flickering. "He *restrains* us." Anna said the word as if it caused her pain. "He will not let us fight – not as we must."

Kyla continued. "Why do you think my grandparents hold our forces in check?"

Anna shook her head, as if she couldn't even consider the question, as if the question somehow cut to the heart of her being. But there was something more, Kyla's training told her. Something *inside* the question, beneath the surface, that strange flicker crossing Anna's face, like a dark beacon in a darker night. In the dragon rider's eyes, Kyla saw frustration, confusion, and boundless rage – all merged. But there was something else, too.

What was it?

Kyla wanted to go to Anna then, to hold her hands, to tell her that she was not alone in that spinning darkness, that she understood too well the kaleidoscope of frustration that engulfed her thoughts. But she couldn't. The gesture would never be seen for what it was. It would be seen as weakness.

So instead, Kyla said gently, "I asked you a question, Captain." She did not relish her own insistence, but she would have an answer. "Why does the High King not give Lord Michael the freedom he seeks to conduct the war as he wishes?"

"Peace." Anna looked up at her, a strange kind of anguish in her eyes, as if the word was torn from her lips. "The High King – Great Sisters honor him – he believes it is possible. He insists, he believes, there's something out there more than war." She lifted her chin at the wall, shook her head, dark hair glossy in the lamp light. "Even now, even after . . . ." She looked away from Kyla and took a breath. "He doesn't understand that those men out there – those soldiers and generals who once served him: Ruge, Serán, Carole, Shu, Taverly, all the others – those men who once swore oaths to uphold his word and lawful authority . . . he doesn't understand that they are his *enemies*. It doesn't matter what they were before. They're his enemies now. And they've proved it." Anna glanced up at Kyla, that strange look in her eye again. "They've proved it beyond all doubt. And every day they kill us. They kill our men, they kill our people in the name of a murderous traitor, in the name of a traitor usurper." She cleared her throat and looked at Kyla. "We cannot fight as we must because the King hopes for peace. And he will hope forever. And while he dreams of peace, his armies will wither and die – and then a different kind of peace will come."

Kyla stepped to her, put a hand on Anna's armored forearm. "Would any peace not be better than this forever war, Anna?"

Anna stiffened. "I don't know. But I do know what your father, Lord Tomas, would've said, Great Sisters sing his praise – before Dorómy's assassins cut his throat."

Kyla blinked, head spinning, suddenly dizzy.

She stepped back.

At her side, Bruno growled softly. In spite of herself, Kyla looked down at her hands. They were icy and clenched, so cold they almost hurt.

She took a deep breath, focused, and looked Anna in the eye.

Kyla had opened this door; it would be difficult to close.

"What," she asked, "would my father say, Anna?"

The dragon rider's eyes were shards of night. "Lord Tomas would say that any soldier who yearns for peace makes a perfect solider – for the enemy."

"Indeed?" Kyla's eyebrow went up.

Anna said nothing, then looked away. And Kyla could tell that the dragon rider regretted her words. But it didn't matter. As much as Kyla cared for Anna, she could not let such a remark go unchallenged, not from a subordinate. She lifted her chin and allowed the barest touch of her power into her voice. "I invited you to speak freely – and you've done so. But I won't hear anyone question my loyalty, even obliquely. Do I make myself clear, Captain?"

"Forgive me, my Lady." Anna bowed. "I spoke out of turn."

"You did not. As always, I am grateful for your honesty. That said, there are many roads to victory and many ways to peace. I prefer that which is shortest, but also that which is littered with the fewest of my family's dead. Now, shall we go? Lord Doldon and Lord Michael await."

5

DEEP IN THE Tarn's Lower Armory, shadowed in the doorway of the Fourth Gallery of Cannon, Captain Fellen Colj, the greatest ogre of Jallow, watched the little boy work.

The boy was shouting as he cleaned, yelling at the great cannon; polishing like a demon, hollering like a madman.

Colj inclined his huge head. He could not understand the boy. But he could understand the boy's feelings, he could understand the boy's energy. This energy was what the ogres of Jallow called a warrior's *ja* – a soldier's fighting heart. The boy's ja was strong. The boy's ja was the reason that Colj had left the High Lords, that he had returned to the gallery. Colj had felt something in the boy. He had sensed something in his ja. And he wanted to be sure.

Colj was certain that he had seen the little boy before. But this was the first time that he had clearly felt the boy's ja. He could not see it, of course. The ja was *sensed*, not seen, like a silent vibration. Colj nodded. Yes. The boy's ja was clean and true. Like a high, jeweled note. And it was strong. So very strong. This strength was not unique; the Tarn was home to many powerful mages, scholars, and adepts. But the Pretender King's siege had drained them, leaving them feeble and spent. This boy, however, had something more than power. He had endurance. Colj could feel it. A special kind of stamina. Very rare. The most determined of hearts. Very rare, indeed. But before Colj mentioned it to Lord Garen, Colj needed to be sure. Lord Garen was wise. Lord Garen would understand what to do. And their need was dire.

The little boy wore a torn shirt and ragged pants. Both these garments were too large for him. The boy had rolled the sleeves of the shirt up past his elbows, but the rolls were so big, he could not put his arms to his sides. The boy needed a haircut, too. He was missing one of his front teeth. His pants hung in tatters. His shoes were too big, the laces broken and retied so many times as to make lacing impossible. The boy's elbow looked swollen. The range of motion was incorrect and he winced as he worked; the work hurt him. There was something wrong with the boy's shoulder, too. Yet he continued his task, continued to honor his oath, continued to honor his duty. Great Sisters, his ja was so bright! He worked as hard as he was able. A little soldier in rags, working alone in the dark.

Colj stepped forward. The boy stopped. He had sensed Colj's presence. The boy looked up at Colj. The skin beneath his eyes was bruised and tired, either from fatigue or fighting, or both. The boy shook his head, mumbled something, and turned away. His head wobbled with exhaustion. He went back to work. He winced with pain, but he worked nonetheless. The boy mumbled once more. Colj could not understand what he said, but his ja was brighter than ever, like a diamond star in the pale lavender of morning.

And then Colj understood what he had recognized.

The boy's ja reminded Colj of his oldest son – Saj.

Great Fellen Saj. Dearest Fellen Saj. The oldest son of Colj. Now gone. Lost to the Great War, like three other sons before him. Only Colj's youngest son, Ponj, remained. Before Saj had been found by death, his ja had shone like this boy's. The same stamina, the same commitment, the same heart.

Since returning from Jallow two weeks prior, Colj and his warriors had not spent enough time with the Tarn's great guns. Colj realized now that this had been a mistake. The songs of the ancient, living weapons were strong and true. Good for the ja. In the past, Colj had made allowance for new warriors to descend into the Tarn's lower galleries to listen, to fill themselves with the great guns' war songs, to fill themselves with the righteous fury of the guns' life force. When dear Saj had arrived at the Tarn, he too had been drawn to the mighty cannon. He had listened to their songs with full commitment. But then he was gone. The siege of the Pretender King went hard. Every woman and man was required, every moment of every day. Their need was dire.

Colj frowned.

Every woman and every man.

Every child?

The thought gave him pause.

Then Colj spoke to the boy. "There is an ancient story that we tell on Jallow. It was the favorite of my son, Saj. Before death found him. It cannot be told in your tongue. But I will share it, all the same."

The boy stared at him.

He did not understand.

But his ja blazed like a white-hot sun.

"On my world," Colj said, in the ancient tongue of Jallow, "we sing the song of a tree that took root near the wall of a garden. It was a lone tree, tall and slender. But it was not of that place. It did not flower. It did not bear fruit. And it never bent to the gardener. As the tree grew, a silver bird came to sing during sunset. On one branch, then another, the bird sang, always higher, as if persuading the tree to grow, sunset colors in its silver wings. For many years, this bird came to this tree, and for many years, the tree grew taller and taller still. A single bird and a single tree, each the only friend to the other. When the gardener cut the tree down, the bird flew around the places the tree's branches had been, inscribing the spaces it had once sang, its flight carving lines in sunset for all to see, higher and higher, so high that the tree finally touched the stars."

Colj took off his gauntlet. He placed his hand on the cannon's side. He closed his eyes and let the cannon's living hymn swell through his mind and heart, its ancient agreements filling his ja with its passion, its fire, and its truth.

He listened for a long while.

When Colj was done, he opened his eyes and saw that

the little boy listened, too. The boy's eyes were closed. His hand was on the cannon. He listened to the weapon's ancient battle song.

Once more, the sight gave Colj pause.

The boy's ja was strong, yes.

But it also seemed that the boy knew and understood the gun's ancient harmonies.

But how could that be?

How had he learned?

How had a mere child coaxed the mighty gun to reveal its holy music? Potent as his ja might be, the boy was no war adept. He could have had no formal training, no proper instruction. Indeed, only the most skilled adepts were chosen by the Order of Alea to commune with the living weapons. And only the most skilled amongst those were picked to learn the ancient counterpoints that could unleash the great cannon's holy fire. Yet here was this boy, a boy who had been accepted wholly by one of the oldest cannon in all the Remain.

Here, alone in the cold and the dark, the great weapon sang for him.

It sang for him, even now.

Colj frowned.

Master Falmon must know this, surely.

Or Lord Garen.

Or Lord Doldon.

But if any of them did know, then why had the boy not been brought into the ancient battle rites? Why had the boy not been taught the correct counterpoints, trained to unleash the weapon's divine rage? The war music was here, swelling the room, waiting for any blessed soldier to hear. Since this was so, why was this little warrior dressed in rags in the freezing dark, cleaning this mighty weapon with a scrap of cloth, his garments falling off him in tatters?

Fury stirred in Colj's center.

He acknowledged its presence and its justice, and let it flow through him. Dear Saj, too, had been humble in his gift.

Perhaps they did not know. But how could that be? And what to do with this little warrior? This little soldier who worked so hard for their cause. This warrior who had within him the power to save them all.

He must be tested, Colj realized.

He looked down at the boy.

The boy looked back up at him.

"Well done," Colj told him. The boy nodded. He was tired.

"Finish your work. Get some sleep." Colj glanced at the great war cannon, then looked back to the boy. "In two days, you will face battle together."

The boy stared up at him. His eyes were glassy with fatigue. He seemed weak on his feet. The little soldier needed his rest. Colj understood. They were all tired.

Colj looked closely at the boy. Through the boy's bright ja, Colj could sense his confusion. The boy did not fully understand Colj's words.

"I will see to it." Colj nodded, speaking slowly so that the boy would understand. "You will be tested." He put his hand on the great cannon. "You will face battle together. You have my word, little soldier."

THE SECOND DAY

6

THE NEXT MORNING, down in his little nest, down under a rickety bunk at the very back of the cleaners' barracks, Little Dan Eadle woke and yawned—.

Or *tried* to yawn.

But he couldn't breathe.

Something stinky covered his mouth.

And he couldn't see, either.

Something pushed down on his face, mashing his eyes shut.

His chest was warm and tingly, almost burning.

He shook his head, as hard as he could. He kicked and tried to roll over – but something held him down.

His pals?

No way . . . .

Monsters!

Scary monsters from the dark!

He had to warn his pals!

"Watch out, Chief!" Little Dan tried to shout, but that stinky thing over his mouth stopped him from yelling.

The monsters had caught him.

They'd spread his arms and legs, stretched him open.

Black wire wrapped his wrists, bit into his skin.

He tried to kick, to move any which way.

But he couldn't budge.

He couldn't breathe.

His head spun. Red shapes wiggled in his eyes.

And he still couldn't breathe.

The monsters – they wouldn't let him breathe.

He thrashed his head back and forth, trying to get a breath.

Impossible.

Lungs on fire.

He tried to holler to his pals, but the monsters wouldn't let him breathe, so how was he supposed to yell? And if he didn't yell, how would his pals know to run?

Whispering now.

Monsters, whispering in the dark.

"Get his ankles there," someone hissed, close to his ear.

Dan went still.

He knew that voice.

It *was* his pals!

It was Chief Tendal and the gang!

Not monsters!

His pals!

Thank the Sisters! For truth!

Then the stinky thing came away from his face. Little Dan took a huge gulp of air and coughed, "Chief, I'm sorry, I thought—."

"Shut up," the Chief hissed and elbowed Dan in the stomach. FUMP! Dan grunted, eyes clamped shut, and tried to double up, but he couldn't because they'd spread him out, tied his wrists and ankles to the lower legs of the bunk. He couldn't breathe again. His face went hot. It seemed kind of early for the beat-up game, but he would try to play right. Yes, sir. Try his best. "Every day's a day to do better," he said in his head in Master Falmon's rough voice. Try to breathe, soldier. Just try to breathe. One of the rules. You had to take it. You can take it, soldier.

"Tighter." Dan heard the Chief order, felt them pull his legs farther down. More twine wrapped around his ankles.

"Stupid cry baby," someone muttered.

Dan gulped for air. The sound was ragged. He *did* feel tears in his eyes, shook his head to get rid of them, and blinked. You couldn't cry.

"Cry, baby, cry," someone said.

"Cry, baby, cry." They started slowly. "Cry, baby, cry."

But he *wasn't* crying. He knew the rules.

Dan tried to take a breath, to show them he wasn't crying. And even if it looked like he was crying, he wasn't really crying. The tears had come on their own because he couldn't breathe, and that wasn't *his* fault. He knew how to play. Yes, sir!

Then he almost did start to cry. But the moment he felt tears coming, he bit the side of his tongue as hard as he could, took a gulp of air, and shook his head. He knew how to play. He could take it. The most important thing to remember in the beat-up game: If you want to win, you had to take it. No flinching, no crying. And there were all kinds of other tricks you could use to play and to win. You could pretend like you were someplace else. He used that one all the time. And if you couldn't do that, then you could pretend that you were *somebody* else. He used that one all the time, too.

"*Cry*, baby, *cry*!" They chanted.

Sometimes, he'd pretend he was big Captain Colj. "A big, strong ogre," Dan said to himself, using Captain Colj's deep ogre voice. An ogre could take lots of hits. Your pals could pound on you for hours, but they'd never really hurt you. Or you could pretend you were Lord Michael, the best fighter in the whole world. Your pals could punch you and kick you all night long, but it wouldn't hurt. Or — best of all — you could pretend you were Stormy, made of magical high silver. They'd tie you up and play the beat-up game on you *forever*, but they'd never really hurt you, not even a little. You can take it, soldier! Dan knew the rules. And he knew how to play. Boy, did he ever.

"*Cry*, baby, *cry*!" The chanting continued.

Little Dan felt a weird, slightly crazy grin spread across his face.

"For the Tarn!" he shouted as they wrapped more twine around his ankles. "For the Remain!"

Someone laughed over the chanting. Little Dan tried to laugh, too. But he couldn't because he still couldn't breathe right.

"*Cry*, baby, *cry!*" Faster now. "*Cry*, baby, *cry!*"

Little Dan looked over at Chief Tendal and tried to smile. Then he said, "I like to play the beat-up game with my pals, Chief. Yes, sir! I *like* it. I'm a good soldier. I can take it. And I'm gonna *win*."

The Chief's eyebrows shot up.

"Shut up," he said to the others.

"Cry, baby, cry!"

"Shut up," the Chief said again.

Everyone shut up.

Dan nodded. That was another really great thing about the Chief. He was always in charge. A good soldier. And a good pal, too. Not like Stormy, of course. Not that good. But still real good.

The Chief looked down at Dan, then shook his head. "Always knew you was a dumb-butt crazy turd, Eadle. But man, you *crazy*. I got some questions for ya, pal. What you doin' down there with Master Falmon and the others last night? Crazy Bill says he saw 'em go down there when you was down there doin' your boot lickin'. What's goin' on? What you see? What they say?"

Dan blinked. His stomach wasn't really hurting anymore so he finally was able to take a deep breath and look around.

They'd surrounded his nest completely. Two of his pals were at each of his feet, one pal at each of his arms, and Chief Tendal there, next to his head. Four or five of the others were standing in front of the bunk. Rost Gonnerdun was above him, looking down over the edge of his bunk, his face going red from hanging his head down like that, not saying anything because Rost Gonnerdun was mute and only made this funny little hooting sound. Dan suddenly remembered a time when the Chief had tried to play the beat-up game with Rost Gonnerdun, but Rost Gonnerdun couldn't really yell right and that was an important part of the game, to yell and scream and stuff, and Rost only made that weird hooting all the time, so he couldn't really play. "Gotta yell while you take it, soldier," Dan had told him later. One of the rules.

But Rost had only smiled and hooted at him.

Someone had taken Little Dan's toolbox from its place in his nest, knocked it over, and kicked his rags and brushes and the rest of his gear all over the floor. His lamp's loop was busted, one of his empty jars of polish was broken, and it looked like someone had tried to break his oil tin. They'd taken his pillow, too. But that was just an old pants leg he'd stuffed with rags, so that wasn't too bad. Dan would never say it out loud, but this was a part of the game that he didn't really like, when they messed with your gear and broke your things and stuff, because it made it harder to do the work. But then again, you couldn't always like everything, and they were his pals. And a pal was a pal, no matter what.

Dan looked around at their faces. He knew them all. He smiled at them. He didn't know all their names, of course. He was real bad at remembering names, anyway. But Benjy Dalter was there, Chief Tendal's second-in-command, holding his own lamp, looking kind of itchy. Benjy Dalter didn't really like the beat-up game, but Benjy was still part of the Chief's gang. And there was Juder Lown and Mateo Zouder and Crazy Bill Femp. Little Dan couldn't remember the rest of their names. He knew those guys because they were always closest, he could see their faces, and because they were always in on the game. Dan knew Crazy Bill because Crazy Bill was *crazy* mean and he liked the crazy bad games. A few of the others carried lamps, too. The flames glowed and smoked and made their eyes glow.

Dan was breathing better now. You had to get your breathing right to play the game good, to take it like a soldier does. Yes, sir! Dan pulled at the twine at his wrists and ankles. It was tight. He hoped the Chief would untie him when they were done playing, because a couple of times — lots of times, actually — the Chief had forgotten about him and Little Dan had been down there in his nest all day until Val or one of the other girls found him and let him loose.

The Chief nodded, like he was reading his mind. "You're not goin' anywhere, Eadle. You gonna stay there 'til we get what we want. Now, *give*. We know there's gonna be action today. Or is it gonna be tomorrow? What you hear, pal? What you see when the High Lords was down there? What they say? Cough it up."

Little Dan smiled. He'd played this version of the game

before. It was one of his favorites. Like a test.

You will be tested.

Yeah. Just like what big Captain Colj had said.

"You will be tested," Dan said to himself in Captain Colj's deep voice.

A test to see if you'd be a traitor.

The way to win was like this: You imagine that the Chief was one of the Evil King's bad spies, and if you told the secret, then you were a traitor, and then Lord Michael would cut off your arms and your legs with his black sword. But if you took the hits, if you *didn't* tell the secret, then you were a good soldier, and then the Silver King would hear about how good you were and say that you did a real good job, and if the Silver King said that you were good . . . .

"Then you is *good*," Dan said.

"Cough it up, little boot-licker." The Chief grabbed Dan's ear and twisted it hard. Dan yelped in spite of himself. The Chief nodded. "Down there all night long, kissin' butts and lickin' boots. Think they gonna like you?" The Chief twisted Dan's ear again, harder this time. It didn't hurt, not really. The Chief would never *really* hurt him. Dan knew that, for truth. The Chief smiled. "I decide who moves up down here. I decide who does what. Now, *give* — you stupid, lying, crazy, little, crazy."

With each word, the Chief twisted Dan's ear harder, still smiling.

"Ain't tellin' you spit," Dan yelped. "I don't tell nobody the secrets. No, sir!" Then, to show them all he wasn't scared, to show he knew the rules, that he was a good soldier, Dan added, "*You* go eat a turd. A big stinky one, you, you traitor spy . . . *you*, uh, you *turd muncher*! Eatin' a stinky old turd like the Evil King eats! With farts on it!"

The Chief blinked, looked from Dan to the others. Then he snorted. Then he laughed. The rest of them laughed with him. They sounded like donkeys. Dan laughed, too. One of the rules. Laugh with the pals.

"Oh, I see!" The Chief grinned. "You know *all* the secrets, eh? I bet Lord Garen made you promise to keep 'em, too, didn't he? Stupid little worm. Smartest lord in the Realm made *you* promise to keep *his* secrets? Makes perfect sense. Perfect sense the cleverest lord spends the time talking to a stupid, lying, little, *crazy*."

The Chief dotted each of those last words with a knuckle rap on Dan's head, each one harder than the last. Dan moved his head back and forth so he couldn't get him in the same place twice. He knew that trick. Yes, sir. The Chief taught him that one last year. It wasn't really a flinch, so it didn't get worse when you did it; it was more like a dodge.

"Yeah." The Chief's grin got bigger. "Makes a lot of sense, Eadle. Now, I'm gonna ask you again. What's goin' *on*? What you hear? What they say? I'm in charge. These're my men, here. They gonna pick to see who goes out today, I know it. Or tomorrow. Whenever it is. I can smell it. We might not see action, but then again, we might. You better spill it. Ain't gonna hurt you, Eadle. We're pals." The Chief smiled. "Just tell me what you heard down there. What you see?"

Dan shook his head.

The Chief cocked his head. "What'd Master Falmon say? Were the High Lords there? Crazy Bill says Lord Doldon and Lord Michael were there, and Master Falmon and Colj, and Lady Kyla and Captain Dyer. Even that dwarf and his dragon – all of 'em down there. That true? What about Lord James?"

Dan shook his head, lips tight. Crazy Bill looked down at

him, his eyes all mean and crazy. Then Crazy Bill licked his crazy lips, winked, and mouthed, "Sweets." Dan sure hoped the Chief wouldn't leave him alone with Crazy Bill. Crazy Bill liked the bad games, the ones you played with a knife or a nail.

"Think you don't have to tell me?" The Chief frowned, pretending to be angry. "Think your boot-lickin' down there makes you somethin'? You ain't *nothin'* down there, stupid crazy. You ain't nothin' *here*. So cough it up." Then he smiled and said real quiet, "C'mon, pal."

Little Dan shook his head. He knew that trick, too.

The Chief sighed. "Gimme that lamp, Dalter." He held out his hand to Benjy Dalter.

Benjy Dalter looked at his lamp, then handed it over.

The Chief held the lamp down by Little Dan's face.

"Ever smell burning hair, Eadle? Or skin?"

The Chief waved the smoky flame next to Dan's eye. Dan pulled away, twisting his face towards the wall. This happened during the game sometimes, too. He still had a scar on his tummy from the last time they'd played with fire together, but that was a long time ago and that had been Crazy Bill's fault. That one had hurt at first, but then Dan had realized that it only was hurting in his head, so he'd pretended he was Stormy and he hadn't felt anything else after that. The Chief would *pretend* to hurt him, but he'd never hurt him for real. He was a good pal.

"It stinks." The Chief moved his fingers through the smoky flame. "Stinks like a burnt turd. Smells like a burnt up little Eadle. Now, tell the truth."

"Ya," Juder Lown snickered. "Tell the truth." Crazy Bill Femp didn't say anything. He just stared at Little Dan like he did with those crazy mean eyes.

Benjy Dalter slapped Dan on the leg, "C'mon, Dan. What you see down there? We just wanna know what's going on, that's all."

"Shut up, Dalter." The Chief smiled. "Just tell the truth, Eadle. Tell the *truth*."

"Tell the truth," they started. "Tell the truth. Tell the *truth*."

As they chanted, the Chief moved the lamp back and forth in front of Dan's face with the rhythm, bringing the flame closer and closer to his nose.

"Tell the *truth*! Tell the *truth*! Tell the *truth*!"

Dan shook his head.

"I'm not kidding, Eadle," the Chief said. "You start talkin' or I'm gonna give this to Crazy Bill, cook one of your ears off."

"For the Tarn!" Little Dan yelled. "For the Remain! I don't tell no secrets! I'm a good soldier! Every day, that's the way, I don't say! No secrets! No, sir! Chief Tendal, sir! No, sir!"

"Tell the *truth*! Tell the *truth*!"

"Hold his head there, lads. You do it, Bill. Start with one of his eyebrows."

Little hands held Dan's face still, nails digging his cheeks. Someone punched his shin to the rhythm of the chant — not exactly fair, but not really against the rules, either. Crazy Bill smiled and licked his lips and took the lamp.

"Tell the *truth*, tell the *truth*—!"

"Let him up, Tendal."

A girl's voice.

Everything stopped, the chanting, the punching, the game, everything.

"Let him up, I said."

Little Dan groaned.

It was the worst thing that could ever happen.

It was Val and her girls.

The Chief stood up, turned around. "How I discipline my men isn't up to you, Val. You got your people. I got mine."

"I like this game!" Little Dan hollered. "I can take it, Val. I'm a good soldier! Get outta here!" He didn't want Val to be there. When Val and her girls came, his pals got hurt.

"See?" the Chief said. "He says he likes it. Keep your stupid nose outta my business."

"You're in my territory," Val said. Little Dan still couldn't see her. Why couldn't she just get into the game? Why'd she have to mess everything up like this all the time?

Val sniffed. "From that bunk there and back to the can is mine, Tendal. Everything. Including the mute, the moron, their stinky-butt beds, all their crap."

"He's *my* man, Val," the Chief said bravely, not backing down. "If he's my man, then he's *my* problem."

"I'm *his* man!" Little Dan yelled. "Leave us alone, Val! Get outta here!"

"Shut up," the Chief said without looking at him.

"*My* people are trying to sleep," Val said. "And ya threw his crap all over the floor. One of my people slip on that junk going to the can, I'm gonna break your dumb head in for ya."

Everyone was real quiet now.

The Chief stepped away from Little Dan's nest. When he did, Dan could see Val. She was taller than the Chief and lanky and thin. She had black hair and dark skin, like the color of tea. She cut her hair real short, except for this tight ponytail, kind of like a topknot, right on top of her head. Behind her, five of her girls stood staring at the Chief. A couple of them carried billy-socks. A billy-sock was a sock filled with rocks or chunks of metal, other heavy stuff. Val didn't carry one. She didn't need to. All her girls were mean and tall. "And they don't have balls," the Chief always said. "Gives 'em the edge." Little Dan had seen his pals get hit in the balls with a billy-sock before. It was no game. No, sir. And if it was some kind of game, then it should be against the rules.

"You gonna break *my* head, eh?" the Chief asked Val.

Dan saw the Chief come up on his toes. The rest of the gang was getting ready, too. From the bunk above Dan, Rost Gonnerdun was staring down at him, making his weird little hooting. Rost had been hanging over the edge of his bunk so long, his face was totally red now. The Chief took another step toward Val. He pointed at her, then at himself. "*You* gonna break *my* head?"

"That's right." Val nodded, all calm. "Torture that idiot all ya want during the day, on your own time. This is rack time. I ain't gonna listen to it anymore."

Then the Chief punched her.

Or tried to.

But she wasn't there, his fist whiffing through the air where her nose had been, throwing him off balance as she sidestepped, grabbed his wrist, and threw him face first — SMACK! — into the wall. She didn't wait for him to get up. Neither did her gang. They jumped all over the Chief and the pals, billy-socks whirling, clumps and snaps and screams coming now, like they always did. Benjy Dalter dove to the side, not trying to attack, just trying to get the heck outta there before one of Val's girls beat him senseless. Val was on top of the Chief now, bashing his face into the floor with her elbow, her knee on his back between his shoulder blades, pinning him down. She'd raise herself up, then slam her elbow into the back of the Chief's head, using all her weight. Not fair! But the good old Chief, he was still fighting. Yes, sir! Brave soldier! Trying to get up.

"You can do it, soldier!" Dan hollered. "You can do it, Chief!"

A billy-sock whistled underhand, and Juder Lown went down, clutching his balls, eyes all glassy. A couple of the pals jumped on the girl wielding the sock – but then a whole pile of *other* girls charged in!

That sneaky Val!

Secret reinforcements, from behind the bunks!

"Cheaters!" Little Dan yelled, twisting against the twine. "Cheaters! Against the rules! Against the rules!"

Not fair!

Then he had an idea.

"Rost Gonnerdun!" Little Dan cried, even though he knew Rost couldn't understand him. "Rost Gonnerdun!" But Rost was looking at the battle now, making those strange little shapes with his mouth when he was excited, hooting and hooting. So Dan kind of kicked at the side of the bunk, not very hard – his ankles were still tied up, so he couldn't build

up any force, just whapping his toe against the bunk leg —
WHAP! WHAP! — and then, by some miracle, Rost looked
down at him. Dan wiggled his hands and feet. "Get me out,
Rost Gonnerdun," Dan said slowly, not yelling, but slowly,
so that Rost could understand what Dan meant by looking
at his mouth. "Get me out." He said the words slowly, then
waved his tied-up hands and feet.

Rost blinked.

"Come down here, Rost Gonnerdun," Dan said carefully.
"Come down here. Get me out. Untie me." He wiggled his
hands and feet again.

A girl screamed as someone pulled her hair. Crazy Bill,
Dan saw, pulling her hair, trying to strangle her at the same
time. Her teeth shone white, and she turned and bit Bill
like some kind of animal, her nails going for his eyes, while
another girl stepped up from behind and clubbed poor Bill
senseless with her billy-sock. The sound was horrible. Crazy
Bill went limp after two hits, eyes rolling into the back of his
head. Dan would never say it out loud, but he was always
pretty darn happy when Crazy Bill got his head clubbed.

The girls had made a circle around the Chief and Val so

that Val could hurt the Chief without his gang helping him. Anyone who came close to the circle got attacked. The Chief was on his hands and knees. Val was still on top of him, had her legs wrapped around the Chief's waist, and she was punching him – these hard, short little punches into the bottom of the Chief's back, on either side of his backbone. Every time she hit him, the Chief winced. But he wasn't going down. No, sir! The brave Chief was fighting hard! What a soldier! Yes, sir!

"I'm coming, Chief!" Little Dan hollered. "Rost Gonnerd-un! Please! Come down here! Get me out! Chief! I'm coming, Chief!"

Rost Gonnerdun seemed to finally understand what Dan was yelling about because he slid down off his bunk and started messing with the twine, cutting at it with a piece of glass from Dan's broken polish jar, cutting away, nodding to himself, hooting in that hooty little way of his.

The Chief flipped to his side, threw Val off, got halfway to his feet – but Val spun low, clipped the Chief's feet from underneath him, and he went down, cracking his chin against the wall. Two of Val's girls had grabbed Benjy Dalter by the ankles, dragged him back hollering bloody murder into the center. They had him on the ground now, and they were beating him with billy-socks, snarling over and over again as they hit him, "Stupid *boy*! Stupid *boy*! Stupid *boy*!"

Rost Gonnerdun had finished cutting the twine off Little Dan's ankles and was working on cutting loose his closest hand. Now that his legs were free, Dan could scoot up and use his teeth on his other wrist. He bit at the twine, sawing at it with his front teeth. His other wrist popped loose as Rost cut through the last thread on that side.

And then Little Dan was up and on his feet, a soldier ready for battle.

He looked around for something he could use as a weapon.

There was nothing there.

So he just charged right at Val, who was kicking the Chief in the gut. Her back was toward Dan, so she didn't see him as he came. Right as she was getting ready to kick the Chief again, Dan tackled her other leg and knocked her down.

She punched him twice in the side of the head as she fell. "Idiot!" she shouted. "Tryin' to help you, brainless fool!" She hit him again — twice in the same place, on the side of his head – hard. He saw stars, but he didn't let go. A couple of billy-sock girls turned around and moved toward him.

"You can't hurt my pal, Val!" Little Dan shouted. He shut his eyes, and got ready for the billy-socks to come, hung onto her leg for all he was worth. He could take it, he knew. But it was gonna be *real* bad. Not like the beat-up game at all. But he could take it. "You girls, you can't hurt him like that!"

Then Val coughed.

Dan opened his eyes.

The Chief had kicked *her* in the gut! He'd knocked her down! Brave Chief Tendal! And now he was gonna give it back to her. But the girls with the billy-socks, they were coming real fast now—.

A loud clang of metal outside in the hallway – the sound of the iron gate, just outside the barracks.

All the fighting and yelling stopped.

All the lamps went out.

Bare feet whispered. Everyone jumped back into their bunks. Dan scuttled like a crab back into his nest. Above him, he heard Rost Gonnerdun trying to pull himself back into his bed, legs cranking in the air, hooting.

The barracks door opened. Master Shum, one of Master Falmon's helpers, shouted into the room, "Muster in quarter bell, lads and ladies. Final polish, buff, and armory sweep. All rooms up for inspection. Up and at 'em! Quarter bell! Not a moment longer!" As Master Shum said this, he whacked the club he always carried on the door frame three times — WHACK! WHACK! WHACK!

The noises of fifty little cleaners rolling and groaning out of bed. But some of the groans didn't sound very sleepy. No, sir, they didn't.

"Gonna be action today, Master Shum, sir?" Dan heard the Chief ask from the front of the barracks, coming forward, pretending to yawn, pretending to be tired. Dan could just see him. The Chief was walking real tender, like he was sore. "Ain't for me to say, boy." Master Shum scratched his stubble. "But yeah, today or tomorrow. Tomorrow more likely. Dunno yet. Now, get 'em out and ready and lined up. Quarter bell. Final polish on all of 'em. Hammer and Oblivion gonna go up. Want the entire lot done again, from top to bottom. Gonna do all the galleries, too. The arcade, the whole thing, top to bottom, halls and doors, hardware, and every other cursed thing, even the pit. Inspection time, lads. High Lords be comin' down, and things gotta be *right*. Out, ready, fed, and lined up, boy. Quarter bell."

"Yes, sir! Master Shum, sir!" the Chief shouted.

Then Master Shum stopped and stepped into the barracks. He tapped his club against the door, spun it once in a circle on its thong, looked at the Chief. "What's been goin' on down here?"

"Rack time, Master Shum, sir!" The Chief saluted, thumping his chest.

"Yeah?" Master Shum tapped his club against the door. That club meant business. "Wouldn't fib to Master Shum now, would ya?"

"No, sir! Master Shum, sir!"

"Everyone alright down here?"

"Yes, sir! Master Shum, sir!"

Master Shum cocked his head. "Clean that blood off your face 'fore you show up." He looked around the barracks. "And your *whole* troop better be sharp 'n tight and clean and fed when they show up for duty. All fifty. Every single one. High Lords comin' down here. Understand me, boy? High

Lords. Your crew don't look right, little clubby here gonna hold you account." When he said this, he touched the Chief in the center of his chest with the end of his club.

"Yes, sir! Master Shum, sir!" the Chief shouted.

Master Shum grunted, scratched his chin, and left.

The barracks door shut. Everyone went crazy, getting ready for the day, as if the battle had never even happened.

"You heard the man!" the Chief yelled. "Quarter bell. Everyone up! Sharp and tight. Wipe that blood off your head there, Crazy Bill. No, dumb-nuts! The *other* side. There ya go. Let's go, lads! Grub carts be comin' any moment! Ain't ya hungry?!

Everyone made some kind of noise. Yes, sir! They were hungry.

"Clock is ticking, lads!" the Chief shouted. "Clock is *ticking!*"

Val and some of the girls jogged by Little Dan on their way to the can, stepping over his box and his gear and his pillow. They always got ready for work in there. When she passed, Val looked at him with disgust and tapped the side of her own head. "Something really wrong with your brains, kid."

"I don't like you either, Val!" Dan hollered at her as he tried to put his shoes on as fast as he could. "You don't hurt my pals, Val!"

And then the Chief was standing there in front of him, looking down at him.

"Get in my business again, crazy little boot-licker, I'm gonna let Crazy Bill hurt you — for *real*. I'm gettin' pretty sick of your crazy."

"Yes, sir! Chief, sir!" Little Dan yelled, not looking up, kind of saluting while he tried to put his other shoe on. "Sorry, sir! I'll do better! Every day, there's a way! Yes, sir, Chief!"

"And clean up this crap before you get your grub." The Chief waved at Dan's gear that they'd thrown everywhere. "'Specially that broken glass. People tryin' to walk here, pal."

"Yes, sir! Chief, sir!" Little Dan saluted.

7

THE PLATOON OF little cleaners marched out the barracks, past the grub carts, out onto the passage, through the iron gate, and up toward the old western stairs. Even though Little Dan had just come down the same way a couple bells ago, the whole place looked different. All the lamps and torches were lit, waving and smoking and bright. So good. Not dark at all. But his elbow was still a little sore, so that part wasn't very nice. But he'd stuffed his box with tons of grub off the grub cart, so that was great. Eat all day long. That's the way. Yes, sir.

The Chief was up at the front of the column, shouting out the count. Val was beside him, marching in good order like a soldier did. The rest of the kids didn't march – not exactly. Least they didn't march like Little Dan had seen real soldiers march. But they didn't just walk, either. It was more like a lined-up, steady kind of stamping. All the cleaners were different sizes, tall and short, fat and skinny, so there was no way their steps came even close to matching. And half of them couldn't count properly anyway, not that Dan could either, he could barely count at all, but some of them didn't even *try*. And some of them were still eating, so they didn't care, and the ones at the back couldn't hear the Chief counting at the front, especially when they went around the corners, so it was kind of a mess. And when the troop got to the western stairs, everything just collapsed. At the stairs, it was every man for himself. The littlest cleaners slowed way down; the stairs were too steep to walk up. The cleaners who carried toolboxes slowed down, too. Unless you were a full-grown soldier, there was no way you were walking up those steps carrying your box. Instead, you had to lift the box up onto the step in front of you, then clamber up the step yourself, then do that again and again, all the way up. Took forever. Being the smallest cleaner with one of the biggest boxes, Little Dan was dead last, every time.

His platoon was already mustering in the central hall with Master Shum and Mistress Croot by the time Dan got there. Because of his sore elbow and shoulder, it'd taken him longer than usual to get his box up the stairs. And one of his feet kept falling asleep, and that didn't help, either. When he'd looked, there'd been this red line pressed into the skin around his ankle from the twine his pals used, deep and shiny; it didn't go away when Dan rubbed at it.

"Eadle!" the Chief shouted as Little Dan hurried into the hall, leaning against the weight of his box. "Ten demerits for being late!"

"Yes, sir! Chief, sir!" Dan shouted.

The Chief yelled, "Don't do it again, soldier!"

"No, sir, Chief!"

The Chief was always handing out these "demerits" when he was in front of the grown-ups. Dan didn't know what a "demerit" was, but he did know that he'd never actually got one. The Chief would say that he could have one, or sometimes ten, but then he'd never give Dan anything. Not even a scrap of paper saying how many "demerits" he had. Dan didn't like that game. If you say you were gonna give something, then you darn well better give it! Yes, sir. One of the rules. He should have *loads* of demerits.

The entire troop was lined up in front of Master Shum and Mistress Croot. Mistress Croot was another one of Master Falmon's helpers. She was a lady Master, shorter than Master Shum, but her head was kind of lopsided, and she had a big hump on her back. Master Shum didn't have a hump. Mistress Croot was the nicest of the Masters, too. Master Falmon was nice, but he was a hard kind of nice. Master Shum was hard, too, especially when his little clubby came out, and he wasn't really nice at all. But Mistress Croot, she was *nice*. One of her eyes was kind of weird, looking off in a different way, but she was always smiling and giving everyone new cleaning rags and little treats and nice stuff like that. She'd helped Dan find more rags to stuff in his pillow. And those treats she gave were good.

The hall was a huge, vaulted place where all the weapons rooms connected. Giant arches went down the middle, one line of big arches on both sides. The arches sat on top of these big pillars. There were torches and lamps everywhere, lots of light and so bright you could see how big everything was. There was a line of big, round windows up at the very top of the ceiling there, and the sun shone through those. The whole place was down underground, Dan knew that, the sun came through tunnels; that's what Val had said, at least. "They use mirrors," Val said. Val was mean, but she knew things. Little Dan couldn't remember the last time he'd seen the sun for real. But he sure did like those windows and that light.

"Alright, soldiers," Master Shum said. "Alright." He whacked his club on a pillar three times – WHACK! WHACK!

WHACK! – and everyone shut up, backs straight, sharp and tight. Dan got into formation beside Rost Gonnerdun, who was always at the end of the last row. Rost hooted at him a little. Dan put his finger to his lips to tell Rost to be quiet. Didn't want to get any more "demerits." Or not get 'em. Or whatever.

Master Shum nodded. "High Lords be down here later this morning, 'bout three bells. When they get here, they're gonna see the cleanest, most well-kept armory in the whole of the Kingdom. Jellan's troop is already up, they're workin' on the southern magazines, top to bottom. Malory's crew is in the main stairs and upper foyer. Chief Tendal, Chief Val, your people gonna start in here. Do the floors, the bases, all of it, 'specially the brackets and other hardware. When you're done with that, your troop's gonna be back on the big guns in the fourth gallery. One half'll work the weapons, other half'll work the room." He pointed his club at Val and the Chief. "You two gonna do Stormhammer and Oblivion – yourselves. Big guns going up later today for some exercise, and they're gonna be clean enough to eat off, or little clubby gonna make someone pay for it. Am I clear?"

"Yes, sir! Master Shum, sir!" the Chief and Val shouted together, backs straight.

"Get to it, soldiers!"

The Chief and Val started shouting orders straight away — the Chief to the boys, Val to the girls — but everybody already knew what to do, so nobody really paid attention to them, everybody just getting to work, some kids throwing their stuff down on the ground right where they were, scrubbing away. Val's girls usually got put to task on the torch brackets and lantern hooks and other hardware, door handles and stuff. The Chief's guys broke into squads, and the Chief sent them to different places in the hall. When the Chief got to Rost Gonnerdun and Little Dan, he gave Rost corner duty, which meant that Rost was to go around the whole hall's edge and scrape all of the dust and dirt and stuff out of the corners with his little fingers so that the sweepers could all sweep it up.

"Eadle, you're in the pit. Work off those demerits." The Chief pointed across the hall, to the far corner, to a dark opening in the wall, a big crack that didn't have a door. The pit didn't have any light, either. You had to bring your lamp down there with you, and there were no brackets to hang a lantern on.

"Hear me, Eadle?" the Chief snapped.

"Yes, sir! Chief, sir!" Dan yelled, saluted, and lugged his box off the floor, got moving to the pit.

"Every rat you bring me, I'll take away *one* of your demer-its, soldier," the Chief shouted as Mistress Croot hobbled by, wobbly hump on her back, that weird eye of hers all shiny. Mistress Croot handed the Chief a bundle of fresh rags, then she gave Rost Gonnerdun a little piece of candy and patted him on the head. Rost smiled and hooted.

"Get going," the Chief continued.

But Dan was already gone, yelling over his shoulder as he leaned against the weight of his box, "Yes, sir! Chief, sir!"

8

THE PIT WASN'T like the rest of the armory or the barracks or Stormy's room. No, sir. In the pit, you walked into a big crack in the wall and right when you were inside, the floor kind of sloped down and made it hard to walk. The walls were nice and smooth but only at the beginning, because

134

they changed after a couple steps, and it was more like a cave. After that, you'd walk down a bit and there would be an arch, and after this arch, the pit would turn and go down these steps, and then you'd be at a dead end with a little iron door that was always locked. It was always real dark, so you *had* to bring your lamp. Dan didn't really understand what the pit was for. That is, what you were supposed to do down there. There was that little door, but that was it. You didn't keep anything down there, and you didn't go anywhere. It still had to be clean, of course. But it would be nice to know what you were cleaning it *for*.

At the mouth of the pit, at the big crack in the wall, Dan set down his cleaning box, opened it up, and took out his clay lamp. He checked the oil, and refilled it from his tin. He inspected his brushes and rags and rubbish sacks. He took a nibble from one of the biscuits he'd grabbed from the grub cart. Then he made sure that his water jar still had water in it, because sometimes it spilled out when he was climbing the stairs since the lid didn't fasten right. When that happened, he'd have to go back down and fill it again from the pump at the can, and that would take forever. But the lid was on and everything was in good shape, so he closed his box and lit his lamp with a splinter of flint and a tuft of cotton. When the flame caught, he hefted his box, and stepped into the crack, down into the dark.

"Best way to clean the pit is start at the end, way back in there, then you work your ways back up to everyone," Little Dan said to himself.

He lifted his lamp to see, but his elbow was so tender he was only able to hold it at his side. Then, in the Chief's mellow voice, Dan said, "You clean that pit, soldier. Bring me a big old rat and work off them demerits."

"Yes, sir, Chief!" Dan yelled, his voice echoing against the rock.

The pit always took a long time to clean. It wasn't a very big place, no, sir. But it was gonna take the whole day, and Dan would still be down there after everyone else had gone back to the bunks. He might miss the night's grub carts. There was always grey dust everywhere down here, even if Dan had just cleaned it the week before. He walked down the little stairs, extra careful with his box while keeping an eye out for rats. There was no end to the darn dust—.

Dan stopped in his tracks.

His lamp flame wobbled, a little orange light surrounded by black.

He was at the bottom of the stairs, at the dead end where the little iron door was.

But the little door wasn't closed and locked like it always was, like it was supposed to be.

The little door was open. Wide open, a little rectangle of even deeper black. Someone had put a stone at the door's corner, so it couldn't swing shut.

Dan held up his lamp a bit.

The doorway's dark swallowed the light.

He cleared his throat.

What was he supposed to do? Leave the door open? Shut it? Go tell the Chief? Master Shum?

And for some reason he couldn't put into words, Dan really didn't like the idea of cleaning the pit with that black door open behind him. No, sir.

"You should just shut it," Dan said to himself in Captain Colj's deep ogre voice. "Shut it, soldier. Then take that stone and put it in front. If somebody pushes it open, you'll hear."

"Good idea," Little Dan answered himself.

He stepped to the door, set down his lamp, made to pick up the stone – but then he heard a distant CLANG! way down there in the dark, like the sound you hear when a cage bangs shut.

Little Dan didn't know what the little door was for, but he was pretty darn sure that nobody was supposed to open it. And that meant nobody was supposed to be going down in there.

"The Chief will say you opened it yourself," Dan said to himself in Captain Colj's slow voice.

"Should I go get help?" Dan asked. "Should I go see?"

Another CLANG! came up from below.

Without thinking, Dan picked up his lamp and stepped through the doorway. The flame flickered. Inside, the walls were just like they were outside, all rough and rocky, like a cave. He walked in, made a turn, then went down a few steps. At the end of the steps, a tunnel went for a while then came to an iron gate. The gate was open, and someone had used another stone to keep it from shutting.

Dan stepped through the gate, walked for a moment, then

found himself in a kind of room that split into three different hallways. You could go straight, you could go left, or you could go right. There was no light down any of them.

"Or you could go back, soldier," Dan whispered to the dark.

He cocked his head to listen.

He couldn't hear anything.

He shut his eyes, listened harder.

There!

Somewhere straight ahead, he heard a soft clicking sound, then another sound, like someone moving around. He couldn't really tell how far the noise was — it seemed pretty far away — but it was up there, straight away. Not left. Not right. Straight.

Then everything was quiet again.

"Should I go get help?" Dan whispered. "I go get someone?"

"Who you gonna get?" Dan answered softly in Master Shum's voice. "Ain't even supposed to be down here, boy. Gotta use little clubby on ya?"

"That's right," Dan whispered. "Who I gonna get?"

He could get Mistress Croot.

"Stand tall, boy," Dan growled quietly to himself in Master Falmon's voice. "Stand tall. What if it's a spy or a bad traitor? What if it's the Fake King?"

"That Fake King eats *turds*." Dan nodded.

But he didn't move.

Instead, he just stood there, cocking his head, listening. His lamp's flame wobbled in the dark. His feet were glued to the floor. He didn't hear anything else, but the hairs on the back of his neck were starting to stand up.

"I'm scared," Dan whispered.

"Do not be afraid, little soldier," he answered himself in Captain Colj's ogre voice.

Dan took a couple of steps down the hallway, holding his lamp up. No noise now. He cocked his head and listened harder. The smoky breath of his lamp was the only sound. This dark wasn't like the dark when he was down with Stormy and the other big guns. That dark wasn't scary.

But this?

This was scary.

Dan started to turn around.

Then he stopped, blinked, and turned back.

"Good soldiers don't run. No, sir."

He took a couple steps forward. Then a couple more. There was a door on his right, then another door on his left. He kept going. More doors. Some of the doors were big, others were small. A few of the doors were *real* small, almost like they'd been made for a little boy. But some of the doors were real big, too. And that made him realize how big the hall was. The roof was way up there, so high he couldn't even see it. And the spaces between the doors were funny, too. Sometimes the doors would be right next to each other, their edges almost touching. Sometimes there was five or ten paces between them. Each door had a different kind of lock, too. Some were closed up with iron bars. Others were locked with glowing locks of high silver.

He touched his front pocket, made sure that his flint and steel and cotton were still there.

He knew what he had to do.

Yes, sir.

It was a trick he'd learned a long time ago.

But then he blinked and looked behind him, back the way he'd come, back toward the hall where all his pals were busy working, back up there in the light.

He shook his head.

And then, without another thought, Little Dan Eadle blew out his lamp.

9

HIGH ABOVE, IN the Tarn's Great Library, at the very same moment that Little Dan was blowing out his light, the mighty ogre, Fellen Colj of Jallow, was waiting outside the iron-bound door of Lord Garen's study.

Colj had just knocked on the door. It was one of six set in the eastern wall of the High Lords' private reading chamber. The chamber was connected to the Library's main reading room by a corridor of polished granite. Five reading tables sat in the chamber's center. Tall bookshelves ran along its four walls, packed with leather-bound volumes of many colors and sizes.

Once more, Colj knocked on Lord Garen's door.

"Come." A soft voice came from inside.

Colj opened the door and entered. It was a tight fit, but he was able to scrape through.

Lord Garen's study was a wide, vaulted room lit by gilt safety lanterns and a huge window of blue stained glass. Bookshelves lined the walls, packed with books of every sort, meticulously ordered and perfectly arranged. Three massive worktables of carved Anorian oak sat at the center of the room. On top of these tables, countless jars and cages and boxes and beakers and other items lay neatly stacked, piled, and arranged. In front of Colj, at the edge of the table closest to the door, a wooden stand held four crystal beakers filled with silvery blue liquid. The liquid glowed iridescent; something seemed to move within its depths. Behind these tubes rested a small, silver clock and behind this rested a bamboo cage. A paper label tied to the cage's corner was marked in a language that Colj could not read. There was an insect inside the cage. It was emerald green, with greenish-blue claws like a sea creature might have. The thing's black eyes swayed on green stalks, eyes pointing in different directions before drawing together and settling on Colj.

"You're a big one, aren't you?" the insect asked, the question blossoming in Colj's mind like a jade lotus. Colj grunted and paid the thing no further attention.

A stack of books rested behind the insect's cage. Two High Cups balanced on top of this stack. Behind these, a large glass bowl was filled with clear water, three translucent fish floating in it. Colj could see their purple innards. Each fish had a single black eye in the middle of its forehead, a small metal tag attached to its tail. Part of some important experiment, no doubt. All the tables were like this. Piled high with carefully organized arcana from over a hundred worlds; a scholar's paradise.

At the center of the study's eastern wall, the only wall not entirely filled by bookshelves, a huge, round window of blue stained glass lit the scene with sapphire light. The window was set at the base of a shaft that penetrated the Tarn's eastern fortifications. A series of mirrors set in the shaft amplified the light of Kon's morning sun. In winter's dawn, the window's glass glowed blue. The silvery sigil at its center was a shimmering, six-pointed sun. At the tip of each sun point, there was a tondo. Each tondo contained a portrait in stained glass, each portrait a member of the ancient founding family, like this:

Of course, Colj knew each of them. The tondo at the sun's top held a portrait of Acasius Dallanar. He was shown pensive and brooding; his eyes were downcast and prophetic. The First Sister, Eressa the Lost, was at Acasius's right. Her face was dark, beautiful, and fierce. She was set in profile and gazed into her token, a silver tear, as if staring into fathomless eternity. Alea the True, the Second Sister, was shown in the tondo beneath Eressa. Her eyes were sad, her portrait set frontally so that the famous scar on her right cheek could be seen. Her eyes looked to the right where her symbol, the silver sword, filled the rest of her tondo. Aaryn the Chronicler was next, at the bottom of the sun, her face set frontally, a serious face, yet one filled with radiant energy and great potential for joy; even in image, Colj could tell that her ja was strong. Aaryn held her token – the great silver book, the Canon which she had begun – but she did not look at it. Instead, she looked down into the study, her eyes seeming to rest on Garen's desk. The Fourth Sister, Kora the Just, came next. Her face was shown in profile, narrow and sharply boned, but with eyes filled with kindness. In her right hand, she held a pair of silver balances, the scales held in perfect equilibrium. Finally, coming full circle, there was the Fifth Sister, Margo the Gentle, a happy, round-faced girl with shining dark eyes and a huge grin. She looked straight out of her tondo, holding her token at her side – a silver cornucopia. To Colj, her eyes had always seemed to gleam with happiness.

Beneath the window, bathed in its blue light, young Lord Garen Dallanar sat at his desk with his two nieces and his nephew. The High Lord was a slender young man of twenty years, dark of hair and eye. He wore ancient reading spectacles of high silver. His young charges – Lady Kyla, Lord Tarlen, and Lady Susan – sat across from him in full-sized chairs, their feet swinging. They were in the middle of an examination of some sort. Unlike the other Dallanar of the royal family, whose features were dark, these children had paler complexions and blond hair, like their father and mother, Lord Tomas and Lady Eíra. Lady Kyla was fourteen, Lord Tarlen had just turned eleven, and little Lady Susan was seven. The children were brilliant, a fact well-known. Indeed, young Lord Tarlen often beat Colj in games of chess, and Colj was considered something of a master among his people.

In the far corner of the room, in the shadows, stood Ponj, Colj's only living son. Ponj was the children's bodyguard. One of the family's cloud mastiffs, Bruno, lay snoring at Ponj's feet. Colj nodded to his son. Ponj nodded in return.

On the table in front of Lord Garen, resting on a blue velvet pad, was the High Cup that Lady Katherine had just returned with from Paráden. As a High Cup, it was a container of memory; the mystical vision it held was the reason for tomorrow's parley. A tiny star tree sat next to the Cup, its roots wrapped in a bright blue burlap sack. The little tree's coppery field swelled and pushed against the edges of the table. Several vials of different shapes and sizes rested beside the burlap sack – Lord Garen experimenting with the roots and abilities of the tiny tree, no doubt.

When Colj stepped forward, little Susan cried, "Colj!"

Tarlen glanced over and smiled. Colj gave them both a formal bow, but his eyes were drawn to Kyla. The young lady looked at him, nodded politely, then looked away. Her ja was troubled. Dark circles ringed her eyes. Her face was pale. Colj frowned. It was well-known that Lady Kyla had been unwell since her parents' murder a year ago. And yet the other children seemed fine.

"See, Ponj!" Lady Susan glanced over at the corner, toward the young ogre. "Your dad *did* come. Now we can all be here together."

Ponj inclined his head but said nothing. Colj also remained silent, then sat on a special-made stool near the door. He did not want to distract them from their lessons. Deep in his nap, Bruno snorted.

"Susan." Lord Garen took off his spectacles, polished them, and put them back on. "Please. I asked you a question. To whom is this shape assigned?"

"Yes, Uncle." Lady Susan gave Colj a wink, then turned back to Lord Garen and her task.

Colj looked closer and saw that Lady Susan was inspecting five silver models, each no taller than a human hand. Each model represented the traditional form of one of the Sisters' High Gates:

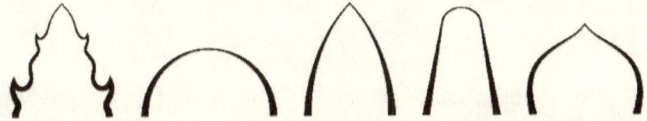

Lord Garen was gesturing to the model in the middle, the one that looked like a tapering arch, heavy at its base, pointed at its peak. Lord Garen tapped his finger and raised an eyebrow. "To whom is this shape assigned?" he asked again.

"That's so easy," Lady Susan said. She yawned, stretched, and finally said, "Aaryn. Like ours, of *course*."

"Good." Lord Garen nodded. "And this." The young lord pointed to a model gate shaped like a narrow doorway, wide at the bottom, its top slightly rounded.

"Kora." Lady Susan bounced slightly, her feet swinging.

Garen inclined his head. "And this." He pointed to a silver gate like a half circle.

"Alea."

"And this?" He touched a model with a profile like a turnip.

"Margo."

"And this?" An intricately formed gate, entirely different from the others, as if almost no silver at all had been used in its making, a fragile tracery governed by neither geometry nor chance.

"Eressa," Susan said. "*Obviously*." She turned and looked up at the Great Sisters in the stained-glass window behind her uncle.

"Good." Lord Garen nodded. "Now the Pendants."

Lady Susan sighed with mock exacerbation and rolled her eyes, looking from Ponj to Colj then back to Ponj again. Colj was happy to see that Ponj refused to indulge her, giving no response. His son understood the value of training.

Lord Garen unlocked the drawer of his desk. From it, he withdrew a thin case of pale korom's wood. The young lord said a few words, the case whispered open, and he took forth a small amulet of high silver on a high silver chain. It was a High Pendant, Colj saw. It gleamed in the window's blue light, a flawless object, a series of seamless arabesques, spiraled curls wrapped and woven into each other with a precision that embodied the mathematical perfection of the Realm.

"Who made this?" Lord Garen asked, hanging the Pendant on its stand.

Lady Susan sighed. "Eressa."

"How do you know?"

"'Cause it's her *style*."

"How many High Pendants are associated with each of the Realm's duchies?"

Lady Susan looked at him for a moment. Then her eyes went narrow. "Are you punishing me 'cause I shouted at Colj when he came in?"

"No," Lord Garen said.

"Then why're you asking me questions I already *know*? Anyway, it's Tarlen's turn."

Lord Garen didn't answer.

Lady Susan didn't say anything either.

The silence continued for a long moment.

"We do need to proceed, Susan," Lord Garen said. "Much to do today. How many Pendants were given to the first High Houses?"

"Five," Lady Susan said. "Five each."

"Who bestowed them?"

"The Great Sisters. Or their emissaries."

"Why?" Lord Garen asked.

"Signs of their authority," Lady Susan droned, rolling her eyes. "So they could travel without using Gates. If you travel by Gate, the Gate's adepts have to sing the Gate open, sing the right song so you can get where you wanna go, and that takes time, and you need adepts and permission, and then everybody will know when and where you went. But if you travel by Pendant, you can do it on your *own*, any time, fast, using your own memory and nothing else."

"Good." Lord Garen nodded. "Now, your best estimate: How many High Pendants are extant?"

"Lots." Lady Susan smiled.

"What does 'lots' mean?"

Susan took an apple out of her pocket and began to eat, looking back at the stained-glass window, swinging her feet. The window's blue light made her eyes seem dark.

"How many, Susan?" Lord Garen asked.

"Four hundred and eighty something," she said while she

ate. "Lots are missing, too. *Obviously*."

"How do you explain the preservation of these artifacts over the millennia?"

Lady Susan paused; her mouth was full of apple. "Well, they're made of high silver, so they can't be crushed or melted or anything like that."

"They can still be lost." Lord Garen steepled his fingers. "We live at the edge of the single longest cultural continuum in human history. Over ten thousand years. A cultural epoch of that length could barely be conceived in ancient times——."

Lady Susan interrupted him with a bite of her apple. "They're the most precious heirlooms we *have*, Uncle. It's not something you leave in the sofa cushions. The High Pendants are *guarded*. You don't just *lose* them."

"How do they work alongside the High Cups?"

"I think you're punishing me." Lady Susan munched her apple.

"Please, answer."

"Fine." She bit into her apple and talked around it. "With a Pendant, you can only travel to a place *you* remember, a place *you've* actually been, using your *own* memory. But

High Cups hold *other* people's memories. So when you drink from a High Cup, you experience the memory it has and that memory becomes yours. Since the memory in the Cup is now your memory, you can use a High Pendant to travel where the memory in the Cup took place. With the right Cup and a Pendant, you can travel anywhere in the Realm. Alright?"

"Good." Lord Garen nodded seriously. "For tonight's work, you'll draft a list – from memory – that gives a brief description of each world that the Sisters visited. You will list them alphabetically. You'll use no more than three dozen words for each description. I'd also like you to give the name of the world's current ruling house as well as their colors and coat of arms. If the duchy is contested, you may simply note that along with other details. You may draw the coats of arms, if you like."

Lady Susan moaned. "Can't I just tell you now? That's a hundred and four *worlds*! I don't want to draw them all, write them all down. It's a *lot*." Then she grinned mischievously. "Besides, one or two sentences for each duchy seems a little superficial. You can't summarize a planet in a sentence."

"Would you like to write more?"

"No." She swallowed a big bite of apple and coughed. "But it's still a *lot*."

"Indeed, it is. You will also give the exact number of High Gates that the Founding Sisters established on each world and the Founding Year in which each world entered the Kingdom as a duchy. This is your last exam on the basic structure of the Realm. If you can demonstrate knowledge and retention now, I won't ask you to repeat it. You are seven years old, Susan; it's time to move forward to more complex subjects."

"Ugh," Lady Susan grunted and took another bite of apple. "I hate memorizing."

"Memory is a skill." Lord Garen looked at her closely. "And the mind is a muscle. A complex muscle with many parts to be trained. Any fool can open a book, find what is needed. That is not knowledge. Memory is how you build knowledge, knowledge of your own. Knowledge is the basis of everything else, tactics, art, philosophy – and more. Remember: Clear thinking, clear memory, and clear writing—."

"Clear writing, clear memory, and clear thinking," Susan

droned. "Yes, Uncle." She sat back in her chair, scowling. Then she turned, grinned impishly, took another bite of her apple, and winked at Colj. Without thinking, Colj found himself wanting to wink back at her, but he stopped short. Like her uncle, Lady Susan was exceptionally intelligent for her seven years and very charismatic. In any other family, it would have been uncanny, but she was a Dallanar. Regardless, it would be inappropriate to encourage lack of discipline.

Lord Garen nodded, took the High Pendant from its stand, lay it back in its korom's wood case, and put the case back into the drawer. Then Lord Garen turned to Lord Tarlen and pulled from beneath his desk a withered branch of dark wood. But it was not a branch, Colj realized. It was a long arm. Fossilized and black, malformed and strange. The elbow was bent backwards and several of the fingers seemed twice their proper length. The middle finger was longer than a dagger and just as sharp.

Lord Garen looked at Lord Tarlen. "What is this?" He set the thing on the worktable.

"The arm of a voidfiend," Lord Tarlen said, lifting the thing for inspection. "A *kalaban*, in the ancient tongue."

"Explain this arm's appearance."

"It was probably caught and killed in the middle of transformation."

Lord Garen cocked his head. "Transformation?"

Lord Tarlen nodded. "A kalaban can take the form of a tall humanoid or a large bird or a combination of both — a sort of hybrid. They can also sort of curl up into a kind of ball, too. Very small. To rest and hide."

"Hide?" Lord Garen raised an eyebrow.

"They're stealth units. Assassins and infiltrators. Not front-line fighters."

Lord Garen pointed at the strange, blade-like finger of the hand. "What of this?"

"Part of its sword," Lord Tarlen said. "Like I said, it was probably caught in the middle of transformation. Their blades are a part of them, built into their templates. In battle, it will appear as a weapon held in hand, but it can't really be 'disarmed,' at least not as we'd use that word." Lord Tarlen looked closely at the dark fossil, clearly fascinated. "If I remember the shape of this particular arm correctly, this kalaban was discovered and killed by Poder Jarlen, on Wenevron during the sixth year of the Founding War, the last year of the siege of that duchy. Mother showed me this two years ago, told me the story."

Colj nodded to himself. Only weeks past his eleventh birthday, and the son was already very much like the father. Young Lord Tarlen's forehead was broad, like Lord Garen's. But that's where the resemblance ended. His hands and gestures were sure and smooth, his shoulders already broad, his blue eyes sharp, all as his father's, Lord Tomas, had been. When Lord Tarlen spoke, Colj noticed how Ponj looked at the young lord with admiration, his son's eyes bright with interest. The young ogre and Lord Tarlen were fast friends, an alliance that would be priceless for Jallow in the future. In the present, Ponj enjoyed the trust, the company, and the education of the most well-trained children in the Realm.

"Eíra told you that, eh?" Lord Garen inclined his head. "What's the story? What does it teach?"

Lord Tarlen nodded. "Jarlen had liberated the duchy in early winter following the voidfolk's retreat. They left nothing behind — except hundreds of sleeping kalaban."

He gestured at the arm. "This thing was hidden in a basket with a false bottom, then placed in the closet of the largest bedchamber of Wenevron's High Keep. It was left to nest, to wait, and then to wake and kill Jarlen, if it could. To murder him in his sleep."

Lady Kyla had been quiet hitherto. But now she stared at Lord Tarlen. Her face was composed, but her hands clenched in her lap; she seemed distressed. Her skin was pale, the dark circles under her eyes more pronounced than ever. Colj had never seen her like this. Indeed, it was very rare for a Dallanar High Lord or Lady to display anything but the most careful training, even in private. Lord Garen had noticed her discomfort as well, but he ignored it.

"But Poder Jarlen knew it was there," Lord Tarlen continued. "He caught the thing. Tried to tame it. But it didn't work. So, he killed it."

"And the lesson?" Lord Garen asked.

"There are many," Lord Tarlen said. "One is that high houses must expect and prepare for all types of incursion. Subterfuge can be more deadly than naked aggression. A single traitor or spy behind your lines can pose a greater threat than ten thousand charging soldiers at your front. The enemy can take many forms, some of them familiar. Be aware of your surroundings at all times; allow trained consciousness to unfold into every space, into every situation."

Lady Kyla looked at her brother and said, "Sleep with one eye open?"

"Yes." Lord Tarlen returned her gaze with a friendly nod. "That's right."

Lady Kyla made to speak again, but Lord Garen stopped her with a raised hand and turned back to Lord Tarlen. "Can you outline for me the deployment pattern of the last kalaban infiltrators at the end of the Founding War, after the retreat of the voidfolk from Golladus?"

"Of course." Lord Tarlen nodded. "The enemy sent thousands of kalaban into the Kingdom, like pollen. Since our forces could respond instantly to aggression on any duchy by way of the High Gates, the enemy's counter was to 'sow' the Kingdom with fiends and attempt to reach unprotected duchies at random. Against an unprepared world, against unarmed civilians, a single voidfiend could be devastating. But it was a useless strategy. If 'strategy' is the word that you'd want to use."

"Why do you say that?" Lord Garen asked. "What's the problem with the vocabulary?"

"Even at incredible speeds — and before you say it, I know our understanding of their navigational lore is limited — it would take a kalaban thousands of years to reach our outermost duchies. At the same time, we could cross to that same world instantly by Gate. It's the core strength of the Realm, the brilliance of Acasius's imperial vision. Then, as now, our troops can respond anywhere in the Kingdom in moments. Theirs was an archaic model, rooted in ancient modes of starfaring. Like the space sailors of Póntokos, for example." He paused, then opened his hands and shrugged. "It's just too slow, Uncle. Too slow and too random to be considered a real threat. Imperial ambition, in the sense that Acasius and the Sisters teach, must be sustained by three pillars: consistently fast communication, consistently fast travel, and the disciplined will to combine that speed with force to maintain order, commerce, and culture. Without these, the Realm as we know it can't be preserved. The voidfolk were desperate. They knew we'd won. It wasn't a tactical move. It wasn't 'strategy.' It was desperation, nothing more. So, they launched countless kalaban into the stars." He gestured at the withered, black arm. "A final, futile gambit."

"You seem quite certain," Garen mused.

"Should we be otherwise?" Lord Tarlen asked. "Thousands of years have passed. The archaeology is clear. As is the history. What evidence exists to the contrary? I *am* certain."

"Nonsense," Lady Kyla said.

She had regained her composure and now glanced from Lord Tarlen to Lord Garen, then back to Lord Tarlen. Her back was straight.

"Nonsense," she said again.

"Nonsense what?" Lord Tarlen looked at her with genuine curiosity. "Which part?"

Lady Kyla ignored his question. "What would the great Poder Jarlen say about 'certainty,' Tarlen? What would Mother and Father have said about 'certainty?'"

Lord Garen looked at Lady Kyla for a long moment. He took off his spectacles, peered through, polished them, and put them back on. He turned to Lord Tarlen, waiting for the boy to answer.

"If they were here," Lord Tarlen said slowly, "they'd say 'certainty is the succor of fools' – something wise like that."

"Indeed." Lady Kyla arched an eyebrow.

"But you can't just—," Lord Tarlen began.

Lady Kyla interrupted him, gestured at the twisted, dark arm. Her voice was calm, trained, and confident. "How long do these things live, Tarlen? How long? Susan? You have any idea?"

Lady Susan shrugged. "I dunno." Lady Susan had been watching Bruno twitch in his sleep as she finished up the last of her apple, not really paying attention to the discussion.

"Well," Tarlen began carefully, as if looking for a trap. "There isn't much known about their biological cycles. But all the evidence suggests a very long lifespan. Millennia, almost certainly."

"And it would have to be that long, wouldn't it?" Kyla continued. "If these things were 'sown into the stars?' Is that not true? By your own reckoning, their journeys would be thousands of years or more."

"What's your point, Ky?" Lord Tarlen asked. He was not frustrated, Colj saw. He was honestly interested.

"My point, brother, is that they need not to have been 'launched' at all in order to be a sustained threat — as your own story proves. How many more of these things have been hidden, left to be found by some unsuspecting traveler, farmer, or child? The nightmare of the Founding War left no duchy untouched; this is common knowledge. But what of the Plague Years? Nearly ten millennia of chaos, a time of incomparable pettiness and cruelty. Don't you find it strange that there are more 'plague years' than 'years of peace' in the Realm's 'great and glorious history'? I do. '*Continuum*' they call it? Ha! I can't——."

"What does that have to do with anything?" Lady Susan piped in, wiping her fingers on her shirt. She shook her head and looked at the dark fossil. "That's not what Tarlen's question was about. I'm hungry. I'm bored."

"These things." Lady Kyla gestured at the black arm. "Could be anywhere. Not spread like pollen but planted like seeds. Left to wait, to wait with patience — invincible patience — the patience of the hunter, the hunter who knows it's just a matter of time."

Lord Tarlen shrugged amicably. "That's not really a

counter to my answer, Ky. The question was about the stra-
tegic value of the voidfolk's last days and moves. I'm sure
that we——."

"You're *sure?*" Lady Kyla shook her head. "Look what
happens now, right now." She gestured out at the blue
stained-glass window. Colj saw her hand shake slightly
before she put it back in her lap. "Outside these very walls,
our people kill each other while we debate the 'tactical
merits' of our enemy's final moments? It's absurd. *We* are the
enemy, Tarlen. The voidfolk – if they're still there – don't
need to attack. Nor do they need to defend. All they need
to do is *wait*. Wait while we cut our own throats, while we
destroy our own people, kill our own family. Wait until they
can quietly step over our corpses, into the fertile ashes that
remain."

10

THE WORDS POURED out of her, almost of their own accord.

And Kyla Dallanar was glad to have said them. She lifted
her chin and looked from Tarlen to Garen.

They were in private.

They were with family.

And the words were *true*.

Tarlen gazed at her, curious and friendly, not at all offended by her ideas. Susan frowned — half listening, but distracted, too — digging in her pockets for another snack. Colj and Ponj looked at her quietly, their calm stoicism the hallmark of all ogres of Jallow. Colj's huge head tilted with attention, as it always was when he was listening intently. Garen nodded thoughtfully, a typical response, neither studied nor judgmental.

And then Garen said, almost out of nowhere, "Good." He gestured at the withered kalaban arm in front of him. "Tarlen, for tonight, I want you to take this back to your quarters, create a scale drawing. Three-to-one should be fine, so long as relevant details are recorded and studied. Or you can make a model, if you prefer."

"I'll draw it, Garen," Tarlen said.

Garen nodded. "You'll also write an essay, a full summary of what is known regarding kalaban tactics, dispersal, and combat metrics. I'd like to see emphasis on the evidence provided by the archaeological material that we have in our collections here. You'll also compile all accounts of Poder Jarlen's attempt to 'tame' his kalaban, distill them into a short precis, and attach it to your essay as an appendix."

Tarlen nodded. "Yes, Garen."

Kyla looked Garen in the eye. "You don't have anything to say about my thoughts, Uncle?"

"In a moment." Garen nodded.

"So." Tarlen cleared his throat and glanced at Ponj. "For tomorrow morning. Where will we watch parley?"

Susan glanced from Tarlen to Garen. "We get to *watch*? Where?"

Ponj was paying close attention. Bruno snuffled, rolled onto his side, and burped, his stumpy grey tale thumping the floor. Susan laughed. Garen blinked, made to reach for his spectacles, stopped himself, and nodded. "You can observe from the western tower. I think that might be best. Filip Toller and his scouts should be back through the sea catacombs this morning. I'm sure Doldon could be convinced to have them stationed in one of the high towers, yes. The Pinnacle, perhaps. If you like, I can have Toller's squad assigned to you as escorts."

At Filip's name, in spite of herself, Kyla felt her cheeks go warm. She cleared her throat and sat up a little straighter.

"Superb." Tarlen glanced at Ponj. Ponj nodded back at his lord and friend.

And then Kyla noticed Susan looking at her, a sly little grin on her little sister's face.

"Filip Toller," Susan mouthed silently and made a silent kissing gesture with her lips. Susan glanced at Garen, then back at Kyla and winked, her grin becoming positively devilish. The little girl was too smart for her own good.

"Don't you dare," Kyla mouthed to her.

Susan giggled, swung her feet, and said aloud, "I wonder if handsome, wonderful, *brave* Filip has any special news. What do you think, Ky? Maybe we want to hear the top-secret reports from the field, straight from his *lips*? Ha-ha!"

The little snot! Kyla scowled, but her frown was half-hearted. In fact, to her chagrin, Kyla realized that a huge smile had crept onto her face and that her cheeks had gone warmer still. Garen didn't seem to notice, neither did Tarlen. But Susan's eyes gleamed playfully as she laughed, swinging her little feet like mad.

Garen nodded, looked to Ponj. "You'll see to the arrangements and security?"

From the corner, the young ogre bowed. "My Lord."

Garen nodded and said softly, almost like he was talking to himself. "The Pinnacle is well within the field perimeter. We can put another tree up there, to be sure." He glanced at the little star tree on his desk, the one with its roots in the bright blue burlap sack; the field around it shimmered like coppery mist.

"'Oh, *Filip*?'" Susan crooned, swinging her feet, her voice taking on a sing-song lilt. "'*Filip*, dear? Can you show me how you handle your *carbine*? Teach *me* how to shoot, Filip.' Ha-ha!"

Kyla, still smiling in spite of herself, kicked Susan's chair under the table, but Susan just laughed and chewed on the core of her apple, munching like a little cow. You just couldn't get mad at such a smart, happy kid.

"Tarlen, Susan," Garen said. "You're dismissed for breakfast. Report to your tutors at the ninth bell, please. And be sure to bring your assignments first thing tomorrow. He took off his spectacles, polished them, and squinted through their lenses. We'll be preparing for parley. But I'll expect to see your work here, before we arm."

Tarlen and Susan nodded, scooted their chairs back, and hopped down. Tarlen went over to Ponj and started talking to him in a low voice, planning. Susan walked to Bruno, stepped one leg over him, and gently lowered herself onto the cloud mastiff's furry side, her arms and legs dangling over the big dog's ribcage. She pressed her face into his muscular shoulder, shutting her eyes, as if listening to his heartbeat. Bruno's fur sparkled like morning mist; he sighed contently with Susan's weight. Colj rose from his seat by the door and stepped to Garen's desk.

"Captain?" Garen looked up at him.

Colj inclined his huge head toward Kyla, in deference to her. "I believe Lady Kyla had a query, my Lord," the ogre said in his huge, slow voice.

Garen glanced at her. She looked straight back at him, letting her gaze do the talking. Garen nodded. "I understand your frustration, Ky. All too well. This is why we meet for parley tomorrow. The High King's command. We must find some end to this."

"And what if you're killed," Kyla said directly, not bothering to lower her voice.

Tarlen, Ponj, and Susan all looked up. Colj gazed at her, an attentive expression on his enormous face, as if carefully considering every word.

Kyla continued. "Parley is a risk. Maybe it's a trap."

"Yes." Garen cocked his head. "It may be a trap. And it's most certainly a risk. But it's a risk worth taking. More to the point, it is the King's command." He paused, looked at her over the edge of his spectacles. "There are many on all sides, including our own, Ky, who would like to see diplomacy fail, for total war to be unleashed."

"We're not at war now?" Kyla's eyebrows went up.

"Of course not. Even with everything that's happened, the King restrains us. He thinks we can find a way. And I agree with him. I thought you would, too, Ky."

"What does the Queen say?"

Just barely, Garen's mouth twitched. To the untaught eye, the gesture would've been imperceptible. But to Kyla, trained from childhood in the arts of perception, it was a silent shriek.

"She agrees with the King." Garen cleared his throat. "We must try. The possibility of peace . . . . A ceasefire, at least. It's worth it."

"Perhaps." Kyla frowned. "And if you're murdered on the Long Bridge?"

The others were listening intently now.

Garen inclined his head. "It is a possibility every soldier of the Remain understands, as you well know." He looked at her closely, then he glanced at Colj. "We have our orders. And we have an opportunity."

Garen turned his gaze to the High Cup resting on the blue velvet cushion in front of him. When Kate had returned, she had brought the Cup back with her, Kyla had learned. Kyla still hadn't seen Kate, she still didn't know what vision the High Cup contained, nor how Kate had acquired it – but she was anxious to hear the tale. But now that Kyla thought on it, why hadn't Kate come to see her yet? To see all of them? And what in the world was Garen hiding, for the Sisters' sake? Because suddenly, once again, Kyla sensed an unstated anxiety floating around her, as if the world had ended and nobody had told her.

"An opportunity that we must take," Garen continued. Then he frowned and looked at her. "Again, I thought you would support this move, Ky. I'm surprised to hear you raise concern."

Kyla looked at the High Cup. It was more like a bowl: It had neither stem nor lip, more like the hollowing of a sphere, a perfect fit for two hands.

"I do support it, of course," Kyla said. "Any chance for reconciliation must be taken. And I understand your duty — *our* duty. I'm just——. I don't want anything to happen to you. That's my concern."

"In that, we're in agreement." Garen nodded and glanced up at Colj. "Colj will be there with me. Michael will be there, too."

Kyla shook her head. "But not *with* you." And upon hearing her own words, Kyla suddenly felt as if she was the youngest of her siblings rather than the oldest. She breathed it out, kept her hands in her lap, and focused.

"You're right," Garen carried on, oblivious to her momentary distress. "Michael won't be with me. But he'll be close. Those are the rules. Formal parley is about trust, ostensibly.

And don't forget: Anna and Moondagger and the rest of the Davanórians will be but moments away. I will have other protection, as well." Garen glanced at the little star tree on the worktable, its coppery field shimmering with other-worldly light. Then he looked at her directly. "We must try, Ky. This can't go on forever. I know you agree."

In her mind's eye, unbidden yet again, she saw him dying on the Long Bridge, blood pumping from that mortal wound. And then she saw her parents, lying on their twin pyre, clasped hands lifeless and cold, waiting for fire's fury to take them into memory. Kyla had held the pyre's torch in one hand, Susan's little hand in the other. Nana had been behind her, hands on her shoulders, singing the ancient dirge; tears blurred her vision, tears that never seemed to end.

"Yes." Kyla cleared her throat. "I see."

Because she did believe in the effort, of course, even if she didn't know how or why the opportunity had afforded itself. She looked again at the silver Cup on its blue cushion and suddenly realized that she *needed* to talk to Nana. Or to Kate. She hadn't seen Nana in days. She hadn't seen Kate in years. Neither of them had any reason to hide anything from her —

and they would know what was really going on.

"What does that contain?" She gestured to the High Cup.

Garen shook his head. "It's too much to discuss right now." He looked over at the others meaningfully. "But I can promise you, for good or ill, all your questions will be answered by tomorrow's end."

She knew him well enough not to keep pushing. And his word was always true.

"Good." Garen nodded, sensing her acceptance. The others had turned back to their own conversations, Ponj and Tarlen whispering and planning the observation of tomorrow's action from the Pinnacle, Susan humming, her cheek buried in Bruno's grey fur.

Garen turned to Colj. "Captain?"

The great ogre looked at Kyla, waiting to be sure she'd finished speaking. Kyla nodded politely at his deference.

Colj said slowly in his deep ogre voice, "There is a boy from below, my Lord. I believe he should be examined. He is gifted. His ja is strong. A small boy. A simple boy. One of the cleaners. I noticed him again last night."

"A cleaning boy?" Garen looked puzzled, as if he didn't

understand the ogre's words. "What do you mean by 'simple?'"

Colj nodded, then said deliberately, "He is simple, as they say." He touched his own temple. "'Daniel Eadle' is the name given in the muster. He has no living parents; no kin. An orphan from Tarntown. He came in with the others as a refugee when the Pretender King took the city; so it is written."

Garen frowned. "Isn't this a matter for Master Falmon, Captain? Perhaps one of his subordinates? Why bring this to me?"

Colj considered for a long moment. When he spoke, his voice was soft and unbelievably deep, as if the words themselves were sacred. "The boy's ja is strong, my Lord. He is something unique. Truly unique. He is gifted." He paused. "He requires your personal attention, my Lord. He requires your examination."

Garen looked at him for a moment, then nodded. "Very well." He paused. "But after parley, if it can wait."

The ogre looked at Garen for a long moment, as if carefully considering Garen's words, then he inclined his huge head. "It cannot wait, my Lord."

"Indeed?" Garen glanced up at Colj, his eyes suddenly penetrating. Colj returned Garen's gaze.

"Very well." Garen nodded. "Speak to Master Falmon, then bring him up today, this afternoon, after council. Check with Ness for the schedule, if you would; he'll need to be present, also."

"Of course, my Lord."

There was a soft knock on the door.

"Come," Garen said.

The door swung open — and it was Kate. Kate was there. Slender, beautiful, her dark hair freshly washed, dressed in clean blue trousers, a white silk blouse, a broad belt of blue Abúcian leather. Garen's secretary, the Tarn's old librarian, Nordo Ness, stood behind her, leaning on his walking stick, a happy gleam in his ancient eyes. A high silver revolver hung from Kate's hip. Kyla knew that her young aunt always wore a high silver blade sheathed at the small of her back.

But Kate also looked different, Kyla realized. A bit older, to be sure. But also . . . what? Two years ago, the gossip surrounding Kate's departure had been savage. Lies, deception, and rumors of the ultimate crime: betrayal. Kyla had never believed any of it, of course — even if some of the others had.

"Auntie!" Susan cried, rolling off Bruno. "You're back!" She ran to Kate, throwing her arms around Kate's legs. Tarlen and Ponj and Bruno followed, the war dog's fur hazing and blurring in that smoky way it did when the big mastiff got excited. Colj nodded at Kate; Kate returned the gesture. Garen grinned from behind his desk, trying not to smile too much, inclining his head at the High Cup on the blue cushion in front of him, a kind of silent acknowledgement.

"Welcome, sister," Garen said. And then his grin broke into a huge, unrestrained smile.

Kate beamed as the kids and dog crowded around her, a close huddle of laughter and love, everyone hugging and squeezing and talking at once, Ponj squeezing them togeth-er, a giant ball of family. Kyla got up to join them, trying to preserve some dignity, but before she knew what was happening, she was running, her arms thrown around Kate's neck, mashing Susan into Ponj's thick legs.

"Hey!" Susan squeaked, then laughed. Bruno barked happily, pacing in circles around them, the cloud mastiff's smoky grey fur shimmering with even more energy, barking, pacing, barking again. Tarlen was babbling something to Kate about some project he and Ponj were working on, Ponj nodding his big head with about as much enthusiasm as Kyla thought she'd ever seen from an ogre.

"Kate! Kate! You want the rest of my apple?" Susan's hand sprouted out of the hugging mass in front of Kate's face, waving a wet, mostly devoured, apple core. "It's from Dayáden. So *good!*"

Kate laughed, grabbed Susan's wrist, bit off a piece. Then she turned to Kyla, kissed her cheeks, and squeezed her tight. And then Kyla felt the tears come, unchecked, unashamed, the relief flooding out and through her like a wave, the anxiety pouring out of her and away.

From nowhere, a thought entered her mind: *This is why it must end, whatever the risk.*

For love. For peace.

For family.

"Auntie!" Susan hollered at Kate from the middle of all the hugging. "Where the heck have you *been?*"

The total rightness – the total artlessness – of Susan's

question struck Kyla as insanely funny, and before she knew what was happening, she was laughing until her sides ached, tears streaming down her cheeks.

11

THE MOMENT LITTLE Dan Eadle blew out his lamp, the darkness swallowed him. Greenish-white shapes danced in front of his eyes.

Dan waved his hand in front of his face, but he couldn't see it.

Not even when he touched his finger to his nose.

So he shut his eyes.

It was a trick he'd learned a while back, when they used to lock him in the barracks with Crazy Bill. You had to shut your eyes, get them used to the dark, then open them up so you could find your way out. The trick was to use your *ears* and to look for that little crack of light at the bottom of the door.

Little Dan kept his eyes shut and listened as hard as he could.

Nothing.

Not a sound.

Eyes closed, he took a step. Then another, soft like a mouse, one hand on the wall, ears open.

Somewhere in the dark ahead of him, he heard another soft click.

Dan opened his eyes.

"There you is, you sweet little thing," Dan whispered to himself in Crazy Bill's crazy voice. "Gotcha."

About forty paces away, Dan could see a crack of light at the bottom of a door. Above that, there was another tiny spot of light, like the light of a flame through a keyhole.

Dan crept forward. When he reached the door, he stood on his tiptoes, put his eye to the keyhole, and peeked inside.

It was Master Falmon.

Little Dan sighed with relief, almost startling himself with the noise.

The Master was standing in front of a cabinet made of silvery wood, lighting some clay lamps. He'd light a lamp, then he'd place it in a kind of silver cradle hanging on a silver chain from the ceiling. But the chains didn't look like any chains that Dan had ever seen. They didn't have any links.

Instead, they looked like silvery vines. They didn't clink or rattle when they moved, either. Instead, they sort of whispered. Master Falmon would light a lamp, say a word, and the silvery vine would whisper back up, lifting the lamp toward the ceiling while other vines dropped down. The lamps shone on the Master's scarred face; you could see every cut and lump and slash.

"Eadle," Master Falmon growled. "If you're gonna stand out there makin' all that racket, might as well come in and gimme a hand." He lit another lamp and didn't look up. "Need to talk to you, anyways. Opened the little side door up there for you, didn't I?"

Dan blinked at the keyhole, then took a step back.

"Come on." Master Falmon grunted and adjusted his eye patch. He placed another lamp in its cradle and spoke a soft word. The silver vine whispered and lifted the lamp toward the room's ceiling. The entire room glowed with warm, orange light. "Let's go, boy. Don't make me ask again."

Dan reached up and pulled the latch, his sore elbow twinging with the motion. The door swung inward. But Dan didn't enter. Instead, he stood at the doorway and looked up at the lamps hanging at the end of their silvery vines.

"Up already, eh?" Master Falmon asked, not looking at him. "Up and at 'em?"

Dan nodded.

Master Falmon glanced at him. "Good thing they always give you the pit, otherwise I'd have had to come get you. Safer this way."

Dan nodded again. But he didn't really understand.

Safer?

Master Falmon grunted. "Good boy. High Lords be down again soon. Big day tomorrow. Big day. Parley. Could mean peace. Could mean more war. Either way, gotta be ready for the worst. Put your lamp down there beside the door, so you don't forget it."

Dan swallowed, crossed his fist against his chest in a silent salute, and put his lamp down where Master Falmon said.

"Well?" Master Falmon grunted.

Dan stepped into the room. It was square and not too big, maybe ten paces across on each side. The ceiling was way taller than he'd expected. Dozens and dozens of lamps hung from the silvery vines up there. The vines came out of these floating silver balls. Each ball was about the size of a fist and each one had these strange designs and patterns carved on them. The balls just floated there in the air, right below the ceiling, moving slowly, warm light all over everything.

Along the walls of the room, there were a bunch of cabinets, all of them set side by side, each about as tall as a grown-up. The cabinets were made of different kinds of wood. Some of the wood was warm and brown, some was pale and silvery, some was golden, some was red. A few of the cabinets on the wall across from the door were made from wood that was almost black. All the cabinets were carved with all kinds of different shapes and creatures and scenes and things. Some cabinets had shields and swords and axes and other weapons carved on them. Some had the Tarn's symbol, the six-point-ed sun. Then there were others that had carved pictures of fighting, each little fight in its own little box.

"Famous battles, all of 'em." Master Falmon nodded, notic-ing where Dan was looking. "Except those." Master Falmon cocked his head at the cabinets made of black wood.

The black cabinets had pictures of scary monsters. Dan had never seen anything like them. Winged things with giant fangs and tails like snakes. Six-legged things with legs like the tree trunks. A huge giant with one big eye in the center of his head, his arms ending with swords instead of hands. A thing like a dragon, but without wings, three heads instead of one, one of its mouths chewing on its own body. A tall thing with a head like an egg. When the lamps shone on the carvings, the monsters seemed to move, as if they were about to come to life. Dan swallowed.

Dan realized that all the cabinets had another thing in common: They were each locked with a silver lock. One of the biggest silver cabinets, there on Dan's right, even had two locks on it. That cabinet looked like it had a whole big war carved onto it, all kinds of different scenes with soldiers and armies fighting on different lands and forests and mountains, and over there was a flat field that ran up against the wall of a big fortress, fighting everywhere, all kinds of different places. He took a step toward the cabinet—.

And stopped dead in his tracks, his eyes wide.

"*Stormy?*" Dan whispered, in spite of himself.

In the center of the battle scene, right there on the carving, there was a huge battle cannon. It looked just like Stormy.

The cannon's mouth was shaped like a dragon getting ready to breathe fire, lips peeled back, eyes just about to close. There was another big cannon right next to him, and that one had a lion's mouth, open and roaring just like a giant lion would.

"Oblivion," Dan whispered, nodding to himself.

It was both of them. For truth!

Dan turned to Master Falmon, pointing.

But the Master was lighting another lamp and paid him no mind.

Stormy and Oblivion, no doubt. Dan blinked and stepped closer. And there were their war adepts, five robed ladies next to each big gun, two on each side, one in the back just like they would be, singing their songs to make Stormy's fire. And they must've just finished singing, because there was a big explosion on the other side of the carved picture, there against the wall of the big fortress where all those soldiers were fighting. There was a silvery line coming out of Stormy's mouth. Without thinking, Dan put his finger into the line and traced it across the battlefield, the wood cool under his fingertip, all the way to the explosion against the giant wall.

"Ka-boom," Dan whispered. "For the Remain."

It *was* Stormy.

He knew it.

Had to be.

The lamp light flickered, and the cannon's dragon eye winked at him.

Dan stared, his mouth falling open.

And then all the figures and the warriors and the cannon seemed to move — to *shift* — as if he was watching the war from above, like he'd climbed a giant tree, or like he was seeing the battle from the sky, how a flying dragon might see it. The whole scene moved at once, each figure at the same time, but slowly, as if they were moving though honey. Dan felt a little dizzy. He closed his eyes; opened them. The battle was still there in front of him, and nothing had changed, everyone moving and fighting and charging at once. And then he heard something in his head. Something familiar, like a battle horn, a set of drums, thumping drums, a deep and ancient blow-ing—.

"Eadle," Master Falmon said gently behind him.

Dan spun, blinked, winced as he saluted, his tiny fist thumping his chest, the pain cutting into his elbow. "Yes, sir! Master Falmon, sir!"

"What's wrong with your arm, boy?"

"Nothing, sir!" Dan put his hand down at his side, keeping his face totally blank as the pain came on like a red light. Take the hits, soldier! You take 'em! But he felt all woozy for a second, then he blinked, took a deep breath, saluted with his other fist. "Ready for duty, sir! Every day, sir! That's the way! Master Falmon, sir!"

The Master gave him a long look with his good eye. Then he adjusted his eyepatch, reached into his belt, and took out a small box of silvery wood. He opened it.

"Here." Master Falmon pinched a dried, bluish leaf from the box, stepped over to Dan, broke the leaf in half, handed one half to him. "Put it under your tongue, lad. Helps. Perfectly safe. If you feel sick, spit it out."

Dan blinked, took the blue leaf, and did what he was told. It tasted like strong mint and seemed to sparkle in his mouth before his tongue went entirely numb. But he was already feeling better. He looked at Master Falmon wonderingly and touched at his sore elbow.

It didn't hurt at all.

Just like that!

Dan smiled.

"You get your front tooth knocked out?" Master Falmon asked.

Dan shook his head. "No, sir! Master Falmon, sir! Fell out, sir! I have it in my box, sir!" He waved back in the general direction of the pit, where his box was. "I can give it to you, sir! Trade is a trade! Yes, sir!" He pointed at his own mouth. "Arm is better! Fair is fair, sir! You want my tooth, for trade, sir?"

Boy, did his elbow feel *better*.

His smile went wider.

Master Falmon raised the silver box at him, nodded, and adjusted his eye patch. "No trade needed. A gift from Lord Garen, now my gift to you." The Master put the rest of the blue leaf under his own tongue, snapped the box shut, tucked it back in his belt. "Take heart, lad. There are people snug in their soft beds right now because hard men like you and me — regular soldiers, strong and loyal — stand ready to bear pain on their behalf. We're not pretty." Master Falmon touched the deep scar in his forehead. "But we're here. A long tradition, and a fine one. You're part of that? Understand?"

Dan didn't really understand all of it, but he nodded and saluted all the same. "Yes, sir, Master Falmon!"

His arm didn't hurt a bit!

Master Falmon grinned, his scarred-up face crinkling. He touched the box in his belt. "Helps, doesn't it?"

Dan nodded.

"Alright," Master Falmon grunted. "Come on over here. Wanna teach you something."

12

As Little Dan watched, Master Falmon took a ring of silver keys from his belt pouch, separated a small one from the others, then put the key into the lock of the cabinet in front of him, a cabinet made of silvery-white wood. Master Falmon turned the key, but it didn't click. Instead, there was a quiet whirling sound, a sound that Dan could barely hear, like a hundred tiny little gears all spinning up together. Master Falmon turned the key again to the left, then all the way back around to the right. Then he took the key out of the lock and stepped back. The cabinet doors swung outward.

Inside the cabinet, sitting on a tall, wooden stand, there was a suit of armor made of high silver. Behind the armor, Dan could see the Tarn's mark, the six-pointed sun, carved into the cabinet's wood. The armor sat right in front of the mark, so all you could see was the sun's six tears coming out like arrows behind the armor's back. The lamp's orange light glowed in the armor's curves; very nice, very smooth. There was a silver helmet, a silver neck guard, silver shoulder pads, a silver breastplate, protection for the guts that Dan could never remember the name for, protection for the legs and the shins, and a pair of what looked like silver shoes that Dan knew would get worn over regular war boots. There were designs all over the gear, shaped right into the silver. These designs sort of followed the shape of the armor, matching the way the armor moved, thin lines and shapes and other kinds of nice patterns, vines and plants and other things. Without thinking, Dan reached up and put his hand on one of the shin guards. The high silver was cool beneath his palm. Felt good. Yes, sir. He closed his eyes and just like that, without waiting, a song – kind of like Stormy's song – came rushing up through his hand and his arm, all the way into his heart—.

"Wait, lad." Master Falmon took Dan's hand gently and pushed him back a little. "We don't touch the gear, not before it's tuned."

"Yes, sir!" Dan took a step back and saluted. "Sorry, sir!"

"No reason to be sorry." Master Falmon shook his head. "You never been down here before. I show you how to do it, then you do it right the next time. Reason I wanted you to come down. The big guns seem to like you, figure you might try your hand at something like this." He gestured at the armor.

Dan nodded. He didn't really understand what the Master meant, but he was starting to think that this might be the best morning in the pit he'd ever had. Yes, sir!

Below the armor, on a separate little shelf, there was a row of about a dozen books. Each of the books was made of blue-colored leather. Some of the books were dark blue, almost black, others were lighter blue. All the books were marked at their tops in silver with the Tarn's six-pointed sun. Master Falmon took the last book off the shelf, the brightest blue one, thumbed it open about halfway.

"Each time the gear comes out . . ." the Master cocked his head at the armor, ". . . we mark it down in here, in the log." He held the book open so that Dan could look. Dan didn't know how to read, not a word, but he saw blocks of writing in little boxes, each box set in a column.

"This here . . ." Master Falmon pointed at the first column. ". . . tells the day and the year the gear was taken out." He touched the second column. "This one here gives the name of the warrior who wore it." He touched the third. "This one tells the world on which the action took place." He touched the last. "And this big one here is where you put your notes and such — repairs needed, damage taken to the undercarriage, padding, straps, that sort of thing. You fill that last one out when the gear comes back."

"Does it always come back?" Dan asked, without thinking.

Master Falmon looked down at him with his good eye. "Always. Been wars fought over this gear. A good soldier either brings it back himself or his mates bring it back. You don't leave high silver on the battlefield, lad. Ever. And if you do, then you go back out and you get it."

Dan squinted. "That's, uh . . . . That's one of the rules?"

"'One of the rules?'" Master Falmon raised an eyebrow. "Yeah, that's right. One of the rules."

Dan nodded. Made sense.

A couple of the boxes in the last columns had words, but they also had a red X in them. There were only a few of those.

"What's them little red marks, there?" Dan asked.

"That's what we put when the soldier is killed in action, when the gear fails its lord."

Dan blinked. There were only two or three red marks on the page – three out of a dozen. Dan nodded. "This silver is strong."

"You speak truth," the Master said seriously. "Some of the finest in the Realm. And tomorrow, it must do its work." He wrote a few things in the book, slid it back into its place, making sure it was perfectly in line with the others. "These logs weren't started until the last millennium of the Plague Years, so nobody knows when this armor was crafted. Some think it was shaped way back in the beginning for Christopher the First, the War-Bringer, at the start of the Founding

War. Others think it belongs later, sometime at the beginning of the Plague Years. Either way, it's strong, as you say. Very strong. But the *record*, lad — that's the real strength." He touched the row of blue books. "The memory is what matters. It's when we *forget* that we lose. And even with these . . . ." He touched the books again. "We always forget."

Dan frowned. He didn't fully understand what the Master meant, but the Master seemed to think it was real important, so Dan nodded.

Master Falmon adjusted his eyepatch, then fixed Dan with his one good eye. "It matters because it's our history." He gestured toward the books and the armor. "Marks and memories like these are our history, lad. And it's our history that makes *us*. Our poems and our tales and our music, they too shape the mind. But history is the foundation for all of that, for everything. You, me, everyone. That's why the best warriors and generals make the study of history their most important duty. They fight with it, they argue about it, and they do their best to learn from it."

Dan frowned. "What do they learn?"

"Most of 'em learn to ignore the lessons of history." Master

Falmon grunted. "But a special few — a very special few — take the lessons that time teaches and try to do it better."

"Every day's a day to do better, sir."

"That's right. Now, attend."

From his belt pouch, the Master took a rolled sheet of oiled leather. The Master knelt to the ground, knees popping, and unrolled the leather sheet on the floor. Inside the sheet, there were five small hammers, each one made of high silver. Each hammer was a bit smaller than the next. The top of each hammer was marked by the Tarn's mark, the six-pointed sun, but on the sides, they each had a different symbol: a tear, a sword, a book, a set of scales, and a weird-looking horn.

Master Falmon spread his hands over the hammers and whispered, "Great Sisters, exemplars of history and time, let us look to our past's best as we forge our future. Let us learn from our mistakes, let us honor our families and our lands, and let us do what is right — always. Great Sister Eressa, patron of quests, grant us the will to begin this war with determination and resolve. Great Sister Alea, patron of swords, grant us the strength to make this war with ferocity and zeal. Great Sister Aaryn, patron of wisdom, grant us the knowledge to wage this war with foresight and reason. Great Sister Kora, patron of justice, grant us the courage to win this war with principle and honor. Great Sister Margo, patron of plenty, grant us the grace to end this war with speed – and to foster lasting peace."

Master Falmon took the first silver hammer, the one marked with the tear, stood up, and tapped the top of the armor's silver helmet. When he hit the helmet, there was a low ringing sound, and the helmet glowed with silvery-white light.

Dan took a step back despite himself.

The sound was new, kind of like Stormy's song, but . . . *different*. It was like no song he'd ever heard before, and yet, at the exact same time, it was somehow familiar – and slightly *wrong*.

And that wrongness seemed to reach right into the center of Dan's chest.

Without thinking, Dan put his hands over his ears.

But that didn't stop the sound.

The sound didn't come from the armor.

The sound came from inside his head.

Master Falmon cocked his head at the armor, like he was listening, too. He tapped the helmet once more, a little harder this time. The glow went brighter. The Master frowned and shook his head, then hit the helmet again, harder.

Dan closed his eyes.

So loud.

So wrong.

He was getting dizzy and kind of sick to his stomach. The sound in his head changed when the Master hit the helmet, and the glow went brighter, and then the Master hit it again, and something seemed to "click." The silver light and the ringing sound joined together and became one thing and stopped being wrong. Dan didn't have the words, but it felt good.

"Ah," Little Dan said.

It felt *right*.

"Yes, sir," Dan whispered, opening his eyes.

The Master grunted, nodded, then looked at Dan. "The great beast from whence this armor came sang the greatest and saddest of songs. Beasts like him sang the mighty hymns for Acasius and his Sisters when they shaped the Realm, when they bound the Remain together. Part of our work before battle, lad, is to ensure that the ancient song rings true." He touched the center of the silver breastplate with his hand, right where the soldier's heart would be. "The harmonies of space and memory are here – *within* – alive and strong. *Living*. Just like your Stormhammer, lad. Each shape, each curve, each line, all born of need, crafted by the ancient shaper's song – and *alive*. So long as the song stays true, no force can kill it." He held the hammer's handle out to Dan. "The tuning is how we know, how we keep the silver song true. Want to try?"

Even though he didn't understand everything the Master meant, Dan nodded and took the hammer. It was very light. The silver handle was cool in his hand.

"Just here." Master Falmon gestured to the right shin guard, where Dan could reach easy. "A little tap at first, just a touch, then listen for it." The Master made a little gesture with his empty hand, like he was lightly hitting the armor. "Just like that. Then *listen*."

Dan looked up at him, blinked, suddenly nervous.

He didn't want to make a mistake, didn't want to do it wrong. No, sir.

He hesitated, swallowed.

The Master put his hand on his shoulder. "It's alright, lad. Just a light touch, and I'll take it from there. Every day, we try new things. Every day's a day to do better. You said so yourself, didn't you?"

Dan nodded.

Then he stepped up to the armor, and lightly tapped the shin guard.

The moment he tapped it, the silver-white glow came, but the sound was all wrong again. So without thinking, Dan put his little hand on the silver, shut his eyes, and sang a bit of how it was *supposed* to sound in his own head, just to show how it *should* be, just how Dan might do with Stormy. And the song flowed from his head, through his chest, down his arm like a warm wave of *rightness*, lining up perfect and strong and true. He nodded and saw that the light and the sound were together and right, just as they should be. Yes, sir! That was good.

"*Real* good!" he said.

But when Dan opened his eyes, he saw that Master Falmon was staring at him. The Master's good eye was wide and slightly crazy looking, and Dan realized that he must've done the work wrong – like *real* wrong to make Master Falmon look like that.

Dan stepped away from the armor, bowed his head, held up the hammer for Master Falmon to take, and got ready for it.

"I'm sorry," Dan said, looking at the ground, still holding the hammer out. "I've got . . . poop in my brains. So sorry, Master Falmon, sir. So sorry."

And he meant it.

But the Master didn't take the hammer.

And the Master didn't say anything, either.

Dan turned slightly so that when the hits came they wouldn't land on his sore arm, even though it didn't hurt now because of the blue leaf. One of the tricks; the way to play if you wanted to take it like a proper soldier. But this was the first time that he'd made Master Falmon mad, so he felt horrible and stupid and wished he could be back to cleaning the pit or even back in his bunk with his pals to play the beat-up game, because at least he knew how to do *that* right.

He shook his head, looking hard at the floor. "I'm a . . . . I don't know how to do things right. I'm very sorry, sir."

The Master touched his shoulder. Dan flinched, then regretted that he'd flinched because it was against the rules, and because if you flinched it was always way worse.

"You did very well, Dan." Master Falmon cleared his throat.

There was something in the Master's voice that made Dan look up.

The Master was looking down at him – and he was smiling. It was a scary smile, because of all the scars on the Master's scarred-up face. And now that he thought about it, Dan didn't think that he'd ever even seen Master Falmon actually smile before, but there it was: a smile. Scary with all those scars, but real! Yes, sir!

Dan made to say something, but the Master raised his hand, and Dan's mouth clicked shut.

"Why don't you finish up these pieces here?" Master Falmon gestured at the other shin guard and the leg protection, gear that Dan could reach. "And then I'll hold you up, and you can do the rest of it."

Dan nodded. Then he pointed at the other hammers lying on the leather sheet. "What we use those for?"

Master Falmon's smile was huge. "Don't think we'll need 'em."

13

So DAN WORKED with Master Falmon on the silver armor for the next bell or so. It sure was easy work compared to cleaning. It made him tired in his head, but his arm felt better. At the very same time, Dan was thinking he needed to get done and back to the pit, or else he'd be in trouble with the Chief, so that part wasn't so nice. But everything else was *very* fine. Yes, sir! Very fine, indeed. Dan would tap the armor with his little hammer, and the armor would glow that silvery glow, its song would come, and then Dan would sing a bit in his head just like he sang to Stormy, and the armor would sing right back until it was all just right. Every time he did it, Master Falmon would smile and nod and turn his ear toward the music and say, "That's just right, Dan. That's just right."

When they were all done, Master Falmon showed him how

to roll up the hammers in their leather sheet so they didn't click against each other. Then he lifted Dan in the crook of his elbow, stepped close to the armor, and placed his scarred hand on the chest of the breastplate.

"Put your hand next to mine, Dan," the Master said.

Dan leaned toward the armor and did as he was told. The silver was cool under his hand.

The Master said, "This isn't part of the real work, but I do it every time, all the same."

Dan nodded.

Master Falmon closed his good eye.

Dan figured he was supposed to shut his eyes, too. But he didn't. Instead, he looked at the Master's scarred face. The Master was quiet for a long time. It looked like the Master was sad. But how could that be?

Then the Master cleared his throat and spoke. "Great Sister Aaryn, binder of words and worlds, protect young Garen tomorrow." His rough voice seemed to go rougher still. "Defend the lad. Let this ancient protection guard him true. Let him return untouched from the fires of war. Let his head touch pillow unscathed. In your holy name, I pray."

The Master opened his eye, adjusted his eye patch, and looked at Dan. "Tomorrow morning, four helpers are gonna go up with Stormhammer and Oblivion, to help the war adepts' squires. One of those helpers is gonna be you, Dan. That means you gotta be up and at 'em and on time tomorrow for muster. And get plenty to eat, too. You're gonna need it."

Dan blinked. He didn't understand exactly what the Master meant. "I'm gonna help?"

The Master nodded. "Yeah. You're gonna help with the big guns."

"We gonna fight tomorrow, sir?"

Master looked at Dan for a long moment. Then he set him down on the ground and stayed down there with him, looking at Dan with his one good eye. He took both of Dan's little hands in his own and sighed. "Yes, Dan. We'll fight tomorrow. They say it's for peace — but neither side wants it. So it'll be war."

Dan didn't really know what to say, but he knew that Master Falmon looked sad, so he patted him on his shoulder and said, "That's alright, sir. Every day, yes, sir! A day to do better! Like you say! It's all gonna be just fine, sir. We fight, that's what we do, eh? We fight. Yes, sir."

"Yes." Master Falmon nodded. But he seemed sadder than before. "It's what we do."

The Master was quiet for a long time. Then he looked at Dan. "You're a braver soldier than I, lad. Maybe wiser, too." Dan shrugged, saluted as sharp and tight as he could. "Yes, sir! I be brave! Like you! Master Falmon, sir! Just like you!"

Master Falmon looked at him for a moment, like he was going to say something else. Then he said, "Best get back to your work, Dan. Important that nothing seems amiss." He gestured at the armor. "I've got more to do down here and others will be coming down soon to take care of the gear for the bear riders and others. We need to keep this a secret for a bit. And we don't want you in trouble with Shum and Croot before the big day." He put his finger to his lips. "Best not say anything about this down here. Not a word. Head on back up, like nothing's happened. Safer."

"Safer?"

"Safer."

"Yes, sir. I be safe! I don't say nothing. A secret, Master

Falmon, sir! Not a word. Do the work! Yes, sir! Don't say a word."

"Know your way back?"

"Yes, sir! Master Falmon, sir!"

14

LITTLE DAN KNEW the way back to the pit and he also knew that he was way behind on his task, so when he got back, he set his lamp on a crook of busted rock, opened up his cleaning box, and got busy, busy, busy. And since his elbow didn't hurt anymore, he could work even harder.

"Feels good!" he yelled.

He started at the back of the pit, close to the little iron door, humming to himself, and worked like a demon from there.

He'd only been working for four or five bells — not too long, but not nothing, either — and he'd just finished up his little afternoon lunch break, when the Chief hollered down, "Eadle! Get your little butt up here, soldier! *Now!*"

On his hands and knees, scooping a giant pile of dust into one of his rubbish sacks, Dan hollered back, "Yes, sir! Chief, sir!" He dropped everything and ran up the stairs. When he came out, Chief Tendal, Val, Benjy Dalter, and a big kid named Zebber were standing there with Master Shum and Mistress Croot. They were talking to a tall soldier. There were a couple of the other cleaners gathered around listening, but kind of pretending to clean at the same time, too. When Dan came out of the pit, everybody looked at him. He stopped in his tracks and didn't step out of the pit's opening.

"Come here, boy," Master Shum said. He spun his club in a circle on its thong. Mistress Croot looked at Dan, too, her bad eye catching the light. Chief Tendal looked mad and gave Dan a mean stare. Master Shum cleared his throat. "Come on now, boy. Some work for you upstairs."

Dan ran over and saluted. "Yes, sir! Ready to work! Master Shum, sir!"

The soldier looked down at Dan. "This him?"

"Yes, sir." Master Shum nodded.

"Very well." The tall soldier nodded. "I'll take him and these others." He waved at the Chief, Val, Benjy, and Zebber. "Special duty. Need some small people, get into some tight corners up top."

"Of course, Captain," Master Shum said.

"Come with me, children," the captain said, and immediately turned to leave.

Dan followed, but slowly. The Chief had gone along with the captain, but he was looking back at Dan with that mean look. It was like the Chief didn't want Dan to come. Dan started to say something, then he shut his mouth and followed, but not as fast as he could.

"Get going, lad," Master Shum said. "Go on. Follow your Chief there."

The soldier turned and looked back at Dan. The Chief and the others turned with him.

Dan stopped, saluted, and blurted, "I'm not done with my work, sir. No, sir! I ain't done down there yet. Gotta do the pit, sir! Clean as spit! And the Chief, he gave me that work, and I do what the Chief says! Yes, sir! Every day! Like Chief say! That's the way! Gotta finish it up, sir!" Then he added for good measure, "I try to do a good job for the Chief!"

The captain looked at Master Shum and frowned. Master Shum glanced at the Chief. Val, Benjy, and Zebber were looking at Dan like he was a total crazy. Mistress Croot rocked on her feet, her strange eye glimmering. Master Shum cleared his throat, stepped up, leaned down, and tapped Dan's chest with his club. "You need to go with Captain Durn, lad. *That's* your job now. Isn't that right, Chief?"

The Chief nodded, gave Dan a weird look. "That's right, Eadle. We're gonna go up there together. Come on, now. Do what you're told."

"My box!" Dan hollered. "Can't do the work without my box, sir!"

Master Shum tapped Dan again on the chest with his club. "You don't need your tools, Dan. You *need* to get going there with your Chief. Don't make little clubby tell ya."

"Let's go, soldier," the captain – Captain Durn – said to Dan. "Gotta get up there." When Dan didn't move, the soldier looked from Master Shum to the Chief, like he didn't know what to do.

"It's an *order*, Eadle," the Chief said.

For some reason, hearing the Chief say it like that made Dan feel way better. So he stood tall and gave his best salute. "Yes, sir! Ready, sir!"

Then he followed the soldier and the Chief and the rest of

them as fast as he could, almost running to keep up.

15

WHEN THE GIANT group hug was over, Kyla Dallanar looked at Kate and grinned. "I missed you."

She didn't realize how true it was until the words were out of her mouth.

"Likewise," Kate said. Her dark eyes reflected the blue light of the study's stained glass window. "Lots to talk about."

"I'll say." Kyla smiled. "Can't wait."

"Yet wait you must," Garen said, trying to hold back his own enormous grin. "Kate needs to bring them down to breakfast." He gave Kyla a pointed look. "You and I have some unfinished business."

"I'm starving," Susan said.

Tarlen laughed. Bruno woofed. Ponj whispered something to Tarlen. Tarlen nodded.

"We're working on something, Kate," Tarlen said, tapping his young aunt on the shoulder.

"So I gathered." Kate put her hand on Tarlen's shoulder. "Tell me over breakfast?"

"Oh, yes," Tarlen said.

"Ponj?" Garen looked at the young ogre. "You'll see them down to table and off to lessons?"

"Yes, my lord." Ponj bowed. His voice was not nearly as deep as his mighty father's, but the basic tenor was the same.

"Anything else?" Garen turned to Colj.

"No, my Lord." The ogre inclined his huge head. "I shall bring the boy after council." He looked at Kate and the others. "And I will join you all for your morning meal."

Ponj and Tarlen looked at each other, then smiled like fools.

"Huzzah!" Susan cried. "Breakfast for all!"

Kate laughed. Kyla laughed, too. She couldn't help herself. It was as if everything was better. Kate was back. Things were better. For a split moment, everything almost felt normal.

"Very well." Garen nodded.

It was the cue to leave, and everyone took it but Kyla, talking and chattering. Bruno circled the group, lending an occasional bark to the conversation. Big Colj brought up the rear. Kyla waved as they left, feeling slightly silly at both the gesture and at the crazy smile she couldn't peel from her face.

When the door shut behind them, Garen said, "Good to have her back." He gestured at the worktable, inviting her to sit again.

"Yes," Kyla said, her smile fading. "It's good to see her. She's the same – but different. She looks older."

"Yes," Garen said. But he didn't offer more.

"Where has she been?"

"Paráden."

"Paráden," Kyla repeated. The founding duchy of Remain, the seat of imperial power, the home of her great uncle Dorómy Dallanar, and the site of the Silver Throne. She focused on her breathing, on her training, willing herself to calm. "All this time, these last years, she *was* with Dorómy after all? And Michael allowed her to return——?"

Garen raised his hand to stop her, then looked at the High Cup on its blue cushion. "Michael has nothing to do with it. Kate's departure, her plan, her entire mission – all was arranged in secret. Michael didn't know. Nobody knew. I didn't even know. So, yes, Kate went to Paráden, to Dorómy – at the command of the High King and Queen."

"And she stayed there with him for two years?"

Garen's gaze was direct. He didn't answer for a moment, just looked at her with penetrating eyes. Sometimes, Garen was like this. Just when you started to believe that he was a bumbling bookworm, an absent-minded scholar, his eyes would reveal the truth – that he was one of the great minds in the Realm. Finally, he said, "The High King has important plans, intricate plans. He'll explain your part himself." He cleared his throat and adjusted his spectacles. "Also, I want you to think about your behavior in front of the ogres and our other loyal henchmen. No matter how close they seem, no matter how close they are, there are some things that must stay within the family, alone."

Kyla frowned at this pivot. Then she took a breath, focused, and released her frustration, feeling her muscles unwind, her mind clearing, her training coming to the fore. It was one of the things that you had to understand when you were a part of this particular family. There were always five or six plans running through and within and around each other at any given moment, with each highborn sibling having a differ-ent take on any or all of them. Garen didn't always agree with Michael, but he'd never oppose him openly, and he was notoriously discreet. Doldon, on the other hand, almost always supported Michael, and you could count on him telling Michael anything he learned or heard. James didn't have the time of day for any of them, except maybe Kate, but Kate had been gone so long that James hardly talked to anyone anymore even when he was around, so his opinion was usually a great unknown. Regardless, the material point was this: If Grandpa and Nana wanted her to know something – or if they *didn't* want her to know something – then that's how it would be. Pumping Garen for information was an exercise in futility. If Garen didn't have the King and Queen's permission to speak, then she might as well try squeezing water from a stone.

"Would you like some tea?" Garen asked, making himself comfortable in his seat.

"No, thank you."

He nodded, glanced at the bell pull on the side wall, seemed to think twice about his own want for tea, then shook his head and continued. "As a family, we must do our best to present a proper picture of unity and strength. The ogres of Jallow are dear friends and valuable allies. But in their presence, we should observe the niceties of rank."

When Garen said this last sentence, something flickered in his eyes, as if he didn't fully believe his own words.

Kyla frowned. It was a weird moment for a lesson in decorum. And Garen looked tired. Of course, they were all exhausted, the endless siege taking its toll. Yet he made no effort to hide his exhaustion from her. And that was strange, too. Because a Dallanar prince could never be tired, never be uncertain, never be weak. Even in front of family.

And once again, that weird dread loomed in the back of her mind, a nagging itch, the tingling sense that something truly horrible had happened.

"In any case," Garen continued, "it's good practice to keep propriety when they're around, especially now. For the best, really—."

"Drivel," Kyla said. "That sounds like something Michael would say. Look at Ponj and Tarlen. They're thick as thieves. They sleep in each other's rooms every night – and just try to tell them different. You think Colj and his men don't know what we're up against? The full measure of the challenge we face? They know who we are. Why pretend?"

"You see the formalities of rank as pretense?"

"Of course not." Kyla shook her head. "I simply suggest we shouldn't perform for them – at least not Colj and Ponj. They know us. They *are* family."

"I'm not thinking of 'us,' exactly. I'm thinking of you, Ky. And not just the ogres. Others."

Kyla raised an eyebrow. "Make yourself clear, Garen."

"I understand you had a frank conversation with Anna Dyer yesterday morning, that you told her—."

"Michael told you."

Garen nodded. "Even suggesting the possibility of surrender to a Davanórian dragon rider is unwise and unbecoming—."

Kyla laughed gently. "Are you listening to yourself? I would understand this coming from Michael. Or Grandpa. Maybe even Doldon. But you? Come Garen, you can't—."

"I'm simply passing the message forward."

"From Michael? And I never said the word 'surrender,' much less suggested it. I'm surprised Anna went running to him."

"She didn't. Michael asked her for the details of your

conversation. She provided them."

Kyla inclined her head. "And she said that I said that we should lay down arms? That's preposterous."

"She didn't say that. She——."

"We talked about parley, yes. The possibility of peace. That's all. It was a rather honest discussion. Quite refreshing, actually. In fact, there was more truth spoken down there in a quarter bell than I've heard up here in a year, our royal masks on so tight, a wonder anyone can breathe. Anna shared her honest opinion. I shared mine. But, of course, that's a crime, isn't it? A Dallanar highborn can't have her own ideas, can she? Everything must seem ordered and perfect and just-so. Can't have the underlings thinking we're real people now, eh?"

"You know better."

"Yes, yes. I know better."

And she did. But even so, it could be maddening sometimes.

Garen looked at her closely. "Several hundred dragon riders will arrive from Dávanor today and tonight." He looked at the small silver clock sitting on one of the work-tables at the center of the chamber. "They come to make war,

Kyla. Not peace."

"Then why meet for parley?" She understood his point, of course. She was just needling him, trying to get to the real reason for the conversation.

Garen ignored her question. "There's also the matter of this scout, Filip Toller, with whom you've been spending time——."

And even though she felt her cheeks go warm, she was proud of her response, which was regal, calm, and immediate, "My friendships are no business of yours, nor anyone else's."

"You can't possibly believe that," Garen said.

Kyla shrugged. "Does Susan ask permission to spend time with Erika Cadence? Does Erika herself ask permission to spend time with that giant young ogre, Doj? Great Sisters, you yourself just now assigned Toller and his squad to *me* for parley tomorrow. I sense some inconsistency here, Uncle."

Garen nodded. "Maybe that was a mistake. Regardless, those examples you give are all quite different – and you know it. Toller is a good fellow. His people are of the strongest stock. But they're——."

She stopped him with a smile. "Filip is my friend, Garen. Nothing more. And I shall spend my leisure time with whom I choose."

He looked at her directly. He wasn't mad — he never got mad — but he was earnest. "Kyla, you're the firstborn daughter of the King's firstborn son. War is imminent. Consider, for a moment. Tomorrow we try one last time for peace. Our chance of success is small. You've said you're worried for me — and I thank you for that. But what if something *does* happen, Ky? To me or to Michael? To Doldon? What if something happens to Kate, Great Sisters forbid? You understand this — even if you don't want to think about it. But you must. Five lives are all that stand between you and the throne. It's quite possible that you will soon command Colj and his men, Anna and her Davanórians, our other henchmen, allies, legions from a dozen duchies — and that you'll command them not as a highborn princess, but as the High Queen of Remain. As much as the ogres of Jallow value truth, as much as the riders of Dávanor value honor, what they value above all else is *strength*. Strength of mind, will, and heart."

"What does this have to do with Toller?"

"Things will change quickly in the next days. You must prepare yourself. There will be no time for anything but the most careful tactical considerations."

She felt the familiar cold seeping into her hands. "We will fight tomorrow."

"Almost certainly." He nodded. "And an heir to the Silver Throne must be prepared to lead, especially in times of war. Look at the List of Kings, sometime. Those dates tell you all you need to know."

"Nothing will happen to you," Kyla heard herself say, the ice in her fingers more frigid than ever.

"Saying does not make it so." Garen smiled sadly. And again, she could feel something beneath his words. Something huge. Something unsayable.

"Nothing will happen," she repeated.

A cold flutter caught her stomach; icy claws clutched at her heart. She clasped her hands in her lap.

"We know something will happen, Ky," Garen said.

"How are you so sure?" she asked calmly.

He looked at her for a long moment, then he nodded. "I'd

like you to listen to something. It'll be a bit hard for you to appreciate, but I want you to try, all the same."

Garen stood from his chair and walked to the low shelf beside the blue stained-glass window. From the shelf, he took a silver box. The box was about seven palms long. He stepped back to the table, set the box before him, and opened it. Within the box there was another box, smaller and beautifully carved from pale korom's wood, closed with an intricate lock of high silver. He pulled a thin chain from under his tunic. On this chain hung four small keys. He selected one, slipped it into the silver lock, and opened the box. Inside, there was a cushion of light blue suede marked with four empty, nest-like hollows. The fifth hollow, however, was filled with what looked like a silver bird curled up asleep, its smooth head tucked beneath its wing. Some sort of ancient golem, Kyla supposed. It was small and would fit in her cupped hand, an artifact from the Kingdom's earliest days.

"Good morning, beautiful," Garen whispered, gently stroking the silver bird's spine, blowing gently over its wings. He took a small perch of high silver from the first box and set the perch on the worktable, touched the perch once with a small silver hammer, like a gentle bell.

The silver bird trembled and gave a tired squeak, but otherwise it did not stir. Its feathers were carved in incredible detail, the sapphire light from the blue stained-glass window glowing azure in its silver wings. Each time Garen touched hammer to perch, the bird would quiver a bit and huddle further down in its nest.

"Sleepy." Garen looked up at her, pushed his spectacles up on his nose. He stroked the bird's back again, gently ruffling the feathers of its head. "Come now, sweet beauty."

The bird lifted its head. When it did, Kyla saw that its eyes were large, round, and slightly too large for its head, not at all like those of a real bird's. Its beak was also strangely shaped, a touch too broad, hooked like a hawk, with strange slitted openings on the top and sides.

"Do you know what this is?" Garen asked softly, gently stroking the little bird's head. It closed its eyes, reveling in its master's touch.

"Some kind of golem."

"Indeed." Garen nodded, not taking his eyes off it. "Much argument surrounds this little darling. There is no doubt that she and her sisters come from the earliest years of the Founding. Some believe she was made by the Great Sister Aaryn herself."

"What does she do?"

Garen looked up at her. "She sees beyond space and memory — *through* it — into both future and past."

As if hearing these words, the little bird gave a low chirp, stretched its silver wings, and stood up in its nest. It looked like a strange little hawk, Kyla realized, its chest round and powerful. It hopped to the box's edge then hopped onto Garen's finger, tiny talons flexing, and gave another squeak.

"Can you share again what you learned last night, little one?" Garen asked it.

The little bird squeaked and cocked its head.

"Not with me, darling," Garen crooned. He looked at Kyla. "With her."

The little thing swiveled its head and looked at Kyla, its large eyes blinking.

Garen nodded. "The conversation that you'll hear will take place in the enemy camp between several of Dorómy's high generals, Ky, about an hour before sunrise tomorrow morning."

Kyla blinked. "In the enemy camp, *tomorrow* morning?"

"Yes." Garen stroked the little hawk, lifting it slightly, as if in explanation. "You'll hear Jon's voice——."

"Vymon Ruge's youngest."

"And most ambitious, by far." Garen nodded. "You'll also hear Corlen Lessip."

"Dorómy's spymaster."

"Marden Julane as well——."

Kyla frowned. "Eleanor's uncle? But I thought Gelánen was with us?"

"Technically, Gelánen has always been 'neutral.' While the Julanes have sent us aid, they've fielded troops for neither Lion nor Fox. But things have changed. Kendal Julane seems to have been killed last week. Kate has been blamed for it."

"Kate *murder* Kendal? That's absurd."

"Of course, it is. But young Lady Eleanor has been convinced otherwise. With her mother incapacitated and Kendal missing, Eleanor Julane is High Lady of Gelánen; she now musters her duchy's full force against us."

It was dark news. Something Nana once said came rushing back to her: "An alliance is only as strong as the will of those who make it."

What had happened?

Garen continued. "You'll also hear the voice of Anthony Carole, James Taverly, the voices of several generals we couldn't identify, and mention of someone we most definitely do *not* know: A 'Lady Valáress.' She's now a person of interest."

"Carole is one of Grandpa's best friends. So is Taverly." Kyla paused. "But where is Vymon Ruge, the Lord of the Siege, himself?"

"You cut to the heart of it." Garen stroked the little bird, then looked at her. "Vymon Ruge is not there. This conversation will almost certainly take place without Ruge's knowledge."

"Yet Jon is there, Vymon's youngest son. Where are Ruge's other boys? Where's Jannon? Where's Jared?" Kyla still had fond memories of playing with the Ruge boys. Only a few years past, the two families had been nearly inseparable. Brash Jannon. Poor, stuttering Jared. Clever Jon — a true genius, crazy ambitious, and thought by many to rival Garen for raw intelligence. Vymon Ruge and Bellános Dallanar had once been the most intimate of friends; Vymon had been Grandpa's most trusted commander, before he'd gone over to Dorómy. Kate had once confided in Kyla that she and Jon had even kissed once, Kate's first kiss, hiding here in the library. They'd both been eleven years old.

"Good questions," Garen said. "We don't know where the other Ruge brothers are during this conversation. Only Jon is present."

Garen lifted the little silver hawk and set it upon its silver perch. The moment he did so, the hawk stiffened, cocked its head as if listening.

"We'll begin in the middle of things, I'm afraid," Garen said, taking off his spectacles, polishing them. "I tried last night to widen the field, but I couldn't. She's old." He looked fondly at the little bird. "So very old. We can't be too hard on her."

"Incredible," Kyla said. And she meant it.

Garen nodded. "Not a typical golem." He stroked the little hawk gently. "The very last of her kind." He cleared his throat. "Now, like I said, this will be hard to understand—."

At Kyla's look, he shut his mouth.

And then the hawk began to sing. It was a strange noise at first, a fluid tooting, not at all hawk-like, a kind of metallic bubbling that seemed to come from the little slit openings on the bird's beak, a low humming under it all, like an impossibly small choir singing at the edge of time. Then the singing became words, blurry at first, woven beneath the song, slowly coming into focus until they were clear, and then a voice: ". . . the High Lord Commander would have this morning's parley conducted with the utmost regard for protocol and honor."

"That's Jon Ruge," Garen said.

Murmurs of assent. Then an older voice: "Of course. Of course."

Garen cocked his head. "That's Lessip."

"And yet," Jon's voice continued, through the golem, "we must be prepared for any eventuality. As the Great Lady Aaryn herself once said: 'To birth a reality, a dream must die.' Lords Garen and Doldon and Michael have shown themselves worthy opponents. Most worthy, most honorable. That said, they'll not miss an opportunity to inflict grievous harm upon us, should the chance present itself. We must hope for an honorable parley, yet we cannot trust it will be so. These are dire times, my Lords. Much hangs in the balance. Should the terms of parley be breached, we must be ready to move – and to move decisively."

There was a low hum, like many voices murmuring in agreement.

Jon's voice continued through the golem. "There's no doubt that Lord Garen will offer Bellános's terms, whatever they may be. He is the logical choice. He's the cleverest of the Dallanar brothers, the most suited to the task. Michael cannot support this ceasefire, nor can I believe he thinks it will succeed. The same will be true of Doldon. James was spotted by agents on Jun four days ago. It's unlikely that he's returned to the Tarn."

There was a shuffling sound, people moving around, low whispers.

Again, Jon's voice came. "The Lord of the Siege has already outlined our plan and position for parley. We'll meet the Dallanar delegation on our side of the Long Bridge, here." A tapping sound. "On their side of the barbican, directly over the Great Seal, as dictated by custom and decree. However,

I would like to move aspects of the Fourth and Ninth Legions around and beside the barbican, a prudent caution with which my father agrees. The recent arrivals from the Silver Guard can be stationed within the barbican itself."

"And if parley is breached?" Lessip's voice came.

Jon's answer was immediate, as if rehearsed. "If the terms of parley are broken, then we must attempt to capture Lord Garen. His value is beyond measure. General Lessip, you've suggested that Lord Marden Julane lead my father's retinue, his defense, and our counter attack, should the need arise to protect him."

"Yes," Lessip confirmed.

More voices. Kyla could almost see the gathering of officers standing around a great map table inside a large tent, nodding, lanterns lighting their grim faces.

Jon's voice continued. "Lord Marden is an experienced soldier. He served with much distinction under General Serán during the Folen campaign on Eulor. More importantly, Lord Marden's wisdom and restraint are known throughout the Realm; he is well-trusted by the Dallanar. I can think of no better man to lead the defense of my father, should it be needed." A short pause. "Lord Marden, will you accept this task offered by the Silver Throne on behalf of your duchy, your people, and on behalf of the High Lady of Gelánen?"

There was a moment of silence, the sound of people shuffling.

"Lord Marden?" Jon's voice came again.

Then a hoarse voice, touched with the unmistakable accent of Gelánen's southern counties. "It is Gelánen's greatest honor to serve the Silver Throne in this regard, my Lord."

Jon's voice came again, without pause. "Lord Garen's no warrior, we know this. Yet his prowess as a scholar is legendary. The Tarn's strange trees, the skill of their High Gate's defense, all depend upon Lord Garen's knowledge of the Realm—."

Garen chuckled. "Nice to be appreciated."

Kyla did not smile.

"– Garen, therefore, must be the primary object of your men, Lord Marden, after the defense of my father. To take him alive would be ideal, but if this is not possible, the High King will understand."

"Of course, my Lord." Marden coughed. "*If* something

should go wrong, my Lord."

"And how likely is that, Lord Jon?" a new voice interrupted.

"That's James Taverly," Garen whispered to Kyla. "In everything we've been able to hear, he's been very quiet. He and Ruge seem to be in accord, but we know that he detests Jon."

"I don't know, General Taverly," Jon answered smoothly. "But for our part, the terms of parley *must* remain inviolate." A short pause. "That said, should parley fail, three matters hold sway: First, we must protect the Lord of the Siege; the safety of High Commander Ruge remains a top priority of the Silver Throne. Is this not so, General Lessip?"

"Indeed," Lessip's voice came.

"Second, if parley is broken, we must attempt to capture Lord Garen. Third, we must penetrate the Tarn and gain access to Lord Garen's strange trees. They've thwarted our guns long enough. Lady Valáress has generously provided an agent that can weaken this aspect of the enemy's defense." A short pause. "General Krodan has suggested that one or two soldiers of the Silver Guard allow themselves to be taken prisoner during the action, should it take place. These men will be equipped with a small measure of an elixir that Lady Valáress has provided. It will take only a few drops of this potion to kill the greatest of Lord Garen's star trees. When these 'prisoners' are taken into the Tarn, they'll use the opportunity to deliver the vials to one or two of these trees, at whatever cost. The trees themselves have been arranged in an overlapping pattern, to ensure their fields have a measure of redundancy, especially around the Tarn's High Gate. If one tree is poisoned, Lady Valáress tells us, the overlapping fields will transfer the toxin to the next tree and so on; all will die. With the trees gone, our big guns can at last do their work. One breach, my friends, and we can all go home."

There was a murmur of agreement.

Jon's voice was silk. "All of you served under Bellános. I know how this feels. The Tarn was as much my boyhood home as was the Ruge family palace on Rigel. Garen Dallanar stood as my second during my rites of passage, he was – and is – one of my closest friends. But as my father has said many times, we *must* end this. We *must* have peace. Every day we fight, more men die, and for less reason. Every day we fight, the Realm itself is weakened. So, we must be ready. And should need arise, we must attack without mercy. It's quite possible, my Lords, should the terms of parley be breached, that we could end the siege today."

"And the High Commander's heir?" a strong, low voice growled.

"That's Carole," Garen said, looking up at Kyla.

Carole's voice continued. "Eh, Jon? Your brother, the Lord Jannon? The Crown Prince of Rigel? You claim to speak for your brother, yet I don't see him here. He agrees with this course of action? These plans of yours?"

"Of course, he does," Jon said. "These plans are his plan, General Carole. They are my father's plans, as well." A long pause. "There's not one man in this tent who wants to be here, my Lords. My brother Jannon shares this view, as does my father. But for the High Laws to live, for the Realm to endure, we must act with vigor and with conscience. If we must fight today, then we fight without restraint, for all our sakes, and for the Remain."

Murmurs of agreement.

"Very well." Lessip's voice came. "You have your orders.

General Krodan, you may pick your detail of Guardsmen for the barbican and consult with Lord Marden as to his own troop selection for the High Commander's entourage. General Carole, your cannon will be ready?"

"Of course, my Lord," Carole's low voice growled.

"And our other cannon?"

No answer came that Kyla could hear.

"Good luck to all of you, then," Jon said.

The shuffle of men moving, the low humming of many voices.

Then Lessip's voice came, like a whisper. "The Silver Throne is proud of you, Lord Marden. Rest assured, the High King will hear of your service."

Marden mumbled something, but it wasn't clear, his mutter turning into a soft blur of low whistles and song, the little silver bird swaying on its perch, its sound fading in a trill of high notes, far and lonesome. Garen took the little bird and set it in its nest. The little thing moved only to tuck its head beneath its wing. Garen shut the box softly, returned it to its place, and sat down.

"They plan for the worst," Kyla said.

"So must we."

"They plan to capture you," Kyla said.

"Or to kill him," a voice said softly.

Kyla turned.

Michael stood there, filling the doorway, wearing a vest of black cloth, that peculiar Labbárkean velvet that seemed to absorb all light. His hair was dark, his neck thick, a body built for war. The perfect soldier. His eyes were tired, yet he himself seemed to radiate a kind of indefatigable force, as if a star had exploded in his center, its energy barely contained. He walked to the worktable and sat, his movements liquid, perfectly balanced, glancing at his brother's neatly stacked piles of books and artifacts, his dark eyes flickering over the High Cup and its blue cushion before coming to rest upon her.

"We must be ready, Ky," Michael said. "For whatever comes."

His charisma was nearly impossible to resist, and it took a moment before Kyla realized that she was already nodding in agreement, her head moving on its own accord, all her training — much of it specifically geared to defend herself from Michael's kind of power — nearly useless.

"You *want* this to fail." Kyla lifted her chin at the High Cup. "Whatever has motivated this move to parley, whatever that Cup contains, you're against it. You say you support the King's wishes – and you'll obey the letter of his commands, of course – but this is an opportunity for you. It's the moment you've been waiting for. You want the war. You want Grandpa to unleash you. And if Garen is in danger, you'll have the excuse you need."

Michael laughed. It was a gentle, potent sound, soft and clear and honest. And slightly mad, she realized. And once again, that strange feeling, that feeling that something was horribly wrong, grabbed at her heart.

"You're right, of course," he said quietly. He glanced at the stained-glass window, his dark eyes shining. "For years, these traitors have ravaged our lands, our peoples, our homes. I would bring our full force against them. I've never counseled otherwise."

"At what risk, Michael?" Kyla asked.

Michael's tired eyes went dark. "They've already taken my brother, Ky. And my sister-in-law."

"You think I don't know that?" Kyla looked away.

"And now," Michael continued, "they've—." He stopped short, looked at Garen.

Garen frowned and shook his head.

Michael cleared his throat. "And now, they've gone too far. So, yes. It's a risk. But it's also the High King's command."

"How convenient," Kyla said.

Michael inclined his head. "Garen will be protected. And if the Pretender and his minions breech the terms of parley, then they will be met with all just force."

"They say the same thing, Michael," Kyla kept her hands firmly in her lap. "The very same thing. Surely you see that? Jon, Lessip, Carole, Taverly, the others – you've heard the golem's words." She inclined her head toward the box where the silver bird lay. "They don't want this to work, either. They don't want peace."

"And in that," Michael said, dark eyes glowing, "we're in perfect accord."

Kyla turned to Garen. "You can't go out there. Send me instead."

Garen nodded absently, fiddling now with the elixirs on his worktable and the tiny star tree in its bright blue burlap sack.

"Vymon and his sons will stand across from me, Kyla. Both families will share the risk. The friendship between our two families is strong. It always has been."

"That may be so," Kyla said. "Yet it seems to me that half a dozen generals stand ready to assume Vymon's role as Lord of the Siege, Jon Ruge first among them."

Garen looked up and gave a crooked smile. "Astute observation."

"And an obvious one," Michael said.

Kyla ignored him. "So, we're in agreement. They don't want this to work. But Vymon does, perhaps? Maybe Jannon does, too? We don't know. We don't really know what Jon is about, either. But we *do* know that killing the Lord of the Siege provides an excuse for retaliation and an opening at the top of their leadership—."

"We're not killing anyone." Michael cut her off. "Listen to me, Kyla. *We* will not attack. If the terms of parley are broken, then *they* will be the ones to do it. And if they do, then we shall respond."

Kyla looked to Garen, to gauge his reaction, but Garen was still absorbed with his tinkering and his little star tree. She turned and looked at Michael directly, doing her best to hold his gaze. "They already plan for it. Just as you do. They say the same words. Just like you."

Michael laughed. "Shall we disobey the High King's command?"

"No." Kyla shook her head. "We send someone else, as I said. Simple. Send me. I'll do it. I know the rules, and I can read. I wouldn't be a threat or a target."

"You can't be serious." Michael grinned. "Other than Kate, you're the most valuable asset we have, as you well know. You or Kate in Dorómy's possession would bolster his claim almost beyond defiance. You saw what happened when Kate left." He looked at the High Cup.

"Ah." Kyla nodded. "So, the uproar about Kate's departure and 'betrayal' has little to do with the deceit of a beloved sister and everything to do with succession."

"They're one and the same. As for parley, Garen has been chosen."

"By whom?" Kyla asked. "Where are Nana and Grandpa? Have they heard what you showed me?" She gestured at the little golem's box. "Do they know what Dorómy and Jon and

Lessip and the others plan out there?" She waved outside, in the direction of the Long Bridge. "I want to see them."

"The High King and High Queen are occupied," Michael said quietly. But the sudden fury she sensed behind his words cut cold down her spine.

Garen glanced up from his little star tree. The brothers looked at each other for half a moment – but it might as well have been an eternity. Garen looked back down at his work.

"What's happened?" Kyla asked softly.

Michael answered, "The High King will tell you soon enough."

Kyla made to speak, but he cut her off. "Parley council will be convened later today," Michael said. "In three bells or so. I have news that couriers have at last come from Lord Jor; he arrives to our relief, finally. There are more details to discuss. I'd like you be present."

She nodded. "Of course."

The arrival of Lord Jor's army would be the first piece of good news they'd had in over a year. Indeed, Jor's presence would force both parties to reconsider the possibility of real compromise. The presence of a massive, loyal army at the enemy's rear could not help but adjust the state of negotiations.

"You should be there, Ky," Garen added absently, repeating Michael's direction, not looking up from his work. "It is important that you're present and seen at these meetings, now more than ever."

"I understand." She stood and turned to go. There was nothing left to say. She would never convince them.

"Also." Michael looked at her, steepling his fingers to his chin. "Watch your tongue around the dragon riders. Think before you speak. And I don't want you spending any more time with the Toller lad. He's a good scout, no doubt, one of our best. You're creating the wrong impression."

She looked him in the eye. "My friends are my own."

Michael smiled, but the air between them seemed to hum with tension, so much so that Garen looked up from his work, peering over his spectacles.

"Get some breakfast, Ky," Garen said. "It's going to be a long day. And tomorrow longer yet. Go down with the others. See Kate. See how she's doing. Eat something."

Kyla looked at Michael. He stared at her. His eyes were

dark and exhausted, but still that black energy sung at the edges of his pupils.

Michael nodded, then looked away to the stained-glass window. The blue light made his eyes seem blacker still. "Good idea, Ky," he said absently. "Eat something."

She turned and left.

She'd never been less hungry in her life.

16

But, as it turned out, that wasn't true.

Kyla could be less hungry.

On her way down to breakfast, right outside the grand mess hall, her appetite coming on at last — the smell of fresh boar bacon and syrup and quail eggs and pancakes nearly driving her crazy — Kyla saw Filip Toller and his squad, fresh from the field, snow on their furry shoulders, faces red with the cold, mittens caked with ice.

She raised her hand in greeting, happy to see him, her entire body unclenching.

"How was it out?" she asked as they approached.

Filip stopped — and then he looked right through her, as if

she didn't exist.

Then he seemed to realize what he was doing, blinked, glanced at her, then looked away, distracted.

"How was it?" Kyla asked again, lamely. She could feel people looking at them as they passed, their eyes barely averted. She stood straight, hands held together before her, composed, waiting for his answer.

He cleared his throat. "Brought in a prisoner for Lord Michael. Looks important, my Lady."

"I'm sure he is." Kyla swallowed. Then she smiled winning-ly, trying to find his eyes.

Filip looked at her, almost as if he was going to say some-thing else, then looked away. His squad had stopped behind him, waiting. She knew all their names, of course. Jordun Sledder, Delen Quine, and Brode Tellerman. Sledder had a fresh cut on his chin. Quine had a new black eye and looked at her in an appraising sort of way that bordered on imperti-nence. Tellerman, also looking a little worse for wear, just rubbed his belly, looking toward the mess hall. Young guys and loyal, dedicated scouts. Filip's crew; his best friends.

Kyla lifted her chin. Her smile felt like it weighed twenty

stone. "Maybe you could tell me about it next time we shoot. After parley, of course. You've been assigned to me. We'll be on the Pinnacle."

"Nice!" Sledder laughed and backhanded Quine on the chest. "Best seats in the house!"

Filip nodded and gave a slight frown. "Of course, my Lady."

"Very well," Kyla said, her stomach folding into itself. She kept her back straight. She took a breath, focused on her training – and kept smiling.

Filip seemed to notice something in her face, because he shook his head, and said, "Would, uh . . . would you like to come with us for breakfast? They sent us up here. Both the lower messes are full."

Kyla knew that Filip asked knowing she had to say no. He knew she could never be seen sitting unattended at the table with him and his lowborn scouts.

"I'm sorry." She clasped her hands in front of her heart and lied. "I have plans to dine upstairs with the High Queen this morning."

"My Lady." He bowed.

She thought her words would wake him up, snap him out of whatever it was, but he looked even more distracted than ever.

So, she turned on her heel and walked calmly away, away from him, away from Susan's delighted laughter in the mess hall, away from her family, away from the delicious smells of breakfast.

She'd grab something small in the family quarters upstairs. She needed time to think.

And she couldn't have eaten a thing, even if she tried.

17

FELLEN COLJ PLACED his jadá cushion on the ground in front of his ancestral shrine and knelt on it. He bowed his head, said a few words, and willed himself to peace. Parley council would begin soon. But Colj had felt the need to commune. So he had finished his morning meal with Lady Katherine, Ponj, and the Dallanar children, met with his ogres, and had then returned to his quarters and his shrine.

Colj had brought the ancestral shrine to Kon many years ago, when he had first come to the Tarn. On the outside, the shrine was a simple wooden box, hinged so it could open outward. Its only decoration was a rough carving of the Fellen family sigil on its side and a plain iron ring on its top. The ring was for transport during campaigns.

Colj opened the shrine. A clay lamp, set in the base of the box, waited for flame. Colj lit it. The orange light flickered, illuminating an array of his clan's memorabilia, tokens, and relics. There was the grey stone taken from Terótan by Colj's great-great-grandfather, Fellen Nonj, during the fourth campaign of Tomas the Second. There was the small painting of a white flower in a delicate silver frame, given to Colj's great-uncle, Fellen Gorj, by Bellános's father, Balmás, after the Battle of Sherrod's Plume. There was the broken dagger hilt that Colj himself had taken from Yor, where he had received his first wound in battle. Dozens of similar items, each with its own story. It had been the Great Sister Aaryn, millennia past, who first had taught the ogres of Jallow the true value of history, the true value of memory. Before her, they had been lost—.

THUMP. THUMP.

A heavy rap on the door.

"Come." Colj did not move to rise.

The door opened. Ponj entered.

Fellen Ponj. Colj's youngest son. His last and only son.

"Father." Ponj nodded, speaking in the ancient tongue of Jallow.

Colj returned the gesture. "Son." Colj took a jadá cushion from beside the shrine, placed it beside him, gestured to it. "Join me."

Ponj knelt beside Colj. Then he bowed, said a few words, and looked into the shrine.

They were quiet together for a time.

After many moments, Ponj said, "Lord Garen summons you, Father. He seeks your words before council."

Colj inclined his head. "We will see battle tomorrow."

Ponj listened, considered, then nodded.

Colj was silent for a long moment. Then he said, "I would speak to you now, Ponj, should death find me."

Ponj nodded but said nothing.

Colj inclined his head, respecting his son's silence. Then he spoke, "You are the last of the Fellen clan, the last of our line of warriors." Colj inclined his head toward the shrine. "We have served the Dallanar since the beginning. Hundreds of generations. But you, Ponj, you are the last. With my death, our clan will be released from our oath, and you will be free to follow your own path. 'Until one remains,' thus it is written and recorded. To the Great Lady Aaryn, we swore a blood oath during the Founding. And for millennia, we have held true. If death should find me, you will be the last and the first. The last of our line, the first free of our clan since the most ancient days. Do you understand?"

Ponj was quiet for a long time, considering. Then he said, "I understand, Father. What are your wishes?"

Colj did not answer for a long moment. To speak without thought was the curse of a fool, such was well-known. But his son's question was of singular import. Colj wanted to answer correctly. It took him some time before he was ready. Then he said, "I wish you to be your own man, my son. I wish you to find a mate, if you so choose. I wish you to find a home, if you so choose. I wish you to walk free, under the stars of Jallow, if you so choose. For thousands of years, our clan has honored its word, honored its history, and honored its promise. When death finds me, we are born anew — in you. I say this not to burden you with expectation, son, but to release you. With my death, you are free. All of us are free. I wish you to feel the truth of that freedom — and to live and to be as you will."

18

THE PARLEY COUNCIL had been going on for a full bell and a half, but nothing about parley itself had been said — nothing real, at least.

And Kyla Dallanar knew why.

Tomorrow's negotiations weren't about peace.

She frowned.

That much was clear.

Everyone — the Tarn's commanders and generals, the colonels and artillery captains, the intelligence officers, the loyal adept liaisons from the Eressan and Alean Orders, the ambassadors and other dignitaries — all of them had been summoned by Michael to the council hall with the alleged purpose of discussing tomorrow's ceasefire.

But they did not plan for a ritualized armistice, which was what parley was supposed to be.

They planned for battle.

Indeed, most of the discussions so far had focused on the tactics, the tricks, and the defenses that the Tarn stood ready to bring to bear should anything happen to Garen — Great Sisters forbid — as he stood before High Lord Vymon Ruge and his sons tomorrow on the Long Bridge.

And the fact that they kept saying things like that — as if a fight wasn't imminent, as if they all didn't want it — was the worst. Everything was prefaced with "should something go wrong . . . ." or "in the event that the terms of parley are breached . . . ." or some other such nonsense. It was as if she was listening to Dorómy's generals talking through Garen's little golem again — but from the other side.

There would be blood.

Everyone knew it.

And Michael practically glowed with the thought of it.

At the center of the council hall sat a massive table on which a huge map had been unrolled showing the Tarn, Tarntown, the port, the bay, the edges of the Sea of Ice, the foothills of the Rakbern Mountains, and the other environs. On top of this map rested hundreds of small flags, tokens, and counters —

the indicators of various corps, regiments, and other tactical fortifications and objectives. Dozens of oil lamps lit the scene, suspended throughout the hall, mounted on wall sconces. Fires blazed in both the room's large fireplaces.

Of course, everyone already knew where parley would take place: on top of the Great Seal, in front of the Tarn's barbican on the opposite side of the Long Bridge, three hundred paces from the Tarn's Great Door. You could see the Seal right there on the map, a massive Dallanar Sun in silver, embedded in the circular pavement before the barbican's main gate. It was a sacred place, one of the most sacred on Kon, perhaps. Legend held that during the Founding it was on that very spot that the Great Sister Aaryn had accepted the final surrender of the last of the old Konungur warlords, the dread Dodrák Kelsrader, after she'd destroyed the highlander's final company of bear riders. Supposedly, the Great Sister Aaryn herself had ordered the High Seal be created as an eternal testament to the power of the Dallanar ruling clan, as a reminder of the peaceful order the Dallanar would establish throughout the Remain. As usual, for Kyla, the ironies were profound.

In the chamber proper, Michael sat at the table's head, his great black sword, the Vordan, sheathed and leaning against the table's edge. On Michael's right sat Garen, Anna, Master Zar and his little dragon, Gregory. Beside Zar sat Master Khondus and several other dragon masters who'd just come through the Gate that morning from Dávanor. On Michael's left sat Doldon, Kate, Kyla herself, Master Falmon, Master Ness, and Colj — in a large, special-made chair. Three of Colj's ogre lieutenants stood behind their commander, as did his son, Ponj.

The rest of the various attendees, perhaps two score in all, crowded around the table. Traditionally, only members of the high family would have had a chair at the table, but Michael had felt it important that their key allies be seated at this particular meeting — seated as if they were family. It was a calculated move, and Kyla both appreciated it and agreed with it, even if it was only for show. And it hadn't been Michael's idea, of course; it had been Garen's, prompted by their earlier conversation regarding the nature of their inter-actions with their closest allies. "The Dark Lord of Kon" was known for his ferocity, not his subtlety. But Michael was still smart enough to take good advice when he heard it, thank the Sisters.

The seating arrangements did highlight one other thing that perhaps Michael did not intend: the notable absence of the High King and High Queen, of Grandpa and Nana.

"Where are they?" Kyla had asked Kate when she'd come into the hall, before council had begun, servants stoking the room's big fireplaces. "I haven't seen Nana in a week, at least. Have you seen her?"

"Not yet," Kate had answered, then she gave her a hug. "Garen says she's busy with some negotiation. Something about an emissary from Peléa."

"Isn't Peléa firmly in Dorómy's camp? That's Lessip's duchy."

"Dunno." Kate had shrugged. "That's what Garen told me. Never underestimate the schemes of the Silver Fox."

"Or the Silver Vixen, apparently."

Kate had laughed in her gentle way and had taken her hand. "Don't worry."

"It doesn't feel right." Kyla shook her head.

"What do you mean?"

"We're planning this parley — a maneuver that Grandpa and Nana supposedly ordered — and they're nowhere to be seen."

"Not so strange, is it? Lots going on. Big duchy, Ky. Bigger kingdom. You know how it is. I remember times when I was younger, I wouldn't see either of them for months. The High King gives this order." She gestured at the parley table. "But he need not be present to know his will is done."

But it *was* strange to Kyla.

More than strange.

Regardless, the fact that Kate didn't know where Grandpa and Nana were either had made Kyla feel better, for some reason.

And then Michael and Garen had come up.

"Ladies." Michael had inclined his head. He looked tired, even more tired than when she'd seen him earlier.

They had both bowed. Then Kate immediately asked, "Where shall I be stationed tomorrow, brother?"

Garen looked at Michael. Michael glanced at Kate and shook his head. "You may arm, of course. But you're not to be part of my company or to leave the Tarn. You may observe from the Pinnacle with Kyla and the children, if you wish." He'd cocked his head at Kyla. "Or from the western ramparts with Zar. I don't want you outside these walls. Especially now."

"'Especially now?' What the blazes does that mean?" Kate asked. Her dark eyes shone. Kate's temper could run as hot as Michael's and she wasn't scared of a fight.

"It means that you will not fight tomorrow, sister – if we fight. That is my command. Are we clear?"

Kate frowned, then nodded – but Kyla could tell that she was having none of it. Michael felt it, too, and quite sensibly pivoted away, turning to Garen. "Has James returned?"

"No," Garen answered.

Michael frowned. "When he's back, we'll need to see him. I want him to take command of our scouts, outriders, and spies in the field, personally."

Kate laughed. "I'm stuck in here and James is sent out? How's that work? Where is he, anyways?"

Michael ignored her. "We must find the Pretender's Gate." And then, without looking at either of them, Michael had called the meeting to order.

And now they were getting yet another report from yet another intelligence officer, this time on the situation in the far northern county of Sonerdun, far north of Aaryn's Cry, where the fighting between loyalist forces and old Konungur rebels had been particularly vicious. Kyla wasn't sure what this had to do with tomorrow's action, until the captain summed up his report to Michael.

"Xyo, Tuck, and Botterfeld weren't able to disengage, my Lord. They can send limited troops within the year, but it's a long journey to the Tarn from Sonerdun by foot. Too long, perhaps."

"What about the reinforcements we requested last fall from Tuck's sister, Alicia?" Michael asked. "Any news there? Those columns should've been here months ago."

The officer nodded. "Yes, my Lord. They didn't make it. Nothing left by the time they got to Aaryn's Cry."

Michael's eyes shone like black jewels.

He's totally exhausted, Kyla realized.

"The 'Mountain King' again?" Doldon frowned.

The intelligence officer inclined his head.

Murmurs ran through the gathering.

"Very well, Captain," Michael said. "We thank you. Please do prepare—."

The council hall's door swung open without announcement. A gaunt, disheveled soldier entered, accompanied by Doj, Colj's largest ogre. Everyone looked up.

The soldier was a tall man, rough-shaven, and almost certainly in a state of shock. Dried blood spattered his armor — and then Kyla realized that he was missing his right hand; his wrist was a white stump wrapped in fresh bandages. His sword sheath was empty. The worn holster under his armpit carried no weapon. There was a line of five precise cuts, recently healed, along his right cheek. His eyes looked glazed. The insignia on his shoulder was torn, but it seemed to mark him as a master sergeant and engineer.

"What's this?" Michael asked, one eyebrow raised.

"From Lord Jor, my Lord." The great ogre, Doj, bowed. His slow voice was impossibly deep. "He has just now arrived."

"Our thanks." Michael nodded.

"My Lord." Doj bowed. The great ogre had two enormous fangs on the right side of his mouth.

"You're Jor's courier?" Michael asked the sergeant, looking him over head to toe.

"Sergeant Daron Eagleton, my Lord." The man bowed. Then he stood tall and held his wrapped stump tight to his chest. He cleared his throat. "I was with Lord Jor, my Lord. I was sent – but not by him."

Michael's eyebrow went up; he shot a look at Garen. "We're grateful for your presence, sergeant," he said. "Please, tell us what has happened. Where is Lord Jor? He is sorely missed. His position is of critical importance for tomorrow's action."

"Your servant, my Lord." Eagleton bowed, stood at attention – but then said nothing. Instead he looked at the floor. He cleared his throat again, clearly trying to stand at attention, holding his wrapped stump to his chest. His lips pressed tightly together.

The man was in shock.

Kyla frowned and glanced at Michael. Michael was appraising the sergeant carefully and had apparently reached an identical conclusion. Michael glanced at Garen, then Anna. Garen frowned. Anna's cool expression betrayed nothing.

Colj and his ogres were impassive, as always. Khondus, Doldon, Kate, Falmon, Zar, and Ness were silent. All the others said nothing. You could have heard a pin drop.

"Sergeant Eagleton," Michael said softly. "How fares Lord Jor? When can we expect him? You are welcome to speak freely."

"Speak, Sergeant," Doldon said, scraping his chair back. He reached for the crystal decanter of mead at the table's center, grabbing a goblet from the silver tray. "Take some refreshment—."

"General Jor is dead, my Lords," Eagleton interrupted. His voice was raw.

Dead silence around the table.

Doldon's hand was frozen, the decanter held poised above the goblet. The mead's sloshing seemed to cease.

From his place on Zar's shoulder, Gregory spread his little blue wings and hissed, showing his fangs.

"Dire news." Michael inclined his head. His voice was calm, but his eyes burned. At his side, the Vordan moaned softly, but nobody else seemed to hear it. Michael glanced at Falmon, who was already pulling a fresh piece of parchment from the bottom of his stack of missives, dipping quill to ink pot. Doldon nodded, filled the goblet, walked around the table, and placed the mead in front of Eagleton.

The room remained silent.

Kyla understood their disappointment. From the outset, Lord Jor had been one of their most stalwart allies and defenders. Lord Jor was Nana's first cousin; his armies from Hakonar had been coming through the Tarn's High Gate since the beginning of the war. For the last year, Jor himself had been active elsewhere on Kon, raising a loyalist army from the southern counties to march overland to the Tarn's relief. Of course, Kyla had known that Jor had been late in coming and that his force was months overdue. But still, it had been an *army*, not some simple relief column. Six full brigades, air support from Dávanor, local scouts, and two dozen batteries of iron artillery from the great Konish city of Konordun.

"We'll need your full report, Sergeant." Michael gestured for Eagleton to drink. "Your bravery has carried you far. We must ask yet more from you."

Eagleton glanced at the goblet, looked into Michael's eyes, and lifted his chin. "I ran, Lord General. I'm not brave. I was captured in flight. He let me live. He let me live to tell you what happened, my Lord – and to give you this."

"Who is 'he?'" Michael asked.

In answer, Eagleton reached into his pocket, brought forth a small package of folded oil skin. He placed the package on the table beside his goblet. One of the Davanórian dragon masters took the package, slid it down the table to Master Khondus, who passed it along to Zar, Anna, and Garen, who finally handed it to Michael. Everyone in the room came closer, moving forward around the table for a better look.

Michael opened the oil skin. It contained a folded piece of white parchment. The parchment was wrapped around something. Michael opened the parchment, placed what it contained on the oil skin – from her place at the table's end, Kyla couldn't see what it was – and scanned the parchment's words. Then Michael handed the parchment to Anna, pushed the oil skin toward her, and looked at her while she read. Anna's eyes flickered with some emotion that Kyla couldn't read. Then Anna looked at the thing held in the oil skin, frowned, handed the parchment across to Doldon, re-folded the oil skin, and pushed it across the table for inspection.

Doldon glanced at the parchment, opened the skin, folded it shut, and pushed the package down to Kate, who looked at it before passing it to Kyla.

Kyla opened it.

The skin contained a long, black thorn. There was a piece of leather thong wrapped around it. The thorn was about the length of her palm — but it wasn't a thorn at all, she realized. Not from plant, but from animal. A weird claw of some sort, long and black and very sharp. Kyla unwound the leather thong and realized that it was attached to the claw, the thong threaded through a hole drilled in the claw's base. It was a primitive token of some sort, like something an old Konungur freeholder or trapper might wear around his neck. Filip Toller would know what it was, probably. She felt her face go warm, then looked at the others. All eyes were on Sergeant Eagleton, waiting for him to continue. The wounded sergeant had taken the goblet of mead and now drank from it deeply.

Kyla opened the parchment.

There was no formal message. Just two lines in black ink,

written in a brutal hand:

Take one of mine, I take one thousand of yours.

Take two of mine, I take everything else.

~ Hone

Kyla frowned. *Hone*. She'd heard the name before. One of Dorómy's oldest friends – Branten Hone, if she remembered correctly. A High General, entirely loyal to her great uncle, who had left royal service many years past. Clearly, he was back in action. She looked again at the claw, held it up on its thong toward the lamp light. It was black and long. Strange. A weird thing. A wrong thing. From what strange beast did it come? Surely, Filip would know. Then Kyla noticed Anna looking at her, at the black claw dangling there from the end of its cord. Kyla wrapped the claw with its thong, placed it back in the skin, and pushed the package back down the table toward Michael. Once more, something flickered in Anna's eyes.

Like all Dallanar children of rank, Kyla had been trained early in the arts of perception, in the arts of observation, in the arts of high consciousness. And there in Anna's eyes – in the eyes of one of the most feared and ferocious soldiers of the Realm, in the eyes of one of the Remain's most ruthless warriors – shone something that looked like the deepest regret. Something that looked like sorrow.

19

"We were almost through the Trange, my Lord," Sergeant Eagleton began. Fellen Colj frowned and inclined his huge ogre head. He had known Eagleton from several actions. The man was a solid fighter. Very tough. A combat engineer; cool-headed. But Eagleton's ja was troubled. He was wounded now, of course. But there was something else in his eyes and voice, something twisted by more than injury. For Colj, the sergeant's ja was like a bird with broken wings.

"Up until that point, it'd been a relatively smooth march. Our outriders had been doing a good job keeping the flanks clear and our dragons had dealt handily with anything the outriders spotted." Eagleton nodded toward the Davanórian captains. "There were constant raids on our baggage, our supply lines, of course. But that was expected. All told, very light action. The enemy didn't have any air power. Too cold up there on the mountain for Tarcerónians, so there was nothing much they could do. Their raiders would come at dusk or dawn, burn some wagons, break up some lines, shoot at the oxen, try to kill some drovers, then they'd withdraw to the forests so our dragons couldn't hit back. Exactly what you'd expect from guerillas tracking a force our size. We were a little over ten thousand men, mind you. And they knew where we were going, knew we couldn't waste time tracking them down. They'd take stabs where they could, mostly action of opportunity, no systematic resistance. They never presented a battle line or massed with enough force to give us pause. They never gave Lord Jor good reason to engage beyond the edges.

"Me and my crews, we were up front, of course. Almost every night, the enemy would knock down some big trees to get in our way; we'd just clear them out. Or they'd blow out the bridges, if they could. But we'd use the trees they'd knocked down to rebuild. The big mountain has no shortage of timber. Me and my boys were far enough in front, we'd usually have the road back in shape for the main column by the time Jor was up. We were making good time. Jor was sending out several dragon squads a day to spot and sow a little carnage of our own if they found an enemy camp. Our scouts kept giving us the all clear. As you can imagine, Lord Jor was disciplined with his reporting schedules. He likes to know what's going on, likes to know where everything is. There was nothing to make us believe we'd see real action until we got through the Trange, past Korfort, at least."

Eagleton shook his head. Colj sensed his ja flutter. "But it was a ruse. They applied just enough pressure to let us know that they were there, just the right kind of sorties to keep us on our toes; no sense of commitment to pitched battle. After a couple of months of marching like that, you get used to it. At least I did. You get into a pattern, into a rhythm. And it was a pattern, my Lords. A rhythm to lull us to sleep. When we got to the Trange, everything went mad."

He took another drink. The room was silent. Colj listened intently.

"Me and my boys, we were down in the gorge proper, in the Trange itself, inspecting the bridge and the foundations. Most of the base of the bridge at the Trange is solid granite, you know. Pillars roughhewn, most of them forty paces wide. Takes real time to break that up, but Jor wasn't in a hurry. He knew the Trange was a bottle neck, a tough place to get stuck if something went wrong. 'Get your lads down in there, Eagleton,' he says to me. 'Check it out, top to bottom. I'm not putting one foot across 'til I know we're good.' And he'd already sent some extra riders and dragons up front, of course. At that point, he had good patrols out three, four days ahead of us, and he had his spies well out in front of that, too. Always knew exactly what was happening. He took pride in that – and rightly so.

"Later that morning, he's down in the gorge with us, look-ing things over, and one of his spies comes in with a young fellow who says he's from you, my Lord." Eagleton nodded at Lord Michael. "This guy says that there's been major action here at the Tarn. Says that Dorómy and Ruge have brought through a third invasion force, somehow, that they've taken up on the southern headlands with a dozen big guns and their war adepts, that they've finally committed their great cannon, not just their local iron. They were pushing hard on the inside, too, through the Tarn's gate, this guy says.

Something had happened with our adepts here, that you were facing hard pressure, inside and out. We had to hurry. That was the point of the message, my Lord: We had to hurry.

"Of course, Lord Jor had been getting messages like this from you for some time, my Lord. It made sense. In fact, it seemed like exactly the kind of message you'd send, if the circumstances related had been true. But again, Jor had that calm sense about him. He listened, then he nodded and said, 'We'll get there. That's what counts.' Not rushed. And we were still at least ten weeks out, even at our very best speed. Even so, he gathered the generals that morning and started making plans to pick up the pace a bit, to push through the Trange the next day. The next day they hit us.

"They came at noon. The sun was bright, just blinding bright. White snow against that sky you get in the high country, that deep, winter blue. Not a cloud in sight. Word had gotten back through most of the column that we were gonna do some real marching, so there was a bit of a logjam at the Trange proper, right there at the bridge. Nothing serious, just enough to block things up a bit. And then — out of nowhere — the enemy's big iron opens up on us from the far side of the gorge, right there — practically on top of us — right there above the far side of the bridge. And not a few guns, either. Must've been a couple dozen batteries. Over a hundred guns, easy. Maybe more. The whole mountain-side, it *erupts*, smoke everywhere, everyone diving for cover, taking hits on the bridge proper, wounded starting to come back almost immediately, our vanguard advancing across the bridge, heading right into that fire, trying to get under some cover — they got torn to pieces. We had ten good squads of dragons for such occasions, however; Lord Jor didn't waste time. He sends half our wing up and out and around, flank-ing the enemy's big iron, burning the forest to cinders — but then it was like the forest *itself* reached up for those dragon riders, a thousand bolts at once — ballistae, if you can believe it — fired together, synchronized, bolt cable strung between them, wing cutters, and there were chained balls coming up from their iron artillery, too. We couldn't believe what we were seeing. The scale of fire was immense. And then our dragons were gone. Only took a moment. This crazy fire from the mountain — and then our dragons are falling from the sky. There were men and bears and guns going off in our middle, too. From both sides, then all at once. Men in furs screaming bloody murder coming down through the forest from every direction, both flanks. It seemed like the enemy was along our whole length. Then from our rear. And the mountain kept thundering. Smoke everywhere. Our guys were getting our own guns unshipped, but the road was narrow, and we were already backed up a little. They had us outmanned and outgunned about two to one, for sure. We didn't stand a chance. There was nothing to do."

Eagleton cleared his throat. His eyes looked strange, almost crazed. Colj appreciated his distress; it was hard news.

"So, I ran. My crews, most of them, maybe two hundred guys, we were still down in the gorge when everything opened up. We had some riflemen assigned to us. My idea was to cross the river, get up on the other side of the gorge – we had all the climbing tackle – climb up there, and get after some of those enemy placements. But the enemy had men in the gorge, too. Down in there, *with* us. They'd been hiding for weeks. Maybe three or four weeks, dug in way deep. Must've been, to avoid our scouts. These guys came charging down the north side of the gorge. Wild men looked like old Konungur berserkers. They knew we'd be down there. My friend Jalen, he got shot through the stomach, I saw his back pop open through his coat, saw him go down. Then they were on top of us; hatchets, logging axes, a few carbines going off here and there, hacking us to pieces . . . and, and I just ran." He blinked, like waking from a nightmare. He looked at Lord Michael, then repeated softly, "I ran."

Nobody spoke.

"How many escaped, sergeant?" Lord Michael asked. "What happened to Lord Jor?"

Eagleton frowned. "Dead, my Lord. There's nothing left. A few got away in the woods, perhaps. But the enemy had the mountain on his side, the land. It was the perfect spot. He'd kind of lulled us into thinking he didn't have the men to engage us, spent *months* singing us to sleep. And then the messenger made it sound like there was real action up here — and even then, Lord Jor didn't let his guard down, not even for a moment. But it didn't matter."

"Where did you get this?" Lord Michael asked, gesturing to the oil skin package and black claw in front of him.

"They caught me, kept me and a couple others tied up.

Tortured us." He touched the five cuts on his cheek. "Asked us questions. But what could we tell? Then their leader came, this huge man. 'The Mountain King comes!' they cried. The 'Mountain King.' And it is a name rightly earned, my Lord. He was enormous, a beast of a man. He rode into camp on a giant, white war bear. Bear albino, eyes like red murder, armored head to toe in the best gear, superb silver. When he jumped off his bear, the ground seemed to shake. He walked to me, looked me over, then orders a tree stump brought close. They bind my wrist, he cuts my hand off, shoves my wrist in the fire – all without saying a word." Eagleton blinked and lifted his stump. "Didn't even ask my name. No questions. Just ordered his men to get me ready to travel. Then he takes out that oil skin and claw and says, 'Take this to the Tarn. Put it in Bellános's hand. Tell him he'd better hope Dorómy gets to him before I do.' Then he mounts his great white bear and leaves, as quickly as he'd come. His men loaded me onto a fast cart, hung a courier banner from the signal pole, brought me to Korfort, then sent me here by zeppelin. That's what happened, my Lord."

Lord Michael looked at Sergeant Eagleton for a moment,

then he frowned. "Hard news. We thank you, sergeant. Stay a moment longer. I would speak with you when we adjourn."

Eagleton bowed and stepped away.

Around the table, the mood was dark. To Colj, it was as if every ja in the room had dimmed – all except Lord Michael's, whose ja seemed to swell. Nobody said a word. Everyone waited for Lord Michael to speak.

"Hard news, indeed," Lord Michael said again. He looked from Master Falmon, to Lord Doldon, to Colj. "Opinions?"

Master Falmon said, "The timing is suspect, of course."

"You read my mind." Lord Doldon nodded.

Colj inclined his head in acknowledgement. He had had the same suspicion.

"Agreed," Lord Michael said. "The very day before parley and we just happen to receive news that our best hope for relief has been butchered wholesale by an army of savages and their 'Mountain King.' If they hope to intimidate us with Hone's army, they'll be disappointed."

Captain Dyer nodded grimly, but her face was pale.

Lord Garen shook his head. "That's only part of the message."

"What do you mean?" Lady Kyla asked.

Lord Garen adjusted his silver spectacles. "The 'Mountain King' is an old Konungur myth. It tells of an enormous, ancient bear that guards Aaryn's Cry from all who would defile it. An ancient legend. Branten Hone has been active against us with his guerillas for years, but he's never had much luck rallying the locals. He's an off-worlder himself, came to Kon from Paráden years ago. He raised a family here, but he's still an outsider; the locals have never trusted him. More to the point, the old Konungur freeholders don't give a damn about Dorómy or about Father – or about the whole war, for that matter. As far as they're concerned, it matters not whether the Tarn – whether all Kon – is held by the Iron Lion or the Silver Fox. They hate both with equal passion; they loathe the Dallanar. But they love their land."

"So." Lady Kyla inclined her head. "Hone engages our forces in his own name, not in Dorómy's, even though the two of them are fast friends, even though Hone has always been loyal to him. Hone then says that he 'fights for the land,' not for Dorómy, even though he's been in Dorómy's service from the beginning. Hone uses an ancient Konungur legend

— the 'Mountain King' — to attract local Konish men and minor houses to his cause——."

"Sounds like it's working," Lord Doldon muttered.

"Exactly." Lady Kyla's eyes were bright. She looked at Lord Michael. "Hone didn't send this message to tell us that Lord Jor is dead, that his army is gone, or that we have no hope of present relief. With this message, Hone tells us that he controls the land *itself*, that he's engaged the support of the countryside's families, that the Konungur freeholders fight for him, and that, by extension, they fight for Dorómy. Hone sends this message to say relief will *never* come."

Colj grunted. Lady Kyla's analysis was sound. The gathered generals and commanders seemed to concur; they murmured and nodded with agreement. And the danger was real. Colj himself had served under General Hone on numerous occasions on several different campaigns. He knew the High General and his family well. Indeed, only eight years ago, Bellános and Dorómy had sent Colj and Zar to Hone's homestead to investigate the murder of Dorómy's adopted daughter, Giácoma Norfell, before the beginning of the war. Colj had seen Hone in battle, both as a commander and as a front-line fighter. There were few in the Realm like him. If Hone had truly raised the old Konungur freeholders against the Tarn, then their situation had worsened ten-fold.

Lady Kyla raised her chin. "We must have peace, Michael. Tomorrow's parley *must* succeed. Surely we can agree on this."

Lord Michael looked at her, nodded, and gazed around the table and room at the gathered commanders. Then he looked at Colj for a moment before turning back to Lady Kyla. "We will do our best tomorrow to come to an understanding, dearest niece. Such is the High King's command. We shall obey it, as always, to the letter. But if we should fail, if our good faith is met by lies, if our honest attempt for armistice is met with treachery, then 'peace' – a false peace procured by the sword – will not be our answer." His dark eyes flashed. "Our answer will be what it should have been from the beginning."

"And what is that?" Lady Kyla asked.

Lord Michael's eyes seemed to go darker still.

"Total war."

20

LITTLE DAN WASN'T very good at counting, but he'd been trying hard to count the stairs as he and the Chief, Val, Benjy, and Zebber followed the tall captain – Captain Durn – up and up and up. Dan would count ten stairs, which was about as far as he could count, and then he'd start over, and then he'd start that over again, too. There were a *lot* of stairs. And he didn't want to fall behind, because a good soldier was a good marcher – but some of the stairs were so darn tall, and he was getting tired even though he was trying hard to keep up. Finally, Captain Durn picked him up and carried him, and that was fine, except that the Chief kept giving him those mean looks, and that was making Dan feel funny.

After a while, they finally got to the Tarn's big Square. It was open to the sky. There were coppery trees on the walls and roofs, and the Tarn's big silver Gate was there in the middle. Captain Durn set Dan down on the ground and said, "Keep up, now."

But Dan couldn't keep up.

He couldn't even move.

Because the big Gate in the Square was *singing*!

Sister's truth, it was!

The Gate's song sounded like Stormy's song, in some ways. But in other ways, it was different. Older and sadder and more tired. There were five adepts in their blue robes at the Gate. They were all singing, too. Two adepts knelt on each side of the Gate like they were supposed to, and one adept stood in the middle, inside the Gate's silvery mist. The adept in the middle was little. Her blue hood was pulled back and her little arms were held out as she sang. As she sang, soldiers and wagons and ogres and oxen and carts and creatures and dragons came through the Gate, stepping and flying and rolling through the Gate's silvery fog. They were coming from other worlds, Dan knew. That little adept in the middle was little, but she was a *good* singer. Yes, sir! Dan could feel her voice through his entire body, from head to toe, her song winding under the Gate's deep music, giving the Gate some help, showing him the way. An image in Dan's mind: A little girl in a blue robe walking down a smooth beach with a giant old man, leading him along with a silver string tied around one of his big fingers. Dan nodded. He didn't understand the little singer's words, but he could feel that her song was good and right, just like when he was singing with Stormy.

Everywhere else in the Square, lots of work was going on, everyone getting ready to fight, the whole place moving with people, shouting and working with the Gate's music below it all. A little snow was falling, but there wasn't any wind. Dan opened his mouth to catch some snow on his tongue. There were big towers above him vanishing into the clouds, so tall he couldn't see their tops, and all those coppery trees, too. He didn't even remember the last time he'd been outside. When had that been? It was cold, but not cave cold. It was that outside kind of cold – nice and clean.

"Real good." Dan nodded and closed his eyes, swaying, listening to the Gate's song, smelling the fresh air. He opened his mouth wider; a diamond of snow landed on his tongue.

"Come *on*, Eadle," the Chief hissed.

"Let's go, lad." Captain Durn touched him on the shoulder. "No time to lollygag."

Dan jumped, then saluted. "Yes, sir!"

They crossed the Square, but it was packed, and the Captain had to yell at people to get out of the way. When they were about halfway across, they stopped, and Captain

Durn talked to another soldier. That soldier took the Chief, Val, Benjy, and Zebber off a different way, across to the other side of the Square to do their work, Dan supposed. Then the Captain picked him up and walked real fast, almost running, in a different direction, way faster than before, through a stone arch and up some more steps, and then they were going up and up and up again, up a big staircase, then across another open courtyard, through a big door, then up another set of stairs. Dan lost track of how many tens he'd counted. Through another set of doors and up another set of stairs that was so darn long Dan was glad he was getting carried, then up and up again.

"You sure are a good marcher," Dan told Captain Durn, patting his shoulder. "I wish I could do it like you."

The Captain grunted and kept marching.

Dan nodded. He understood. No time to talk when you were on the march.

They kept on going up until they got to a wide hallway, then they went down that hallway until they were standing in front of a door guarded by two big ogres in armor.

Captain Durn set Dan down on the floor. "This is the boy

Lord Garen summoned."

The ogres looked down at Dan, then looked at the Captain.

Captain Durn didn't say anything else, so Dan stood tall, saluted the biggest ogre, and said, "Ready to work, sir!"

The ogre blinked at him, then nodded and returned his salute, his huge fist crossing his armored chest. He really was the biggest ogre that Dan had ever seen. Bigger than Captain Colj, even. Two big fangs stuck out of one side of his mouth.

"They're done," the big ogre rumbled slowly. He tilted his huge head at the door. As he did this, a pair of men in fine clothes came out, talking together in low voices, not looking up, walking past them, down the hall. Then another man came out. One of his hands was missing, wrapped up in a white bandage. There was a grey-haired man at his side talking to him about something, something about dragons; the man with the missing hand looked real sad.

"Go ahead." The big ogre pushed the door open.

Captain Durn touched Dan's shoulder. "Come, lad."

It was a long room with a big table in the middle and lamps and lanterns everywhere. There were banners hanging from the ceiling in all sorts of different shapes and colors. A bunch of armor and weapons hung on the walls with little signs next to them. There were some shelves running around the sides, too, but short ones, filled with little blue books like the ones Dan had seen down with Master Falmon. Some soldiers stood around the table talking in little groups, and a couple of people sat at the table, moving things around on it; Dan couldn't see what they were doing because the tabletop was above his head. The blond lady with the ponytail he'd seen down with Stormy yesterday, Lady Kyla, was talking to the purple dwarf, Master Zar, and his little blue dragon. There was another lady who had darker hair who Dan had never seen before. The black-haired lady in silver armor was there, Captain Dyer, but she wasn't talking to anybody. Lord Doldon and Lord Michael were talking at the end of the table. Big Captain Colj was over there talking to an old man in a black robe with a big scar on his forehead, the old man leaning on a crooked walking stick.

Captain Durn walked Dan across the room, and then Dan saw Master Falmon. The Master was talking to a man wearing a blue vest and silver spectacles. The man with the spectacles had to be Lord Garen, Dan figured. Dan had never seen Lord

Garen before, but everyone said that he wore silver spectacles like this man did, so that's who this had to be. When Dan saw Master Falmon, he smiled and waved, then put his hand down because that's not how a proper soldier did it. But then Master Falmon waved back, so Dan ran to the Master, looked up, and saluted. "Ready to work, Master Falmon, sir! Don't have my box, but I can do it! Tight corners, I be ready for 'em, sir! Yes, I be!"

Lord Michael, Lord Doldon, and Captain Colj looked up and came over. Then the rest of the people came over. All of them looked down at him, and Dan got nervous. But then he remembered that *they* had told *him* to come up there, so he saluted again. "Ready, Lords! Ladies! Yes, sir! I do a good job!" Then he bowed way down, because they were the High Lords and Ladies, and he remembered hearing something about bowing, so he did that.

"This is the boy?" Lord Garen looked at Captain Colj.

Both Captain Colj and Master Falmon nodded. Master Falmon gave Dan a serious look, as if to say, "Do it good, soldier."

Dan nodded back. He'd do it good, as good as he could.

For truth.

"Ready to work!" Dan saluted again.

Lord Garen bent down and brushed Dan's hair away from his eyes. Dan flinched at this touch, then looked at Lord Garen for a moment, blinked, and bowed again.

"You're Daniel Eadle?" Lord Garen asked.

Dan started to say that nobody called him that name, but then he realized that that wouldn't be right, so he stood tall, saluted twice—thump-thump little fist on his heart—and nodded. "Yes, sir! I'm Eadle, sir! Eadle is me! One, two, three! Ready to work, sir!"

All the other folks in the room were looking at him now, but Lord Garen just smiled, took off his spectacles and polished them with the corner of his vest. "Glad to hear it, Daniel. There's some special work we need done up here." He paused, glanced at everyone else in the room, then looked at Lord Michael. "I think we're done here."

Lord Michael nodded. "Gentlemen," he said. All the talking in the room went quiet, and everyone turned to look at him. "I think we've accomplished what we can for today. We'll reconvene three bells before dawn. Thank you for your wisdom and good council."

All the other soldiers and men and everyone nodded and started moving toward the door, talking and murmuring. Master Zar and his little dragon stayed. Lady Kyla, the other dark-haired lady, and Captain Dyer stayed, too. So did Captain Colj, Master Falmon, Lord Doldon, and the old man in the black robe with the crooked walking stick.

When the last person left, Lord Garen looked down at Dan. "Captain Colj and Master Falmon say you're a good worker, Daniel. Very trustworthy. They say you're one of the most dedicated workers we have."

Dan knew what "good" meant, but he didn't quite know about "dedicated." But everyone said that Lord Garen had the big smarts, so if he said that Dan was "good," then that other word must be a good word, too. So Dan nodded, bowed again, and kept his eyes on the ground.

Lord Garen touched his shoulder. Dan looked up. "Colj tells me you sing to the big guns. Falmon told me about the armor earlier this morning." Lord Garen lifted Dan's chin so he could look him in the eye. "He says you sang to the armor, too. Is that true?"

Dan frowned, squinted at Captain Colj and Master Falmon, then nodded quickly because it was true, then looked at the ground again. But it really wasn't fair. Master Falmon had said not to say anything. "Not a word," Master Falmon had said. And that meant it was a secret that you shouldn't tell anybody. But the High Lord was asking, and you had to tell the truth. So Dan just nodded again, stood tall, looked Lord Garen in the eye like a good soldier would, and said, "Yes, my Lord, sir! I sing sometimes! I try to do it good!"

"Dan?" Lord Michael knelt in front of him. "Can you tell us about your songs?" Lord Michael's voice was tired and real soft, but it reached right inside Dan's chest. Lord Michael took Dan's hands in his own, looked into his eyes, and Dan went dizzy, like falling down a well — no noise, just falling into those dark eyes, like nothing you could do about it. Dan's face got kind of hot, and his head was spinning, so he just blurted the first thing that came into his head. "I'm not a crazy, sir!"

Lord Doldon chuckled. Dan's face went hotter still. Lord Michael looked at Lord Doldon, and the chuckling stopped. Lord Michael didn't let go of Dan's hands, just squeezed them real nice. Lord Michael's hands sure were warm. Master Zar and his little dragon, the ladies, all of them were looking at him. Captain Colj nodded his big ogre head at Dan, as if to say, "Stay strong, soldier."

"You're not crazy, Dan," Lord Michael said gently. "We know that. I know that. We want to hear about your songs, isn't that right, Master Falmon?"

"That it is, my Lord." Master Falmon cleared his throat. "A good soldier tells the truth, Daniel. You've done no wrong. Your Lord asked you a question. You need to answer with your most honest words."

Dan looked at Master Falmon. Master Falmon nodded back at him, as if to say it was all good. So Dan lifted his chin. "I sing to keep warm, my Lord, sir."

"Keep warm?" Lord Michael asked. He looked up at Master Falmon. Master Falmon nodded. Lord Garen glanced at the old man in the black robes with the crooked stick. The old man turned and went to the side of the room, walking stick tick-ticking, bent at one of the shelves, and came back with a long box made of silvery wood. Everyone came closer.

"Put him here." Lord Garen patted the tabletop.

Lord Michael picked Dan up and set him on the table. There were papers and drawings all over the table, and a huge painting that looked like a kind of map with little markers all over it.

The old man gave the silvery box to the dark-haired lady that Dan didn't know, then opened it. Inside the box, there was a small high silver hammer, like the one Master Falmon had used down with the armor, and five weird tools made of high silver, all resting on a blue cushion, like this:

"Dan," Master Falmon said, "this is Master Ness." He nodded to the man in black robes with the stick. He looked at the dark-haired lady beside him, the one holding the box. "And this is Lady Katherine."

Dan bowed where he was sitting and saluted Master Ness and Lady Katherine. Master Ness looked real old. He had a scar on his forehead that started at the top of his nose and went up between his eyes. He was leaning hard on his walking stick, like he could barely stand without it. Lady Katherine looked at Dan curiously. Next to her, Lady Kyla was smiling at him. Dan smiled back.

Master Ness took the silver hammer in one hand and took the first silver tool out of the case.

"Can you hold this, lad?" Master Ness put the tool into Dan's little hand.

Dan took the tool and held it. It was very light and cool to the touch.

"Hold it up in front of you, just like this." He made a gesture like he was holding the tool in front of his heart.

Dan did as he was told.

Master Ness nodded. "Now, listen."

Dan got ready to listen. Everyone was staring at him. Master Zar and Lady Katherine and Lady Kyla were looking at him. Zar's little dragon was looking at him, its tiny eyes like yellow jewels. The Masters, Captain Colj, Captain Dyer, and the High Lords looked at him, too. Dan felt his face go warm, but then he looked over at Master Falmon. Master Falmon nodded at him, one soldier to another. So

Dan nodded back and got ready.

And then Master Ness touched the hammer to the tool and everything around Dan went dead quiet, like his ears didn't work anymore, and it was as if a door had opened inside Dan's head, and he was staring at a silent night sky. But not at it. *In* it — silvery stars weaving together and dancing in the black, like he was looking into his own head, and his head was full of stars from the inside out. Then a song came real soft, not like Stormy's really, but the same sort of *feeling*, just sadder — so much sadder — and he couldn't help but hum along. He closed his eyes, following the soft song through those stars, feeling the way, a quiet rush in his ears, but not really ringing, more like a vibration you could feel but not hear, the tool going warm in his hand.

Then it stopped.

Dan opened his eyes.

Master Ness was staring at him, holding his hand over Dan's little hand that held the tool. The tool was glowing silver-white, like the light of the moon. It wasn't hot, just warm. Everyone looked at each other — then back at Dan.

Master Ness nodded. "Very good, very good," he said.

He took the tool from Dan. It stopped glowing right away. Master Ness put the tool back in its box.

Everyone was still looking at Dan, so he saluted and tried to say something, but he suddenly found that he couldn't really talk and that he was *real* tired.

Master Ness gave him the other four tools in the same way, taking them from the case that Lady Katherine held, one after the other. Each time, there was a different song, and a different kind of feeling, and each time Dan kind of sang along and got more tired, like he could barely keep his eyes open. Each time, there was that bright light from the tool when the song stopped, and the tool would be warm in his hand. Everyone had gathered close around him. But he was so tired now, he could barely sit up straight.

"You take it, soldier," he mumbled at himself, trying to keep his eyes open. "You take it, boy." But the words didn't come out right; they sounded like he was trying to talk with his mouth full of pebbles, and he was just so darn *tired*. And then, before he knew what was happening, Dan pitched forward off the table, and Lord Michael caught him and held him close and said something that Dan didn't understand, but the words sounded gentle and soft and kind.

21

KYLA DALLANAR BLINKED. She was standing in front of a miracle. Then she looked around and was grateful to see that she wasn't the only one astonished by Dan's display of power. Michael held Dan to his chest, whispering softly, "Good solider, good solider." Garen's and Kate's eyes were glassy, as were those of Falmon and Ness. Even Zar, Anna, and Colj seemed to have been touched. Little Gregory gave a soft squeak from Zar's shoulder, then nuzzled the purple dwarf with his blue snout.

"It's true," Michael said softly, looking over Dan's head at Garen and Ness. "He has it?"

Ness nodded. "He both feels and knows the bases of the ancient songs – naturally, with no training."

"How is that possible?" Kate asked.

Garen said, "Such savants are rare, but they've existed in the past."

"When?" Michael asked.

Garen didn't answer but instead looked to Ness. Ness

leaned on his walking stick. "The most recent example we could find was recorded by Venara Godol during the reign of Julia the Third."

"'The Siegebreaker,'" Zar murmured.

"Indeed." Ness nodded.

"Fortuitous," Doldon grinned. "We're due for a bit of siege breaking ourselves."

Kyla looked from Ness to Garen. "Julia reigned over seventeen hundred years ago." She looked at Dan, who now snored softly against Michael's shoulder. "'Rare' seems likes an underestimation."

"Extremely rare, then." Garen shrugged. "Remember, that case was documented. There could have been — there could *be* — many examples that are not known."

"What do we know from that earlier instance?" Michael asked.

Ness nodded. "That early case was very much like this one, apparently. A young boy, ten years old, quite 'simple' as they say, like our young Daniel here — but in complete tune with the Realm's ancient songs. He was discovered by chance on Dayáden, brought to Paráden by Julia, and used there to annihilate the forces then laying siege to the Káladar. Also, unlike our war adepts, who are nearly all women, a savant's ability seems to manifest almost exclusively in men. It also appears to be linked to brain development — and to memory, somehow."

"That makes sense," Kate said. "The High Gates, High Pendants, and High Cups are all tied to memory."

"What do you mean?" Anna asked her.

Everyone looked to Garen. He adjusted his spectacles. "While the processes are poorly understood, when you travel the Realm by High Pendant, you first visualize a location where you've been — you recall the memory of a place — and then the Pendant moves you into that memory, through space-time. Likewise, High Cups allow an individual to 'deposit' memories within specially tuned vessels, thus preserving those memories for eternity. High Gates join key principles of both Pendants and Cups, allowing Gate adepts to conjure stable connections between known destinations that can be used by others. The High Gates' songs, when properly tuned, provide 'cues' or 'prompts' back to the primal memories generated when the Gates were first created by Acasius and his Sisters. In all three cases — Pendant, Cup, and Gate — *memory* forms both the binding tissue, the primary element used to 'activate' the particular artifact."

Anna frowned and smoothed a lock of dark hair behind her ear. "So, in Dan's case, he 'remembers' songs he's never heard?"

"Precisely." Ness nodded. "His discovery provides an unprecedented opportunity for further study. In some ways, the great cannon are like the High Pendants, Cups, and Gates: alive and profoundly mysterious — living tools." Ness looked at Daniel. "Much could be learned, if he is willing to teach us—."

"Can he fight?" Michael looked down at Daniel. "Can he engage the enemy?"

Kyla's hands went cold. She shouldn't be surprised by Michael's question. She knew that. But still, it chilled her to the bone.

Nobody spoke for a moment.

"Can he fight?" Michael repeated.

Ness bowed. "I would think so, my Lord. But whatever action he does take, it will be wild, untrained."

Michael nodded. "Was Julia's savant 'wild' and 'untrained' when he was discovered?"

"Yes, my Lord."

"But it worked, somehow," Michael said. "Julia was able to harness her savant's energy, to destroy her enemies?"

"Yes, my Lord." Ness bowed. "The records are clear: The destruction was catastrophic."

Michael's eyes flashed, but he said nothing more.

Kyla shook her head. She would not – could not – keep silent. "Can we, in proper conscience, unleash this boy when we don't understand his abilities? When we don't know what he can do? We don't even know who he is, where his family is."

"With respect, we do know something, Lady Kyla," Ness bowed. "Our assistants have looked into the records. The muster taken of children brought into the Tarn during the Pretender's initial assault lists his name as 'Daniel Eadle, an orphan.' No living relatives. The surname is uncommon. There were only two Eadle families recorded during the census of Tarntown conducted ten years ago. Those two families belonged to two brothers, both laborers. Both lived in Port's View. Daniel was the only child of the older brother, Bodun Eadle. The other brother, Bradun, had no children. Daniel's mother, father, uncle, and aunt were all killed in the Pretender's assault."

"He has no living relatives, then," Kate said.

Ness inclined his head. "No lineage, no family."

Kyla frowned. "That does not answer my first question. Can we use him when we don't know what he can do?"

"Of course, we can," Michael said. "And we *must*. The majority of the Legion's generals are with Dorómy, Ky. So too are most adepts of the Alean Order. Our own adepts and cannon are exhausted. Dorómy's army grows daily. And by your own reckoning, we have no chance for relief; Hone has demonstrated this. For two years, we've been pressed into a corner." He held Daniel to his chest. "This is the moment to break free."

"Whatever the cost?" Kyla raised an eyebrow.

"What is 'cost,' when it brings victory? And this——." Michael touched the top of Daniel's head. "This is victory."

Kyla frowned. "He's a little boy who sings in the cold to keep warm. And, with respect, Michael, tomorrow is not battle. Not yet. It's parley. It's a chance for peace. At least some kind of ceasefire, to help us come to an agreement."

She looked at Dan, then noticed that everyone was staring at her. She lifted her chin, cleared her throat, and gestured to Daniel. "I understand the tactical advantage he might provide. But we don't know what we're asking him to do, what he *can* do. We don't know what will happen."

"That's true," Michael said. "But he will go out, nonetheless." He looked at Ness and Garen. "What steps must we take to activate him?"

"But—," Kyla began.

Michael's gaze silenced her. "I appreciate your thoughts, Kyla." He looked back at Garen and Ness. "What must we do to make use of his abilities?"

Ness frowned. "The accounts are . . . unclear. It is a risk, as Lady Kyla notes."

Michael said nothing for a moment. When he did speak, his voice was quiet, but seemed to fill the room with unspeakable power. "What must we do to make use of his abilities, Master Ness?"

Ness bowed. "I have marked and read all relevant passages.

I have also marked the scholia. The accounts are consistent: Julia brought the boy forward in the heat of battle, the boy laid his hands upon a great cannon, and the result was devastation. In all versions, it seems that battle *itself* was the prompt that joined boy to living weapon."

"So, he just needs to be present?" Michael asked.

"Unknown." Ness inclined his head. "But that is what the sources seem to relate."

"Not much to go on." Master Falmon frowned. Kate nodded. Kyla could tell that neither Falmon nor Kate were entirely pleased with the direction the conversation had taken.

"True," Doldon said. "But can we risk not taking full advantage of what he might be capable of?" He looked from Michael to Garen to Kate. Garen inclined his head, but it didn't look like he was full agreement, either.

"The point is moot," Michael said. "We *will* take advantage. He'll go up with the adepts and squires as a helper, as Master Falmon suggested. He'll stay close. Doldon and Falmon will be there with him. We'll brief our war adepts as to his potential. When battle commences—."

"*If* battle commences," Kyla interrupted him. "Isn't that what you mean, Michael? *If?*"

"Of course." Michael smiled. "*If* battle commences, Falmon and Doldon will move him into alignment with our adepts, as they see fit." He glanced at Anna. "We will, of course, rely on our traditional forces, should something occur. We'll neither expect nor depend on anything else. If Daniel's ability manifests, then we'll stand ready to use him."

Kyla began to say something else, but a knock on the chamber door interrupted her.

"Come," Michael said.

Colj's great ogre, Doj, opened the door. A Davanórian dragon rider entered and moved toward the table, saluting when she arrived. "My Lords. The last flights are ready to come through." She turned to Anna and Zar. "Captain Dyer, Master Zar, your presence has been requested."

"Very good," Michael said. "We were just wrapping up." He stood and carried Dan to the far side of the room, blowing out lanterns and lamps as he passed.

Anna and Zar bowed and departed with the dragon rider. Kyla watched Michael get Dan comfortable on a settee beneath the far window, tucking a cushion beneath his head.

Kyla turned to Ness. "I have some questions for you, Master."

"As do I," Kate added

Ness bowed. "I thought you might, my Ladies. I am at your disposal, of course – but my knowledge is limited, I am afraid."

"What happened to Julia's savant?" Kyla asked. "When the battle was done, what happened to him?"

"My question, exactly." Kate nodded.

Michael returned. Everyone looked to Ness, waiting for his response.

"All accounts agree." Ness looked at her. "Julia's savant died on the war field. Killed by the effort."

Kyla shot a look at Michael.

Michael returned her gaze emotionlessly. "Such is the life of a warrior."

"He's not a warrior," Kyla said.

Michael's gaze was dark. "He will be tomorrow."

Kyla glanced at the others. Falmon and Kate looked concerned, but they wouldn't challenge him. Garen made notes in one of his books, showing what he wrote to Ness. Colj looked on, a pensive look on his huge ogre face. Doldon poured himself a glass of wine; he would be no help. And what argument could she herself make? Kyla knew what they faced. She knew what was required and she understood the necessity. But still, something seemed wrong.

"We can't hurt him – or others – needlessly, Michael," she heard herself say. "We can't bring suffering without cause."

"Agreed." Michael nodded.

But when she looked into his eyes, she felt a sudden pang of fear.

Michael continued. "Let me share with you something the High King once told me and your dad, when we were little, Ky: 'A great leader,' he said, 'needs not be a person who does great things; a great leader needs to be a person who stirs her people to do great things.' And sometimes, Ky, great things are terrible things. Yet they must be done."

"I know." Kyla held her hands close in front of her.

"Then why do we debate?"

She sighed. "This isn't a debate, Michael. I know I can't convince you. I'm not sure I want to, either. I understand what compels this thrice-cursed war. But I must speak the truth, as I see it. Would Grandpa and Nana – the High King and Queen – would they take this risk, when so little is known? And if the power Daniel holds is as great as they say—." She gestured at Garen and Ness. "Then perhaps we shouldn't risk it at all."

"Maybe you're right," Michael said. "But I must finish this. We must finish this—."

Kyla shook her head. "But it won't be 'us,' Michael. It will be a little boy – a simple, good, little boy. He won't know what he's doing."

Michael looked over at Daniel, his eyes eternally dark. "Such is the nature of war."

22

WHEN DAN OPENED his eyes, he was laying on a soft couch with a pillow under his head. He was in the same big room, but most of the lamps and lanterns were out. Lord Michael, Lord Garen, Captain Colj, Master Falmon, Lady Kyla, Lady Katherine, and Master Ness were all over there, talking softly around the big table. Master Zar, his little dragon, and Captain Dyer had left. Lord Doldon was walking to the table from the door.

Dan didn't feel too tired anymore, so he swung his legs off the couch, slid down, and walked over, knees wobbly, then bowed and saluted when they turned and looked at him. Lord Michael picked Dan up, set him on the table's edge. He lifted Dan's chin, brushed his hair away from his face, and looked into his eyes. Dan bowed and saluted but didn't say anything because looking into Lord Michael's dark eyes made him dizzy.

"How are you feeling, Daniel?" Lord Michael asked.

Dan nodded a couple of times, blinked, then saluted. His fist had never felt so heavy. "Good, sir." He cleared his throat. He was real thirsty. "Ready to work, sir," he croaked.

Lady Kyla poured water into a cup and handed it to him. Dan took it with both hands, drank, and it was so good. Best water he'd ever tasted.

"Easy, Daniel." Lady Kyla took the cup from him. "Not all at once." She handed the cup to Lady Katherine.

Dan wiped his mouth and nodded. "So good! That's darn good water, right there!"

Lady Kyla smiled at him. Lady Katherine smiled at him, too.

Lord Michael put his hand on Dan's shoulder, made like he was going to say something, but then he just squeezed gently and looked up at Lord Garen. "Should he stay up here with us?"

Dan didn't know what that meant, but Lord Garen frowned, took off his silver spectacles, polished them on his vest, then looked at Lord Doldon, Captain Colj, Master Ness, and Master Falmon. Master Ness shook his head. Master Falmon said, "I'd recommend not, my Lord. Let's send him back down. As if nothing's happened."

Lord Michael nodded. Captain Colj listened, paused for a long moment, then he nodded, too.

Lady Kyla gave Dan the cup again, and he drank. Water dribbled down his chin. Lady Katherine dabbed it with a napkin.

"That's so *good!*" Dan nodded, looking into the cup. The ladies smiled. "For truth!"

Master Ness ticked his crooked stick against the floor. "We know they have one or two agents inside, my Lord. One or two, at least. They'll be waiting for something like this." Master Ness tilted his head in Dan's direction. "He was brought up to clean something. That was the pretense. So, he cleaned it — and now he's done with his work and he's going back down to bed. A little late, but nothing remarkable. He came, he did his work, and now he's going back. Nothing out of the ordinary — that's how it must appear."

"Routine," Lord Doldon nodded.

"Agreed," Lord Garen said. Everyone else was nodding, too. Captain Colj looked at Dan for a long moment, then nodded.

"Is the threat that serious?" Lady Kyla asked.

Master Ness looked at her, ticked his walking stick, then shrugged.

Dan didn't understand what any of this was about, so he kept his mouth shut like a good soldier should. But he did understand what "back down to bed" meant, of course. And he was ready for that part. He was dog bones tired.

"Very well," Lord Michael said. "We'll return him to his place. He will go out tomorrow as we discussed. A simple squire's helper. Our adepts will tend him. We'll bring him up later, depending on tomorrow's action."

Everyone nodded.

Lord Michael looked at Dan for a moment, then glanced at Master Falmon. "You'll see to it?"

"Of course, my Lord," Master Falmon said. Then he turned to Dan. "You ready for bed, Dan?"

"Great Sisters, yes!" Dan nodded and gave a loud burp because he'd drank so much water. "Ready, Master Falmon, sir! Always ready for rack time, sir!"

"Big Dan." Lord Doldon laughed and patted Dan's shoulder. "My kind of soldier."

THE THIRD DAY

23

Deep asleep, Little Dan dreamed.

He saw a workshop. A workshop filled with little boys and girls and silver machines. It reminded Dan of that place where they made the swords and axes and armor. He couldn't remember what that place was called, but this place had the same kind of clumping and banging and loud noises.

But it was different, too.

They didn't make swords or axes or armor down here.

No, sir.

They made something else.

Those silver machines thumped and clanked, opened and

shut, opened and shut. Big silver cogs turned on long silver tubes. Clunk-whump. Clunk-whump. Clunk-whump. The machines smelled like lightning. Silver steam hissed from silver holes. The pipes, the gears, the floors, the walls, the machines, all glowed the same silver glow. Like Stormy, Dan realized. That same silver light.

The little boys and girls worked at the machines. They wore silver cloth on their feet and walked with tiny steps. They were all Dan's age, but some looked even younger. They had silver mittens on their hands and silver bands over their hair. Silver cloths covered up their mouths. Dan nodded. He understood. The silver cloth protected the work.

The work must be protected, someone whispered behind him.

Dan turned.

But there wasn't anybody there.

A little boy placed something in his machine and pulled a silver lever. The machine clumped shut. When it opened, a silver tear sat in the machine. The tear was hot, silvery-white, and perfectly smooth, about the size of the little boy's fist. The boy took the tear from the machine and turned to Dan. He held the tear up with both his little hands. Inside that tear, Dan heard a song. It was like Stormy's, but different. Older and slower and way stronger, too.

Dan listened and for a moment he imagined something else under the music, something hidden and dark. Like a secret. A big secret.

We can't hide forever, the whisper came.

"Hide what?" Dan asked. "Is this a game?"

The little boy jumped at his voice and dropped the tear, and it broke on the floor. From the pieces, a black thing like a black bug hissed. Its hands were hooks, like little knives ticking the floor as it clicked out of the shards and scuttled toward the drain, dropping down into the dark.

Somewhere below, a big door banged open, and a sound echoed up. It was the sound of big hooves pounding on an old road, of deep monsters who worked down in the deeper places. That thing in the tear had set them loose.

The door crashed open, and a pack of monsters ran into the workshop. They were wearing black robes. Oily black slime dripped everywhere. Their hands were bird claws. But the worst was their faces: They were like eggs. Grey eggs. Smooth, toothless mouths opening. They didn't have eyes.

A monster grabbed Dan, drove a knife into his heart, and dropped him dead to the floor.

But Dan didn't die.

It didn't even hurt.

Not a bit.

Dan looked down at the wound and saw silvery liquid coming up out of his chest.

But still, he didn't die.

All around him, the monsters killed. They held the little boys and girls down, ripped the cloths from their faces, and cut their throats, their legs, their arms. Bad games! Bad!

But there wasn't any blood.

All the kids were just like Dan, and silver came out of them when the monsters hacked and stabbed and howled. There was another sound, too — a low cry. The voices of the little boys and girls. The voices came together, became one voice. More of those bright tears shattered. More of those weird black things crawled down into the dark. More hooves came up from below. More monster egg-heads crashing through doors, those weird mouths with no teeth. And the bad games kept going on and on . . . .

The promise must be kept.

Another tear shattered to the floor.

But this time, a black crow flew from the pieces then landed and hopped across the floor until it stood near Dan's hand. It cocked its head side to side, then gave a loud CAW! CAW!

The monsters came around the crow and looked at it.

The crow cocked its head at Dan. "You must choose," it cawed in its crow voice.

"Choose what?" Little Dan asked.

"Who lives." The crow cocked its head. "And who dies."

"Bad games!" Dan shook his head. "I don't want to play that game. No, sir!"

The crow blinked, hopped, and cocked his head back and forth.

A monster knelt on the ground in front of Dan. From his robe, he brought a small silver tear.

The tear sang, but you could barely hear it.

And Dan knew the song instantly.

"That's Stormy's song!" he cried.

The crow cocked its head at the tear, then back to Dan, as if asking a question.

"Choose!" it cawed. "Choose!"

"You don't hurt my friend, crow," Dan said. He wagged his finger at the bird and saw to his amazement that his whole arm was made of silver — pure, shiny silver.

The crow squawked. It jumped to a new perch.

The monster squeezed the silver tear.

The song began to die.

"You don't hurt my friend, you darn egg monster!" Dan shouted. "You don't hurt Stormy!" He pushed his silver hand at the thing — and a funnel of silvery fire shot out of this hand and hit the monster in its chest, its black robes burning up in white flame.

He could save Stormy!

Dan moved his silver hand and melted the monsters with his silver fire. The monsters' robes rushed up in flames, weird egg-shaped heads hissing and splitting, cracking, darker things coming now from the cracks, weird black things clawing out of the egg heads, flashing black blades.

"Even you," the crow cawed in a strange voice, like it came from a thousand throats. "Even you have chosen."

"I didn't choose! No, sir! I didn't *want* to play!" Dan yelled.

"*You* made the bad games. *You* hurt Stormy. He made his hand into a fist, silver-white flames sizzling around his knuckles, and aimed at the crow.

But the crow just jumped aside and cocked its head, and then there was nothing but rising out of sleep into darkness and pain.

24

WHEN DAN WOKE, he was tied to his bunk, again.

His arms were stretched out above his head, his legs were pulled all the way down, twine biting into his skin, black cords wrapped tight around his wrists and ankles, just like before. And it was cold.

"Chief!" Dan hollered.

But there was nobody in the barracks.

Dan could tell because there wasn't any noise, and the little lamp in the can was blown out. That lamp was never blown out unless everybody was gone for the day.

"I gotta be out there for muster!" Dan yelled. "Hey! *Hey!* I gotta go muster, Chief. Today's the day! Chief! *Chief!*"

The darkness swallowed his voice.

And he had to go to the bathroom.

Real bad.

"Should be against the rules," Dan muttered. Not a fun game. No, sir. And how was he supposed to get out now? Master Falmon had said sharp and tight, not to be late. Dan shook his head. He must have been so tired from the night before, slept through everyone getting up. Why didn't they wake him up?

Dan pulled on his wrists. He pulled on his ankles. The twine was super tight. His sore elbow was real sore again, too. He wished he had some of that blue leaf that Master Falmon had.

"Darn it," he whispered.

Then he stopped and took a deep breath.

"Think, soldier," Dan said to himself in Colj's deep voice. "Think."

"Yes, little soldier." Crazy Bill's whisper came from the dark. "*Think.*"

Dan froze. The hairs on the back of his neck stood on end.

There was the scrape-scrape of flint and steel, a white spark in the black, then the orange glow of an oil lamp. A big shadow held the lamp, wobbly and huge. The shadow came toward him, lifted its lamp, and showed Crazy Bill's crazy eyes glowing blood orange.

Little Dan started to say something, but Crazy Bill touched his finger to his lips. "Shh, little soldier. Shh. They's all gone now. It's just you and me, soldier." Crazy Bill pointed at himself with his thumb and then Dan with his finger. "Just *you* – and *me*."

When Crazy Bill said these last words, he smiled. His teeth seemed long, and the way his eyes glowed made him seem crazier than ever.

Dan swallowed. "I – uh, I gotta get up with Stormy, Crazy Bill." Then he added. "I gotta go to the can."

Crazy Bill shrugged. "Maybe you do that after we're done. They already gone." He looked up at the ceiling. "Nobody said nothing 'bout a stupid little crazy going up there. Big day today. Everyone up and out and ready to watch. Ready to fight, maybe? Ain't nobody gonna be down here for a long time." He stepped closer to Dan's bunk, squatted down beside it, and set his lamp on the floor. "Just *you* and *me*."

Crazy Bill crouched there for a while, kind of hunched over. Then he sat down cross-legged beside Dan and took a weird little knife out of his pocket. It looked like something that he had made himself. The blade was tiny, but it looked super sharp.

"All day together." Crazy Bill looked him over from head to foot, pulled on the twine at Dan's wrists, making sure they were tight. "Beautiful day."

Dan blinked. Then he said, "The Chief won't like it if you do the bad games on me, Crazy Bill." But in his head, Dan was already starting to think about himself like he was Stormy, sliding out and away from his own skin, down into Stormy's silver skin, going away from his own body. Nobody could hurt Stormy. No, sir. He just had to be like Stormy – to *be* Stormy – and then the bad games wouldn't hurt. That's the way. Yes, sir. The way he always did it when it was gonna be like this. Dan just closed his eyes and saw himself changing and turning into a big silver cannon with hard cannon bones and no brains inside, just the high silver that could never be sore or hurt or cut. Stormy never felt bad. No, sir.

"The Chief? Ha!" Crazy Bill laughed from what sounded like very far away. "Chief the one that tied you up, kid. You been a bad soldier. Been up there talkin' all *kinds* of crazy. Chief is sick and tired of your stupid, boy. Sick and tired of your crazy."

But Dan could barely hear him now; he was sinking faster down into his new body, down into his new Stormy skin.

"You been up there, thinkin' you is *so* good. Chief says you needs a lesson. I gonna give it to you. Me and you, Dan. Big day. Big lesson." He patted Dan's stomach, but Dan didn't feel it. In his head, he was almost entirely Stormy now; big Stormy didn't feel anything. No, sir.

Crazy Bill smiled. His eyes glowed. "Big day——."

Then Crazy Bill coughed.

And made a weird, wet noise.

Dan opened his eyes, but he couldn't really see properly because he'd been so far down inside his Stormy skin. He did see bright red blood running down Bill's shirt and there was a hooked bird's beak pushing *out* of Bill's throat, a black beak, like a beak digging through a crunchy egg, pushing through the skin. Blood squirted on the floor. The black beak was moving up and down in Bill's throat, more blood running down his shirt, the beak turning this way and that. Bill waved his hands. His eyes rolled white, his teeth opened and shut, opened and shut. The beak was all the way through Bill's throat now, blood dribbling on the floor between his knees. And then the beak disappeared. There were a couple of wet slaps; Bill jerked with each one. Then Bill fell on his side and Mistress Croot moved up into the lamp glow, her weird eye rolling off in the wrong way. Crazy Bill gurgled once, then didn't gurgle any more.

Mistress Croot looked down at Dan, at his wrists and ankles. Then she shook her head, the weird hump on her back bobbing. Her weird eye caught the light.

Dan blinked and started to come back from where he had been in his head, to come back from being Stormy.

This is what they do to their best.

Mistress Croot frowned.

Dan looked at her.

He'd never heard Mistress Croot speak before because Mistress Croot never talks. But she wasn't talking now, either. Instead, her voice was inside his head, soft and kind.

Her good eye looked sad. Mistress Croot knelt at his side, put her hand on his chest, right over his heart.

This is how they respect their greatest strength.

Then her bad eye seemed to change, to focus on him, to shrink and become how a normal eye would be, dark and pretty, and she didn't have a hump anymore either, and she wasn't all old and hobbled. She was a beautiful lady, white skin so smooth. There was a black stone in her forehead, a black egg that didn't shine. Her teeth were white, her hair was black, like the black you see at night. But how could that be? Dan blinked. Maybe he *was* a crazy, after all. He blinked again. This didn't make any sense.

The beautiful lady looked down at him and smiled. It was the saddest smile Dan had ever seen.

She took something from the floor. It was a black knife. Its point was hooked and nasty, like a bird's beak. She used the knife to cut the twine at Dan's wrists and his ankles.

Then the beautiful lady looked at him.

Her eyes were dark, like Lord Michael's, and Dan could feel himself falling up through them. Her voice in his head was like a song he'd always known.

You are needed today, war singer. Needed as never before.

Dan nodded, but he didn't know what the lady meant or how she could be talking in his head.

And you see us as we are, do you not?

Dan frowned at her question, but then nodded to himself because he saw her, and that's what she was asking, right?

She smiled her sad smile and touched his chest again, his heart.

Because of this, I tell you truly: We would never harm you. But we will not stop you from harming yourselves. When you fight, you fight for us. When you win, you win for us. And when you die, you die for us. The work must be protected. The promise must be kept.

She looked at Dan for a long while. Then she rubbed his wrists and his ankles for a bit, and he was already feeling better, coming all the way out of his Stormy skin, his head a little foggy but better. And when he looked up at her again, she was just Mistress Croot, nodding and bobbing. She handed him a little treat. He didn't know where the other lady was, or really what had happened; it was like another dream. And then she was gesturing for him to follow. So he got up, went to the bathroom, and followed.

324

25

THEY WALKED FROM the barracks, Mistress Croot wobbling in front of him, out into the lower passage, past the food cart. Dan grabbed a muffin, eating as they walked to the iron gate, up the western stairs, up to the main hall. He still wasn't sure what he'd seen, or what it meant, but he was hungry – he knew that much.

When they got to the main hall, Dan saw that all the cleaning crews were out, hundreds of little cleaners all lined up, sharp and tight. Master Shum and Master Falmon were there at the front. Master Falmon was wearing silver armor, talking to everyone about something, all the kids at attention in rows. There were four big kids standing up there in front with Master Shum and Master Falmon. Dan didn't know who three of them were, but one was Chief Tendal.

Dan and Mistress Croot came up to Master Falmon. Master Falmon glanced at her, looked down at Dan, and frowned. Master Shum tapped his club against his chin. When the Chief saw Dan, he gave him a dirty look and looked away. The Chief seemed mad – but kind of scared, too. Master Falmon nodded to Mistress Croot. Mistress Croot just kind of bobbed and nodded. Dan had this crazy vision of her — kind of like a memory — but it was already fading, and it didn't make much sense anyways, so best it be gone for good. No crazies down here!

Master Falmon turned away, looked over the army of kids, adjusted his eyepatch, and said, like he was wrapping things up, "Let's do our best this morning. The High Lords are counting on us. For the Remain."

Master Falmon put his fist across his chest, and all the little cleaners did the exact same thing. Dan saluted, too.

"Master Shum," Master Falmon said, turning things over to the Master.

Master Shum saluted. "Yes, sir."

"Let's get these soldiers to work."

"Yes, Master Falmon, sir." Master Shum turned to the crews and yelled, "Let's get to it!"

All the other chiefs and their top girls turned around and started yelling at their crews, and all the cleaners started milling around and going where they were supposed to go to start the work, but the Chief and the other big kids at the front didn't go anywhere.

Master Falmon turned and knelt in front of Dan. "Told you to be on time, sharp and tight, Dan."

Dan saluted and raised his chin. "Sorry, Master Falmon, sir! I do it better, sir! My fault, sir!"

Master Falmon looked at Mistress Croot and Master Shum, then back to Dan. "How's the arm?"

"Good, sir!" Dan saluted again, even though his arm hurt. "Thank you, sir! Very good, like tough old wood!" Then he added, for good measure, "Ready to work, sir!"

Master Falmon looked him over, then his eyes went narrow. He took Dan's sore arm and looked at his wrist, at the red lines made by the twine the Chief had used to tie him up. Dan's face went red, but he couldn't pull his hand away, because that wouldn't be what a soldier would do. Master Falmon lifted Dan's wrist to show Master Shum. The Chief and the other big kids looked at Dan's wrist, too. Master Shum frowned, tapped his club against the side of his head. The Master gently squeezed Dan's wrist and let go. Dan blinked and saluted.

Master Falmon stood up. "I don't want to see something like this again," he growled at Master Shum. There was something in Master Falmon's voice that Dan had never heard before, and suddenly Dan was real scared for Master Shum. The Master continued, "I see something like this again, you're done." Master Shum saluted without a word and walked away, over to where Val and Benjy Dalter were giving the pals and the girls their orders for the day, swinging his club in a circle.

Master Falmon looked down at the Chief. "You know anything about this, boy?"

"No, sir! Master Falmon, sir!" the Chief hollered, his chin up.

The Master frowned. "And why not? He's your man, isn't he?"

"Yes, sir, Master Falmon!" the Chief yelled, but he looked confused and nervous.

Master Falmon turned to Dan, knelt in front of him, and took his wrist, holding the red line up to the light. "Who did this, Dan? Who tied you like this?"

Over Master Falmon's shoulder, the Chief was staring at Dan. Mistress Croot was staring at the Chief, her weird eye catching the light.

Dan didn't know what to do. He couldn't say bad things against the Chief, that was against the rules. But you couldn't lie to Master Falmon, either.

"You tell me right now, soldier," Master Falmon said. His voice was real quiet. "Who did this?"

Dan nodded. "My fault, Master Falmon, sir. We were playing. Just playing. Looks worse than it is. I didn't see the Chief do nothing, sir. For truth." That *was* true. "We just playing, that's all."

Master Falmon looked at him for a long moment. There was a strange look in his eye. Then he nodded. "Alright. You hungry? You get anything to eat?"

"Yes, sir! Master Falmon, sir!" Dan saluted. "Ate a muffin!"

Master Falmon nodded. Then he motioned Chief Tendal and the other big kids to come closer; they did. The Chief was looking at Dan like he was gonna kill him. But why? Dan didn't do anything but help the Chief out.

Master Falmon said, "You five are gonna be up today, helping out the war adepts' squires on the big guns. It's hard work, but it's safe, you'll be inside the star trees' perimeter. If battle comes, you'll need to keep the squires' water buckets full, keep the ladles clean, keep fresh towels and supplies at the ready — anything those squires call for their adepts, you need to be there, sharp and tight, fast as the bunny, get me?"

"Yes, sir! Master Falmon, sir!" the five kids shouted together.

Master Falmon nodded. "Gonna be two helpers for each gun. Tendal and Stef, you're gonna go with Stormhammer. Gilda and Jass, you're with Oblivion. Dan, you're gonna be the runner. Know what that means?"

Dan thought about it for a moment, then shook his head.

"It means you go between both of the guns, and if something comes up, if the other helpers or the squires need something for their adepts or their cannon, then you step in and help." Then Master Falmon leaned down and whispered in Dan's ear, "And if the time comes to sing, Dan, then you do what the adepts tell you — *exactly* what they tell you. They know you're gonna be there. They will tell you what to do. Hear me?"

Dan stared at Master Falmon, then nodded. Then he stood tall and saluted. "Runner gets the water, keeps it clear, Master Falmon! Do what them adepts say! Do a good job!

Help out!" None of that sounded too hard, and he was gonna be up there with Stormy fighting, so he was happy about that. "I'll do a good job, sir!"

The big kids were looking at him like he was a crazy, and Chief looked angrier than Dan had ever seen him, so he shut his mouth. Mistress Croot wobbled and bobbed and patted him on the head.

Master Falmon looked at Dan for a moment. Then he nodded, adjusted his eyepatch, and touched the deep scar on his forehead. "I know you will, Dan."

26

LITTLE DAN FOLLOWED Master Falmon and the Chief and the other kids up and up and up. But it was hard to keep up with them, and finally Master Falmon told the Chief to pick him up, and the Chief did, looking mad and carrying him all the way until they got up to the big Square.

Up there in the Square, there were all kinds of folks moving around. The place was more packed than before. A little bit of snow was coming, too. They went through a couple of big doors and down a big hall, Master Falmon yelling at people to get out of the way. Then they went through another passage, into a smaller courtyard – and right there, Dan saw Stormy and Oblivion waiting by a huge door with a bunch of war adepts and squires and bear riders and ogres. Lord Doldon was there, too, talking with one of the war adepts. The adepts wore blue robes like they always did. The bears and riders and ogres wore their silver armor. When Lord Doldon saw Master Falmon, he walked over, clasped arms with the Master, and then looked down and winked at Dan. Dan put his heels together and saluted. Lord Doldon looked at the other helpers, then back at Master Falmon.

"We good?" Lord Doldon asked.

"Yeah," Master Falmon grunted. "How goes it here?"

"Guns and adepts and everything up and ready to go." Lord Doldon cocked his head over at the big door. "Riders are ready. Michael's up, too. Last minute check on the gear. Garen and Colj getting set to head out." He glanced over at the big door, then looked at the sky. A single snowflake landed on his cheek. "Any minute now, I should think."

"Our adepts ready for our young friend, here?" Master Falmon touched Dan on the shoulder. Dan didn't know what he meant.

"Of course. They're ready to guide him, should something manifest." Lord Doldon looked down at Dan and winked at him.

"What about our batteries?" Master Falmon asked.

"Mortars and big iron crewed and stocked and ready. Fire all day, every day, for a week, if we need 'em."

"Dragons?" Master Falmon asked.

"Anna's been up and away for the last bell, out of range, waiting our signal. Never seen such a flight. Must be six hundred dragons, in all. Been coming through most of the night."

"Zar?"

Lord Doldon laughed. "He and Gregory are up there with their 'regiment,' guess you'd call it? Up on the western rampart. Gonna be big action today. Big action."

Master Falmon frowned. "Big gamble."

Lord Doldon looked Master Falmon in the eye but didn't say anything for a bit. Then he glanced down at Dan and the other helpers. "This elite squad ready?"

"Yes, sir!" all the helpers yelled and saluted.

Lord Doldon looked down at Dan. "You ready, Big Dan?"

Dan nodded and saluted again.

"You're gonna do great." Lord Doldon looked over at Stormy and Oblivion by the big door, toward the adepts and bears and ogres. "Better get in line with our big guns there. Time to get started."

27

HIGH ATOP THE Pinnacle, the tallest tower on the Tarn's western side, safe beneath the coppery leaves of one of Garen's smaller star trees, Kyla Dallanar looked out over the Long Bridge.

They were waiting for parley to begin.

Tarlen and Susan stood in front of Kyla, their furs bundled against the cold. Bruno lay on the granite pavers at the tower's western battlement, muscly legs straight in front of him, snoring away. Ponj stood behind Kyla, just in front of their star tree, the young ogre's thick arms crossed over his armored chest. Also present on the tower's top – for good or ill – were Filip Toller and his scouts. The whole crew had been assigned to them as escorts, just as Garen had promised, their long carbines hidden under some old banners beneath the tower's crenellation.

The entire situation was awkward, for a couple of reasons. First, Filip was still ignoring her, but at least this time, she could understand why: His eyes were locked onto the Long Bridge, below. Kyla had learned that Filip had indeed returned with a prisoner of some value earlier that morning, at least that's what people were saying. But Kyla still didn't understand why that should mean anything or why that would have changed his behavior toward her.

Second, and more importantly, Filip and his scouts were most definitely armed. Garen and Doldon had specifically told Kyla *not* to bring weapons to the Pinnacle. Of course, she and Tarlen had objected to the order, but her uncles had been firm. "We can't give any excuse for aggression, Ky," Garen had said. "You know this." And then Doldon had pulled her aside and told her that Michael had forbidden it. "A weapon is a target, Ky," he had said. "Michael doesn't want you and the children drawing fire." And yet here were Filip, Sledder, Quine, and Tellerman – all toting guns. Garen and Doldon were right, of course. The enemy's spotters and sharpshooters would be watching for any sign of deceit, any hostility. A glimmer of silver from rooftop easily could be misunderstood. Which made it even more annoying that the scouts had their weapons and she didn't have hers.

Kyla rubbed her shoulders through her furs. She looked up to the cloudy sky, then leaned over the tower's battlements, gazing out over the Long Bridge, over the sprawl of Tarntown, up to the high western ridge, the harbor's stone breakwater to the north. Everywhere she looked – across the headlands, around the barbican, even across Tarntown's great docks – she could see the enemy's men, cannon, and war machines. The entire town was filled by Dorómy's army. It was a force the likes of which she'd only read about. Thirty thousand men, perhaps more. Armor, guns, horses, men, and thousands of other creatures from who knows where. Over there, near the city center, a big squad of giants from Okógon, each twice as big as Colj, were busy tearing down part of Tarntown's old fortification wall, using the material for new gun ramparts. Over there, on the northern mole, some new siege fortifications were going up. And over there, on the southwestern embankment, a thick wall of rough-cut logs now blocked the Tarn's vantage of that side of town. Hundreds of war pennants hung limp in the cold air, banners from a dozen duchies. Far to the north, a few rebel angels from Tarcéron soared lazily in the distance, black wings like huge black birds, sharp against the grey horizon.

Below, on the Long Bridge proper, nothing moved, of course. Several moments ago, everything and everyone had stopped, as if frozen in time. Formal parley was about to begin. The Tarn's men, the enemy's men — both sides — neither would stir until negotiations were complete. Yet even in stillness, the presence of the enemy's vast host filled Kyla with a strange mix of rage and dread and sadness.

She shook her head, looked down below her toward the Tarn. Everywhere she looked, she saw Garen's star trees, a coppery canopy throughout the fortress. Wherever there was room — in courtyards, on towers, on the walls — the trees' thick trunks were tucked into massive root-boxes, clay pipes running everywhere, feeding their strange soils, their coppery leaves, and the near-magical fields the trees produced. Even the little tree up here with them on the Pinnacle was accompanied by a water barrel which Ponj diligently tended. It was as if the Tarn had been transformed into a great forest of copper trees. Over there, in the High Square, Kyla could just make out the peak of their High Gate, huge and proud, ten times the height of a man. Even now, with parley only moments away, the Gate burned with silent silver light, the Square a flurry of activity.

"When will we see Uncle Garen?" Susan whispered, using her softest voice. She'd stepped up onto Bruno, on her tiptoes, straining to look over the battlements, out at the surrounding army. The big cloud mastiff didn't seem to notice the weight of a seven-year-old girl. Susan didn't seem to be asking her question of anyone in particular. "Will Uncle Garen convince them to leave?"

The air smelled of snow, stray flakes dancing here and there. Filip Toller glanced at Kyla, then at Susan, then back again at Kyla, as if he was waiting for her to answer her little sister's question. It was the first time their eyes had really connected since he'd been back. Kyla looked away. Filip turned and knelt before Susan. "Lady Susan, your High Lord uncle is the smartest man in the Realm, believe you me. If there's anyone who can send those armies on their way in peace, it's him. You watch."

"But *how* will Uncle Garen do that, specifically?" Susan asked, not so easily satisfied.

"That's why we're meeting, Sue," Tarlen said, taking his telescope out, extending it, the oiled brass segments clicking, not looking away from the Long Bridge. "Garen wants to stop the fighting so everyone can talk and try to come to some arrangement. But it's complicated. There are strict protocols."

"I get it." Susan nodded matter-of-factly. "Rules."

"Exactly, my Lady," Filip said. "Everyone on the bridge will say the right words, and those words will open the parley. But everyone will want to say everything just the right way. It's important that the honor of both sides be observed. That's why they say their lines just so."

"I understand." Susan nodded. Then she glanced at Filip, then Kyla, and gave a little frown. She turned back to watch. "I suppose it's like a play."

"Except nobody's pretending," Tarlen said, not taking his eye away from his telescope.

"Is Garen going to get hurt?" Susan asked.

"No, my Lady," Filip shook his head. "High Command-er Ruge is a friend. A friend to Kon and to the Tarn. You remember Lord Ruge and his boys, my Lady? Lords Jannon and Jared and Jon? They're good friends. They'd never hurt Lord Garen."

Susan nodded, understanding perfectly, still frowning down at the bridge.

"W-w-we l-l-like J-J-Jared," Tarlen said, using a playful, stuttering voice, mimicking Jared's stutter. He winked at Kyla, then looked back through his telescope.

Kyla smiled, despite herself. She did like Jared. And she liked Jon and Jannon. She cared for all the Ruge boys, actu-ally. In that, Filip spoke true. Jared did have a horrible stut-ter, but he didn't take himself too seriously; he was a normal person, not some highborn twit. The oldest brother, the rascal Jannon was the same. Jon . . . well, he was a little snooty, but still a good fellow. At least she hoped that was still true. After what she'd heard from Garen's silver golem, Kyla was no longer so sure. She shook her head. Why assume the worst? The truth was, Filip was right. Ruge and his sons *were* their friends, but the thought gave little comfort. She looked out at the vast army. Despite her training, her careful breathing, her stomach and hands still felt cold and clenched.

Kyla noticed that Filip was looking at her again, gauging her reaction. She gave him a polite smile.

"There they are!" Susan cried. "There they are!" She hopped up and down, forgetting that she stood on Bruno. The cloud mastiff growled softly. Susan leaned down, patted his thick grey fur. "Sorry, Bruno." But she didn't step off him.

Everyone moved to the battlements for the best view. The star tree behind them seemed to sigh, its coppery leaves tinkling. Kyla reached for her pouch and took out her own telescope, a special gift from Garen years ago. She trained her eye on the Long Bridge. Filip and his scouts had done the same with their own, less expensive, spyglasses.

There they were.

At the Great Door, just below them, Garen and his retinue were marching forward onto the Long Bridge. Garen was at the front of his party. He wore ornate high silver plate and a heavy blue cloak trimmed with sable. He was flanked by two squires and two standard-bearers. One standard-bearer carried the banner of the Duchy of Kon: high blue with the Dallanar Sun embroidered in silver at its center. The other standard-bearer carried the banner of the Tarn itself: midnight blue with a silver book stitched in its middle. Kyla hit the moonstone button on her telescope's side, activated the telescope's ancient magic, and immediately heard the scrape of armored boots on bridge's granite, as if she was standing there beside Garen. The ancient artifact would allow her to both see and hear the coming action.

In front of the standard-bearers, right behind Garen himself, one of his squires carried a silver box. Kyla focused her telescope on it. The box was made of pale korom's wood and locked with a mechanism of high silver. She frowned. She didn't know what the box contained. The banners fluttered softly as they moved down the bridge. A few more snowflakes danced around them. Colj and a double squad of ten ogre guards followed Garen and his retinue, serving as his honor guard. Such squads at high level parley were always from a different duchy than the principals, Kyla knew. The ogres did make for an imposing sight. Each carried an enormous, ogre-sized shield of high silver and wore a great suit of ancient, high silver plate. Concealed beneath their blue capes they carried massive, ogre-sized axes of the best Konish iron. The High Laws did not forbid ceremonial arms at parley, of course. But they must remain unseen.

Kyla swung her telescope down the length of the Long Bridge, toward the barbican, about three hundred paces in front of Garen. There, High Lord Commander Vymon Ruge and two of his sons, Jon and Jared, had walked out of the barbican's gate and had stopped to wait for Garen on the edge of the Great Seal. Like Garen, Ruge was accompanied by two squires, two standard-bearers, and an honor guard. One of Vymon Ruge's standard-bearers carried the banner of Rigel: dark blue with the Dallanar Sun emblazoned in silver at its center. His other standard-bearer carried the imperial banner of Paráden: creamy ivory, marked again with the Dallanar Sun, this time in gold. As custom dictated, Ruge's honor guard was not of his own House, but rather came from an allied duchy, in this case House Julane of the Duchy of Gelánen, just as Kyla had heard from Garen's golem. The men of Gelánen wore dark green. With royal Dalla-nar suns on nearly all the banners, with the once-loyal men of Gelánen standing at attention behind Vymon Ruge, the meeting looked more like a summit between friendly allies, not a conference between the belligerents of a civil war.

Kyla moved her telescope, looked more closely at High Lord Ruge. The commander seemed much the same as when she'd last seen him four years ago. Perhaps a touch greyer in the beard, but still tall and broad of shoulder, his movements smooth, like a man half his age. He was a true warrior, that was certain, a legend in his own time – and he looked the part. His mail was some of the most storied in the Realm, a gift from Grandpa over two decades past, ornate high silver plate reflecting grey winter sky. He wore a cloak of dark blue, the color of his high House, the sides of his cloak properly covering his sidearm and sword.

Garen was well along the Long Bridge now, about twenty paces away from the Tarn's Great Door, when a second squad of ogres exited the Tarn. At the center of this squad, the mighty Doj, Colj's biggest ogre, pulled a small, ornately carved wagon. Inside this wagon, set in an engraved wooden root box, was a sapling star tree about ten palms taller than a full-grown man, just a bit shorter than a full-grown ogre. The little star tree's coppery leaves clinked like a thousand tiny bells.

"Look at that." Filip pointed.

"What is it?" Susan asked, staring. "I can't see."

"Uncle Garen set a star tree up in that wagon, Sue." Tarlen's eye was pressed firmly to the telescope. "They're bringing it over with them. Ostensibly, a gift for the High Lord Commander."

"Doj is pulling the wagon by himself," Quine said.

Ponj grunted.

"A present for Vymon Ruge." Kyla nodded, the genius of the plan dawning on her.

His eye at his telescope, Tarlen grinned.

"Interesting gift, Lord Tarlen." Filip cleared his throat. "If you'll permit me, my Lord."

Tarlen nodded, still not looking away from his telescope. "It looks like the little tree's field will shield them as they exit the Tarn's defensive perimeter."

"Hmm." Filip nodded.

"The best gifts serve both sides of the exchange, as you said, Master Toller," Tarlen said. "Lord Garen is the son of the Silver Fox, after all."

"Of course, my Lord." Filip bowed. Kyla could tell that Filip approved of how Tarlen carried himself – like a proper Dallanar prince.

It took Garen several long moments to cross the rest of the bridge's length – three hundred paces in all – to reach the far side and the Great Seal there. The second squad of ogres and their little tree stayed ten paces behind him, every step of the way.

"They're starting," Tarlen said.

Kyla wiped the oculus of her telescope, put her eye back to it.

Garen had stopped on the near side of the Great Seal, five paces in front of Lord Ruge. One pace for each of the Great Sisters, Kyla remembered. The protocols were precise. Each party would take two steps forward, but only after they'd re-affirmed the preliminary terms of the meeting. Their handshake would bridge the final distance over the Great Seal, and then parley itself would begin.

The squire on Garen's right began the ritual. He bowed to Vymon Ruge and his two sons, then called out for all to hear: "High Commander of the Silver Legions, Lord Vymon Ruge, Duke of Rigel, Master of Aaryn's Cry, and Lord Protector of Remain, we bid you peaceful greetings in the names of the Five Sisters and the Silver Kingdom. We stand with you here, over the Tarn's Great Seal, under the protection of the Realm's High Laws, to reach terms for formal parley."

Ruge and his sons bowed to Garen.

Then Lord Ruge's squire answered:

"High Emissary of Kon, Lord Garen Dallanar, Duke of Jallow and Lord Librarian of Remain, we honor your peaceful greetings in the names of the Five Sisters and the Silver Kingdom. We stand with you here, over the Tarn's Great Seal, under the protection of the Realm's High Laws, to reach terms for formal parley."

Garen bowed to Vymon Ruge and his sons.

Still looking through his telescope, Tarlen said, "Lord Ruge's squire called Lord Garen 'Lord Librarian.'"

Kyla nodded, not looking away. "And Garen addresses Ruge as 'Master of Aaryn's Cry.'"

"Both are older titles," Tarlen said. "Given before the war began."

Kyla nodded. "'Master of Aaryn's Cry' is a Konish honorific, while 'Lord Librarian' is a title that belongs to the Kingdom as a whole."

"A good sign," Tarlen said.

Kyla felt herself unclench a little. With their formal greetings, both Garen and Ruge appealed to past attachments, to the friendships that bound their two families together.

Both squires took two steps back. Garen took two steps forward. As the representative of the party initiating parley, these first two steps were his right and duty. Ruge would then step forward and respond with his own formal list of terms.

"High Commander," Garen said, his voice clear and strong. "For the Realm's people and its peace, we beg parley from your High Liege and Lord, Dorómy Dallanar. We seek your terms, High Lord Commander, so that we might end this conflict for one day, a day of peace that might model years of tranquility for the people of Remain."

Ruge took his two steps forward. A few snowflakes caught in his grey beard. "High Lord Emissary, as a servant of the Realm, I am privileged to receive your honorable request and to speak on behalf of my High Liege and Lord. It is Lord Dorómy's deepest wish to end this conflict for one day so that we might sit in free and fair discussion. In so doing, my Lord hopes not only to find a way to peace but also to strengthen and guard the Realm against those who would do her harm. Thus, in accordance with the High Laws and in the names of Acasius and his Great Sisters, we offer the following terms."

Jared Ruge stepped forward with a silver tube, uncapped it, and withdrew a single sheet of thick parchment lined with a densely written order of protocol. Jared handed the tube to one of the squires and then, with his familiar stutter, he began reading the formal terms of parley.

28

WHEN FELLEN COLJ marched with Lord Garen down the length of the Long Bridge, when he and his fellow ogres arrived at the High Seal, when Colj looked into the eyes of the enemy, he saw deceit.

And the war song blossomed in his heart.

It was a trap.

It had always been a trap.

There would be battle today.

Lord Michael, Lord Doldon, the others — all had said it would be so. Colj had believed them. But now that Colj saw it with his own eyes, it was obvious.

The enemy lied.

Most of them, at least.

A few did not.

The stuttering young man, Jared Ruge, the young man who now read terms of parley, he did not lie. The father of the stutterer, High Lord Vymon Ruge, grey-bearded and solemn, Dorómy Dallanar's High Commander, the Pretender King's Lord of the Siege, he did not lie. The soldiers in the honor guard behind them, those in dark green livery, Lord Marden Julane and his men from Gelánen, they did not lie. Indeed, there were many here who thought they met for peace. But the young man beside Vymon Ruge, the youngest son of the High Commander, the young man with narrow eyes, Jon Ruge — he lied. And there were many others with him, also.

The war song hummed in Colj's heart. He wanted to fight. And he was ready. He had been ready for months. But the war song made it hard to think, the savage side of his ja overcoming reason. Colj took a breath, let it out, felt his huge muscles flex like living stone beneath his armor.

"War is truth." So his father had taught him. A lesson passed down from father to son, all the way back the beginning. An ancient truth, and like all truths, eternal. A truth that would be revealed once more today.

Colj looked at Jon Ruge, at the deceit in the young man's eyes. It was easy for these people to lie. Colj knew that. But it was hard to make eyes match tongue's deception.

Colj flexed his fingers. His gear felt good, solid and tight. Beneath his cloak, slung on his wide leather belt, he carried a double-bladed axe of the finest high silver. The rest of his ogres carried strong Konish iron. Only he, Fellen Colj of Jallow, carried the Tarn's silver into battle. "You've been chosen, Captain Colj," Lord Michael had said. And then Master Falmon had opened the cabinet, had given him the axe, and had told Colj that the ancient weapon had been carried by the dread Hakon Dallanar, Hakon the Terrible. "Lord Hakon was a big man," Lord Garen had said. "He could only use this axe with two hands."

Colj used one.

Jared Ruge still read from his parchment, stuttering. The young man did his best. A good man. An honest man. He would surely die.

And then Colj realized another truth.

The reason why the stuttering Jared Ruge spoke for the enemy.

It was part of the trap.

The Pretender King used Vymon Ruge and his son Jared to speak truly, to speak the truth as they saw it, to hide the lie *inside* the truth of past friendship. The Pretender understood the old bond that lived between Vymon Ruge and Bellános Dallanar, the ties of loyalty that linked their families. Lord Michael and Lord Garen would never have asked to meet with any other High House. And so the Pretender used Vymon Ruge and his sons, their honesty and their honor, as weapons to bait the snare.

Colj grunted with disgust. He was not surprised. He would be glad to fight today. His ogres would be glad to fight today. They had waited a long time. Today was a day of release. There would be some signal. Some word. The attack would come. And they would fight.

And with this thought, the war song swelled in his mind, filling his ja with holy music.

29

L ITTLE D AN WAITED behind Stormy with Chief Tendal and the other helpers. The helpers were standing behind their squires, and the squires were standing behind their war adepts, and the adepts were standing behind Stormy and Oblivion. They were waiting by the huge door, waiting to go out and fight. The adepts' hands were on the big guns, humming. Stormy and Oblivion hummed right back – but it was *off* to Dan's ear, something not right, but Dan didn't know how that could be. He did know that Stormy wasn't happy about it. Dan wanted to give Stormy a little pat on the side, tell him it was gonna be fine, but that wouldn't be how a proper soldier did it. So, Dan just stood there humming a little song himself, hoping Stormy would be alright and that he'd hear Dan humming.

The whole place by the big door was packed with bears and riders and soldiers and ogres and lords and guns and all the other things you needed to fight a war. Lord Michael was there at the front, by the big guns' noses, wearing his black armor, looking through a little peephole. Lord Doldon was there beside him. Nobody was saying anything, but the bears were grunting and swaying around, their armor crunching. Master Falmon stood behind Lord Michael. He carried a silver spear with a blue ribbon tied at its tip. The sky was grey, a bit more snow was falling now, but it wasn't cold. Dan stepped out of the roof's shadow, opened his mouth, and caught a flake on his tongue. Lord Doldon turned away from Lord Michael. Master Falmon walked back past the cannon and the adepts, toward where Dan was. The Master was saying this and that to folks, patting the war adepts on their shoulders, his eyes sort of glowing.

"Every day, a day to do better," Dan whispered. Then he hummed a bit more of his song and swayed a little. He wasn't nervous for himself, but he was nervous for Stormy. Lord Michael looked again through his peephole. Lord Michael's war bear was the biggest bear Dan had ever seen; it waited and grunted behind Lord Michael, covered head to claw in silver armor. There was something scary in its big bear eyes. Dan swallowed and took a step back in spite of himself, but he bumped the Chief and said he was sorry. The Chief told him to shut up, to calm down, and to get ready, even though the Chief didn't look too calm himself.

Dan tried to be calm, but it didn't work.

So he just got ready.

30

THEN COLJ SAW something move.

It was well behind Vymon Ruge and his sons, behind their squires and their banner-men, behind Lord Julane and the green-clad honor guard from Gelánen, back in the shadows of the barbican, in the dark mouth of barbican's gate.

Something large in the dark.

Something moving forward.

The war song swelled in Colj's mind, his ja ringing with righteous cadence.

It was beginning.

Colj took a deep breath, felt the tension rush out of his enormous muscles.

Then he deliberately shifted his shield on his shoulder.

The movement was the signal to his ogres, to the Tarn's

batteries, to Lord Michael behind them at the Tarn's Great Door.

The sign was simple – as was its meaning.

Treachery.

31

"There it is," Lord Michael whispered at the big door. But when he whispered, it was like he was whispering right into Little Dan's ear, real soft, but somehow everyone else heard him, too. "It's happening. Prepare."

A kind of sigh went through everybody. Armor crunched, harnesses jingled. Then Lord Michael threw the scabbard off his black sword and climbed onto his giant war bear. The bear growled. It was probably the scariest sound Dan had ever heard. Lord Michael's sword had a black blade; its edges crawled with smoky things. It was hard for Dan to look at it, but hard *not* to look at, too. The sword made a strange noise, kind of like a song, but underneath that, it was more like a hungry buzzard locked away from its meat, a sort of black sizzling.

We thirst, all of us.

"Ready the door," Lord Michael said softly. "On my mark."
Four soldiers at the door got ready. Lord Michael put his eye
to another peephole, this one high up so that a soldier on a
bear could look out of it.

Lord Michael turned around and looked at them. His
eyes were black, and it looked to Dan like there was smoke
around them, like the smoke from his sword.

Lord Michael said, "We must not move until battle is
joined, until the enemy's intent is certain. But when we
move, we move with force. Cannon out first. Soften them
up. Five shots. Then we ride like a storm."

32

Jared Ruge was still stuttering his way through the terms
of parley. For Kyla, high on the Pinnacle, it was painful to
watch Jared try so hard. Her heart went out to him—.

And then Kyla saw Colj shift his shield.

The gesture was barely noticeable, a simple tilt of the
shield's bottom away from the ogre's huge, armored legs.
But to Kyla, it was like a blood-red flag waving before a wall
of white ice.

Treachery.

But from where?

Colj shifted his shield again, tilting its front forward, toward the barbican.

It was a subtle, natural gesture, almost unnoticeable.

But to Kyla, it might as well have been a child's scream.

Treachery from the front, from the barbican. Behind Ruge and his entourage. But Kyla couldn't see it.

An icy claw touched the back of Kyla's neck. She ignored it, breathed deeply, allowed her training to unfold around her, moving her telescope over the barbican, to the ridge above, north and south, the bridge, back to the barbican again.

Nobody stirred.

At least not that she could see.

Her breath came more easily now. She tried to will warmth into her fingers. Jared still stood in front of Garen reading, stuttering, still trying to get through it, oblivious to anything other than his task.

What did Colj see?

"What is it, my Lady?" Filip asked, as if hearing her

thoughts. "I thought I saw Captain Colj—."

"Quiet," Kyla commanded. And there must've been something in her voice because Tarlen, Susan, Ponj, Bruno, all the scouts turned to her, their mouths clamped firmly shut.

But she was still looking at the bridge, scanning, scanning.

Filip cleared his throat. "Shall we arm?"

"No," Kyla said.

She still couldn't see what the danger was.

In her eye, her telescope's round image was a blur, the sounds from the ancient instrument a jumble of sighs, creaking armor, men's breath, scraping metal on stone. She scanned the bridge, the barbican, the headlands again, the new fortifications on the southwestern embankment, then back to the barbican again.

Colj *had* given the sign.

He had given the direction.

Treachery.

From the front.

She was certain.

And now Colj's ogres were responding, shifting their own shields, loosening their shoulders, preparing. Beside her on the tower's top, Kyla could feel the scouts, everyone, looking at her, then turning and straining their eyes and scopes toward the gathering below, looking back to her.

"What's going on, Toller?" Sledder grumbled.

Tellerman nodded. "Can't see spit."

But Filip's eye was pressed firmly to his own telescope now, his other eye clamped shut, looking as hard as Kyla was. "Something . . . ," he muttered.

"Gear up," Sledder whispered and turned toward the hidden carbines.

"Don't touch those weapons," Kyla said calmly, not taking her eye from her telescope.

In the corner of her eye, Kyla saw Sledder freeze, then look to Filip. Filip mouthed to Sledder, "Are you mad?" Bruno growled. Susan stepped off him. The big cloud mastiff stood on his rear legs, shoved Sledder out of the way, and looked over the fortifications, his wet jowls resting on the battlement's granite, grey fur hazing like silver fog, preparing for a fight. Behind them, the star tree shivered, as if sensing a change in the weather. A bit more snow was falling now. Ponj stepped forward and lifted Susan to his armored chest, so that she could see over the battlements, cradling her on his armored forearm, the other arm protectively across her middle.

"Careful," Tarlen said absently, not moving his spyglass from the barbican.

Susan held the edge of the front paldron of Ponj's armor. "Happy?" she asked. Tarlen ignored her. Susan patted Ponj's huge armored forearm. "You'd never let anything happen to me, would you, Ponj?"

There was a short pause. "No," Ponj said in his voice deep. "Never."

"Do you see anything, my Lady?" Filip asked, his eye pushed hard against his telescope.

She frowned. Because now there were some murmurs from Ruge's side, behind Ruge's entourage, behind the honor guard, inside the barbican's gate. Some frowns as well from the green-clad soldiers of Gelánen. Vymon Ruge said something. Kyla didn't catch the words. But they weren't part of the parley ritual, that was certain.

And then she realized that it didn't matter.

That words didn't matter.

Because Colj and his ogres were bracing for battle.

And there *was* something now . . . .

It was something Kyla couldn't quite see, a kind of tension in the eyes of the standard-bearers and squires behind Lord Ruge, in the eyes of the men of Gelánen. Jon Ruge looked at his father. Jared looked down at his parchment, then up at Garen with complete sincerity, still stuttering, the effort of reading straining his face as he tried to complete the final terms of parley.

Then Jared finished. Garen nodded and gestured back to his own entourage, to the squire who held the pale korom's wood box. This squire stepped forward. Garen took the box, opened it, and took out the High Cup that Kyla had seen in Garen's study. The Cup glowed silver-white in Garen's armor. Even through Kyla's telescope, at this distance, the Cup seemed alive, ready to reveal the memory it contained.

"What is that, my Lady?" Filip asked.

Kyla did not answer.

"The High Cup from Garen's study," Tarlen said. "The Cup that Kate brought back from Paráden. The memory it holds must be the reason for parley."

Kyla nodded but said nothing.

The enemy soldiers in the barbican shifted again. The men from Gelánen looked at each other, then to Marden Julane, their commanding officer; he shook his head. Another elusive movement, back there in the barbican's gate.

There was something big in the door shadow behind them.

Kyla trained her telescope on it.

"There." Kyla cleared her throat. "There. The barbican, the barbican's gate."

All the telescopes swung together, in unison.

"That's a great cannon," Tarlen said calmly. The scouts muttered. Bruno growled, the sound pure menace.

And it was.

Floating, silver, alive, accompanied by the Pretender's war adepts, two golden-robed young women at each of the big gun's sides, their lead adept in gold at the rear. Kyla could just see the cannon's nose, the yawning mouth of a great sea monster, hidden still in the shadow of the barbican's gate, but coming, aiming straight down the axis of the Long Bridge, aiming straight at the two retinues.

"Treachery," Kyla said, a distant calm in her voice. "High

treachery all along."

The plan was so simple, so obvious: Some commander would say that he'd seen some signal, maybe even Colj's signal, that they had merely responded to a threat from the Tarn, as was their right.

"What is it?" Susan asked.

Kyla heard Tarlen murmur something, but she couldn't take her eye from her telescope. There was no way to warn Garen. But Colj had seen the great gun. And Kyla couldn't look away. It was like she was frozen. In the gate's shadow, the great cannon seemed to crawl forward with infinite slowness, still partially hidden in the darkness of the gate's mouth.

"High Lord Commander," Kyla heard Garen say through her telescope. Garen held the High Cup out to Ruge, looking at him. "We beg you to see this tale, for the good of the Remain and its people – a tale that once known, might set things right for all. In the name of my Father, High Lord Bellános Dallanar, the Silver King, in the names of the Great Sisters and their songs, I swear to this High Cup's truth."

Ruge looked at Garen for a long moment. Then he looked

at the High Cup.

Back in the dark, the big cannon crept forward, slowly.

Ruge didn't know that it was coming behind him.

Kyla stared, frozen, unable to move.

Then Colj took a step forward, toward Garen, his armored ogre step enormous and heavy.

And then everything seemed to stop.

Kyla realized that she was holding her breath. She also realized, quite suddenly, that her hands weren't cold anymore.

They were warm.

Ruge looked up from the High Cup to Garen. He blinked slowly, something new coming into the Lord Commander's face.

He understood something.

But what?

It didn't matter, Kyla realized.

Regardless of what vision the High Cup contained specifically, Ruge understood what it *might* hold — what it *could* hold.

Once upon a time, Vymon, Bellános, and Dorómy had been the best of friends. Between the Dallanar brothers, of course, all trust had disintegrated. But faith still lived here, in the eyes of Vymon Ruge, in the heart of Dorómy's Lord of the Siege. And just like that, Kyla saw something open in the old general's face, open like a dawning answer.

Ruge stepped to Garen and spoke softly, "High Lord Emissary, in the name of the Silver Throne and its rightful King, I am honored to see any vision High Lord Bellános places before me."

Ruge took the High Cup from Garen's hands, lifted it, and inspected it.

Behind them, still in shadow, the cannon moved up again, its great maw nearly out in the light, the snow coming a bit harder now, flakes swirling chaotically.

Jon stepped forward and smiled – but his smile was venom.

Jon put his hand on Garen's arm.

And then Colj was there, swinging his arm like an armored tree trunk, his massive high silver shield crashing down in front of Garen, its edge buried in stone. Colj backhanded Jon, the young lord skidding back across the granite pavers, clutching his arm. A single shot cracked out, everything happening at once.

33

FROM COLJ'S VANTAGE, the enemies' reactions to the High Cup that Lord Garen revealed were varied. Some were surprised, some were confused, others were angry. Vymon Ruge was startled — and then hopeful. Jared Ruge was puzzled. Jon Ruge's eyes narrowed, suspicious. Behind Vymon Ruge's entourage, in the barbican's gate, the cannon's mouth was huge, the maw of a monstrous kraken. The big gun was almost in the open now.

The attack would come in moments.

Colj took a step forward.

Vymon Ruge took the Cup and inspected it. Then he said to Lord Garen, "High Lord Emissary, in the name of the Silver Throne and its rightful King, I am honored to see any vision High Lord Bellános places before me."

Jon Ruge stepped forward, smiling.

But his smile was a lie.

Jon Ruge put his hand on Lord Garen's arm.

His touch was the enemy's signal.

Friendship as betrayal.

A smile as treachery.

The kiss of a serpent.

The open maw of the enemy's gun pushed out into the light.

And then it was happening, everything at once, war song blossoming hot in Colj's, and he swung his shield in front of Lord Garen, knocked Jon Ruge back. A single shot cracked the air.

34

"It's happening," Lord Michael said. "Stand ready."

But Little Dan had heard the noise out there, a noise like a little firecracker, and Stormy and Oblivion wanted to go *now*, their humming coming louder and louder, even though the songs weren't quite right, and Dan felt something move inside his head, a kind of hot craziness, the cannon songs getting louder in his ears.

"Stand ready," Lord Michael said.

But Dan didn't want to stand.

Little Dan wanted to fight.

35

KYLA SAW THE bullet hit and disintegrated against Colj's high silver shield, a tiny nova at the center of her telescope, just as Colj backhanded Jon, the young lord skidding across the pavers, armor scraping, clutching his arm.

A few more shots broke the quiet – CRACK! CRACK! The dark blue standard of Rigel fell to the bridge, its bearer hit by friendly fire. Vymon Ruge looked around, confused – then furious. He yelled an order, something Kyla couldn't hear until she focused her telescope on him, "Cease fire, curse you—!" Jared Ruge looked back at Jon, frowned, looked at Colj, uncertain, then moved to help his injured brother.

Kyla moved her telescope away. There were more shots coming now. Colj's ogre phalanx had surrounded Garen, their shields turtling, a wall of impenetrable high silver. Colj's second squad came up with the wagon, the field of the wagon's little star tree moving forward to protect the phalanx. Carbine fire from the southwestern flank, the rounds winking against the star tree's coppery field. Big Doj pulled the wagon forward, while another ogre at the wagon's back pumped water into the little star tree's roots. Another spattering of fire. Colj crouched behind his huge shield, holding Garen safely to his chest, high silver flashing, glowing with reflected force. And then the wagon was up with them, the little tree's coppery field enveloping the phalanx. Garen shouted something to Colj, tried to straighten his spectacles, shouted something Kyla couldn't hear.

"What's happening?" Susan asked calmly, a strange note in her voice. "What's happening?"

More guns were firing now, from the barbican, a heavier spatter, but still just warming up. Around the phalanx, the little tree's coppery field shrank with the impacts, the tree's branches trembling, its misty field dwindling as it absorbed incoming rounds, then growing once more – but smaller.

And yet all the shots came from the opposite side of the Long Bridge, from the enemies' forces. Kyla frowned. She knew that Michael, his mighty war bear Okros, his bear riders, and two of their own great cannon waited at the Tarn's Great Door. She knew that the citadel's countless artillery batteries stood ready. She knew that Anna and their dragons were only moments away.

Why did they wait?

A horrible suspicion rose in her mind, but it was blotted out by another bright flash that struck Colj's shoulder guard, an ancient high silver round making its way through the little star tree's field, the flash blinding white, the impact deflected by chance.

"That was high silver," Tarlen said calmly

But the enemy was just getting started. The Pretender's great cannon floated out of the barbican now, floating in plain sight, a bit faster now, its great maw aiming down the Long Bridge proper, its golden-robed adepts surrounding it, priming the living weapon's song and fire. And it was a most lethal axis of fire. Garen and Colj had no cover save the little tree's field and their ogres' shields. And the little star tree's field was still shrinking, already half of what it had been. It might be able to take one cannon shot — maybe. But even if it could, it would be finished after that, and Garen would be left entirely unprotected.

But then, as she watched the entire army across Tarntown begin to move, like a giant beast waking from slumber, she realized that the attack wasn't really about Garen. In fact, it might never have been about him at all.

"It's an all-out assault," Kyla heard her own voice say, distant in her own ears, her eye pressed to her telescope. "They mean to end us now. They mean to take the Tarn."

And quite suddenly — seeing Garen trapped beneath Colj's shield, watching Colj and his ogres huddle protectively around him in the face of the enemy's thirty thousand men, the little star tree withering under increasing fire — something hot began to uncoil in Kyla's mind, a kind of worm, a kind of seething, furious worm.

Below, on the Great Seal, Ruge still shouted. "No! No!" Hands up, turning to his honor guard, shouting back at the barbican, holding the silver High Cup. "Cease fire!" The green-clad honor guard from Gelánen looked uncertain. They glanced at each other, then glanced to their commander, Lord Julane.

Kyla stared, blinked, forced her eye from her telescope, looked around the tower top, to her little brother and sister, to Ponj and Bruno, to their own little star tree, to Filip and his scouts.

Tarlen and Ponj still watched the action, Tarlen with his telescope, Ponj squinting, trying to make things out. Bruno had shoved himself even further up on the battlement, thick hind legs between Tarlen and Ponj, mouth clamped shut, staring down at the bridge, sniffing, eyes scanning, ears swinging, his growl more frightening than ever, grey fur alive with tendrils of smoky mist. From her place in Ponj's arms, Susan calmly watched the swelling chaos. Another volley of shots cracked from across the water, from the southwestern embankment and the new wall of logs there. The field of Colj's little tree seemed to cave in on itself, the coppery field shrinking to almost nothing, the high silver armor of the ogres' phalanx lighting up like suns, before the tree's field expanded again to cover them – but still smaller, so much smaller. Kyla looked at Filip. He and his scouts were staring down at the bridge, strange looks on their faces as they realized the full extent of what was happening, grasping that Garen and Colj and their tiny squad now stood virtually unprotected against the onslaught of the Pretender King's entire army.

"Lord Michael will come," Filip said to nobody in particular. "Anna and Moondagger will come."

Tarlen and Ponj looked at each other, then they turned

and moved for the tower's trapdoor, Ponj gently lowering Susan from his chest as he moved, Filip and his lads seeming to wake from a dream, diving for their guns, pulling carbines from beneath banners.

The furious worm opened in Kyla's mind, a lashing white flame.

"Stand fast!" Kyla cried.

And her voice carried with it the force of her training, her lineage, and her power. It was the voice of a highborn Dallanar lady, the voice of the Silver Kingdom's greatest nobility, the voice of a future Queen of Remain.

Ponj and Tarlen stopped in their tracks, staring at her, waiting her orders, Ponj actually frozen in place at her command, Susan dangling from his huge ogre hand, little feet brushing over the tower's pavers. The scouts looked as if they'd been locked in ice, hands frozen at their guns.

"Put me down, Ponj," Susan said.

Ponj lowered her to the floor.

"Quine," Kyla ordered. "You will take Susan below to her quarters." He moved to obey; Susan did not protest. "Tarlen, take your scope and step to the battlements, you'll spot for me. Ponj, tend our star tree. I want to ignore fire from their snipers."

"My Lady." Ponj bowed.

Kyla turned, stepped, and held her telescope out to Filip. "Filip, you'll spot for Sledder and Tellerman. Give me your weapon."

He bowed and handed it over without pause.

"Fire only on my mark. You'll target their sharpshooters, every sniper on the barbican. You'll then work your way across the headlands, starting with those riflemen by that new log fortification at the southwest. I want a hundred notches on the stocks of each those weapons when we're done today, gentlemen."

The scouts saluted, heels snapping together. "My Lady!"

"What's our plan?" Tarlen asked, turning back with her to the battlements.

"We're going to cover Garen and Colj." Kyla glanced down at the bridge. "Kill anyone who comes close."

Tarlen nodded.

She looked down at the carbine she'd taken from Filip. The gun wasn't his, she realized. It was an ancient weapon of high silver, its design fluid, timeless, lethal – and entirely beyond his station. He must've taken it as a prize somehow, from his last trip out.

She checked and primed it.

Where it came from didn't matter.

It was a perfect weapon.

And she knew how to use it.

36

ANOTHER HIGH SILVER round punched through the little tree's field, struck Colj's shield, and flashed bright. Colj was still huddled down with Lord Garen, shield up, using his body to protect him.

"We need that Cup," Lord Garen said calmly, pushing his spectacles onto his nose, as if oblivious to the danger.

"Stay down, my Lord," Colj grunted, bracing against the enemy's fire, the war song swelling his veins, leaning into it.

"The Cup, Colj," Lord Garen repeated.

"That it is not possible, my Lord," Colj said.

"No!" Vymon Ruge shouted, turned and shouted. "No! No!" Colj glanced out from the phalanx and saw that the Lord Commander was looking from side to side now, his face furious, all decorum lost. At Jon Ruge's side, Jared Ruge turned to look up at the barbican. He put both his hands up, as if trying to settle a raging horse, as if he could stop the coming fire with open palms.

And more fire was coming in, vanishing against the little tree's field. Mostly small arms and carbines, mostly sporadic, mostly coming from soldiers behind Vymon Ruge's retinue, up on the barbican, and from the southwestern embankment, as if it was unplanned. The men of Gelánen were still unsure what to do, still looking to their commander, Lord Julane.

Colj was not worried about infantry fire. His ogres were there, they had their star tree, and they had their shields. And Lord Michael and Captain Dyer would be coming soon. Colj was worried about the Pretender's great cannon at the barbican, its maw a dark hole of burning death.

"Back," Colj ordered.

With perfect coordination, the ogres kept their formation intact and withdrew, backing away from the Great Seal toward the Great Door and the Tarn at a slow and steady pace. The little star tree's field wavered, shrunk with the incoming fire, then rebounded — but still shrinking, big Doj rolling it back, Rudj pumping cold water into its roots, the little star tree trembling with effort. The Pretender's great cannon was almost entirely out of the barbican now, its adepts in position, the mighty cannon glowing deadly with silver light. Only Ruge and his entourage stood between them and it.

"Stay tight," Colj said. "Stay together. Back."

The enemy's infantry would not charge. Colj knew that. Nor could their great cannon fire down the axis of the bridge. Not without destroying their own commander and his entourage.

Unless the Pretender King wanted to kill Vymon Ruge and his sons.

"The Cup," Lord Garen said again. Colj ignored him, kept the formation moving backwards, shields scraping granite, other shields held high. The little tree's field took more fire from the southwestern embankment; for a moment, its field shrunk to almost nothing.

"The Cup," Lord Garen said. He grabbed Colj's arm. "Colj. We *must* have it."

Colj looked over the edge of his shield.

Vymon Ruge, High Cup in hand, waved and shouted, "Stop! *Cease fire!*" Jared Ruge looked at his father, said something Colj couldn't hear. The green-clad men from Gelánen were finally drawing their weapons, moving past Vymon Ruge, toward the ogre phalanx, but not with much enthusiasm. Their commander, Lord Julane, looked from Jon Ruge to Vymon Ruge, as if trying to make up his mind.

And then the great cannon moved fully out of the barbican's gate, a silvery sea beast, surrounded by the golden-robed adepts of the Pretender King.

"No!" Vymon Ruge cried, running straight at it. "Stop!"

Colj did not pity him.

Only fools screamed against a storm.

And the storm was almost upon them.

37

"Stand ready." Lord Michael's eyes were pure black. Little Dan blinked and nodded.

Then Lord Michael raised his groaning sword and crossed his chest with his black armored fist. Master Falmon raised his spear, and everybody else raised their weapons and guns and shields, returning the salute. Dan crossed his chest with his fist and felt his heart pounding there. His head spun with the humming songs of the big guns; they wanted to get out the door so badly, to get out there and do the work that weapons do.

Lord Michael's giant bear growled, and Lord Michael turned the beast to the door, looking out the peephole again. Outside, Dan could hear more noise, like a whole bunch of firecrackers – then even louder firecrackers. Everyone jostled and moved. More snow was falling now.

Lord Michael said something that Dan couldn't hear. Lord Michael's black sword was all smoky.

We thirst, all of us.

A big hand touched Dan's head. Dan glanced up.

Lord Doldon stood behind him, smiling down at him.

"It's you and me today, Big Dan," Lord Doldon said. He glanced over at Stormy. "Right?"

Dan nodded. But he couldn't really say anything because his heart was hammering in his chest so loud, and the cannon's songs were starting to ring through his head – not right, but loud — so he nodded again. The Chief looked over at him, his eyes mean and jealous.

Lord Michael whispered something again and looked out the peephole. The smoke from his sword was spreading over everyone, covering the fresh snow on their shoulders, everyone's eyes going black like murder.

"Good lad." Lord Doldon pounded Dan on the shoulder with his fist. Then he stepped up and whispered something to Stormy's lead adept. She looked at Lord Doldon, nodded. And then Stormy and Oblivion rose up off their carriages, floating, that silvery glow coming from their skins, their songs coming louder than ever — still wrong in Dan's ears — but *way* louder, winding together, joining and rising, the songs loud and strong, but still wrong. Lord Doldon turned around, looked at Dan, and saluted. Dan saluted back.

"You sing for 'em, Stormy," Dan said. His head was starting to hurt a little. "You sing like you never sung before."

"Shut *up*, Eadle," the Chief hissed.

But then, all at once, the big door crashed out and open and everything was moving forward, the great cannon moving out onto the bridge, their songs louder and louder, the war thumping coming like it'd never come before, the war adepts singing, guiding the big guns out the door, barely able to hold them back.

38

THE PRETENDER'S SOLDIERS were coming out of the barbican now, Colj saw. Moving past Vymon Ruge, who still stood in front of the Pretender's great cannon and its golden adepts, pushing past him, moving toward Colj's phalanx, firing sporadically as they came. Jared Ruge looked around in confusion. The poor, stuttering boy wasn't in on the trap, of course. He never had been. Indeed, the whole advance, such as it was, was meant to look disorganized and uncoordinated. But Colj could tell that the opposite was true. It was all part of the deception. With Jared's help, Jon Ruge had gotten to his feet and had drawn his high silver revolver; he stood well behind the advancing soldiers, his injured arm held to his chest. Then, as if sensing Colj's gaze, Jon Ruge looked up at him, raised his weapon, and fired. The silver bullet hit Colj's shield, a blinding star, high silver deflecting killing force.

"Charge!" Jon Ruge shouted, waved his pistol overhead, a

bit of snow whirling around him. "Charge! Protect the Lord of the Siege! We need Garen alive!"

Lord Julane and the men from Gelánen began to move forward, a bit tentative at first, but now with more vigor. Vymon Ruge stared at his youngest son like he didn't know him. Then Vymon Ruge shouted something at Jon, but Colj couldn't hear it.

"The Cup," Lord Garen said. "Colj, listen to me. We *must* have that High Cup. When Michael comes, we will push forward with him. We *must* retrieve it."

Colj bowed in acknowledgment. But Lord Garen was no soldier. And Lord Michael had made clear that the High Cup was of secondary importance. Lord Garen's life was what mattered.

A few more bullets hit Colj's shield, priceless high silver rounds punching through the star tree's field. A well-placed rifle shot hissed through a gap in the phalanx, burning past Colj's shoulder. Then the big iron guns of the enemy opened up from the southwestern ridge, from placements in front of the new log fortifications, orange fire and black smoke bellowing. The enemy's iron in town started, too, from everywhere at once. Sharpshooters fired from all four towers of the barbican, from everywhere. The coppery field of the little star tree shuddered and shrank, absorbing the incoming salvos, unable to recover, coppery leaves beginning to wilt, detonations all around them, big Doj pulling the cart, Rudj back there pumping water as fast as he could into the little tree's roots. The field of the tree barely covered the phalanx now.

And then, from behind him, Doj called in his deep voice "Our great cannon come."

Colj glanced back and saw their own great cannon coming out of the Tarn's Great Door, floating out, blue adepts in their positions, the living guns aiming to either side of the bridge, ready to clear the flanks, Master Falmon and Lord Doldon there beside them, ready to cover Lord Michael's sortie. Stormhammer and Oblivion, the oldest of the Tarn's mighty cannon, ready to return fire. Lord Michael was astride the great Okros with his bear riders, behind the great guns, ready to go, waiting only for their cover, holding the charge back.

And then the silvery maws of the Tarn's great guns came

to life, like the living things they were, silver lips pulling back, silver fangs opening, lion and dragon, and together they thundered – SHOOM! SHOOM! – flaming silver meteors blazing over bridge and water, thunder, white light, the headlands erupting in a haze of tumbling lumber and bodies and dirt. Then came the screams of dying, the shrieks of burning men. Lord Doldon and Master Falmon spotted for the Tarn's great cannon, pointing. The flanking war adepts in their fugue states, lead adepts behind each cannon singing to her weapon, heads back, elated, battle ecstasy, hands on the great guns as they sang their war songs, the guns singing in return – SHOOM! SHOOM! – more searing silver fire blasting into the enemy, and there was nothing the enemy could do about it save watch as the Tarn's great cannon rained silver fire upon them from within the protective perimeter of the citadel's star trees.

"Keep an eye on the Cup," Lord Garen insisted.

Colj looked over his shield. There it was. Vymon Ruge still held the High Cup as he stood in front of the Pretender's great gun, blocking its path and its fire. Vymon Ruge grabbed a soldier, a group of soldiers, pointed back to the barbican, pushing them back. His hand was on the maw of the great weapon now, still trying to stop what had already started. Others moved past him. Jared Ruge was trying to lift the Ruge family standard off the ground. Jon Ruge took two steps forward, aimed his pistol at Colj and the phalanx, looking for another shot. Jared Ruge picked up the dark blue banner of House Ruge and looked from side to side, as if he didn't know what to do with it. Jared Ruge looked toward Colj and took a step forward. And then a carbine shot – CRACKED! – and a fleshy hole was blown in Jared Ruge's throat, blood leaking between his teeth. He'd been shot in the back of the neck, a bullet from behind, from his own side, perfectly placed, right beneath the high silver of his helmet. Blood guttered from his mouth. His head wrenched at an odd angle. He took a step, then dropped bonelessly, blood spreading over the bridge's stone. Jon Ruge stared wide-eyed, looked at his older brother, and lowered his revolver. Vymon Ruge ran to his dead son, Cup and cannon forgotten, screaming: "Cease fire! Oh, Sisters! *Cease fire!*"

But his words were impossible to hear.

True battle had been joined.

The storm had commenced.

The men from Gelánen and the Pretender's soldiers were pushing past Vymon Ruge, firing, drawing up formal ranks in the middle of the bridge. Behind the enemy infantry, at the barbican, Lord Corlen Lessip – a fat, red-haired general – gestured and pointed past Colj, at the little star tree and its wagon, giving orders, preparing the golden-robed adepts to fire along the bridge's axis. Vymon Ruge turned and shouted at Lessip. The Pretender's soldiers and the men from Gelánen were getting nearer the ogre phalanx now, almost on top of it, pushing forward, the green-clad men from Gelánen beginning to fire systematically, still blocking the line of fire of the great cannon, small arms not doing much. Lord Julane had not even drawn his weapon.

Then Lord Lessip pointed at Vymon Ruge and cried, "Protect High Lord Commander Ruge! The Silver Fox has killed Lord Jared! The Tarn has killed Lord Jared! Forward! For the Silver Throne! For the Silver Kingdom! Protect the Lord of the Siege! Forward! For the Remain!"

As if in answer, Stormhammer and Oblivion fired again – SHOOM! SHOOM! – a barrage of silver flame and the hills of Tarntown exploded, screamed, the great guns' living fire voracious. Jon Ruge grabbed his father, pulled him off his dead brother. Vymon Ruge struggled against him, cursed him, cursed his own son. He still held the High Cup. More soldiers came, pulling Vymon and Jon Ruge back toward the barbican, their shields up and around the High Lord Commander, the old man's face stricken with sorrow and rage.

The snow came harder now, swirling. Through it, Lord Lessip pointed a fat finger at the Tarn's great guns, signaling at the new timber fortifications on the southwestern embankment. A black flag waved in return. Lord Lessip turned back along the bridge. Fresh soldiers advanced out of the barbican. But these men were different, Colj saw. They wore high silver armor and carried high silver guns. The elites of the Pretender's Silver Guard. The source of the high silver rounds. Their faces were grim and battle-hardened. Colj grunted as a bullet punched through a gap in the phalanx, hitting his shoulder guard with a silver flash. Stormhammer and Oblivion thundered once more – SHOOM! SHOOM! – the enemy lines bursting again, clotted dirt and men, screaming silver fire, the great guns alive and unstoppable, their ancient song filled with righteous fury. A bullet struck granite beneath Colj's shield. Vudj, his first lieutenant, took a bullet in his calf, right above the joint in his armor. Blood spattered. Vudj grunted, laughed. "Something bit me!" Another volley hit the ogres' shields, the enemy's fire more focused now, the Guardsmen well-coordinated, perfectly trained. They were still being cautious, however. They still wanted to take Lord Garen alive, it seemed — but that meant hand-to-hand combat with the ogres of Jallow.

"Stay tight," Colj said. "Stay together." The star tree's field was almost gone, its edges well smaller than the phalanx now. The Tarn's Great Door was just over two hundred and fifty paces behind them. The ogres picked up the pace. Storm-hammer and Oblivion thundered — SHOOM! SHOOM! Smoke wafted over the bridge, the rising hills of Tarntown, a silvery fog laced with a tendril of black.

39

LITTLE DAN WAS out on the bridge with Stormy and Oblivion and Master Falmon and Lord Doldon, and he could barely believe what he saw. There were enemies all around the city, so many enemies everywhere. And the city was *burning*, smoke rising all around. The cannons songs blazed in Dan's head, but they were still all wrong, and he was dizzy, so dizzy. Stormy and Oblivion sang and roared. It was so loud Dan could barely stand it, and his head was really starting to hurt. He put his hands over his ears. How was he supposed to be a good helper when he couldn't think straight, the songs so loud and so wrong?

And then something even louder came.

It was Lord Michael's voice.

It came — changing, growing, thundering into a giant's roar — a lion's roar that reached its claws for Dan's heart.

"FOR THE REMAIN!"

40

"As you will!" Kyla cried, hot exultation lighting up her mind. "Weapons free!"

And it was as if the entire Tarn heard her command, everything at once, the mighty fortress's great iron batteries opening together, all the big iron on the lower bulwarks, the upper ramparts, the eternal towers — a thundering storm, the citadel raging to life. Sledder and Tellerman fired on the enemy snipers in the barbican, solid and accurate. Snow swirled. Hundreds of other sharpshooters blazed from the Tarn's countless towers, the Tarn alight now, burning, like a living thing, a slumbering giant finally roused. And Kyla's own weapon was a part of it, one with it, smooth and steady, the action of the ancient gun perfect, snug against her shoulder, her focus absolute.

"Call them out, Tarlen," she said.

Tarlen nodded, eye pressed to his spyglass. "Ten paces in front of Garen's phalanx, charging."

"Got him."

Her sight tracked the target.

"Goodbye." She breathed — and put a high silver bullet through the charging soldier's skull.

41

AND THEN COLJ heard the Vordan shriek and the Tarn's mighty batteries opened, a thunderous rush of holy might.

"Lord Michael comes!" Colj roared, more for the benefit of

the enemy's men than his own. "Lord Michael comes!"

In front of him, on the bridge, every soldier heard and paused.

The Vordan's black scream came once again. The enemy – even the men and women of the Silver Guard – seemed to waver, to hesitate. But the green-clad men from Gelánen did not wait; they were grim-eyed and resolute now. Lord Julane charged to their front, his jaw set, drew his pistol, and cried, "For Kendal! For Lady Margaret! For Gelánen! For Gelánen!" The men in green took up the call, surging forward, pushing against the ogres' shields, jabbing swords in the gaps, firing into cracks where they could. Vudj laughed, "Another bite!" A charging Guardsman ran along their flank – and dropped dead, shot through the head by a sharpshooter high on one of the Tarn's towers. Colj glanced behind him and saw that the enemy advance was too late.

Through the smoke and haze, through the fog and the fury came High Lord Michael Dallanar, the Dark Lord of Kon.

At first, he was a shadow in fog. And then he was there behind them, the great war bear Okros grunting, black armor like the dark between stars, a horde of grim bear riders following, two columns of raging death driving fast down either side of the bridge, charging headlong for the Great Seal and the Pretender's cannon there.

"*FOR THE REMAIN!*" Lord Michael roared, his voice shaking the heavens.

As one, the ogres and bears roared in return, and the war music burned in their veins.

"To the right," Colj ordered.

The ogre phalanx shifted, cleared the path, gave the enemy a view of what came: Bear riders crouched low behind silver shields, guns and lances ready, bears' eyes black with blood lust, Lord Michael at the front. And then a bear went down, shot through the ear, its rider jumping clear, throwing off his lance, drawing a high silver blade, still charging. The Vordan screamed. A rider threw her shield into the air as she was hit, blood spraying from her face. Another bear went down, a perfect shot through its mouth, the Silver Guardsmen accurate and calm in the face of certain death. Stormhammer and Oblivion thundered again – SHOOM! SHOOM! Tarntown burned, the headlands burned, smoke everywhere. Colj grunted as more bullets hit his shield. Then the fire slowed for a moment. Colj saw the green-clad men from Gelánen hesitate, the Legionnaires and Guardsmen holding, pushing them forward, hardened veterans bracing for Lord Michael's coming charge. Lord Michael raced toward them, too fast for the enemy artillery to track, the Vordan screaming for blood.

"Captain!" Doj shouted, his massive ogre finger jutting down the bridge. "There! At the barbican!"

The Pretender's great cannon was on top of the Great Seal. Lord Lessip pointed down the axis of the bridge, conferring with the lead adept in her golden robes, nodding, ready to fire.

If they could kill Lord Michael, it would be worth it to sacrifice their own men.

The Great Door of the Tarn was just under two hundred paces behind Colj and his phalanx.

"Back," Colj said calmly. "Pick up the pace."

42

LITTLE DAN CLAMPED his hands over his ears, wobbled, dizzy, then fell down in a heap. The guns' songs were so loud. The

Chief kicked him and told him to get up and get the water. But Stormy's song was so *wrong*, so loud in his head, it felt like his skull was gonna burst, his brains boiling in there. It was so bad. He wanted to help, but it just hurt so bad.

So he tried to hum something *right*, because the adepts didn't sing the right song, but he could feel a black pain coming into his head. He wanted to throw up. The Chief kicked him again, kicking him to move out of the way.

"Stupid idiot! Damn you, crazy!"

The Chief's kicks didn't hurt. Dan could take those hits easy.

But the hits in his head were something else.

It had never hurt so bad.

And even when he tried to hum and make it right, his little song got lost somehow in Stormy's roar, and it felt like he was falling into a black, endless hole.

43

THE WAR SONG of the enemy's cannon filled the air as it prepared to fire. Colj could hear it, clear as day. And then Lord Michael was there and past him. He was there and then he was gone, a blur of black armor and rage through the snow, his face a mask of fury. Okros roared. The Vordan shrieked, the black mist around the dread blade devouring all incoming fire. Lord Michael was in front of them now, in front of his own column, tearing through the men of Gelánen like they weren't there, heads jumping from bodies, geysers of black blood erupting. The Vordan screamed again and Marden Julane of Gelánen went down, his shoulder hacked off at the joint. Michael plowed into the men of the Silver Guard, a dozen men killed in a blink. The bear columns merged, Lord Michael at the head, a wall of the Tarn's best bears and swords and guns and lances and armor.

They would be at the enemy's great cannon in moments.

"Down!" Colj shouted, holding Lord Garen to his chest. "The enemy will fire!"

Stormhammer and Oblivion roared again, light and thunder – SHOOM! SHOOM! Silver smoke everywhere. It was getting hard for Colj to see.

Lord Michael killed everything in his path. He was almost at the enemy cannon now, twenty paces out, cutting a blood-soaked road through the enemy.

Ten paces: Lord Michael charging straight at the open maw of the enemy gun.

Five paces: The heads of the golden-robed war adepts tilted back in holy battle song.

And then their cannon fired – THOOM! – and Lord Michael turned great Okros's broadside into it and lifted his shield to show a tiny star tree hanging at his belt, roots wrapped in a bright blue burlap sack, the coppery field of the tree only four paces wide, but exceedingly powerful, strengthened by Lord Garen's lore. The enemy's fire hit the tree's field, exploded around it, and the little tree withered to dust.

Then Lord Michael was among the enemy's golden-robed war adepts. The Vordan screamed. Okros roared. Lord Michael threw himself at the great cannon, cutting the adepts to ribbons, golden limbs spinning, spewing as he hacked, the Vordan's screams echoing against the front of the barbican.

Near the center of the bridge, the rear of Lord Michael's column was deep among the Silver Guard. A rider leapt from his mount, shot a Legionnaire in the face. Red blood spattered fresh snow. Stormhammer and Oblivion fired again — SHOOM! SHOOM! A dark-bearded legionnaire fired his pistol into the eye of a charging bear, the great beast collapsed, its rider coming up, swinging a two-handed sword of high silver. Bullets bounced off armor, high silver glowed like living suns. A tall, red-haired Legionnaire ran up behind the swordsman, shot him in the armpit before she was killed in turn by a sharpshooter from the towers of the Tarn. Empty guns were dropped, broadswords and long daggers came out for close work. Everywhere, the artillery on all sides had opened up. Everywhere, the headlands were alive with smoke and fire, the Tarn's batteries giving it back with unprecedented fury, freed at last, black smoke drifting, mingling with silver. The war bears were wild with rage, Legionnaires fighting and falling to tooth and claw. The soldiers of Gelánen had fallen dead everywhere, green livery littering the bridge. Blood sprayed, the screams of the killing and dying merging, rising together in one wailing, pitiful cry as silver blades flashed. And there, a squad of Silver Guardsmen led by a blond sergeant rallied and swarmed over a pair of dead bears. Lord Michael was inside the barbican's gate now. Stormhammer and Oblivion, fangs wide, wreaked havoc upon the enemy batteries – SHOOM! SHOOM! – like earthquake's living thunder, silver smoke, white fury, the sound deafening as Lord Doldon, Master Falmon, and their war adepts poured on the holy fire.

And then Lord Garen was up and out and away from him, sliding between Colj's legs, around in front of the phalanx, running as fast as he could, *toward* the barbican.

Colj shouted to his ogres, "After him!"

But it took the big ogres a moment to get out of their defensive stance. A bullet grazed Colj's arm, drawing blood. An ogre, young Kudj, went down, a hole through his cheek. Lord Garen charged into the throng of the bridge's insane melee, trying to get through the swarm of battling Guards-men and Legionnaires and riders to Vymon Ruge, who was nowhere to be seen. One of the Tarn's bear riders, who'd been staying close to the phalanx, dismounted and ran past Colj to the defense of Lord Garen, drawing a vicious sabre of high silver. The rider's closed-faced helmet was topped by a blue plume, that streamed as he ran to Lord Garen's side, into the thick of battle. But Lord Garen did not notice. Instead, he ran straight ahead, flinging greenish vials anywhere there was an enemy. When Lord Garen's vials broke open, small, tentacled things covered in bumpy eyes reached for throats and mouths, clamped down, squeezed, and burrowed. A bald lieutenant leapt from the bridge, clutching his face. An enemy jumped at Lord Garen and was promptly shot through the temple by a Tarn sharpshooter, then gutted by the blue-plumed rider. Colj ran up behind Lord Garen, his giant axe swinging like a scythe, cutting a man in two. The squad of Silver Guardsmen saw Lord Garen from their cover behind a dead bear. Their blond sergeant pointed her finger at Lord Garen, shouted something, and charged. Vudj roared and leapt to Lord Garen's defense, only to be shot between the eyes by the blond sergeant; he dropped. The Guardsmen leapt to the attack and met death at the hands and blades and teeth of ogre and bear and rider. The living roar of the Tarn's guns was impossibly loud – SHOOM! SHOOM! Through it all, the blue-plumed rider was amid everything, beside Colj and Lord Garen, a blur of speed and precision, one moment here, the next there, his weapon red from tip to hilt, a razor's line of silver death, sniper fire from the towers of the Tarn seeming to mark the blue-plumed warrior's path, searing bolts from above coming fast and deadly with inhuman precision. The enemy sergeant fired straight at Lord Garen. The bullets hit his breastplate, flashed white with deflected force. The sergeant could not get past his armor, so she dropped her pistol, drew her blade, and took a bullet in the neck from the Tarn's heights, blood spraying. The blue-plumed rider finished her off before leaping at the next enemy, a pouncing lion through swirling snow. Colj finally managed to stop Lord Garen, to get him turned around.

"Please, Lord Garen!" Colj shouted over the battle's roar. Lord Garen looked at him, pushed his spectacles up on his nose. "I will help you look for the Cup!" Colj said. "Only stay with me! *Stay* with me, Lord Garen!"

But how could he do this and obey Lord Michael's order to protect his brother? Ahead of them, deep in the guts of the barbican, Lord Michael and the Vordan and the war bears killed, the screams of the dying rising in a dread wail. At the Great Seal, a squad of bear riders had dismounted and had turned the great cannon of the enemy toward the Pretender's iron on the southwestern headlands. It was a perfect line of fire at the enemy placements.

Then five bear riders threw off false gear to reveal the sky-blue robes of war adepts of the Tarn, and the song of the Pretender's gun came immediately, a symphony of blood and silver. And then the great gun fired – THOOM! – and the enemy artillery on placement in front of the timber fortifications exploded in a shower of gore and iron. Soldiers screamed. The enemy gun crews realized they were flanked, that they were not able to turn their iron fast enough. Storm-hammer and Oblivion thundered in unison from the Great Door – SHOOM! SHOOM! – white death and fire raining down. The enemy gun crews ran.

And then there was a loud, close shot and a blinding flash of light at Colj's side. Lord Garen grunted. Colj turned and raised his shield – too late.

Lord Garen was hit.

He did not move.

He did not breathe.

44

"GAREN IS DOWN," Tarlen whispered.

"From where?" Kyla asked, keeping her voice calm despite the flutter in her heart.

"Up there." He pointed, holding his telescope to his eye. "Lesser cannon. Top there, on the barbican's southern tower."

Bruno barked savagely, barely able to contain himself, his fur a hissing haze of silver-grey static.

Kyla scanned, found the small cannon, found its crew — fired.

CRACK! CRACK! CRACK!

And the cannon's crew died.

She was a trained machine.

A killing machine.

It was a strange kind of joy.

45

LITTLE DAN COULD barely stand it, his head hurt so bad. Stormy's song was so loud and so wrong, and the other noises — the blood and the screams — it hurt. He knew he was supposed to be helping, but it hurt so bad. Tears streamed down his face. He tried to get up, but he was too dizzy. He fell.

46

Colj knelt at Lord Garen's side – and then Colj smiled. Lord Garen breathed. The high silver had done its job. Lord Garen was only dazed. The armor had been perfectly tuned. Lord Garen blinked, his eyes foggy. He adjusted his spectacles, but he could barely speak. "That . . . that was a big gun." A crooked grin. His eyes went out of focus. "Don't tell Michael, he won't like it . . . ."

Colj looked up and saw that Michael's column was through barbican now, on the other side, killing. Some of his bear riders were also within it, on the roof, throwing men from the heights. Guns went off, bears slashed, the great batteries of the Tarn taking a terrible toll on the enemy positions on the headlands, the docks, the center of Tarntown. On either side of the barbican, the enemy was running in headlong panic. But the batteries of the Pretender were still firing, and other battle groups were coming up, fresh war banners waving.

The fight was just beginning.

"We must get back." Colj looked to his ogres. "Lord Garen is injured."

". . . the Cup," Lord Garen whispered. And then his eyes rolled back in his head. A snowflake landed on his spectacles and melted. Doj was there behind them with the wagon, the little dead star tree in it, the blue-plumed bear rider panting beside them now, his high silver shield raised over Lord Garen. The rider opened his visor, and it was Lady Katherine, of course – never one to obey orders. Stormhammer and Oblivion fired again at the headlands – SHOOM! SHOOM! Colj could no longer see Lord Michael, but he could track him by the Vordan's black scream, the war bears moving with incredible speed, speed their only chance against the numbers of the enemy as they sought the Pretender's soft center while the Tarn's great batteries pounded the enemy's front and flanks.

"Move," Colj said.

Doj and Lady Katherine and the ogres nodded.

Colj picked up Lord Garen.

The ogres formed their phalanx around him——.

And that was when the Pretender's new timber fortifications on the southwestern embankment fell open to reveal seven enormous silver battle cannon, floating, great mouths alive with holy fire, ancient fangs wide and primed and deadly, the song of the Pretender's golden-robed war adepts a chant to end all wars.

And then a strange, black lightning arced silently toward the Tarn's Great Door, a black lightning with no sound, yet somehow painful to the mind. A black-robed war mage stood high on a newly built podium behind the Pretender's great guns, her black hair streaming. In one hand, she raised a battle staff, a shard of obsidian topped with a lightless black egg. Another black stone shone in the center of her pale forehead. Her dread lightning forked toward the Great Door, passed through the coppery fields of the Tarn's star trees, and cracked soundlessly into the heads of Stormhammer and Oblivion – killing the great guns instantly, the guns' glow and mighty songs winking out like blown lamps, the guns dropping dead, rolling and crushing their blue-robed adepts beneath their lifeless weight.

47

THE BLACK LIGHTNING wasn't quiet for Little Dan. It came screaming across the sky, a kind of high, freakish boiling. Dan saw the black branches coming for Stormy, and he got up despite the horrible pain in his head and shouted and pointed, but the Chief just shoved him aside.

"Shut *up*, you idiot!"

Then the lightning hit Stormy and Oblivion on their noses, and they both stopped dead and crashed to the ground, rolling, crushing the adepts at their sides. Master Falmon and Lord Doldon jumped clear. The eyes of the lead adepts went black, black lightning in their robes and hair, frying skin, black lightning crackling out their mouths. Lord Doldon got up, reached for Oblivion's lead adept, touched her, and dropped; his eyes went blank and blood came out his nose. Master Falmon tried to help Stormy's adept, touched her, and the black lightning shot into his eyes, and he fell like a stone. An adept on the ground screamed and screamed, her blue robes splashed with blood. She looked around, looked Dan in the eye, but it was like she didn't see him at all. Stormy's huge, dead body slowly rolled over her legs like an iron log, crunching bone. She screamed something at Dan, something that he couldn't understand. Blood popped from her knees and legs and then her mouth, and then she stopped screaming.

"Stormy!" Dan yelled and ran to his friend. He put his hands on Stormy's skin. There was a black jolt, a crackle in his head, and his hands tingled, but it didn't really hurt. He pushed against Stormy, but he couldn't stop him from rolling, because there was nothing inside Stormy's skin except cold metal.

Dan looked around.

He didn't know what to do.

The adepts were dead

Stormy was dead.

Did that mean there was no way to help?

No!

It was just like Master Falmon said!

This was the time to sing!

"Stormy!" Little Dan cried. "Stormy! It's alright, big boy! I here for you! I help you, Stormy! Little Dan's here! Little Dan's here!"

48

"G<small>REAT</small> S<small>ISTERS</small>!" T<small>ARLEN</small> cried. He touched Kyla's shoulder, pointing at the southwestern embankment, at the seven great cannon there, the golden-robed adepts, the dark war mage on her podium, her staff alive with black energy. "They . . . they *killed* our big guns! Ky! You see! They—!"

"Focus your fire on her," Kyla said calmly, giving the order to the scouts.

"My Lady." Sledder and Tellerman pivoted. Filip took bearing on their new target.

"What're you waiting for?" Kyla asked Tarlen.

Her brother nodded and collected himself. "There's a bit more cross wind at this line, Ky. A bit more snow." He cleared his throat. "Visibility's down."

Kyla aimed, the snow swirling, the battle clarity still pure, placed her sight on the center of the black-robed mage's forehead, on the black stone that nested there.

And then the war mage looked at her — *into* her — and it was as if the entire battle vanished.

All the noise and smoke gone, the distant shriek of the Vordan cut off like a knife, the constant thunder of the armies' big iron silent.

Across a quiet chasm, their eyes locked together, the woman's eyes dark and beautiful and pure.

Kyla's finger froze on the trigger.

We see you, child queen.

Kyla's breath locked in her throat.

In her mind's eye, she saw Garen and Colj alone, unprotected, on the Long Bridge, only the Tarn's batteries and Michael's mad sortie providing cover for their return, the Pretender's great cannon turning down toward Garen and his ogres, the enemy's golden-robed war adepts lifting their voices in song . . . .

And we know you, child queen.

Tarlen, one eye pressed to his spyglass, the other eye shut. "You're good, Ky. You're good. Looks like they're targeting the bridge. Looks like she's sighting for them, too. You're good to fire. Ky? Ky!"

But Kyla could not pull the trigger.

And the war mage aimed her black staff at the Pinnacle's heights, just as she pointed the Pretender's great cannon toward the bridge below, her eyes locked onto Kyla's.

Black lightning crackled silently up from that staff of night. It moved through the swirling snow, black fractures against grey cloud, skeletal black hands jittering, coming, but slowly, as if in slow motion, the black lighting jumping here to here to here, branching toward them, silent, slower, closer . . . .

And we know you see us.

49

"BACK," COLJ ORDERED. "Quickly."

Lady Katherine nodded.

But the Pretender's great cannon still turned together, seven living guns aimed as if guided by one mind, the Pretender's golden-robed war adepts alive in their own righteous song, the power of the great weapons unstoppable. Together they turned, pointing down at Colj and his little phalanx, the seven mouths dark holes from which death would issue.

Then the big guns stopped and together swung toward the sky, toward the countless war dragons of Dávanor diving from heaven.

50

"ANNA!" TARLEN CRIED. "It's Anna! Ky! Our dragons!"

Sledder, Tellerman, and Filip hooted and popped off a pair of shots, then hooted some more.

But Kyla still couldn't move.

The war mage's voice came to her and her alone.

Watch, child queen.

It was not an evil voice, Kyla realized.

It was no voice of darkness.

It was kind — and almost sad.

Watch your best and last burn at the hands of your last and best, child queen. Watch your failure unfold.

Kyla's eyes turned up on their own. She saw over a hundred squads of diving dragons, Anna and Moondagger, blinding white and resplendent at their lead, countless Davanórian war banners streaming, hundreds of dragons diving toward the enemy, straight at the great guns.

But the maws of the Pretender's living weapons rose to meet them, the great bores opened, swelled, lips peeled back, silver fangs wide, their swelling war songs like the end of everything. Kyla saw Anna atop Moondagger, Anna's black hair flying behind her, Moondagger's great white wings folded to his side, plummeting, Anna standing high in her saddle, her silver armor glorious, her silver sword raised overhead, a primal war scream like the savage edge of dawn, dropping into death.

And then the Pretender's guns fired — THOOM! — a single, enormous noise that shook the earth. And a quarter of the dragons of Dávanor were erased from the sky. Smoking ash, scores gone, dragons of every color careening, dying, hissing into the Sea of Ice. A triumphant cheer rose up from the Pretender's host, fresh energy for the enemy, loyal dragons and riders falling in charred fragments but — but no, oh Great Sisters, no! Kyla couldn't look away. There, a blue heavyweight flapping one enormous wing, desperately trying to stay aloft, to save its rider who dangled lifeless from her saddle, fragile bones snapping as it succumbed to gravity, its dying cry pure sorrow. And there, a massive red, its leg and tail missing, trailed blood across the sky like a falling meteor, its rider trying to unclip, falling into Tarntown noiselessly as the rain of color and blood and dragons continued.

The Pretender's great cannon prepared to fire yet again,

on center this time. Anna and Moondagger were still out front, still diving.

They had realized what had happened — what *will* happen.

A strange expression came onto Anna's face, and she leaned forward and whispered something to her dragon. Moondagger's blind eyes glimmered with knowledge, with fearless determination, and then it was as if Kyla were there beside them, riding the sky.

"This and only this, forever," Anna said.

Where is your joy now, child queen? Is this not what your people sought? Time now, child queen. Time to reap what your people have sown.

At Kyla's side, Tarlen whispered, ". . . they're gonna kill them."

51

HIS LITTLE HANDS on Stormy, Dan hummed a tune. It was just a little song. He closed his eyes, rocked back and forth, hands tingling with the black cold in Stormy's skin, pushing a bit of his own warmth down into the big gun — pushing, but gentle — trying to find the heat at Stormy's center, because

Dan could still feel Stormy down in that cold metal. He was sure of that now.

"You take it, Stormy," Dan said. "You take it, boy."

He pushed harder, pushing his little heart down into the big gun, pushing his own warmth down into his friend, humming his song, eyes clamped shut.

Then, out of nowhere, Dan felt Stormy *pulling* at it, and he willed his own heat into Stormy's center. It was starting to hurt a little in his chest and hands, but it was alright because Stormy was his friend and that's how you're supposed to do it. He just sang his song – the *right* song this time, the song like it was *supposed* to be.

A song of silver and blood.

Stormhammer's song.

And then the Chief came up and punched Little Dan hard in the face.

"What did you *do*, crazy idiot?! *What* did you do?! Get your stupid hands *off*!"

52

"THEY'RE GONNA KILL them all," Tarlen said again.

Watch, child queen.

Kyla saw the dragons falling toward the Pretender's great guns. She heard Anna's scream. She felt Moondagger's roar.

The mouths of the mighty cannon opened, as if to devour them, ready to blast them into ash.

And there was nothing she could do.

Watch and learn. See the true flower of your people's dark seed.

53

"MOVE," COLJ SAID grimly.

Lady Katherine nodded.

But they couldn't go much faster. They were still taking sporadic fire. And the phalanx could only go so fast.

"Move," Colj repeated. "Anna buys this time with her life."

54

THE CHIEF HIT Dan again. Dan felt his nose break with a little pop. Dan tasted blood, but he couldn't let go. And he couldn't protect himself, either, because his hands were warming up and sort of *sinking* into Stormy's side, as if Stormy's skin was a warm cushion. That was good, Dan knew. Stormy was starting to wake up, starting to take what Little Dan gave.

"What did you *do*?!" the Chief yelled. Another punch, this time to the side of Dan's head. Dan saw stars and tried to say something to the Chief, but he couldn't really say anything because he had to concentrate on the song, and his words came out like a crazy mumble. Then the Chief hit him again — *real* hard this time. So, Dan just closed his eyes and kept humming and let himself become like Stormy, let himself flow down into Stormy's skin like he'd done so many times before. The Chief hit him again — but this time he cried and fell away.

And then the Chief was gone.

And everything was gone.

And Dan just *pushed* his warmth into Stormy.

It hurt, but it was what Stormy needed, and that's how a good soldier did it.

And then Stormy *pulled*, heat flooding out of Dan's hands, his own little chest going cold, all his good song, his good warmth pouring into the big gun.

"You take it, Stormy," Little Dan whispered. "You take it, big boy."

He was still humming, but then — suddenly — the warmth came *back* to him.

And the song came back, too.

Kind of soft at first. Real soft. Right there, where you almost couldn't hear it, a kind of low beat, a kind of low thump — like the beat of a big drum calling soldiers to war. There was a jingling noise, too, like weapons and armor and gear, the snuffling snorts of dragons and animals, the hiss of sharpening swords that stops as soldiers get up from their tents, buckling on gear while the drum keeps thumping like a big monster's heart. Other sounds came, too. A creak, a grinding clank, the beat thumping faster now, a bit more warmth in your chest, the metal turn of wheels and iron clattering over mud and bones, ground shaking, pebbles jumping, iron creatures puffing smoke, rising slow and sleepy, stopping, starting, stopping, then starting up again, crawling like metal ants into battle. The drum thump louder now — and *warmer*, too, louder and warmer, louder and warmer — *way* warmer, the iron monsters riding their burning bellies and metal feet, the stamp-stamp of heavy boots taking up the beat, iron-shod war boots spiked with stud and claw, stamping-stamping-stamping now into battle's maw. And ho, there! Yes, there! Far away at first, then louder, louder, louder still, rising 'til they burst above: the crying horns, the sighing horns, their cry of blood and tears, their sound the moan of lowing beasts fed by ancient fears. Faster now, faster now, the drum-thump comes and booms, a million hungry brutes of war, marching to their dooms! Then — *kreeeEEE! kreeeEEE!* — the war flute's jagged scream, a screaming bolt of lightning's fire, a war flute's olden scream and fall, scream and fall, the cry of raging war, a hundred children crying now, cursed with savage lore — and then the song *broke* inside Dan's head, it didn't hurt any more, it was more like a soft snap, like a kind of *opening* into something huge and warm, something beyond Dan's words, the war flute's scream rolling up into an endless cry, the cry becoming a shriek, the thumping drums coming down to meet it, the tempo lost and strange, so far beyond his words — but so right, *oh so right at last!* A rush, a stampede, a wave of arms and men and blood and teeth, pounding faster and faster, hotter and hotter, so hot now, so hot! Louder now, the song opened. Louder! It grew! It swelled! Louder still! Hotter still! A thousand voices — a million voices — crying together, colliding, exploding, a storm of victory and sacrifice, a trumpeting rout whose fiery roar shook Dan's little heart like the thunder of armored giants, everything he was, everything he had to give — and more.

"It's alright, Stormy," Little Dan whispered, accepting, knowing what it meant. "You take it. You take it, boy. You sing for 'em. You sing for 'em, Stormy."

And then he let go of everything inside himself, kept one hand on Stormy, pointed his little finger at the place where the bad black lightning came.

And then he *asked*.

It wasn't a demand.

It was a simple request.

A high, shining question:

"Can you sing for me, Stormy?"

55

From Behind Colj and his ogre phalanx, at the Great Door, a sudden war song rose from nothing.

It was unlike anything Colj had ever known.

A clarity of heart.

The ultimate song.

The ja of the purest warrior.

The power and fury of its fire was beyond imagination.

Colj turned.

There he saw the little warrior — Daniel Eadle — standing beside the mighty Stormhammer. The little boy's eyes were shut, one hand on the great weapon, the other pointing at the Pretender's guns. Daniel was surrounded by the mighty cannon's holy light, the great gun alive with silver radiance, floating off the ground, barely contained, the gathering power unspeakable. The little boy's mouth moved over and over, as if repeating a whisper, as if repeating a song.

"Get down," Colj ordered calmly. His ogres took a knee, Lady Katherine and the unconscious Lord Garen at the formation's center. "Brace."

"Are you mad?!" Lady Katherine cried, pointing at the

Pretender's battle cannon. "We *can't* take that fire, Colj! Anna gives herself for *us*! We must get back! On your feet, now!"

"Not that fire, my Lady." Colj shook his big head. He lifted his huge chin toward the Great Door, toward the little boy and his weapon, toward the swelling song which could save and destroy a world.

Lady Katherine saw and heard and said, "Great Sisters save us . . . ."

56

"CAN YOU SING for me, Stormy? Can you sing?" Little Dan asked and hummed, kind of singsong. He was so tired, just so darn tired now, but he understood what had to be done, what had to be given. The fire was so hot, it hurt bad, and he was almost empty inside now, hollowed out, getting cold. But still, he gave his all. His chest was caving in on itself, like all the air was being pulled from his lungs. Didn't matter. He was ready, ready to give what he had, to show the way, to point where Stormy needed to go.

"Can you sing for me, Stormy? Can you sing?"

57

FROM THE TOP of the Pinnacle, Kyla saw the dark war mage's face open with surprise — and then with utter terror. And then the spell broke, and the mage pointed her staff at the Tarn's Great Door, raw panic in her eyes.

"I see you, now," Kyla whispered.

And then she aimed.

58

"CAN YOU SING for me, Stormy? Can you sing?"

Little Dan's lilting question, high and true.

"Can you sing for me, Stormy? Can you sing?"

59

"IT WON'T *MATTER*, Ky!" Tarlen cried as Kyla readied to fire. "They'll butcher them!"

Kyla didn't answer, she just sighted down the barrel of her high silver carbine — her aim real and perfect and divine — and then she fired.

60

AND STORMHAMMER ANSWERED.

Stormhammer sang.

61

FOR COLJ, THE noise was catastrophic and, at the same time, accompanied by a strange, otherworldly silence, as if Storm-hammer had drawn all the planet's air into a mighty set of lungs – a strange swelling at the front of the gun, something growing in the air before it – then *blasted* it forth in a blinding column of pure-white dragon fire.

VOMMM!

The Pretender's great cannon on the southwestern head-lands vanished.

They were there – seven great guns on thick, timber embankments, golden-robed adepts singing their holy songs, great silver maws pointed to the sky, ready to fire, ready to destroy Anna and her dragon riders, the black-robed battle mage high behind them all – and then they were wiped away.

Gone.

Leaving nothing behind but a smoking channel in the earth,

black soil instantly flecked by the white of falling snow.

62

KYLA'S BULLET DIDN'T hit anything.

There was a silver-blinding flash, a flash like the sun, a thunderous noise like the end of everything, and the Tarn shook on its foundations.

She steadied herself, recovered her aim, readied to fire again, but there was nothing to hit.

There was nothing at which to aim.

Kyla blinked and took her weapon from her shoulder.

Filip, Sledder, and Tellerman were cheering like lunatics, hugging each other, pounding each other on the backs. Bruno barked like mad, smoky fur phasing grey. Even stoic Ponj ogre-hollered, thick ogre fists raised in triumph, the whole Tarn rising in song, in glory . . . in what?

In victory?

"What happened?" Kyla asked.

One thing was clear: The dark mage, her podium, the Pretender's great artillery placement, all were gone.

Blasted from existence.

From her vantage atop the Pinnacle, Kyla saw a scorched furrow some thirty paces wide running through the south-western headlands, through Tarntown itself, ending in a perfectly round hole in the foothills of the Rakbern Mountains, a hole through which she could see a pinpoint of daylight.

"Tarlen." She blinked wonderingly, pushed a lock of blond hair from her face. "Tarlen?"

Time came back into focus.

"What?" He said the word as if stunned, staring over Tarntown. Then he blinked, the full extent of the devastation dawning at last, realizing the number of homes and shops and streets and people that had been vaporized.

"What—?" he started.

Kyla swallowed.

Thousands of dead — *tens of thousands* — most of them civilians.

Who else has died along that path of destruction?

Tarlen blinked. "What did we do?"

Then Filip pointed. "Our dragons!"

Sledder screamed, "Burn 'em to *ash*!"

63

From the bridge, Colj watched Anna and her Davanórians drop upon the enemy's center, strafing dragon fire from hundreds of open jaws, the screams of the enemy rising like a wave. In moments, the center of Tarntown was an inferno of smoke and fire. Then Michael and his bear riders burst into view on the enemy's flank, driving toward the center. And then a cloud of thousands of messenger dragons swarmed from the Tarn's western rampart. It was Master Zar's scourge, an army of tiny dragons led by little Gregory, a murderous flock of tiny fangs and claws, sent to finish the enemy, the wounded, and the fleet-of-foot, to dissuade the fallen angels of Tarcéron.

And then began true slaughter.

At last, after two years of siege, Michael Dallanar and Anna Dyer had been unleashed.

Colj looked to the Great Door. There was Daniel. He stood at Stormhammer's side, one hand on the big gun, the mighty weapon floating, the cannon's great dragon maw seeming to pant like an enormous dog, loyal beside its little master. Daniel's eyes were wide open, unseeing. His knees wobbled. He was breathing hard, his other hand held out, palm up, turning, searching for enemies, the great gun turning freely, as if it weighed nothing, effortlessly joined to the little boy's gesture.

"We need to get back," Lady Katherine said.

Colj nodded. They moved toward the Great Door and the little warrior who protected it.

64

"THEY'RE COMING IN," Tarlen said. He pointed down at the Long Bridge. "Let's go."

Kyla nodded, then she looked to Filip, Sledder, and Tellerman. "Stay on station. Apply fire as needed."

But there was no need. For all practical purposes, the battle was over – the *siege* was over. And if she couldn't understand that fact from the scouts' beaming faces, then all she had to do was look out over the war field from whence the enemy ran. The enemy host – all of it – was fleeing Tarntown in headlong terror, the battle standards from a dozen duchies thrown to the ground and trampled, lines of men streaming away from the city. For Kyla, the enemy's terror was entirely justified; they were mercilessly pursued by Michael and Anna's forces, the two legendary warriors finally free to release their rage. And with no air support to defend them, with Daniel Eadle standing watch on the bridge ready to obliterate any threat, with Master Zar's army of tiny dragons swarming the headlands, there was nothing for the enemy to do but run like hell and pray.

But Kyla didn't think it would matter.

They wouldn't escape.

They couldn't escape.

None of them.

Michael and Anna would show no mercy. Already, most of Tarntown burned, smoke and screams rising while Michael and Anna sowed their carnage, the cries of the dying matched only by the howls of triumph from the Tarn, the great iron batteries ceaseless as they pounded the retreating armies, a constant accompaniment to the savage roars of war bears, the blasts of vengeful dragon fire.

Kyla paused, took a breath, and forced herself to examine her own feelings. She was relieved, she was horrified, she was elated — all at once. But behind it all, one burning question:

What does this day mean for peace?

"Come on," Tarlen said. "Let's go, Ky. What're you looking at? It's over. It's totally over."

Kyla nodded. "The battle, yes."

65

COLJ AND HIS squad of ogres approached Daniel. As he did, the boy turned toward them, one hand on Stormhammer, the great weapon swinging toward them, its dragon lips quivering around the vast hole that was its mouth. A low hum filled the air, the sound of barely restrained wrath. Daniel's eyes were open, but they were blank, like silver pearls. As he neared, Colj realized that the boy shook with effort, barely able to stand. Something was wrong with him. It was as if his muscles and tissue had been consumed by the effort. His little legs were skeletal sticks, even thinner than before. His arms were nothing but skin and bone. His neck was reed thin, as if it could barely support the weight of his head. Behind Daniel, Master Falmon helped Lord Doldon to his feet. Both men were shaken, barely able to stand; their noses were bloody, their eyes glazed. Stormhammer and Oblivion's lead adepts were dead, eyes burnt from their skulls, black scalps smoking ruins. Several of the flanking adepts had been crushed when the cannon fell, others did not stir.

Master Falmon coughed, then grunted when he saw Colj approach. "Gotta get some carriages out here." He adjusted his eye patch, touched the scar in his forehead, and leaned against Lord Doldon. Master Falmon looked from Daniel to Colj. "Right away, Captain. Carriages. He can't hold it but a few moments more. We're gonna need your boys to help lift Oblivion."

"Yes, Master Falmon," Colj said.

"Aye." Lord Doldon winced, then he grinned. "Get the carriages." Both their faces were dark with smoke, teeth white in wrinkled black faces. "Then Colj, if you can, maybe you can tell me what the blazes just happened."

66

KYLA, TARLEN, PONJ, and Bruno had made their way down to the High Square just as Colj was bringing Garen back into the Square from the Great Door. Kyla had been sure to retrieve

Susan on the way down; she'd sent Quine back up to the Pinnacle with his mates. And she'd kept Filip's high silver carbine. The ancient weapon was hers now, not received as a gift, but taken as a right.

"Dallanar! Dallanar!" The High Square thundered, the place swarming with men, women, children, soldiers, ogres, bears, everyone. Dallanar banners streamed high blue against the clean falling snow. The High Gate blazed with silver light. Every so often, a dragon squad would blast overhead, and the crowd would cheer and clap, crying, laughing, exultant. Coming in behind Colj, through the passages from the Great Door, Doldon, Falmon, Kate, and several big ogres rolled the mighty Stormhammer and Oblivion on carriages into the center of the Square. Soldiers kept dragging in the spoils from the Long Bridge, dead Legionnaires and Guardsmen clad in priceless high silver.

It had been an incredible victory, but the price had been high. In Colj's arms, Garen did not look well. Falmon carried Daniel; the little boy was unconscious and looked starved, near dead. And that did not count the innumerable corpses of soldiers, bears, ogres, and dragons outside the Tarn's walls, a body count that could only climb.

"Dallanar!" the High Square roared. "Dallanar!"

Everywhere around them, the mighty star trees seemed to sway with a kind of celebratory rhythm, their coppery leaves like tinkling bells. Kyla watched Garen open his eyes, touch at his spectacles, then say something to Colj. Colj frowned, set him down, and looked him over, top to bottom, as if inspecting a young athlete back from his first wrestling match. Garen looked up at Colj, said something, then steadied himself against the great ogre's arm. Colj gave Garen another long look, summoned a servant with some water, and shook his head. Kate was staying close to her brother, her high silver armor covered in blood. Then Kate looked around, saw Kyla and the rest, and waved them over. They didn't need encouragement. Susan and Bruno ran to them, straight through the crowd; Kyla, Tarlen, and Ponj followed.

"You're alive." Susan patted Garen's side. Then she paused, looked up at Colj. "Good job."

The soldiers around them laughed and shouted and lifted their weapons, slapping each other on the back, gathering around the High Family, the whole Tarn cheering with one voice, the citadel's mighty batteries still firing in the distance, the roar of dragons echoing the walls. "Dallanar! Dallanar!"

Once again, Kyla was confused by her own feelings. She was beyond relieved that Garen was safe, that the enemy had been driven from their gates. But, in the very same moment, she was haunted by the knowledge of the whole-sale slaughter that continued as the celebration ensued. The strange joy she had felt as she'd fired from the Pinnacle had been replaced by a cold hollow at her center. The mighty batteries of the Tarn still thundered, pounding their own city to dust; the distant roar of dragon fire was unmistakable, even over the closer cries of jubilation. Above her, on the towers, she could see her family's soldiers and artillery-men watch and point and cheer, no doubt as Michael and Anna continued their pitiless hunt. It was a bizarre mix of sounds and emotions and thoughts. Did it make her weak to pity the men and women whom Anna and Michael now butchered? Or did it make her strong? Had she herself not taken part in the battle with righteous zeal? Were these questions themselves not a luxury? She blinked and looked at her family. The soul-searching would have to wait. She hurried to Garen.

"You alright, Garen?" Kyla asked. Clearly, he was not. His eyes looked out of focus, and he kept trying to fix his spectacles, even though they were on perfectly straight. From the tower tops, from every window, high blue pennants and scarves and flags waved and swung, the Dallanar Sun flashing silver in winter's light.

"Dallanar! Dallanar!"

Garen looked at her. His eyes cleared. "The Cup."

Kyla frowned, shifted her new carbine from one elbow to the other. "Ruge had it. He must still have it, I think. I saw him take it with him."

Garen shook his head and seemed to go dizzy with the gesture. "No. You don't understand. Michael, he . . . ." He frowned. Doldon came up, gave Kate a sideways hug, winked at Tarlen and Ponj, then pounded Garen on the shoulder, nearly knocking him down. Doldon's face was black with smoke and grime, his eyes and teeth pure white. There was dried blood beneath his nose and ears, a slightly mad expression on his face. He shouted and smiled and pointed all around. Kyla couldn't hear half of what he said over the noise of the crowd, and she doubted whether Doldon could hear himself either. Even so, it was impossible not to smile at those crazy white teeth grinning in Doldon's dirty face. He said something about getting a drink, then laughed when three sloshing cups appeared before him, as if by magic.

"Need some help here," Master Falmon said hoarsely. His voice was soft, but everything seemed to go quiet. "Need some help."

He held Daniel to his chest. The little boy had become a strange, withered thing, like a skeleton, his large skull prominent, blue veins bright under translucent skin. He barely breathed.

Garen stepped toward them, steadying himself as he went, and knelt beside Daniel. He touched the boy's thin neck and wrists, looking for a heartbeat, peeling the boy's eyelids back to expose sightless silver orbs.

Garen looked at Doldon, then steadied himself against Falmon. "I have something that may stabilize him. But we must get him to the infirmary."

With a blast of wind, Moondagger landed above the High Square on a dragon perch. Everyone looked up and cheered.

Michael sat behind Anna in her dragon saddle, the blind drag-on's white wings wide, folding down as he settled. Michael leapt from the saddle, jumped to the perch's walkway, and slid down the brass pole into the Square. When he ran to the family, the crowd opened before him. He held the Vordan sheathed beneath its cross guard, the black blade singing sweetly, as if sated at last.

Kyla blinked.

As Michael approached, it was if a strange silence descend-ed in her own mind. It was as if the sounds of victory had been suddenly muffled, while the dark sword's song became clear-er. Michael didn't smile, but his eyes were wild and terribly bright. His black armor was covered in ash and blood. As he came to where Garen and Falmon knelt with Daniel, Michael nudged Kate aside, not noticing her, everyone pounding him on the back, all decorum forgotten. Michael knelt, touched Garen on the shoulder, and looked at Daniel.

"He did it," Michael said.

Garen nodded, still a bit groggy, and reached for his belt pouch, fishing for one of the countless vials he kept there. "It cost him."

"Never seen anything like it," Michael said. "It came right in front of us, about five hundred paces or so. You could *feel* the heat from where we were, even at that distance, it pushed us back." His eyes were bright. "This changes everything, you know."

Garen frowned and said nothing. He pulled a small vial from his pouch. The liquid within was thick and silvery-gold. He unstopped it and held it to Daniel's lips, tilting the contents gently into his mouth. The effect was immediate. The little boy took a deep breath. His eyes were still shut, but new color came into his cheeks.

And still, through all of this, the black sword sang in Kyla's mind.

Doldon tousled Tarlen's hair, called for more drink, and lifted Susan up so that she could see. Ponj was there next to Colj and the rest of the ogres. Bruno paced around Garen, sniffing at Daniel's feet.

"The Cup," Kyla asked. "What happened to the High Cup, Michael?"

Michael looked at her. His eyes went dark. The cheering seemed louder, but somehow — bizarrely — harder to hear.

In Kyla's ears, her own voice was more muffled than ever, farther away. Every sound was muted, save the Vordan's low, satisfied song. It sang there under the cheering, a dark melody, hauntingly familiar, an ancient tune long forgotten, just remembered, as if the sword sang for her and her alone.

"The Cup, Michael!" Kyla said again, louder. Garen looked from Daniel to Michael, and frowned. Falmon adjusted his eye patch, a strange expression on his smoke-covered face. Kate watched closely, as did Tarlen.

Michael ignored Kyla's question, instead looking up to the perch where Moondagger had landed, where Anna now dismounted. Doldon lifted his goblet and drank, clearly deafened, that crazy white smile beaming from his smoky face. He leaned down, put his hand to Garen's ear, and said something. Garen nodded but kept his attention on Kyla and Michael. In Falmon's arms, Daniel had started to open his eyes. Falmon cradled the boy's head in the crook of his elbow. Michael looked back at Kyla, then looked again toward Anna who was just sliding down the pole from Moondagger's perch. The crowd opened and Michael went to her. The sword's song rose. When Anna reached him in the Square's center, Michael lifted Anna's fist in victory, and the crowd went crazy. Moondagger roared his triumph to the sky. Michael and Anna walked back to the family, the Vordan's song going quiet. Michael took a saddle bag from Anna.

"Ruge had it!" Kyla stepped toward him, shouted at him over the cheering. "Do you have the High Cup? Do you know what happened?!"

Doldon stared at her blankly, then smiled, looking from her to Michael.

"What?!" Doldon shouted, his hand at his ear.

Kate stood behind him, listening intently.

Kyla shouted again at Michael. "The Cup!"

"Sure!" Doldon shouted. He grabbed a cup from a passing soldier and handed it to her, nodding madly, turning to kiss Susan on the cheek, raising his own cup. "We'll feast and drink tonight, dear niece!" Susan giggled. Kyla shook her head and handed the cup to a passing solider.

Michael opened the saddle bag he'd received from Anna. From it, he took the High Cup – in two pieces. The silvery bowl had been cleanly split, right down the middle, as if by a cleaver. The Vordan's crooning swelled. The Cup no longer glowed.

"Dallanar!" the crowd chanted. "Dallanar!"

Kyla stared at the Cup. Garen frowned. Kate's face had gone dead white.

"We tried!" Michael shouted over the celebration. He put his arm around Kyla's shoulder. She shook her head. He had destroyed it. Only the Vordan or a similar ancient blade could cleave high silver like that.

Garen stared at him. Kate frowned. Doldon looked confused. Behind Michael, Anna nodded. Her emotions were difficult to read.

"It's my fault!" Michael shouted over the crowd. He looked to Garen, then to Kyla. Michael wasn't smiling, but he wasn't upset either. His expression seemed strange, his frowning mouth failing to match the wild, dark light in his eyes. He shouted over the crowd. "Ruge dropped it! I didn't see him! One of Lessip's squires had it. Held it up like a shield as I rode him down. I didn't aim for it. An accident, but my fault."

Kyla frowned. Whatever memory, whatever vision the High Cup held, Michael wanted none of it.

So, he had destroyed it.

Kyla looked at Garen, saw the disappointment in his eyes. Kate looked like she'd been kicked in the gut. Two years with Dorómy on Paráden to retrieve that High Cup and the tale it contained — gone in a moment. In Kyla's head, the black blade's song seemed to become more enthusiastic, as if celebrating its own triumph. And, in a way, it was Michael's triumph as well. The crowd chanted and waved, but still, it was as if the sound was muted in Kyla's ears. Around her, things continued to slow. The sound of the crowd was almost gone. And then there was only the black blade's song. Kyla looked at Doldon and Michael. Then to Kate, to Falmon, to Colj and Ponj, to Tarlen and Susan.

They didn't hear it.

A song of victory.

A song of lies.

But none of them heard it.

Kyla shook her head. But still, her eyes were drawn to the Vordan. It seemed to sing to her and to her alone.

Come, child queen.

Like a forgotten whisper . . . .

Michael knelt beside Garen, Falmon, and Daniel. He held the pieces of the Cup out to Garen. Garen took it, blinked, put the pieces into his pouch, then turned back to Daniel. The little boy's eyes were open. The black sword's song rose higher. Doldon clapped Michael on the back; his grin was huge. Michael kissed Susan on the top of her head.

"I'm hungry!" Susan cried.

Doldon laughed. "Good idea! Let's get something to eat!"

Michael nodded and——.

A gunshot CRACKED! A woman screamed. There was a shout, and a flurry of movement across the first courtyard, near the passage to the Great Door; elsewhere the celebration continued, oblivious. Anna, Kate, and Michael stepped protectively in front of Garen and Daniel, looking around. Then a stocky Legionnaire in high silver armor was running, stumbling toward one of the giant star trees. Blood ran from her nose and ears. Her young face was haggard, her mouth a grim line. As she ran, she fired into the crowd behind her, downed a cheering spectator. Another shot. Another scream. Someone fell. In her hand, the Legionnaire held a small crystal vial. The vial held a measure of black liquid. Her eyes were set on the large star tree in front of her.

Michael was already moving, smooth and lethal. Anna was right behind him, her silver sword out, low as she ran, more like a lynx than a young woman, both trained from birth in the arts of war, eternal hunters.

"Michael, don't kill her!" Garen shouted, struggling to make himself heard. "We need her alive! She'll have information! Michael, no! We need her!"

Garen looked at Kyla, as if for help.

She nodded, turned, and shouted, "Michael! Don't kill her!"

Michael didn't respond.

And as he moved away, the Vordan's song grew even more urgent. The Legionnaire was almost at the star tree, stumbling and wounded, but still fast. Some infantrymen shot at her, potshots. A few pointed and laughed, drunk with triumph. They didn't see the vial the Legionnaire carried. Bullets bounced off the Legionnaire's high silver armor, ancient gear flashing white with reflected force. A pair of ogres near the star tree moved to intercept.

But they were too slow, Kyla realized.

Then Kyla looked from the black vial to the great star tree swaying near the wall, its delicate coppery leaves waving happily, a timeless, ancient being recruited to their cause, literally uprooted from its home to serve them . . . .

Before she knew what she was doing, Kyla lifted her carbine to her shoulder, sighted in on the Legionnaire's unprotected head.

The black blade's song was a howl.

Kyla didn't know how much longer she could stand it.

Then — just like that — the sword's song stopped.

It was as if Kyla had gone deaf.

Her finger moved to the trigger.

Michael threw the Vordan.

Pure silence.

Kyla didn't fire.

As the dark sword flew end over end, it was as if another image imposed itself over the black blade, the shape of a vulture-thing, a hunched beast with hooked wings, hissing fangs. The black beast hit the Legionnaire in the chest, just as the young woman reached the star tree's root crate, the creature pinning her to the crate's logs, the creature feasting, tearing out her throat, feeding on her neck, dark wings fanning air, its back hunching, convulsing. But the young soldier took no real wounds from the beast, at least none that Kyla could see. The black vial dropped harmlessly to the flagstones and broke.

"We must save anything we can from that vial," Garen said softly.

And then the Vordan screamed. It was the hideous shriek of a slavering carrion-eater. The young Legionnaire looked down at her chest where the Vordan had spiked her to the crate. Her face was pale. Her hands trembled; they went to her own throat, as if to protect it. Her head thrashed back and forth, hands clutching at her neck, pawing at the high silver collar there. And then Michael was at her side, leaning down, whispering something to her. The Legionnaire stared at him, as if in recognition. Then Michael jerked the sword from the young woman's chest and lopped her head off in one smooth motion, a jet of dark blood arcing into the snowy air. Michael turned and looked back at his family, his eyes black with madness, fury, and joy.

And still, somehow in Kyla's mind, everything was silent.

There was no noise.

People were moving and cheering and screaming, as if in slow motion.

But Kyla couldn't hear anything.

No crowd.

No Vordan.

Nothing.

Nothing at all.

Kyla blinked.

Great Sisters save us.

Michael strode back to her, to the family, his eyes glittering cold fire. A squire tossed him a rag. Michael caught it absently, wiped the black blade as he walked. The smooth black stone on the Vordan's pommel absorbed all light.

Michael slammed the blade into its sheath, and the noise of triumph roared back, euphoric screams, cheers, and celebration.

"Dallanar! Dallanar!"

"'Don't kill her?'" Michael snarled at Kyla as he passed. "What do you think this is?"

Kyla shook her head. "Garen wanted——."

But he ignored her. Beside Michael now, Anna said nothing.

Then Michael stopped, paused, and turned back to Kyla. The stench of blood on his black armor was overpowering; it was all she could do to keep from backing up as he walked up to her.

"We don't need to interrogate our enemies, Ky," Michael snarled. "We know what they want. We know what they've chosen." He pointed at the dead Legionnaire. "She *chose*. And after today, I will command the Kingdom's loyal hosts. No more questions, no more waiting, no more talking. Are we clear?"

Kyla tried to lift her chin, to meet his gaze, but the insane, barely restrained fury she saw in his eyes was so terrifying, all she could do was bow and say, "Yes, Michael."

Standing at Michael's elbow, Anna's expression was undecipherable. Michael gave Kyla one last look, then turned back to the rest of the family, leaning down at Falmon's side, checking on little Daniel.

Kyla blinked. She felt dizzy. Across the courtyard, the crowd had raised the Legionnaire's body over their heads, dancing and cheering around the star tree. Then they threw the body against the wall and began to strip the young woman's high silver armor. Behind Kyla, Doldon shouted something to one of his men, already on his third cup of wine. Tarlen looked at Kyla from his place at Ponj's elbow, a puzzled expression on his face. "Bring me the bottle, for the Sisters' sake!" Doldon laughed. Susan frowned. Kyla stared, confused by her own thoughts, the pinwheel of emotion swirling in her mind. Again, she was thrilled and sickened and miserable and happy, all at once.

Is this who we are now?

And then Kyla realized what was really missing here, what was really wrong: Grandpa and Nana.

The ultimate moment of triumph — and the High King and Queen are nowhere to be found?

Kyla stepped to Kate. "Where are Grandpa and Nana?"

"Dunno." Kate frowned. "They should be here."

Garen looked up at her question, then away, as if he knew the answer. Kyla frowned, then gestured at the celebrating crowd. "This was their doing. Their plan. You don't think it's strange—."

"Told you before." Kate took her hand, put her arm around her, and silenced her with a squeeze. "Never second-guess the maneuvers of the Silver Fox. Let's see how our new hero is doing." She moved toward Falmon and Daniel. Kyla hesitated. That dark itch at the back of her mind was worse than ever; then she followed.

67

When Little Dan opened his eyes, there were people all over the place. He was lying on the ground. He felt weak and dizzy, but Master Falmon was there holding his head, so that was nice. Lord Garen was there, too, and Lord Doldon and Captain Dyer and Lord Michael and Lady Kyla and Lady Katherine and all sorts of other highborn folks and a whole mess of ogres and bears and soldiers. That big grey dog was barking, and everyone was yelling — "Dallanar! Dallanar! Dallanar!" — cheering like crazy. Dan could still hear the guns firing from the walls, but they were real far away. The coppery trees were everywhere, too, swaying and tinkling. There was a huge white dragon up there on the top of a tower, stretching its white wings. Boy, was he thirsty! And tired, too.

"Gonna sleep like a baby tonight, for sure," he muttered.
"Yes, sir."

He didn't know exactly what had happened. But he knew he'd worked hard, that Stormy was alright, and that everyone seemed happy, so that must mean they'd done a good job. And even though he couldn't see him, Dan could still hear Stormy over there behind him somewhere, the big boy's song echoing inside his head.

"How're you feeling, Dan?" Master Falmon asked.

"Thirsty," Dan croaked.

"Water here!" Master Falmon ordered. Someone came with a cup. Dan drank, and it was so good. Then that big grey dog came up and licked his face sloppy wet. Master Falmon smiled down at him; it was a sad smile. The big dog licked his face again, from top to bottom.

"Ha-ha!" Dan laughed, but it kind of hurt to laugh, and it made him feel even more tired.

Lord Michael knelt next to Dan and put his hand on Dan's chest. Then he whispered something to Lord Garen and Master Falmon that Dan didn't really understand: "He changes everything, gentlemen." Then Lord Michael looked at Lord Garen, then over at Captain Dyer and the other ladies. "I'll pay any price to keep them safe. They'll not take one more. Not *one* more. Not when we have him." He patted Dan's chest.

Lord Garen frowned. Master Falmon bowed. Lord Michael got up and looked around at everybody.

"Where's Kate?" Lord Michael asked. "I saw her."

Captain Dyer pointed to Lady Katherine, who was standing there with Lady Kyla. Lady Katherine wore silver armor; Lady Kyla carried a long silver gun. Lady Katherine's eyes glowed. Her face was all sweaty from fighting, and there was blood on her armor. Dan waved at her, she waved back, then she and Lady Kyla came over. Lord Michael took a step toward them.

"Leave it be," Lord Garen said to Lord Michael's back. "You knew she'd go out, one way or another."

Lord Michael didn't reply to Lord Garen. Instead, he whispered to Lady Katherine, "You disobey me? You risk yourself in battle, in defiance of my command?"

Lady Katherine looked Lord Michael in the eye.

"Answer," Lord Michael hissed.

"We're all loyal, Michael." Lady Katherine gestured at the high lords and ladies around. "More important, we all love one another. It's always been so with our family. We've always cherished each other; we've always lifted each other up. *That* is our true strength, Michael. Our real power. It's a power that we all possess. I'm a warrior, the same as you. I love the Tarn, same as you. And I'm a part of this, same as you. Yes, I was gone. But now I'm back. And I'll protect what is ours as fiercely as you — as fiercely as anyone."

Lord Michael blinked, frowned, and then he looked at her for a long moment. Dan didn't really know what she'd meant by those words, but she'd said them real good. Then, all of a sudden, Lord Michael gave her a giant hug, lifted her up off the ground, and spun her around. She smiled, and everyone cheered. The big grey dog barked and all the high ladies and lords gathered around and started hugging. Lady Katherine was smiling so big, there were tears in her eyes, but they were happy tears. Master Falmon was holding Dan and patting his chest all gentle and that was nice, too. And then Lord Michael smiled and lifted his sword, and Lady

Katherine lifted her sword, too, and Lady Kyla lifted her gun, and Captain Dyer lifted her sword, and Lord Doldon lifted his cup, and everyone cheered for the High Family, all the soldiers and ogres yelling; the white dragon up there roared so loud.

Then Lord Michael looked down at him. Dan blinked and gave him a weak salute from where he lay. Lord Michael looked at Master Falmon and asked, "May I?"

Master Falmon helped Dan to his feet, but he was dizzy. All wobbly and tired, and his head felt like it wasn't on right; there was a funny taste in his mouth. He almost fell over, but Master Falmon steadied him and said, "Easy there, soldier." Dan nodded and took a deep breath and saluted, but it wasn't a good salute because his arms were *tired*, like floppy noodles. Lord Michael reached down, picked him up, and held him to his armored chest. Captain Dyer stood behind him. She looked kind of sad, but kind of happy, too. She stepped up and whispered in his ear, "You saved us today, Daniel. You saved us. You understand?" Then she kissed him on the cheek. The white dragon roared.

Dan nodded and tried to salute. "I'm a good soldier, lady.

I sure try my best . . . . Every day, for truth."

Lord Michael and Captain Dyer smiled, and everyone laughed around them, but it was a nice kind of laugh. And then, before Dan could say anything else, Lord Michael lifted Dan high above his head in one hand and roared like Dan had never heard before: "*DALLANAR! DALLANAR!*"

Everyone went wild. The ogres yelled, and the big white dragon spread its wings and roared again, all the soldiers shouting and holding onto each other, everyone hugging and jumping. Those big copper trees waved and made their pretty tinkling sounds. Little Dan wasn't sure what to do, so he just lifted his little fist and gave everyone a proper salute, and people went totally crazy-bonkers saluting back to him. Even though he was tired, it was still pretty darn nice to have everyone cheering together. Dan looked down at Master Falmon. Master Falmon had tears in his eyes, but they were the happy kind, for sure. Then Dan looked over at Stormy, and Stormy seemed to kind of smile at him, so Dan raised his little fist one more time and yelled as loud as he could, "For the Remain!"

"FOR THE REMAIN!" Everyone roared. "FOR THE REMAIN!"

So, Dan yelled it again and they all hollered and yelled like total crazies, and the big white dragon roared to the sky so loud. Then Lord Michael brought him down to his chest, looked at him, and said, "You're going to be with us now, Daniel. You're going to be here with us. We'll take care of you, and you won't have to worry about anything, alright?"

And then Captain Dyer, Lady Katherine, Lady Kyla, Captain Colj, Master Falmon, and everyone were all around them hugging. Captain Dyer kissed him on the cheek again and Dan's face went red, but he nodded and said to Lord Michael, "I'm a good worker, sir. You can count on me! I can do it! I'm a good soldier!"

"You are, Daniel." Lord Michael nodded. "The best we have."

THE THIRD NIGHT

68

FOR COLJ AND his ogres, for everyone, the celebrations lasted long into the night. They had lost adepts, they had lost dragons, and they had lost bears. But compared to the grievous damage done to the enemy, their honored war dead were but few. And much had been gained. An unprecedented victory. A new hope for peace — or at least hope for war's end here on Kon, for the time being. And, most important of all, the revelation of a young savant unlike anything seen in nearly two millennia. Truly, Colj mused, the wisdom of the Great Sisters still guided the Tarn's path.

Colj lifted his great cup to his lips. He rarely drank. He

seldom allowed his men the luxury, either. But tonight was different. Tonight was special. For the first time in years, they had something to celebrate.

Daniel Eadle had spent the rest of the day with Lord Garen in the infirmary. By sunset, however, both were feeling better, up and about, walking together with Master Falmon, slowly making the rounds, both a bit tender. The High Lords of the Tarn were presenting the young soldier to all the troops and the people. Celine Quay, the Captain of Lord Doldon's Guard, had made a victory wreath out of star tree leaves which Daniel proudly wore. The little boy was exhausted, but he also seemed to enjoy it. To every person he met — dragon rider or ogre, lady or lord, captain or commoner — he said the same thing: "We did a good job today, didn't we? Every day, there's a way! Yes, sir!" These words would be met by a solemn salute, a raised glass, friendly laughter, a loud cheer, or a combination thereof. Already, Daniel was the stuff of legend. Exactly as it should be.

Colj took another sip from his cup.

A good drink after a good fight.

There was really nothing quite like it.

"Captain Colj."

Colj turned. It was Lady Kyla, resplendent in a simple high blue dress of Eulorian silk. She carried a large folio of blue leather in her arms. "May I speak with you, Captain?"

"Of course, my Lady." Colj inclined his head. "How can I be of service?"

She walked him across the hall, to an antechamber free of revelers. There, she turned and looked up at him, her stance and posture formal.

"Captain Colj, Lord Michael commanded me to give you this as a sign of our appreciation and respect." She lifted the leather folio. "We owe you Lord Garen's life. A great debt. Lord Michael hopes this will go a small way toward repaying it. There will be many awards and honors bestowed in the coming weeks. He asked me to present this to you now, without delay, so that you might enjoy the fruits of your loyalty as soon as you are able."

She held the folio out to him.

Colj did not take it.

"What is it?" He inclined his huge head politely.

"Title and land in the Duchy of Jallow, Captain. To be

placed in your name and the name of your heirs in perpetuity. Also herein are documents that release you and your clan from their blood oath sworn ages past. Lord Michael would speak to you in detail about this tomorrow, if you are willing; he offers it now for your attention."

Colj considered for a long moment. It was significant, of course. And, depending on the precise contents of the folio, it would mean important things for young Ponj. Then Colj said, "The Lords of Remain are generous."

Lady Kyla looked at him thoughtfully. "They can be," she said. "But this is not generosity. This is justice. Long overdue."

She held out the folio to him once more.

He took it. "Thank you, my Lady."

"No." She shook her head. "We thank you, Lord Fellen Colj of Jallow."

Lord Garen approached, holding Daniel Eadle by the hand. The little warrior looked tired, but he still smiled. He wore a new doublet of blue Eulorian silk, a small Dallanar Sun embroidered in silver over the heart. He tugged at the doublet's bottom, as if the new clothes itched.

"Lady Kyla," Lord Garen said. "This young soldier is a little tired. It's been quite a day."

Lady Kyla smiled. "Your talent for understatement remains unmatched, Garen."

Lord Garen inclined his head. "I wonder if you might be willing to escort him to the family chambers. Jeremy's old room has been prepared."

"Of course. It would be my honor." Lady Kyla looked down at Daniel and smiled. "Shall we, young sir?"

Daniel smiled up at her; he looked so tired. "Ready to work, Lady. Yes, ready I be. You can count on me."

69

"And this is your room," Kyla said, swinging the door open. A servant had been up earlier to light the lamps, but the huge window's curtains were still shut.

Daniel looked up at her, blinked, craned his neck, and peered into the room – but he didn't move to enter. Kyla could understand his reticence. The little fellow was probably overwhelmed and exhausted. All this must be quite a change from what he was used to. And right then and there, she made up her mind to make him feel totally comfortable, entirely welcome, and completely at home.

So she stepped into the room, walked straight to the far wall, and pulled the blue velvet curtains open with a flourish, walking each curtain back to its place, moonlight streaming through the huge window, silver dust motes dancing, the room's wool rug glowing azure and green and blue with its vibrantly woven pictures of sea animals from across the Realm's oceans.

"This is your window, Daniel." She turned to him and smiled. "One of the best views in the Tarn. You can see out across the water and a bit up toward town, too. That's the Sea of Ice." She looked back out the window, gestured at the leaded glass, then turned and smiled at him again — but he hadn't moved from the doorway.

Actually, he seemed to have taken a step back.

"Just there. If you'd like to look? The moon is full tonight — beautiful." She gestured again and smiled. But he didn't budge.

"If you like, you can see the eastern breakwater — the mole, there — and a bit of Tarntown. Here's your seat. During the summer, you can see the ships sail into port." She patted the long bench below the window, then gestured at the three model ships sitting on the bench top, each of them a perfect replica of a famous vessel of the Tarn's summer navy, brilliantly painted in their proper colors, little wooden sailors ready to be walked about the decks. Dan blinked and kind of nodded, but still didn't move.

"And this is your library." She gestured below the window to the shelf built beneath the bench. The shelf was made of polished Anorian oak and packed with leather-bound books, gilt titles shimmering in the moonlight. Kyla touched the books. "All kinds of stories and pictures from across the Kingdom that you can read. And look at this." She withdrew a volume bound in luxurious Abúcian hide, dyed blue, the Dallanar Sun emblazoned silver on its spine. "This is your copy of the Silver Book, the Canon of Tarn, Dan." She paged through it, nostalgia touching her heart, the old pictures taking her back in time. "It used to be my uncle Jeremy's, of course, James's twin – but now it's yours. Not all the stories are here, of course. But there are amazing pictures. Would you like to see them? There are other books here that you can look through, too, if you like."

From the doorway, Dan stared at her with tired eyes and nodded, understanding seeming to come at last — thank the Sisters! — but also kind of biting at his lips, a strange look on his face, kind of like he was nervous. But no, that wasn't it. It was like he understood, but also like he didn't know what to do.

Or was he afraid?

She couldn't tell.

In fact, Kyla realized, she couldn't really read his face at all. She put the book back, gave him her gentlest, and most winning smile, and turned determinedly to the rest of the room.

"This." She touched the bronze-bound chest in the corner. "You'll like this, Dan. This is your toy box. Do you like toys?" She opened the chest — turning the false lock twice to the right and once to the left, then flipping the real latch on the chest's side. "It has a secret lock, see here?" She patted the side. "Only *you* can open it. And inside, all these amazing toys from all over the Kingdom." She reached into the chest and pulled out a wooden soldier about a palm tall, an ogre from Jallow, carefully carved and perfectly painted in every detail. She held it up to Dan. "This looks like Captain Colj, doesn't it? Look at his fangs and his armor. Just like him, huh? His arms move, and he can hold different weapons and things. There's a whole squad of little ogres in here for you, if you want to see?" She hopped the little ogre up and down, then growled in a deep voice, "For the Remain!" And immediately felt a little silly.

Dan nodded and tried to smile. He was so sleepy, but he was getting it at last, she saw with relief. At the same time, however, his gesture was perfunctory, like he was obligated to agree with everything she said. He was holding the front of his new doublet with both hands, clenching the fabric in his little fists. He still looked at her, but every once and a while he'd look around the room, then glance back down the hallway, like he was looking for something. That strange, nervous expression on his face was becoming more pronounced — but he was still nodding, still agreeing with everything she said.

It was late.

Perhaps he just needed a good night's sleep?

Great Sisters knew *she* did.

"And this——." She stepped away from the toy chest and hopped onto the bed. It was covered with a thick white bear's skin. She patted the spot beside her patiently. "——this is *your* bed."

The bed was the perfect size for a boy his age, its pale korom's wood headboard intricately engraved with naval battle scenes, framed by aquatic creatures. From each of the bed's four posts, the silvery smooth head of a porpoise flowed up from carved water as if diving over the bed, perfectly rendered, their porpoise eyes wide as they jumped, leaping over their sleeping charge. The top of the headboard was carved as a silver sea dragon, its wings spread over endless waves. She touched the dragon's claw. "Kind of like Moondagger, see?" She gestured at the carved porpoises. "And they'll watch over you as you sleep. And this dragon here." She gestured back at the dragon. "You can rub his nose and tell him what time you want to get up in the morning, and he'll wake you. This wood is very old. Ancient scholarship. They call it 'korom's wood.' An ancient master crafted this bed long ago for a little boy to sleep in, just like you. Do you want to come and try it? Be sure you like it?"

He'd taken a step forward and was almost inside the room now. That strange expression was still on his face, but now he seemed to be frowning, too. Nodding but frowning. He kept looking back down the hall. His frown deepened, his brow wrinkling, swaying a little bit now, as if he was having a hard time standing up.

"You can come in, Dan." She smiled patiently, resolute not to give up. "This is *your* place. That door over there is for your toilet, and there's another room through there for you to take your bath – you share that one with James. This was his brother's room a long time ago. And that door there." She pointed. "That's a closet with your clothes."

His eyes moved over both the doors, he nodded, but his frown went even deeper. Then he yawned and muttered something that she couldn't understand.

She walked over to the closet and opened it. Inside, neatly lined outfits perfectly tailored for a boy his age hung on polished hangers. They might take a little adjustment, to be sure – but the quality was the very best in the Realm. She didn't think that Dan would care that they had been Jeremy's before, but maybe he'd like to see how nice they were? Surely, he could appreciate the fine material and the colors. She gestured at the rows of hanging clothes. "All for you, Dan."

Dan nodded, then looked at his feet and mumbled something again, shrugged, pulled at the front of his new doublet.

Kyla closed the closet door firmly, walked across the room, knelt on the floor in front of him, took his hands in hers, and tried to look into his eyes.

He wouldn't look at her.

"This is your room, Dan. *Yours*. Do you understand?" She squeezed his little hands. They were so small. And scarred, she realized. Old and new cuts overlapping, a scab on the knuckle of his little index finger. "This is where you'll be now. Up here, with us. With me and my brothers and sisters, right next to James, when he returns." She gestured back into the room. "This is your place."

He nodded, still looking at the floor, muttering.

Gently, she touched his chin with one hand, lifting his eyes to hers.

His eyes were glassy with fatigue, the skin around them marked by old bruises. He was trying not to cry, she realized.

Biting his tongue to keep the tears away. Trying to be strong, to be tough, to be a soldier.

"This is your place, Dan." She nodded again, her throat starting to go thick. "*Your* place." She touched his chest.

". . . my box." He nodded, stammering. Then, as if remembering himself, he cleared his throat and saluted. "Yes, Lady Kyla. I can do it. Yes . . . yes, Lady. I can. Sorry, Lady. Every day, there's a way. But . . . but—." He shook his head. "I need my *box*."

"Your box?" She held his shoulders gently, nodding, smiling, encouraging him to continue.

"My box? My – uh, my tools? In my box. Yes, Lady Kyla. My toolbox."

"Your things? Oh, of course." She smiled and laughed and wiped her eyes. "Of course! Of course, Dan. I'll send for your things right away. First thing tomorrow morning. First thing, that's a promise."

Dan nodded, kind of smiled, nodded again, then frowned and looked at the floor. "I do a good job. You'll see, Lady." He looked up at her and grinned. He was missing a front tooth. His smile was pure. "You'll see. I do good. *Real* good for you, Lady. Just need my box, *then* I can start."

Kyla grinned back at him — and stopped short, the truth coming at last, a punch to the heart.

She took a deep breath, held him by the shoulders, and looked into his eyes. "Dan, I want you to listen to me. You don't work here. You don't clean here. You *live* here. With us. With me. We're your family now. You're my new, most favorite cousin. You don't work here, understand? You live here. You live here *with* us."

He blinked, frowned, shook his head, so tired, his face screwing up with confusion, almost desperation. "B-but I do a *good* job, Lady. I'm a *good* worker. All the pals know . . . . For . . . for truth . . . ." He cast around, yawned, then saluted out of the force of habit. "I get my box, Lady. If I——. I get my box and you — you'll see. Yes, ma'am. Please. I'm sorry. I'm a good worker. I'm good."

And then she was holding him to her heart, holding him so tight she could barely breathe, her arms around him, kissing the top of his head, tears hot in her throat and eyes. "You *are* good, Dan. You're perfect."

70

KYLA INTRODUCED DAN to his servant — which took another quarter bell to explain — and had another servant go fetch his box — which, upon arrival, turned out to be a half-broken piece of junk packed with rubbish, which Dan promptly hugged and shoved into bed beside his pillow, the happiest smile on his face. The box was home, she realized. And now that it was here, he understood. He was amazed and over-whelmed and exhausted, but he understood.

And he was irresistible, she realized. He never lied, he never spoke an unkind word, and his simple, missing-toothed smile was joy. She stayed the entire time the servants were getting him situated, then dismissed them, and tucked him into bed.

"I see you tomorrow, right, Lady?" he asked, fresh covers pulled tight under his chin.

She kissed him on the forehead. He smelled like clean soap and little boy. "Of course, we'll have breakfast together with everyone and then I'm sure you'll be starting on your lessons with Garen and the other tutors."

"Lessons? What's 'lessons?'"

She smiled. "You'll have teachers, and they'll show you things. You'll work on your reading and your writing and your numbers and your history, logic, weapons, everything — all kinds of wonderful things."

"I'm a good worker," he nodded, eyes drooping. Then he gave a giant yawn.

It was infectious, and she yawned herself, the length of the day coming on at last.

"Yes, you are, Dan." She smiled and touched his cheek.

"This is the nicest bed there is, in the whole world . . . for truth . . . ."

He slept.

And it was time for her to do the same.

She blew out the lamp, made sure the little safety lantern was lit in the toilet in case he needed to go in the night, and left for her own quarters just a little way down the hall. Bruno was there, as always, snoring away on the foot of her bed, upside down, his floppy jowls wide, one eye peeking open as she entered. Her bed beckoned, and it took all her willpower to actually undress before crawling into those cool, clean covers. Bruno wiggled his furry warmth against her feet, the last thing she felt before sleep took her into sweet darkness.

71

KYLA WOKE AT the sound, at the knocking, and reached for Bruno, but the cloud mastiff had already shifted silently from her bed, blinking across the room to appear at her bedroom door, his fur shimmering like magical fog. He didn't growl, but his ears and posture showed he was on highest alert.

The knock came again, a soft rapping.

Kyla blinked, reached for the dagger beneath her pillow, and glanced at the clock beside her bed. Pale moonlight reflected its dials: three bells after midnight.

Bruno sniffed at the bottom of the door, his stumpy tail moving now, back and forth — back and forth. He knew who it was.

Kyla pushed the covers away, slipped on her robe, and slipped her feet into her house shoes. She lit the lamp beside the bed and walked to the door, her dagger held pommel down, the blade following the line of her forearm. She listened for a moment, hand on the latch, looked again at Bruno's moving tail to be sure, then cracked the door. Bruno promptly shoved his fat head into the gap, stumpy tail wagging now.

It was Nordo Ness.

Kyla's eyebrows went up. "Lord Librarian?"

"My Lady." Ness bowed formally. He was an ancient man, stooped and wispy-haired, grey skin pulled snug over old bones, leaning, as always, on his crooked walking stick. He now wore a faded blue robe and cowl, the wool clean but threadbare, smelling of cloves and mint tea. A strange scar ran between his dark eyes, from the middle of his forehead to the bridge of his nose. While the old scholar's commitment to the Tarn's collections was legendary, it was also known that he performed other tasks, special errands for the High King and Queen . . . .

"It's late, Lord Librarian." Kyla looked at him pointedly, breathing deeply, focusing on her breath, holding at bay that nagging suspicion, that lurking sense of dread.

"That it is, my Lady." Ness nodded. He scratched Bruno's back as the big mastiff snuffled around his feet. Then he looked her in the eye. "The High King has asked for you."

"Of course." She nodded.

At last.

"Bruno is invited, as well." Ness leaned over a bit, put most of his weight on his walking stick, and scratched the mastiff behind his floppy ears. Bruno closed his eyes, savoring the attention, jowls glistening.

"Very well," Kyla said. "Give me a moment."

Ness bowed.

She shut the door, quickly dressed in practical pants and a tunic, then belted her dagger to her waist. Before she returned to the door, she opened the small box on her night-stand, took from it a plain silver ring – a gift from Nana – and slipped it on the index finger of her right hand. The ring wasn't a ring. It was an ancient golem that only looked like a ring, just like Garen's future-speaking silver bird only looked like a bird. With the right touch, the ring-golem would shape a small needle from itself, a needle laced with a deadly vari-ety of Marsinion poison that had been woven into its essence millennia past. When the needle was out, Kyla could kill with the touch of her hand.

72

BRUNO LEADING THE way, old Ness's stick ticking the pavers, they walked down the hallway, past Daniel's new bedroom, up a short flight of stairs, past Tarlen and Susan's quarters, up another flight of steps, finally past a junction guarded by two of Colj's ogres. There, a short hallway led to a bronze gate that marked the entrance to the royal apartments. Two Targead assassins, wearing the traditional golden robes of their duchy, stood on either side of the gate. Their fingers were steepled in front of their chests, fingertips just touching. Their skin was tan, a color that perfectly complimented the collars of gilded bronze they wore at their necks. Each was armed with a falchion of high silver belted at the waist and a high silver revolver slung across the chest in typical Targead fashion. The assassins' golden robes were wrapped tightly around their limbs, ready for instant action. Their eyes were bright and vigilant.

Ness stopped and asked one of the Targeads, "Has Lady Katherine arrived?"

"Yes, my Lord," the assassin answered. His accent was thick. He looked at them, then at Bruno. "Just a moment ago. She asked the same of you."

Ness nodded. The Targead opened the gate. They stepped through, walked down a long hallway, up a final flight of stairs. Another pair of Targeads waited at the top of this staircase, at the edge of the foyer just outside the door of the royal bedchamber.

Kate stood at the foyer, talking quietly with the taller of the two assassins, waiting. She wore a jerkin and pants of blue Abúcian hide. A leather messenger bag was slung over her shoulder. It looked like she was ready for travel. Kate didn't smile as they approached, but she did give Bruno a good thump on the side when he trotted up to her.

What was all this? Kyla frowned.

"Lady Katherine." Ness bowed.

Kate nodded, then looked at Kyla, stepped forward, and hugged her. When she stepped back, her face was deadly earnest. The Targead assassins looked on with merciless eyes.

Something was wrong.

The cold in Kyla's hands threatened, but she took a breath, allowing her trained awareness to unfold.

Kate had been gone two years, and she'd changed, that much Kyla had already seen. But now, here — in the middle of the night, standing outside the royal bedchamber waiting for only the Sisters knew what — Kyla was finally able to put her finger on the precise nature of the difference: Kate looked *worn*. It wasn't just that she was older. It was as if ten years had passed, not two. Indeed, Kate's face, posture, movements, her entire presence, was more precise, tighter — and tired.

Kate took Kyla's hands in her own and looked her in the eye. "Everything you see and hear beyond this door must be held in the closest confidence, Ky."

There was something wrong with Kate's voice, Kyla realized.

"Not a word," Kate continued. "Not to anyone. Do you understand?"

"Of course." Kyla lifted her chin and pressed her heels together, unconsciously standing at attention, meeting Kate's gaze. Her whole body was freezing. Bruno leaned hard against her knee.

"The High Queen is dead." Kate cleared her throat. "My

mother is dead."

The bottom dropped from Kyla's stomach.

Her breath caught in her throat.

Her gut clenched, and she felt her mouth begin to open.

Bruno growled.

On their own accord, as if the icy tremors had never left her, her hands began to shake.

"What—?" Kyla began.

Kate continued without pause, squeezing her hands, her eyes glowing with a strange mix of unspeakable sorrow and barely suppressed rage. "High Lady Adara Dallanar is gone, Great Sisters sing her praise. Assassinated one week ago. Nobody knows, Ky. The family, the inner circle, they all know, of course. But no one else. It must stay that way. The next months will see the end of all this." Kate lifted her chin at the hallway's walls, at the Targead assassins. "The end of the killing, this war – all of it. But until then, no one else can know." She looked at Kyla directly. "*Nobody*."

Kyla nodded, her head spun with disbelief and sadness, a strange taste rising in her mouth, copper and ash.

Her legs felt weak.

Impossible.

Nana?

How could she be gone?

And yet everything became perfectly clear.

That strangeness she had sensed in Michael, in Anna, in Garen, in Falmon, in Colj – in all of them this last week. The odd glances. The sudden silences. That feeling that they were hiding something, that the world had ended, it now made perfect sense.

Because they *had* been hiding something.

The world *had* ended.

The High Queen was dead.

She'd been dead for a week.

Kyla's head spun faster. She reached for Bruno. He leaned harder into her leg.

And they couldn't tell her.

They wouldn't tell her.

And it was Michael's doing.

Of that, Kyla was certain. "Give her time," she could almost hear him say. "She was Nana's favorite." But more specifically, he'd point to her age. She was only fourteen.

She hadn't completed her rites of passage. Legally, Kyla was still a child and thus not to be trusted — at least that would be his excuse. The truth was that when Kyla turned sixteen, Michael knew she'd be a threat to his plans and his ambition. She could never challenge his claim as heir, of course. But there were other ways to resist. So he isolated her now, planted those seeds of doubt . . . .

My family is killing itself.

Kyla blinked, tried to take a normal breath, and willed her training to come. Kate cleared her throat, squeezed Kyla's hands, then cocked her head at the door of the royal bedchamber.

"If our allies hear of the Queen's death, if others learn, peace will be impossible—."

"'Peace?'" Kyla whispered, words tumbling out. "What 'peace?' The High Queen is *slain*. Nana is dead." Her voice hitched. "This morning, they tried to kill Garen, to kill us all. Hundreds of our soldiers and riders and dragons are dead. To say nothing of the uncounted thousands — tens of thousands — that Anna and Michael and Daniel slaughtered today. You think Dorómy and his commanders — Lessip, Serán, Ruge,

Taverly, the others — you think they'll consider another parley after a child annihilates their entire army? You *know* what they're thinking, Kate. 'The Silver Fox has played us all, yet again.' Can't you hear Lessip say it? 'The ultimate trick.' That's what they think. This whole time, we've had a hidden ace up our sleeve, an asset of legendary power, a prodigy, a savant that the Silver Fox had been waiting to deploy, parley nothing more than a trap, baited for our enemies." Kyla shook her head. "Jared Ruge was killed on the Long Bridge, Kate. I saw him die. And Marden Julane, Eleanor's uncle. Dead. How many other Legionnaires and Guardsmen did Michael and Anna and their men kill today? How many high-born officers were lost? *'Peace?'* Yes, we must try; I know we must, but . . . ." Kyla shook her head. Her face flushed, tears threatening to blur her vision, her head spinning. "But *how*? How can we—?"

"Be quiet," Kate said softly and squeezed her hands again.

Kyla shut her mouth. Bruno growled at her side, worried.

"The High King waits." Kate cleared her throat. "We were summoned to receive his orders. We must trust in him, as we always have, especially now."

Kyla swallowed, nodded, and breathed. She willed her training to come — but it was hard. So hard.

The High King has orders.

Kate shook her head and looked at her closely. "Father is tired, still weak from his wounds." Kate looked at Ness. "Is that not so?" Ness nodded. Kate continued. "There's no time, Ky." She cleared her throat and lifted her chin. "We'll mourn later. Now, we act. And we obey. For our family. For the Remain."

But there was something else behind Kate's words.

It wasn't just that Kate spoke these words to herself, that she sought solace in duty . . . .

"You yourself haven't seen him yet," Kyla breathed, knowing it was the truth the moment she'd said it. "Since you returned, Kate. He wouldn't see you. Or couldn't. And there's been no time. Not with parley, not with everything that's happened. When we saw you in the library, you'd only just returned, and parley was less than a sunrise away. You don't know what this meeting is about." She inclined her head at the door to the royal bedchamber. "You don't know what he wants."

Kate nodded. "I know that he wants us, Kyla. More specifically: He wants you."

73

THE ROYAL BEDCHAMBER was warm, its ceiling low and comforting. In the left wall, the chamber's huge fireplace lit the room with a steady, orange glow. Colossal pillars squatted in each of the room's four corners, monoliths set deep within layers of ancient masonry. The pillars were some of the oldest elements in the fortress, Kyla knew, erected by some Konungur monarch millennia past on a holy site near the peak of the world's great mountain, Aaryn's Cry. During the Founding, it was said that the Great Sister Aaryn herself had ordered the pillars be taken from the mountain top, moved into the throne room of the Tarn — her new imperial fortress — as symbols of her power. Some centuries later, the great stones had been moved here, when this room had served as the private audience chamber for Katherine the Second, the pillars once again serving as symbolic testament to the Tarn's strength. Indeed, it sometimes felt to Kyla as if the royal bedchamber and these enormous stones held the weight of the entire Kingdom on their shoulders.

"Lady Kate. Lady Kyla," a hoarse voice croaked from inside the bedchamber. Kyla looked past Kate as they stepped forward.

The voice belonged to old Gart, Grandpa's steward. The old man sat beside the royal bed in a fur-covered chair. As they approached, Gart put his finger to his scarred lips – shushing them – cocking his head at the bed where Grandpa slept, snoring softly. Gart was a short man, but stocky, his thick arms covered in tattoos and scars. Most of his right ear was missing, lost years ago when he'd rescued a pair of youngsters, Bellános and Dorómy Dallanar, from a gang of Konungur poachers up past Korfort. Gart had aimed his chair at the door. He held a high silver pistol in his lap. An ancient dagger rested on the bedtable beside him. His right hand and wrist were set in a plaster cast.

Sorrow swelled once more in Kyla's throat, but she pushed it back.

Four Targead assassins stood guard in the hall, yet still old Gart watched over his Lord and Master, watched over his dearest friend.

Kate stepped closer. Kyla followed. Gart made a move to get up, but Kate gestured for him to stay.

Kyla realized that Gart had pulled everything – all the room's furnishings, the bearskin, the chair, Grandpa's night table, the royal bed itself – all closer to the fireplace. A clay pitcher and mug rested on the bedtable next to an ivory statuette of the Great Sister Aaryn. Grandpa's sketch book and his copy of the Tarn's Canon were there also, several pages marked in both. The bearskin rug faced the fire, the flames warming the bear's dark nose, his eyes closed as if in peaceful dreams.

Kate took off her boots, stepped across the bearskin, and knelt before the High King's dearest servant. Kyla did the same.

"Gart." Kate took the pistol from him, placed it on the bedtable, and held his uninjured hand in hers. Gart looked at her, then he turned his eyes to Kyla. Kyla placed her own hand on top of Kate's. Bruno sat at Gart's side, nuzzling the old man's knee. Ness stood in the door's shadow, a silent witness.

"I tried my best to help, Ladies," Gart said. His voice was

raw. He cleared his throat and raised his chin, but he didn't look at their faces. His voice wavered. He pressed his lips together, glanced at the statuette of Aaryn, then back down at his lap. "Great Sisters know I did. But they killed her."

Gart withdrew his hand from theirs. He took the pistol from the bedtable and held it to his chest.

It was Nana's gun, Kyla realized.

There was a jagged bruise on the left side of Gart's face, near his temple. Kyla hadn't noticed it until now. The bruise was greenish-yellow.

About a week old.

Gart looked away from them, into the fireplace. "I tried my best," he whispered to the flames. "So did Lily. Good old Lily girl, best dog we ever had." He closed his eyes. "We tried so hard; we did." He absently patted Bruno's head. "Didn't make no difference."

"Can you tell us?" Kate asked, her voice strangely monotone.

Gart nodded and cleared his throat. "They'd gotten in here somehow, see? Killers. Used old magic, for sure. Pendants, must've been. But even so, we don't know how so *many* got in at once. But they did, all dressed in black. Good Lily, she was sleeping there by the fire, snoring away like she did. She knew something was wrong right away. She gave a loud bark, and I came running, and they hit me and knocked me down. I saw them moving around the bed there. Didn't hit me hard. Stupid old man, not even worth killing. Lily already got two of 'em, blinked and tore their throats out. The Queen had killed another one, already. But I could see it in their eyes, both Lily's and the Queen's. They knew they couldn't save him. They were both trying their best, fighting so hard. This way and that Lily went, shifting as best she could, fur like lightning clouds. She'd go to one of them, then the other, biting and trying to get in the way. The Queen was the same. She was like an angel of death, spinning, daggers like liquid silver, painting the walls with blood. But they're both older, see? They fought, killed so many, but there were *more* than that. If it had been twenty years ago . . . if Bruno had been here." He patted Bruno's big mastiff head. "Might've been different."

"I tried to get up, but one of 'em had his cursed foot on my back. I couldn't move. Lily and the Queen, they were fighting. But there were just too many. The King, he was already up when I come in. Standing in the middle of the bed, he was, Lily and the Queen in front of him. They were all around, maybe a dozen in all, coming at him from all sides, silver daggers and swords. The King must've shot one or two of them himself, a few moments after they arrived. He was probably up and firing at Lily's first bark, just like the Queen — you know how he was in a fight." Gart glanced at Ness. "He was young again, blazing away, that calmness in his eyes, cursed jackals dropping at his feet, the Queen leaping to protect him from every side, she must have taken another two or three in those next moments. Never seen anything so fast. Her blades, they glowed with her speed — but she didn't have this." He clutched Nana's gun to his chest. "And then they just *mobbed* them. The King, he got another one with his gun, then another one with his blade, but then they changed tactics. A bunch of 'em went after the Queen. Lily shifted right in front of her, just like a good dog, took the first knife in her side. I could tell by her breathing they'd got Lily in the lungs. Good dog, didn't howl, just leaned into it and bit at the man, got his arm, nearly tore it off. Queen threw her knife, caught him in the jaw, still trying to protect the King. Then a big one came up, clubbed Lily on her head. I could see Lily's fur starting to mist, getting ready to shift out, to get him, I could see the Queen trying to move, too . . . but then Lily pushed her back, to protect her. She almost shifted to kill the man, see? But then it was as if she remembered that she couldn't leave the Queen. Good Lily. She was bleeding from her nose and her ears. The Queen was bleeding, too. And then they stabbed Lily again, her fur was covered in blood. And good Lily, she just leans back, and they keep stabbing and stabbing. She didn't even try to bite, after that. She was bad hurt, I could tell. She knew. They were trying to get the King now, they were trying, but Lily and the Queen kept getting in the way. Then one of them got past them; he hit the King and knocked him out. Then they just swarmed on top of them, Great Sisters curse me. I couldn't see what was happening. But I could hear. Great Sisters curse me, I could *hear* it, hear them stabbing the Queen, stabbing Lily, still trying to get at the King, those two dying for him, trying to give him a few more moments for help to come . . . ."

Out of nowhere, Kate grabbed Kyla's hand and squeezed

it, squeezed so hard.

But Kyla could barely feel it.

She could barely see, her eyes hazed by hot tears, her throat thick, the crazy spinning in her head threatening everything with madness, a fury near overpowering.

"Then I hear this voice," Gart continued. "– this cursed *voice*. Couldn't hear what he was saying. But I could hear his voice. I could hear Lily wheezing, and I could hear this cursed voice whispering to the Queen. She could barely breathe herself. The voice asking her something. Couldn't hear the words." Gart looked up at Kate. "Then your mom, she said something in that quiet way of hers, talked to him, for a long moment, but I could tell by her voice she was dying—."

Gart stopped, swallowed, looked from Kate to Kyla.

"The voice said something – and then, oh Great Sisters curse me, the bastard cut her throat."

Gart dropped the pistol to his lap and covered his face with his good hand, shuddering.

"I could hear the Queen gasping – Sisters forgive me. I could hear our guards coming up. Too late. It was already over. They'd killed her, they'd tried for him, but they'd killed her and her mastiff. The one standing on me, he stomped my hand." He lifted his cast. "Then he ran. Guards broke down the door. The killers all ran over there." He lifted his chin toward the eastern antechamber. "And then they were gone the same way they came in. Ancient magic – High Pendants, for sure, but we don't know how they got so *many* in here." He looked at Ness for a moment. "Either way, they left more than half their number dead behind. I got up and went to the bed. The guards came in. Blood was everywhere. But the King, the King was breathing. They'd hurt him bad, hit him hard, blood all over his head, but they hadn't managed to kill him. He was still breathing. He couldn't see. And his hand kept patting at the bedclothes. He found the Queen's hand, and he touched it and said something like 'There, there' – just like that, like everything was just fine. He thought the guards and Lily had saved them, see? He didn't know she was gone. He didn't know. He just kept patting her hand. 'There, there.' They fought so hard. The Queen, Lily, they tried so hard." Gart bowed his head and seemed to cave in on himself. "I can't believe it——." Then he looked up at them, his eyes bright with misery. "I am to blame. *I* am——. Stupid,

useless old fool. Forgive me, Ladies. Forgive useless Gart."
He closed his eyes, tilted his head back, and let out a strange
noise, a kind of sob.

Kate was squeezing Kyla's hand so hard, but even so, Kyla
still couldn't feel it. She was dizzy. Her head spun, the images
coming again and again and again. She could see it – but she
didn't want to see it. She closed her eyes, tears still coming.
Her throat was hot; she could barely breathe. And the rage .
. . the unquenchable rage.

Gart cleared his throat and looked up at them. "Lord
Michael, he went mad, by the Sisters he did. Michael had
brought the Vordan home to the Tarn five years ago. But the
King and Master Falmon always kept it locked up. Michael
would use it for sorties, for missions. But he would always
bring it back down to Falmon when he'd return from the
field and Falmon, he'd lock it back up. Michael was up here
only a moment after the guards. He took one look, he saw
his mom lying there, saw Lily on her lap, his dad holding her
hand, blood everywhere – and he went *mad*, I tell you. He
went to Falmon, took the Vordan and the key to the blade's
vault. Falmon didn't dare oppose him. Not even Master

Falmon. Who would dare, I ask you?

"Then Michael went to the stables, had Okros and the rest of the war bears clad in their best armor. He went into the pen with great Okros, talking to him, talking to him for a long time, for bells it seemed. The Vordan was in there with them, whispering its black whispers. And the more Michael talked to that great bear, the more enraged Okros became. It was black death in that pen, I tell you. Garen and Colj and Anna — they all went down, tried to talk to him, to get him to come back, to talk to the King. Michael wouldn't speak to them. Told Garen to get out, to get out and tend the King's wounds. Told Anna to prepare the Davanórians for action, same for Colj and his ogres. But Colj and Anna, they refused — on account of the High King's command. The King had ordered them to stand down. They had words, horrible words.

"So, Michael went out with his bear riders alone, two full companies. All of them in disguise. No marks, no flags. Supposed to look like a rogue sortie by one of our allies. But how could it, with the Vordan screaming for blood? They left through the deep catacombs, undersea. Came up on the far side of Tarntown, on the other side of the mountains, came in from that way, killing everything in sight. And not just soldiers. They won't say it, but it's true. Nobody will say it. Anyone who stood in his way – man, woman, child, merchant, soldier, friend, or foe. Our people, theirs – didn't matter."

Gart looked from Kate to Kyla. "He killed our people out there, Ladies. Michael cared not. He was *insane*, I tell you. He killed his way through town, through to the Pretender King's center. The Vordan was screaming. All of them were screaming – Okros, the war bears, the riders, Michael, everyone. Everyone here in the Tarn heard the sounds of battle, but they didn't know what was happening, nothing had been planned, and they saw no flag or standard of the Tarn. The enemy was trying to sight their big iron on Michael from the ridges, turn the guns on the headlands around, but Michael and his men were moving too fast, the enemy blasting holes in their own lines, total chaos. Then Lord Doldon ordered our own guns to open up, ordered the greater cannon brought up. Says he didn't know the King had forbidden it. Madness. Those men out there, on the headlands, the town, most of them were *our* men, Ladies. And Tarntown is *our* city. Those good people took terrible fire from the front and the rear. Michael and his riders were in their middle. Everyone here ran to the walls and the towers, some of 'em cheering like cursed idiots. But even at that distance, over the guns, you could hear the Vordan's shrieking. And I could hear another scream, I tell you. I could hear *Michael* screaming. Don't know how. It was like his scream and the scream of the black blade, like they were one and the same."

Kyla remembered this, even though she hadn't known what it was about at the time, a week ago. "A skirmish" Garen had told her later. "Nothing of consequence."

My family is killing itself. The thought came unbidden.

"When they came back through the catacombs, every one of them was drenched head to toe in blood. Everyone inside here was going crazy, screaming like demons from the walls and the towers, like they'd gone crazy with the dark blade's blood lust themselves, the whole column dripped with gore. Okros's coat was soaked through. And when he came back, Michael wouldn't lock the Vordan away. He wouldn't put it back in the vault. He kept the key himself. Master Falmon stopped asking him for it. Now Michael keeps the black blade with him always, always at his side.

"Next morning, Michael sent young Lord James through the High Gate. Gave him free reign to hunt the Queen's killer, told him not to come back without the assassin alive, in chains. Falmon and Ness, they think they might know who the killer was, where he hid. But I tell you true: that thrice-cursed dog, whoever he is, he is nothing to our young High Lord. You should've seen James, Ladies. His eyes were razors, high silver vest worn under travelling clothes, ancient pistol of the deadliest make. Garen gave him one of our last Pendants, a pouch full of coin, and a bag of his dirtiest tricks. Even Falmon gave him one of his own blades. James took a knee in front of Michael. Swore he wouldn't come back without the murdering dog. Swore he'd die trying.

"Then Michael called in Garen, Ness, Doldon, and Colj. We still don't know how the assassins got in here, see? Those five had strong words, they did. Completely private and none of them would ever let on, but Michael all but accused 'em of letting the killers in here. I was there, I heard it. Michael was in the wrong, but that didn't stop him. I heard it all.

'Where were your cursed men?' Michael asks Doldon. He's holding the Vordan, squeezing the cursed thing. 'They were there,' says Doldon. 'Why weren't they outside the door?' Michael asks. 'Father asked for privacy,' Doldon says. Colj just listened. The Tarn's defense and interior is Doldon's sphere, see? Then Michael asks Ness and Garen to explain how the killers had gotten in; when they had no answer, he cursed them, too. They all took Michael's rebuke, but you could tell it was hard. Now we've got Targeads on the watch, the best killers in the Realm. They won't get in again so easy. Curse me and my stupid bones. Not that it matters now. She's gone. The Queen is gone."

From the bed, Grandpa whispered softly: "It's true."

Kyla and Kate leapt to their feet.

"She is gone." Grandpa continued, "But we must not despair. She wouldn't like it." There was a long pause. Then his voice changed, became strange. "Is Tomas here with you? I thought he said he'd come . . . ."

Kyla and Kate looked at each other, confused, then they rushed to the bed, each to a side.

Grandpa was covered in blankets and furs. His eyes were closed.

And he looked entirely different, Kyla realized with rising horror.

She'd seen him about two weeks ago — but it was as if decades had passed. It was as if the High King of Remain, Bellános Dallanar, had been replaced by a dried-out husk, a withered doll made in his image. Grandpa's thick, silver-grey hair and beard were now white and thin. His once proud cheeks were sunken and hollow. Both of his eyes were bruised purple and yellow. His lips were cracked and dry. When his mouth opened slightly, Kyla could see at least two broken teeth. A thick bandage swathed his head, making his neck and face seem smaller still. He took shallow breaths, as if anything more caused pain.

Kate took one of his hands. Kyla took the other. His hand was bony and dry. Scabs and scratches marked his knuckles, blue veins running between prominent tendons.

"Father." Kate stroked his hand. "Dad?" His eyes were still closed. He didn't stir.

It was as if his words had come from someone else.

"Grandpa?" Kyla raised his hand to her lips, kissed the back of it. Bruno was at her side of the bed, up on it, sniffing and whining, his black nose wet.

Grandpa's eyes fluttered, his eyelids heavy and translucent.

Then his eyes opened, and he looked at Kyla.

His right eye wouldn't fully open; it was deeply bloodshot, hardly any white remained.

Grandpa looked at her. Then he turned and looked at Kate for a long moment, then turned his head back toward Kyla. "Kyla?"

Kyla nodded; her lips pressed tightly together. She didn't know what to say, so she kissed his hand again. His good eye searched her face, moving back and forth over her features. He didn't look into her eyes. Kyla squeezed his hand, fighting the terrible sorrow – the terrible anger – that threatened to come once more.

"Father . . .," Kate said again.

"Kate." He sighed and closed his eyes.

He swallowed dryly.

Then he cleared his throat, opened his eyes, and looked from Kate to Kyla, back to Kate again. "Kate, you're home. Home at last. Did you find it? Do we have it?"

Kyla's eyebrows went up. She looked across the bed at Kate.

"It's here." Kate nodded and reached into her messenger bag.

From it she pulled forth a High Cup of high silver.

Kyla recognized it immediately.

It was the Cup that Kate had retrieved from Paráden. The same High Cup that Garen had had in his study, the same Cup that had prompted parley. The same Cup that Garen had supposedly presented to the Lord of the Siege, Vymon Ruge. The same High Cup that Michael had destroyed.

That Michael *thought* he had destroyed.

Kate had been gone over two years to retrieve the Cup – or, more accurately – to retrieve the memory that the Cup contained. That had been her mission: to retrieve this Cup, to protect this Cup.

To protect this Cup from Michael?

For here the Cup was, yet again.

Had Garen even offered the real Cup to Vymon Ruge? Or had the Silver Fox known all along that he'd be met with betrayal from his own son?

"It's here, Dad," Kate continued. She pressed the Cup into Grandpa's bruised hands. "Michael drank from it. So did Doldon and Garen. So did Ness. So did I. It's true, Father. It's exactly as you said. He lives, Dad. His name is Christopher. He *lives*, Father. The last Dallanar in Alea's line—."

Kyla stared, her head spinning. "*That's* what this is? *Another* heir to the Silver Throne?"

"A *rightful* heir." Kate nodded. "A *neutral* heir, if the High Laws are to be observed."

"Ah." Grandpa sighed and closed his eyes. He held the Cup to his chest. "There's hope."

Gart stepped toward the bed, a clay mug held in his good hand.

Kyla looked at Kate, the import of what she heard dawning.

Grandpa's mouth moved soundlessly, as if he'd fallen back into a silent dream.

Kyla said, "You know Michael won't stand for it, Kate. 'Rightful heir' or not, 'neutral heir' or not, he'll have his war. We can't stop him."

Kate frowned, but Kyla could tell that she knew it was true.

Kyla continued. "I don't know if *anyone* can stop him. Nana is gone. We can't keep that secret forever. And yesterday, we killed thousands with a weapon no one has seen in millennia." She shook her head. "For Michael, there can be no peace. Maybe, if Nana was alive, we'd have a chance for diplomacy, some new treaty based on a just heir, a neutral outsider, fully supported by the High Laws. But now? How can we convince him? With everything that's happened? Michael won't have it."

"I've restrained him thus far," Grandpa murmured, out of nowhere, his eyes still shut. "Is that not so? Even though he has no talent for peace. Even though he forgets his role in the start of all this."

Kyla didn't know what Grandpa meant, but his tired voice closed her mouth. She nodded, almost to herself.

Kate turned to Grandpa and stroked his hand. Grandpa looked at Kyla, his eyes suddenly and absolutely clear. "Did it feel good to kill yesterday?"

The abrupt lucidity of his gaze, the strange angle of the question threw her off. "I — what?" Kyla asked.

"The killing." His gaze was razor sharp. "During battle. Did it feel good, Kyla?"

She blinked.

He continued, like his old self, "Think back on the battle for a moment, Ky. The mighty battle, the roar of the guns, the smoke, the noise, the dragons. Think about the excitement you felt, the joy of combat, the thrill of watching things unfold from your vantage, the pleasure of firing from on high, watching your enemies crumple beneath your aim, the *joy* of killing. Remember that?"

Kyla's face went warm. She nodded.

"Did it feel good?" Grandpa asked.

Kyla nodded again.

Grandpa reached his hand out for hers.

She took it.

He looked deep into her eyes. "Against that most ancient pleasure we fight."

He looked at her for a long time, then squeezed her hand. "And it will take all your cunning, all your resourcefulness, all your power to hold it back. It's a thing they never tell you when you're young, even as nobility. *Restraint*. The highest virtue of royalty, the most difficult use of power. But you see it now, don't you? You see it. You understand why we cannot continue this madness? Why it *must* be stopped? You see the real reason. Why we *must* try?"

"Yes," Kyla whispered. "I see."

Grandpa nodded; his eyes fluttered. "That's why you're the hope we seek, Ky." He held the silver Cup over his heart. He closed his eyes. "That's why it must be you. You will seek him out."

Kate looked at her. Kyla lifted her chin, but she didn't know what Grandpa meant.

"What do we do, Father?" Kate asked. "Dorómy went to great lengths to conceal this Cup. In the end, he tried to destroy it. He's committed to hiding the memory it holds. He's scared of it. He knows what this Cup means. What are your orders?"

Grandpa shook his head. "Dorómy's not scared of this Cup, child. He's not afraid of anything, living or dead. His children are gone; he thinks I killed them. The only thing Dorómy fears now is losing a chance for vengeance."

Grandpa's eyes were still closed. Then he opened them and looked at Kate, then turned to look at Kyla again. "Might

I trouble you for more water, dearest?"

"Of course." Kyla looked to Gart, who stood at the ready. He handed the clay mug to Kate, who set it to Grandpa's lips.

Grandpa nodded and closed his eyes. "Hmm." He was silent for a moment, breathing with difficulty. He opened his eyes, tried to scoot up toward the headboard, winced with the effort, waved them all away when they tried to help, then settled back into his pillow.

"Can we make you more comfortable?" Kate asked. Ness had come forward also, standing at the foot of the bed. Bruno sat at Kyla's side, his dark mastiff eyes bright with concern. Grandpa shook his head and said nothing for a long moment. Then he opened his eyes and frowned.

"What were we saying?" he asked. His eyes looked glassy. Kyla held his hand gently, gave it a squeeze. But when Grandpa looked to her, she saw no recognition in his face. None. She looked again at the mass of bandages around his head, a horrible thought coming once more to mind.

"We were talking about the Cup." Kate leaned over and kissed his forehead. "The Cup?"

"Yes? Well . . . right. That's fine," Grandpa nodded absently. "Fine." Then he shook his head. "I understand your brother's reasoning . . . . I must confer with him. Where is Tomas? He said he would come. Or Michael? Where are they? They don't come often. You must convince Tomas to come, Kate." He cleared his throat and looked at the clay mug in Kate's hands, as if not remembering how it got there. "A sip, please? Hmm. My thanks. Now—." Then he blinked again, shook his head slightly, and looked around, confused. He smacked his lips aimlessly. But then his eyes came suddenly into focus. He cleared his throat and looked at Kate. "You drank from the Cup?"

"Yes," Kate said, but she looked to Gart, then to Ness, then to Kyla, concern spreading across her face.

Cold dread threaded its fingers around Kyla's heart.

Had his mind been damaged in the assassin's attack?

She looked again at the wide swath of cloth wrapped around Grandpa's head.

Had they injured his brain?

Grandpa was nodding. "Thank the Sisters. You drank . . . and what did you see?"

509

"I didn't see things clearly, Father," Kate said slowly, carefully. "I did see the young man: Christopher Dallanar. But I didn't see what Michael or Doldon saw. Garen saw something else entirely. As did Ness." She looked at the old librarian, who inclined his head. "We've all seen Christopher. He does live. Yet we've all seen him differently."

Grandpa made to speak, but then he coughed. Kyla dabbed his lips with her sleeve. He took a deep breath, then took another sip of water. "That's better." He ran the back of his hand across his mouth. "Christopher Dallanar, eh? Not the most fortuitous name — but no matter. Perhaps the name itself is a good omen. Twice before, a High King with that name has been cursed with bad fortune. Perhaps, this time, the name will be redeemed."

Then Grandpa paused, nodded, and looked around — that vacant expression dropping down across his face. "Tomas has been here, then? Yes . . . yes. You'd said he had. And where's Adara? Where's Mother? She wants to speak to Tomas; I remember that she wanted . . . . He said he'd come. Yes . . . yes . . . . She wants to see Tomas, isn't that so?"

Kyla looked across the bed to Kate.

Kate's eyes were closed.

"Yes, Dad," Kate said softly.

Gart and Ness looked at each other.

Their silent faces spoke volumes.

Grandpa shut his eyes, nodding for a long while.

Kyla held his hand, her mind spinning.

Oh, Great Sisters, save us.

And then, just like that, he was back. "Not the best name — Christopher — but, yes. Eh? And you drank from it?" He held the silver Cup out before him.

"Yes," Kate said patiently. "We saw different visions."

"That's to be expected, these days." Grandpa nodded. "It's not the past we see in this thing — not memory. Christopher is alive, *now*, just as the Queen thought." He nodded. "Now, tell me: the voidling, Sles. He's dead?"

"Yes." Kate nodded.

"You're certain? Absolutely certain?"

"Both he and his kalaban are dead at my hand." Kate nodded. "And I took this, as you instructed." She reached into her bag, pulled forth a black, oval stone about the size of a robin's egg. She handed it to him.

Grandpa nodded, held the stone between thumb and fore-finger, inspected it, then handed it to Kyla.

The stone was cool and smooth. It reflected no light.

Grandpa cleared his throat. "It was Sles who first told Tomas of this Cup, over two years ago." He lifted the High Cup from his chest. "And it was Sles who told Dorómy of Tomas's knowledge – of that I'm certain." He trailed off for a moment, then blinked. "It was also Sles who stole the Cup from Dorómy using Fo Darrídan. And it was Sles who made Darrídan appear to be working for us, who maneu-vered Dorómy to try to find it. All with one purpose: to sow chaos within the Realm's ruling class, to weaken us from within, to further stoke the fires of war." He shook his head. "The feeble plotting of a dead race. It matters not, now." He patted Kyla's hand and looked at her. "We were fortunate that dear Tomas acted so boldly. Your father's heroism and sacrifice may have saved us all, Ky." Grandpa looked from her, to Kate. "I don't know how this High Cup originally came to be found, or whence it comes, but I do know that Sles's death was well-deserved. You did well." He squeezed Kate's hand. Then he glanced over at Kyla and looked at the black stone in her hands. "Give that to Garen, he'll want it for study."

"Yes, Grandpa," Kyla said, but she didn't know what was going on.

Grandpa nodded, cleared his throat. "You know, Kate, it was your Mother's plan to send you to Paráden. Not mine. She understood the full value of this Cup — what it could mean, the opportunity its vision could afford, long before I did. One last chance for peace. She gave me the credit, as always. But the idea was hers."

"I suspected," Kate said, something different coming into her voice. Kyla looked up, saw tears welling in Kate's eyes.

Grandpa nodded. "The rest of the strategy was hers, too. They call me the Silver Fox, but it was always her. It was her idea that your brothers be left out of the plan. It was her idea that you present yourself as a defector from our cause. It was her idea that you present yourself to Dorómy as a misguided child hoping to stop a war, fleeing her family on a fool's errand. It was her idea that you become a part of Dorómy's household, that you prove yourself loyal to him and to his claim. I didn't want to send you. We argued about it for days.

Finally, she said, 'This is what we've trained her to be, Bell.' And that was the end of it. And she was right, of course. Never underestimate the schemes of the High Queen. She did it. *You* did it, Kate. You found it. You brought it home. You've taken us halfway there."

Grandpa turned his head, looked at Kyla, a strange gleam in his eye. "And you'll take us the rest of the way, Kyla."

Kate, Gart, and Ness looked at each other.

Kyla squeezed Grandpa's hand. "Command me, sir." She swallowed. "What can I do?"

Grandpa nodded, took the silver High Cup in both hands, then held it out to her.

Kyla took it, looked down into its center.

The Cup was very smooth, bowl-like, and weighed almost nothing. And as she looked into it, shapes seemed to form, silvery blue shapes dancing in front of her eyes, her mind beginning to fall into it, stars rushing toward her. She blinked and looked back up at him.

Grandpa's eyes were bright, almost luminous.

"What can I do?" Kyla asked.

Grandpa nodded. "Dearest child, you want an end to this

as much as I. Only the Queen wanted it more, Kyla . . . ."

His eyes clouded again, losing focus, the darkness threatening to come.

Kyla squeezed his hand. "What can I do, Grandpa?"

Bellános Dallanar blinked, nodded, then shut his eyes. His voice was soft. "You can find a lost king."

74

IN HIS VISION, in his dream, Michael Dallanar raised the High Cup to his lips — and drank.

At first, all he tasted was puddle water, dank and cold. But then the water *changed*. It became metallic, as if he drank from a helmet of war. There was a chalky bitterness also, like powdered bone, a sweetish tang at the base of your tongue, the stink of charred flesh. He drank more deeply, and the water changed yet again, now tasting of copper and blood, now of honey and clover, like the most carefully crafted of cordials — at one moment sweet, at the next bitter. But always real.

Oh, yes.

Beyond real.

In his dream, Michael looked deep into the Cup.

And saw stars.

Rushing stars, everywhere.

He was pulled through them at incredible speed, racing faster than the fastest of ancient ships. The dungeon had disappeared, and all around there was nothing but the black of space, the milk of stars, and countless diamonds of light. He burst through a scintillating cloud of pink and gold, beautiful beyond all reason; he flew past a throbbing pulsar, flashing its signal to the deep; he raced toward a pillar nebula rearing white against the black, the stars forming in its cloudy head countless, brilliant eyes, the eyes of a great dragon, a white dragon that curled and grew . . . .

What joy it would be to sail this silent void for a time, he thought, to see all that the Great Sisters had seen, to sing the sacred songs of old, to sing the songs of travel and battle, the songs of space and memory . . . .

But was this some kind of trick?

Kate.

His sister's name came to him from nowhere.

She'd been gone so long – two years, too long. And she'd

returned with this High Cup and the memory that it held.

Had his sister infected his thoughts?

Poisoned his consciousness?

Or was *that* the true poison?

The mere *thought* that his sister could turn to treachery? That she could return after so long to destroy him? To undermine her own family?

My family is killing itself.

The thought slipped into his mind quietly, without effort.

And was that not the most lethal venom of all?

Doubt?

Maybe so – but to what end, this strange vision?

What memory did this High Cup hold?

An icy planet rushed past him, and he began to slow. A massive gas giant rolled by, orange and red and swirling, heavy with its constellation of moons. Much slower now, Michael swung down and around the fiery titan, guided to his left. There, in front of him, a fine yellow star burned fitfully.

He banked toward it and something caught his eye.

A small, blue world.

And something caught his ear.

A song.

An ancient song.

The oldest of melodies.

The singing world circled the yellow star, winking just inside a ring of debris, a silver-blue gem warmed by the yellow sun's glow. An old world, a living world – beyond ancient, a world whose life was measured in units yet unimagined by men.

Michael flew closer, and as he did, the world's song echoed through the void, a primordial horn, sad and powerful, a lonely war horn bellowing at the sun. The song pulled at his heart, and for a moment Michael longed to join that ancient song, to fight against the world's ancient enemies, to push its foes back against entropy and time.

And then suddenly – but kindly, like a gentle grandfather – the world's song came to him, reminding him of things he had forgotten, singing of his duty and his strength, his honor and his love.

You are powerful, the world sang. *You have only forgotten.*

Here, alive inside this ancient song, there was no need to hide, to be afraid, to stare into himself with uncertainty.

There is no need to retreat, my son.

In moments, the song reminded Michael of everything he had been and could yet be — strong, determined, and just. But more importantly, the song reminded Michael of his lust to fight, to win, to crush the enemies of life and love beneath his grinding heel! Oh, Great Sisters! There could be no defeat with such a song!

The song rang out, and Michael soared around the little world, like a trailing moon. Yes, the song was old, but it was majestic, the sun warming the world's ancient body, a mighty crown of spires at its head, four strange burning stars in its wake, comets with tails of blood. What a city that crown must hold! A shining capital of silver towers and warlords, ruled by a great Dallanar king! And these little red stars that trailed it? What strange power might they hold? What might they offer to this wise and ancient place?

Michael circled once more, closing further, moving through the warmth of the world's skin, a tingle of heat and light at the edges of his vision. And then he was flying over the land, a grey patchwork of ancient fields and silver forests, ruins and valleys, old rivers run dry. The world was ancient,

ancient beyond reckoning, but still it sang for its people, still it lived for its children.

And there below, Michael could see them – a scattering of villages whose denizens still cared for the world's arid lands and pastures. A dry farm here. A dusty gulch there. And ahead, the grey-blue walls of a city rose up, topped by the spires of a crown. But the city was small, Michael saw. Instead of massive towers, these spires were wrinkled and bent, some broken, no more than stumps. The world was old, so old; so proud, so huge, and so lonely. There could not be many of the world's children to tend his fire, to tend his sacred song. And without that ancient song, the four red stars that followed carried nothing but death.

Michael banked toward a maze of blue streets. Curved homes and boulevards shining turquoise in the yellow dawn.

A flash of gold and an avenue rushed up toward him.

A boy.

A young boy.

A young boy stood there in the avenue, in the doorway of his family home.

Michael could tell he was a Dallanar – he knew it the

moment he saw him. His hair was dark blond and disheveled. His nose was slender, his chin small. His eyes were very dark, a cobalt blue like the deepest of oceans. He could only be in his mid-teens, yet his eyes looked old and sad, the eyes . . . those eyes – dear Sisters!

It was Tomas!

Tomas is not dead!

His brother, dear Tomas, as a young man! Alive!

What was this memory, this vision?

"Tomas!" Michael cried suddenly, despite himself. "Tomas!"

But no sound came from his lips. Yet still, in front of him, he saw his older brother standing as if he'd been cast back in time.

It took Michael a few moments to notice the differences.

The wider breadth of the boy's shoulders, the tilt of the boy's head, the frowning brow, the strange darkness of his blue eyes. These traits were the boy's own. And yet, even so, the boy could've been Tomas's twin.

Then the boy turned to his home and spoke, "Thank you, Mother. Thanks, fellas. I'm off."

His voice was not like Tomas's either.

But to Michael it didn't matter.

And then, Michael was transfixed — transfixed with fear.

Cold claws touched his scalp.

In his mind's eye, he saw Doldon leaving to retrieve Tomas's and Eíra's bodies. Doldon returning, bringing them back. Tomas's face — it had been so young in death.

This Dallanar boy looked like Tomas at that moment, at the moment Michael had seen Tomas's dead body.

And then those four bloody stars fell from the sky. Dark things moved toward the boy, dark things from every direction.

No.

Not things.

Thing.

One thing.

A kind of slavering demon, gibbering and winged, terrible from the shadows, fallen like a red star risen up, the thing crawling out of its black egg, up behind the boy, hunched and hooked and lethal . . . .

Michael dropped to the avenue and charged, swinging his

sword overhead. His arm was a black, razor-tipped horn. The shadow-thing raised its sword, a mock salute, then charged with a shriek, and then it became a green-clad artillery officer from Gelánen, and they were on the Long Bridge, the soldier's eyes going wide as Michael cut his face in two, the Vordan splitting his smile, Michael singing a dark song all his own.

The thing could no longer hurt the boy!

Michael laughed.

Oh, the joy — the endless joy — of killing for those you love!

"You are safe, Tomas!" Michael screamed at the soldier's cloven skull. "You are safe!"

He was the Vordan.

The Vordan was he.

A living weapon.

And the Realm would tremble.

So Michael turned from the Long Bridge to the barbican and went to work on the rest of them, the scurrying soldiers that surrounded the enemy's gun. Great Okros was there with him. Okros understood. He crushed and tore and mauled, and when Michael leapt from the great bear's back, into the midst of them, the war bear went madder still. The enemy soldiers fell, screaming, dying, fleeing like pale insects, their faces white with horror, dripping blood, raised hands, supplicants, Legionnaires down on silver knees, Guardsmen, young and old, all died before the Dark Lord of Kon.

"Dallanar!" Michael howled as he cut them down. "Dallanar!"

The spray of coppery warmth – the elated slaughter; intoxicating.

Michael licked his lips, looked up at little Susan and young Tarlen. And smiled. Felt his lips pull back against long teeth. And then he was cutting Susan in half, the grey ropes of her guts spilling slippery to the pavers. He grabbed Tarlen by the throat. His dark hand was a raptor's claw, the boy staring at him with horror and confusion, the crunch of small bones. And somewhere, somewhere far away, Kyla screamed high in the dark—.

Michael's eyes snapped open.

Green shapes flew past his eyes.

Frigid sweat shined his chest and shoulders.

His bedclothes were damp with sweat.

His bed.

His bedroom.

The Tarn.

Home.

THUD! THUD!

Another knock on the door.

His bedroom door.

And it was not Anna's knock.

He reached for the Vordan. It was there at his bedside, its grip cold to the touch.

A cold that burned.

He brushed his fingers against its hilt, its black pommel stone. The blade stirred and moaned, like a lover wakened from a cruel dream.

It was not like other swords.

He almost laughed at the thought.

Oh no.

Michael had carried many of the Realm's most storied blades, and they were all the same: In battle, regardless of the weapon, a kind of holy fire would overtake his mind, the war field's fury.

But no longer.

When he carried the Vordan, everything was cold – icy cold.

And in that cold, a crystalline purity would come. A purity through which he could see and hear and smell everything with absolute precision. Even the smallest details were clear. When he killed with the Vordan, he saw everything, he heard everything, he smelled everything.

And he remembered all.

Another knock on the door. Even louder this time.

THUD! THUD!

Michael rose from bed, wiped his face, and lit a lamp. He took the Vordan in hand and opened the door.

Stephen Yates, the captain of his personal guard, stood outside. Doldon stood behind him, talking to a servant.

Normally, Yates was about as emotional as a stone, a ruthless rider and cunning soldier; a professional killer. But now he was worked up about something. Indeed, the man looked like a child on a birthday morning.

"Yates?" Michael asked. "Know what time it is?" He looked past Yates as Doldon dismissed the servant to whom he spoke.

"Aye, my Lord." Yates grinned. His canines were sharp. "The prisoner that Toller and his scouts brought in is awake, my Lord. You asked to be told."

"You've told me." Michael nodded. "Who is she?"

Yate's grin widened. It was the smile of a feral wolf. "High Lady Jane Taverly, my Lord."

Michael paused.

The import of the name swirled in his mind.

Jane Taverly.

Only daughter of High General James Taverly, one of Father's closest friends, one of Vymon Ruge's most trusted commanders.

Doldon stepped up beside Yates. Michael acknowledged him. His brother looked tired, but excited as well.

Michael looked from Yates to Doldon. "What would General Taverly trade for the life of his only daughter?"

"The location of the Pretender's Gate?" Doldon grinned.

Yates's eyes gleamed.

Michael nodded. The Vordan seemed to writhe in his hand. He looked at Doldon. "Did you wake Garen?"

Doldon shook his head. "I saw no need. Not yet, at least."

"Good. I'll speak to Lady Taverly first."

Doldon nodded. Michael turned to Yates. "Have her ready for questioning. Meet me there in half a bell."

"My Lords." Yates bowed again and turned to go.

"Yates," Michael said, stopping him. "What did Toller say about her, when he brought her in?"

"That he'd taken a prisoner. That he thought she was of high value."

"That's all?"

"Aye, my Lord."

"Toller doesn't know who she is?"

"No, my Lord. Don't see how he could."

"Who else knows that she's here, who she is?"

"You, me, Lord Doldon, couple of the wardens down there, Filip Toller and his lads."

"Let's keep it that way."

"Aye, my Lord." Yates bowed and left.

"Interesting news." Doldon scratched the side of his jaw.

Michael waited until Yates had turned the far corner, then he nodded. "Indeed. Dorómy's Gate cannot be far, not with the pressure Vymon Ruge brought to bear, not with his new arrivals reaching the front so quickly. If Taverly can be persuaded to provide proper intelligence, we could move soon, by the end of the week, even. We don't have Lord Jor's reinforcements. But most of our dragons are intact, and we do have an unstoppable new weapon."

Doldon nodded. But Michael could see something in his brother's eyes, something like concern.

A hint of impatience stirred at Michael's center, and he tried to quell it. The Vordan was cold in his hand. Within the family, Doldon was his most trusted ally. In a fight, there could be nobody better. They were more than brothers; they were best friends. More to the point, Doldon hated their uncle Dorómy almost as much as Michael did himself. Their positions were thus totally congruent.

"Something bothering you, brother?" Michael asked.

Doldon blinked, inclined his head, then looked both ways down the hallway to be sure they were unobserved. He stepped closer and lowered his voice. "Just wondering how you're doing, that's all. Haven't really had time. It got pretty close there."

It took Michael a moment to suppress an irritated sigh. There was no time for this. "Indeed. But we pushed through. And now we have this good news. It is time to act."

Doldon nodded, but then continued, oblivious to Michael's annoyance. "How's Anna?" he asked. "The Davanórians took it on the chin today. Over a hundred and fifty dragons and riders, dead. Anna lost——."

"She's a soldier," Michael cut him off. "And the enemy paid for it."

"Yes." Doldon nodded. It looked like he was about to say something else, but then he stopped himself.

Michael took a deep breath. He loved Doldon – he loved all of them. But sometimes, it could be maddening. "Out with it, Doldon. Yates is waiting."

Once again, Doldon looked down the hallway. "Some of the Davanórians are saying we suppressed the intelligence on the enemy's great cannon, their strength and placement. Zar asked me about it. Unofficially, privately."

Michael took another deep breath. "What did you say?"

"That it was nonsense, of course. But they do know we asked Anna to wait on her assault, to time it correctly.

There's a rumor that she ordered the Sundaggers and some of the other riders to stand down, to be held in reserve."

Cold fury blossomed in Michael's heart, but he laughed. "All these rumors, this cursed second guessing – *after* the fact, *after* I deliver one of the most crushing victories in recent memory. I wonder what they'd say if I'd lost?"

Doldon looked down at the floor. Michael was overcome with a sudden urge to grab his brother and shake his brains loose. How could he not see? The Vordan began to coo at his side, a kind of dark longing pushing through his hand and arm, into his heart. Doldon seemed not to hear it.

And suddenly, Michael was tired.

Just so tired.

He tried to take a deep breath, but it hitched in his chest and Doldon looked up, something like alarm on his face.

"Michael—," Doldon began.

Michael looked up. At his gaze, Doldon shut his mouth.

"Brother," Michael said. "There is much more to do. We're close to the end of this. I know you feel it, too. It's hard. There's nothing harder. But we can't wait, we can't stop, and we most certainly cannot waste our time listening to these weaklings who would idly gossip while the Kingdom burns. We *must* end this, now."

"Yes, Michael. I know, of course. I—."

Michael raised his hand, a dark kind of spinning coming into his mind. "Zar asked if we knew about Dorómy's big guns. Of course, we did not. But why don't they ask where those guns came from? Why don't they ask whence Dorómy recruited his battle mage? Our traitor uncle seeks aid from the darkest of quarters, yet *my* decisions are questioned, *my* reasoning is doubted? Was *I* not there, at the tip of the spear? Was my own life not forfeit to protect our people, our home, our family? I am no madman, brother. I never wanted this. I do not risk my own life or the lives of my men without cause. This is *war*. And it is *my* war now. And I will act as needed. We can have no doubt and we cannot wait. Great Sisters, how can this not be clear?!"

Doldon nodded, looked him in the eye, but said nothing. He looked like he was ashamed, and Michael was overcome by a strange split within his own heart: He wanted to hug his brother close, to tell him that he loved him – and choke the life out of him in the same moment. At his side, the Vordan whispered sweetly.

Michael closed his eyes, willed himself to calm. "Do you remember when we were kids, you were ten, I was eleven? Mother and Father had hired that sculptor from Aradan?"

Doldon nodded. "Tarana Glenfeld. I think I was in love."

Michael nodded. "You spent all that time, working on that figure of an ogre, a big warrior of Jallow. You built the maquette and got that set. Then you built the armature, and then you started working on the final piece. You were obsessed. I'd never seen you so excited about a project."

"I was just trying to impress her."

"When you were more than halfway done, you'd spent two weeks modeling that thing——."

"It fell over." Doldon laughed. "The table I'd set him up on had a bad leg. The whole cursed thing went down."

"What did Mother do?"

Doldon looked up at him; his eyes were bright. He cleared his throat. "She helped me start over, from scratch, got me back to where I'd been in no time. She . . . she was in the workshop as much as I was."

"She loved you, Doldon. She loved us all. In ways we could

never understand in the moment."

Doldon nodded.

Michael looked him in the eye. "And Dorómy killed her."

Doldon blinked like he'd been slapped.

Michael continued quickly, his voice soft. "Just like he killed Eíra. Just like he killed Tomas. Just like he tried to kill Father. Dorómy doesn't just want the Silver Throne. He wants the throne uncontested. He wants his family – *our family* – dead. So I ask you, brother – not from the heart, but from the head – from the perspective of cold, hard logic: What should our response be? Shall we wonder at Dorómy's intent? Should we wait until his armies have reestablished themselves here on Kon? Shall we second guess ourselves and our allies at every turn? Should we wait for the siege to resume? Shall we offer our throats to be cut, one by one? Or do we *fight*? There's no time for discussion, for delay, Doldon. Look me in the eye and tell me I'm wrong. Look me in the eye and tell me I'm a madman."

Michael realized that he was shaking, that his grip on the Vordan was almost painful, a kind of cold ache pulsing through his knuckles. And he was exhausted. He blinked. He was just so tired. He felt suddenly dizzy. And then he saw Mom on her bed, her throat cut, and a kind of low moan rose from the base of his throat. When he killed, he couldn't see her. He didn't want to see her anymore. He shook his head, tried to shake the vision loose, to let the dark thoughts come. At his side, the Vordan seemed to writhe in his grip, hungry once more.

"You're right, Michael." Doldon's voice came. "Of course, you are. You're right. I didn't mean to disturb you. I knew Yates was coming. Thought I'd see how you were."

Michael blinked. Then he nodded, put on his best smile, and stepped forward, pounding his brother on the back, then pushing him away. "I can always count on you, brother. I know that. Now go and get some rest yourself; you earned it. You even been to bed yet?"

Doldon smiled sheepishly. "Almost."

Michael forced himself to laugh. "Well, get going. I'll see you in council chambers at the seventh bell."

Doldon smiled. "Need anything else? Want me down there when you talk to Jane?"

"No." Michael shook his head. "I don't need a thing – other

than for you to get some rack time. I'll want to talk to Filip Toller sometime tomorrow, to hear more about Jane's capture. I think I have another assignment for him. But that can wait."

"Very well." Doldon nodded. "Tomorrow, brother."

"Tomorrow."

Doldon turned and walked down the passage, his wide back seeming to fill the hallway.

Michael stepped back inside his bedroom and shut the door. He sat on his stool, pulled on his boots and pants. Yates would be waiting below with Jane Taverly. He nodded to himself, then drew the Vordan from its sheath and quickly wiped the black blade with a red silk cloth. It cooed at his touch, so he spent a few extra moments on it, working its smooth surfaces from point to pommel stone. The dark stone did not shine, but it did feel good to clean it; it was about the size of a large egg and fit his palm perfectly – although there'd been moments during the last few months when he'd thought it had grown . . . .

Suddenly, Michael had never felt so exhausted.

Even more tired than a few moments before.

He shut his eyes and continued to polish the Vordan.

Perhaps, this new business could wait — just a few bells.

He was so tired.

We thirst. The cold voice came. *All of us.*

"I know," he said absently, forcing his eyes open. "I know."

The Vordan purred and swelled under his touch, its icy surfaces so beautiful, so cold.

Michael shut his eyes.

And then he breathed a single word, a single word not entirely his own, a word so soft that only the sword could hear, an exhausted whisper, a poem to a lover.

"Soon."

Epilogue

Deep asleep, deep in that glorious sleep that comes only to the truly exhausted, Little Dan dreamed.

And it was absolutely *wonderful*.

His bed was fresh and warm. His pillow was fluffy and clean. His belly was full. And he had his box. Yes, sir! Right beside him. It was the perfect room and the perfect bed – the perfect place for dreaming the very best dreams.

In this dream, Dan sat next to Stormy on a green hilltop under a strange tree on a warm summer day. A sparkling blue creek wound its way through the grass below, trailing off toward a little village, happy smoke rising from its chimneys. Below him on the green hillside, a herd of wooly sheep bleated; above, a little silver bird sat singing in the tree. The breeze smelled of hay and flowers and sunshine. Beside him, Stormy was quiet – at peace, at last. Every so often, Dan would reach up and give the big boy a little pat on his side. Then he'd look over the fields and let the golden sun pour into his bones and warm his toes while he listened to the silver bird's song. Did it ever feel good! Yes, sir! There was something darker over there, an angry thundercloud on the horizon, but it was a long way off. Besides, Stormy had earned this. It was alright to take the day together, to spend the time.

Dan sat with Stormy like that for a long while, until an ogre came from across the field and walked up the green hill toward them. It wasn't Captain Colj or any of the other ogres Dan knew, but that didn't matter.

Dan waved and yelled, "Up here, sir! Sure is fine! Yes, sir! Mighty fine up here!"

The ogre came up, nodded to Dan, and sat down on the other side of Stormy, resting his huge ogre elbows on his huge ogre knees. Then he leaned back and closed his eyes, warming himself in the sun. The big ogre looked a bit like Captain Colj, but it wasn't him. Dan patted Stormy, rested his elbows on his knees exactly like the ogre did, and enjoyed himself. It felt so good. Sun warm and bright against your face, the gentle breeze just perfect, the smell of green every-where.

"This sure is the best up here, ain't it?" Dan asked, keeping his eyes shut. The sunlight was red and warm against his eyelids.

The ogre didn't say anything but instead gave a deep,

satisfied grunt.

"Yeah." Dan nodded. "The best. The *very* best."

For a long time, they didn't say a thing.

Stormy didn't say anything, either.

Then the ogre sat up and gave a big, ogre-sized yawn.

"I'm tired, too." Dan yawned and looked over at the ogre. "I'm gonna sleep like a baby tonight, for sure! Are you sleepy?"

The ogre looked at him for a long moment. Then he smiled his big ogre smile, put his hand on Stormy's side, and closed his eyes.

And then the ogre started to hum.

The sound was low and deep, a big rumbling sound from his big ogre chest.

Dan blinked.

The ogre kept humming, not opening his eyes.

Dan sat there, looking at the ogre. Then he reached out, put his little hand on Stormy's huge side, bowed his head, and listened to the ogre's deep song.

There was something in the song that Dan recognized.

Something simple and pure and good.

Something sad and true and holy.

A song to himself, from himself, from his own heart:

Rest well, dear child, you have done your work. Tomorrow will come, and you will do your best. Have no worries, for you are true. In this land of dreams, you will always be welcomed, you will always be safe, and you will always be loved. Your song is no song of war or killing or blood, it is a song of peace and hope and joy, of green grass and tall trees and gleaming silver memories. You have earned this rest, dear child. Enjoy the calm. Enjoy it deeply. For you are true, dear child, you are true.

In his new bed, Dan nuzzled deeper into his pillow, a slight smile touching his face, sinking warm into the music's gentle rhythm, losing himself at last within the very best of dreams and the song the ogre sang.

Appendix 1

The Duchies of Remain

as Recorded by Susan Dallanar

High Lady Susan Dallanar composed the following list of the Realm's fiefdoms in the Third Year of Dorómy III, Founding Year 12,040. At that time, she was seven years old. Lady Susan's roster is a succinct account of the Kingdom's constituent duchies. Her record consists of a catalogue of the Remain's worlds in alphabetical order, organized by founding Great Sister. (All names are given in the Kingdom's Common Tongue rather than the duchy's local dialect.) Each entry begins with a brief description of the character and/or the notable features of the named principality. This is followed by the year in which the duchy was annexed (its so-called "Founding Year"), the number of High Gates known to have been established on the world, and the name of the duchy's then current ruling family. The colors and sigil of the current High House are also included. (While the illustrations printed here are based on Lady Susan's original drawings, they have been adjusted and cross-checked to precisely reflect the specifics of each duchy's coat of arms.) The world of Paráden is not included. As the Remain's Founding World, humanity's First Home, and the royal seat of Acasius Dallanar, it is the only world known to have been inhabited before the Five Sisters began their Great Expedition. Five High Gates were established on Paráden in F.Y. 1, by Acasius Dallanar. These five High Gates are the only Gates known to have been created by the Great King.

— Nordo Ness, Chief Librarian of the Tarn
Fourth Year of Dorómy III, F.Y. 12,040

The First Great Sister, Eressa the Lost
53 worlds recovered

Amágos

A world of vile pits, stench, and decay; violent hills and castles of iron.
Founding Year: 11; two High Gates.
Ruling House: Gokór.
Color and Sigil: A scimitar of bronze on a split field *(par fess embattled)* of red and black.

Anis

A world of frost with three moons of fire; the toughest soldiers in the Realm.
Founding Year: 21; one High Gate.
Ruling House: Kellson.
Color and Sigil: Three red discs on a field of pale silver.

Anótos

A world of dreams, dreamers, and magic; soundless, mystical, and enchanted.
Founding Year: unknown; one High Gate.
Ruling House: Wanten.
Color and Sigil: A silver crescent over a lavender mountain on a field of deep purple.

Asarnór

A world of clean, green waters and seas; glass cliffs, diamond shores, and scintillating coasts.
Founding Year: 12; two High Gates.
Ruling House: Moráldan.
Color and Sigil: A jumping, silver fish on a split field *(per fess engrailed)* of lime green and aqua blue.

Árcdoth

A world rich in gold, silver, and copper; productive mines and cunning engineers.
Founding Year: 5; three High Gates.
Ruling House: Dérenno.
Color and Sigil: A golden miner's pick on a split field *(party per pale)* of dark brown and dark tan.

Atlósios

An unsoiled world of green plains, vast trees, and windy steppes; home of the tree shamans.
Founding Year: 9; two High Gates.
Ruling House: Barnard.
Color and Sigil: A silver tree of many branches on a field of high green.

Batládea

A night world of thieves and assassins, bathed in perpetual twilight.
Founding Year: 27; three High Gates.
Ruling House: Torg.
Color and Sigil: A silver bull's skull on a black field.

Callón

A world of foggy swamps; low sad hills.
Founding Year: 1; one High Gate.
Ruling House: Veticar.
Color and Sigil: Two copper snakes entwined on a split field *(party per pale)* of sad green and melancholy lime.

Cathanósa

A world of turbulent storms; lightning fields of sparks and chaos.

Founding Year: Unknown; one High Gate.

Ruling House: None (Contested).

Color and Sigil: None. At least four "high houses" currently claim dominion of Cathanósa.

Colodóx

A near dead world; a ruined husk of blighted misery and sorrow.

Founding Year: Unknown; one High Gate.

Ruling House: Landown (Contested by Jahoryn).

Color and Sigil: A white disc crossed by a black sword on a field of red.

Danarcion

A world of orange and brown sunsets; the merchant's nest and trading center of the Realm.

Founding Year: 11; four High Gates.

Ruling House: Tacir.

Color and Sigil: A crescent harp of gold on a field of brilliant orange.

Dunsáor

A flooded world with eternal seas and oceans; home of the sea folk and their kin.

Founding Year: 22; one High Gate.

Ruling House: Garosh.

Color and Sigil: A silver sea-beast with eight tentacles on a field of deep blue.

Exarkiha

A world with deserts of obsidian sand; sharpest blades in the Kingdom.

Founding Year: 26; two High Gates.

Ruling House: Saan.

Color and Sigil: Crossed silver daggers on a split field *(party per fess)* of black and emerald green.

Ebum

A world of madmen, fanatics, and criminals; low, whispering hills; silent, cold mountains.
Founding Year: Unknown; one High Gate
Ruling House: None (Contested).
Color and Sigil: None. At least six "high houses" currently claim dominion of Ebum.

Egáton

The largest and most bountiful world in the Realm; a farmer's paradise.
Founding Year: 15; three High Gates.
Ruling House: Nelleron.
Color and Sigil: Crossed pitchforks in gold on a field of light green.

Egókontos

A world with ageless mountains of iron and granite; the most ancient forges in the Realm.
Founding Year: 4; two High Gates.
Ruling House: Von.
Color and Sigil: A jet black hammer on a field of pale grey.

Ekor

A frozen, barren rock inhabited almost entirely underground; home of the tunnel men.
Founding Year: Unknown; one High Gate.
Ruling House: None (Contested).
Color and Sigil: None. At least three "high houses" currently claim dominion of Ekor.

Escódon

A luminal world of eternal twilight; second only to Anótos with regards to the arcane.
Founding Year: Unknown; one High Gate.
Ruling House: Porró.
Color and Sigil: A silver quarter moon and two stars on a field of pale lavender.

Espónyo

A world with cavaliers and ladies; the best drink in the Kingdom.
Founding Year: 7; two High Gates.
Ruling House: Dontaigne.
Color and Sigil: Crossed golden rapiers on a split field *(party per fess)* of crimson and white.

Elágios

A world of song, dance, and merriment; the musician's haven; a world of eternal sunshine.
Founding Year: 15; two High Gates.
Ruling House: Zappata.
Color and Sigil: A lyre of white on a split field *(party per bend)* of dark orange and dark yellow.

Eupóseol

A merry world, with primitive shores of crystal and gold.
Founding Year: 16; one High Gate.
Ruling House: Lan.
Color and Sigil: A golden fish on a split field *(party per pale)* of white and green.

Eureok

A world with black seas, blood red moons, and vast, blank continents.
Founding Year: Unknown; one High Gate.
Ruling House: None (Contested).
Color and Sigil: None. At least eight "high houses" currently claim dominion of Eureok.

Evalok

A world of wind storms and typhoons; a tropical maelstrom.
Founding Year: Unknown; one High Gate.
Ruling House: Liau (Contested by Tak).
Color and Sigil: A black crane over a black mountain on a field of blood red.

Farámor

A world of vast, grey oceans and huge, grey skies; clever sailors and navigators; best boat builders in the Realm.

Founding Year: Unknown; two High Gates.
Ruling House: Hannér.
Color and Sigil: A grey kraken on a field of black.

Gellátek

A dying world near the Kingdom's edge; supposedly visited by the voidfolk.

Founding Year: Unknown; one High Gate.
Ruling House: None (Contested).
Color and Sigil: None. At least two "high houses" currently claim dominion of Gellátek.

Golladós

The frozen moon of a massive gas giant; vicious; last world to be reclaimed in the Founding War.

Founding Year: Unknown; one High Gate.
Ruling House: Svonsorn.
Color and Sigil: a white bear on a split field (*party per bend sinister*) of black and grey.

Gunorica

A world of huge, flat hills; huge, broad men; some of the best infantry in the Realm.

Founding Year: 17; two High Gates.
Ruling House: Yordán.
Color and Sigil: A dark brown war hammer on a split field (*party per pale)* of tan and crimson.

Hakonar

A world of savage, brutal cliffs and mountains; relentless, ruthless, and cunning.

Founding Year: 14; two High Gates.
Ruling House: Jor.
Color and Sigil: A double-bladed axe of blood red, lined with silver, on a field of black.

Helvanthíos

The high sky land of the floating folk; rainbow dawns and polychromatic seas.
Founding Year: 13; one High Gate.
Ruling House: Holte.
Color and Sigil: A silver falcon *(passant)* on a field of high blue.

Indónok

A world of razor blade storms; uninhabitable save the mountains at the southern pole.
Founding Year: Unknown; one High Gate.
Ruling House: None (Contested).
Color and Sigil: None. At least three "high houses" currently claim dominion of Indónok.

Itáteos

The smaller library world; second only to Genonea for the size of its collections.
Founding Year: 4; four High Gates.
Ruling House: Cuon Sach.
Color and Sigil: A copper chalice on a field of brown.

Jaga

The world of the snake lords – and their pets; pale green sunsets; eternal marshes.
Founding Year: 14; two High Gates.
Ruling House: Soness.
Color and Sigil: A coiled silver serpent on a split field *(party per bend)* of pale and emerald green.

Jun

A world of burning, dry, red sands; an untamable wasteland governed by violence.
Founding Year: 20; two High Gates.
Ruling House: None (Contested).
Color and Sigil: None. At least eight "high houses" currently claim dominion of Jun.

Lábbarkos

A world of strange animals, melted mountains, and ashen fields.
Founding Year: Unknown; one High Gate.
Ruling House: Vyre.
Color and Sigil: A black wolf (*passant*) on a field of dead grey.

Lythéntor

The mercenary world; a land of professional soldiers, scouts, spies, and saboteurs.
Founding Year: 6; three High Gates.
Ruling House: Rorvik.
Color and Sigil: A blood red, spiked mace on a field of white.

Marsinion

The land of eternal war; also known as "Acasius's Folly."
Founding Year: 2; seven High Gates.
Ruling House: None (Contested).
Color and Sigil: None. At least nineteen "high houses" currently claim dominion of Marsinion.

Mercal

A world of death, graves, tombs, and dark scholarship; rumored alliances with the Voidfolk.
Founding Year: Unknown; one High Gate.
Ruling House: Fando Myre.
Color and Sigil: A skull crowned in red on a field of black and mustard (*per saltire*).

Nelor

A world of green, soft fields; high harvests; honorable customs; "Acasius's Rest."
Founding Year: 15; one High Gate.
Ruling House: Nellerman.
Color and Sigil: A white lion (*passant regardant*) on a field of high green.

Norága

A world with a sky of a thousand colors; the nursery of stars and suns; once bred dragons.
Founding Year: 7; two High Gates.
Ruling House: Mong.
Color and Sigil: A golden dragon *(rampant regardant)* on a split field *(party per pale)* of red and purple.

Olóros

A world of pure white ice; blinding skies; frozen tundras and steppes.
Founding Year: Unknown; one High Gate.
Ruling House: Ty (Contested by Tuk).
Color and Sigil: Crossed black axes on a split field *(party per fess)* of grey and white.

Peléa

A world of hard warriors and sly slavers; steel grey skies and blood feuds.
Founding Year: 6; two High Gates.
Ruling House: Lessip.
Colors and Sigil: Crossed, curved falcions in silver on a field of iron grey.

Somákos

A world of liars, thieves, and assassins; violet skies and sunsets; four moons.
Founding Year: Unknown; one High Gate.
Ruling House: Bostrok.
Color and Sigil: A straight, black dagger on a field of bruise purple and black *(quarterly)*.

Swozox

A world with dark caverns of glowing stones and skies with dark moons.
Founding Year: 4; two High Gates.
Ruling House: Mordán.
Color and Sigil: A crescent in silver on a field of dark purple.

Tarcéron

The world of the flying cities; winged men of white and gold and copper.
Founding Year: 9; two High Gates.
Ruling House: Clarán.
Color and Sigil: Acasius's Star in deep gold on a field of pale ivory.

Terelag

A world with high brown grasses and deep, eternal fields; endless plains and rolling hills.
Founding Year: 3; one High Gate.
Ruling House: Xiang.
Color and Sigil: A golden stag *(rampant)* on a field of light brown.

Terótan

A word with twelve weird moons; bizarre, dark creatures unlike anywhere else in the Realm.
Founding Year: Unknown; one High Gate.
Ruling House: None (Contested).
Color and Sigil: None. At least three "high houses" currently claim dominion of Terótan.

Tóvonok

A small red moon, like a demon's eye; some of the cruelest soldiers in the Realm.
Founding Year: Unknown; one High Gate.
Ruling House: Xath (Contested by Modán).
Color and Sigil: A blind red eye on a solid field of midnight black.

Ugásur

A world of eternal forests; high cities of the trees; home of the tree folk.
Founding Year: 3; one High Gate; sister world to Ugátria.
Ruling House: Sur.
Color and Sigil: An oak of black on a field of silver.

Ugátria

A world with low hills; grey plains; dreary and primitive, but full of undiscovered secrets.
Founding Year: 3; one High Gate.
Ruling House: Gatron.
Color and Sigil: A silver-grey sun with seven rays on a field of black.

Ursobór

A massive and dark world; giant brown sun; ancient warrior traditions.
Founding Year: 12; one High Gate.
Ruling House: Anor.
Color and Sigil: A disc of deep brown, crossed with two blades in white, on a field of tan.

Wasondí

A world with caravans of spice, bronze, and sand; pale green moons.
Founding Year: 6; four High Gates.
Ruling House: Faraní.
Color and Sigil: Two green discs over a bronze griffin *(rampant regardant)* on a field of tan.

Wenevron

A world of ashy darkness; painfully grey and bloody.
Founding Year: 10; one High Gate.
Ruling House: Shakán.
Color and Sigil: A double headed lion in red *(rampant)* on a field of dark grey.

Zeloros

A burning world on the farthest edge of the Void.
Founding Year: Unknown; one High Gate.
Ruling House: None (Contested).
Color and Sigil: None. At least three "high houses" currently claim dominion of Zeloros.

The Second Great Sister, Alea the True

22 worlds recovered

Akrivor

A world of nightmare skies and demons, blood red suns, and warrior clans.
Founding Year: 7; one High Gate.
Ruling House: Tallyn.
Color and Sigil: A hawk's head in black over a disk of red, on a field of dark grey.

Albotos

A world with cool waves and sunny islands; an idyllic haven for hedonists and philosophers.
Founding Year: 12; two High Gates.
Ruling House: Bonón Tor.
Color and Sigil: A dark blue sea turtle on a field of silver.

Amá

A world of grey wastes; tough, melancholy, and dire; home of the beast men.
Founding Year: 40; two High Gates.
Ruling House: Konter (Contested by Dor).
Color and Sigil: A grey lion's head on a field of brooding black.

Amótros

A world with friendly hills, blue flowers, and a huge, silver moon.
Founding Year: 8; one High Gate.
Ruling House: Hylor.
Color and Sigil: A silver circle on a split field *(party per bend)* of light blue and deep blue.

Anortion

A world of hard edges and broad, pale mountains; great hunters, trackers, and scouts.
Founding Year: 21; one High Gate.
Ruling House: Maeleon.
Color and Sigil: A black boar *(passant)* on a split field *(party per pale)* of white and grey.

Anor

A world of iron hills and strong, stocky, broad trees; home of the purple dwarves.
Founding Year: 14; one High Gate.
Ruling House: Nor.
Color and Sigil: A broad plain tree in iron grey against a field of deep purple.

Asada

A world of smiling clouds and skies; a sandy, open world of merchant princes and traders.
Founding Year: 25; one High Gate.
Ruling House: Asanar.
Color and Sigil: A radiant, silver star on a field of brilliant, light green.

Básadon

A world with a wide archipelago; teal seas and shores; great beasts of the lurking deep.
Founding Year: 37; one High Gate.
Ruling House: Kerek.
Color and Sigil: A copper octopus on a split field *(party per fess engrailed)* of teal and dark green.

Brotunaeon

A world of volcanic chaos and lava flows like the veins of a molten giant.

Founding Year: 7; one High Gate.

Ruling House: Lorno.

Color and Sigil: A black mountain peak crossed by a double tipped spear on a field of orange.

Corícea

A world of honor and principle; fine cities and towers; the finest steel in the Kingdom.

Founding Year: 38; one High Gate.

Ruling House: Reneé.

Color and Sigil: A high silver tower on a field of clean, radiant blue.

Dalíos

The most tragic world in the realm, haunted by memories of lost loves and dreams.

Founding Year: 42; one High Gate.

Ruling House: Dalían.

Color and Sigil: A circle of braided black and silver on a field of blue.

Dalonás

A world with lonely, pale shores; seven pearl moons, also inhabited; intricate politics.

Founding Year: 39; two High Gates.

Ruling House: Han (Contested by Tros).

Color and Sigil: Seven circles of silver over a mountain of gold on a field of pale blue.

Ebavia

A world of fierce warrior women; fertile plains, fields, and streams.

Founding Year: 40; one High Gate.

Ruling House: Bavian.

Color and Sigil: Five crossed war spears in red on a field of dark blue.

Eborium

A world of underwater cities, island ports, and deep coral islands of glass.

Founding Year: 7; one High Gate.

Ruling House: Ebor.

Color and Sigil: Acasius's Star on a split field *(party per pale)* of deep blue and healthy green.

Ephak

A world with wide clouds of pink and gold; seas of grass; home of the roc riders.

Founding Year: 10; two High Gates.

Ruling House: Phak (Contested by Lenow).

Color and Sigil: A falcon in silver over a field of ruby pink.

Ferragias

A world with a mother-of-pearl moon; towers of light and diamond. Once bred dragons.

Founding Year: 23; two High Gates.

Ruling House: Jang.

Color and Sigil: A silver dragon *(passant)* crossing a silver crescent on a field of mother-of pearl.

Genonea

The world of scholars, philosophers, historians, and poets; eternal, grand libraries.

Founding Year: 22; two High Gates.

Ruling House: Scolum.

Color and Sigil: The ancient letter "A" in silver on a field of high blue.

Okógon

The land of the giants; vast mountains, deep rivers, and ancient seas.

Founding Year: 40; two High Gates.

Ruling House: Gorók.

Color and Sigil: A war hammer in silver on a split field *(party per pale)* of high white and blue.

Panávion

The Realm's only truly divided world; lavender skies and cities; land of the eternal men.
Founding Year: 15; two High Gates.
Ruling Houses: Jyran and Kylon; contested since the Founding.
Colors and Sigils:
House di Jyre – A circular silver shield on a field of high blue.
House di Kylo – A golden, double-bladed battle axe on a field of blood red.

Spárunok

A world of grunting beasts and brutal villages; a freakish, primordial hell.
Founding Year: 6; one High Gate.
Ruling House: None (Contested).
Color and Sigil: None. At least six "high houses" currently claim dominion of Spárunok.

Teládon

A world of high blue glaciers; deep, clean rivers and pure mirrored lakes.
Founding Year: 5; one High Gate.
Ruling House: Serán.
Color and Sigil: Acasius's Star in white on a field of glacial blue.

Yor

A raspy, harsh, barren, and hot world.
Founding Year: 10; one High Gate.
Ruling House: Krodan.
Color and Sigil: Twin, curved daggers in black, crossed on a split field *(party per fess)* of burnt orange and blood red.

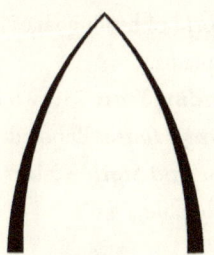

The Third Great Sister, Aaryn the Chronicler

14 worlds recovered

Abúcia

A world with rich soils, strong men and women, and dark, bountiful earth.
Founding Year: 10; one High Gate.
*Ruling House:*Ción.
Color and Sigil: An ox in white *(passant)* on a split field *(party per pale)* of brown and tan.

Dávanor

A world with high, white peaks, stony vales, and eternal forests; home of the dragon riders.
Founding Year: 21; two High Gates.
Ruling House: Dradón (Contested by Fel).
Color and Sigil: A roaring white dragon *(rampant)* on a sky blue field.

Dorn

A world with huge mountains, tan fields; strong and implacable; home of the iron dwarves.
Founding Year: 10; two High Gates.
Ruling House: Beln.
Color and Sigil: A broad mountain of deep brown on a field of tan.

Ethené

A world of healing lakes and trees; gentle farms and plains.

Founding Year: 23; two High Gates.
Ruling House: Benford.
Color and Sigil: A silver plow on a field of gentle blue.

Farák

A world of wailing winds and frozen rains; merciless and unforgiving.

Founding Year: 22; one High Gate.
Ruling House: Nyr.
Color and Sigil: A silver lightning bolt across a split field *(party per fess)* of bruise blue and black.

Gelánen

A world with great rivers, green grasses; clean, bountiful, and pure.

Founding Year: 17; one High Gate.
Ruling House: Julane.
Color and Sigil: A braided circle of white on a field of high green.

Horizon

A world with fine sands; wind farms; silk trade and unsurpassed hospitality.

Founding Year: 13; two High Gates.
Ruling House: Dallanar.
Color and Sigil: Acasius's Star in silver on a split field *(party per fess)* of high blue and golden yellow.

Ibittion

A world of madmen and lunatic moons; longest continuous High dynasty in the Realm.

Founding Year: 28; one High Gate.
Ruling House: Goylen.
Color and Sigil: Four crescents *(white, blue, silver, and grey)* on a field of black.

Jallow

A hard and honest world; deep lakes and rivers; mighty mountains; home of the ogres.
Founding Year: 31; one High Gate.
Ruling House: Dallanar.
Color and Sigil: Acasius's Star in silver on a split field *(party per pale)* of high blue and deep brown.

Kon

A world with icy seas; snowy forests and mountains; a world of near perpetual winter.
Founding Year: 9; one High Gate.
Ruling House: Dallanar.
Color and Sigil: Acasius's Star in silver on a field of high blue.

Pénulen

A world of gritty dust and yellow hills; low valleys of shame and hauntings.
Founding Year: 32; one High Gate.
Ruling House: Len.
Color and Sigil: A dog *(rampant)* on a field of dusty, burnt yellow.

Póntokos

The home of the star sailors; a world with rainbow river boats and prismatic sunsets.
Founding Year: 12; three High Gates.
Ruling House: Evenór.
Color and Sigil: A golden boat on a split field *(tierced per pall)* of red, orange, and purple.

Rigel

A world with platinum sands and lakes; fish of silver and gold and copper.
Founding Year: 33; one High Gate.
Ruling House: Ruge (Vymon).
Color and Sigil: Acasius's Star in brilliant white on a field of dark blue.

Sparáton

A world of stern hills and fortresses; pale, cruel warriors of the most lethal cunning.
Founding Year: 36; one High Gate.
Ruling House: Stenegard.
Color and Sigil: Two crossed scimitars of silver against a field of pale grey.

Utarcton

The Kingdom's prison world; a baked husk; completely subterranean.
Founding Year: 9; one High Gate.
Ruling House: Konnór.
Color and Sigil: A flat black key on a field of pale, lifeless silver.

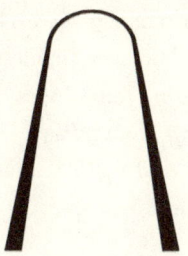

The Fourth Great Sister, Kora the Just

9 worlds recovered

Aradan

A world of soft hills and fields; flowers of silver, yellow, orange, and pink.
Founding Year: 15; five High Gates.
Ruling House: Aradak.
Color and Sigil: Acasius's Star in white on a split field *(party per fess)* of deep pink and gold.

Borádon

A world of violent caves; underground lairs of the deepest and strangest dark.
Founding Year: 27; one High Gate.
Ruling House: Rondan.
Color and Sigil: A battle axe in black on a split field *(tierced per pall)* of purple, red, and green.

Bentór

A world with eternal stonewood forests; towering jade peaks.
Founding Year: 13; one High Gate.
Ruling House: Kentón.
Color and Sigil: A green serpent wrapped around a silver mountain on a field of light green.

Kesst

A world of high waves; blue-green skies; eternal breezes; timeless sunsets.

Founding Year: 26; two High Gates.
Ruling House: Ruge (John).
Color and Sigil: Acasius's Star in silver on a split field *(party per fess)* of cobalt and white.

Nordán

A beautiful, azure world with an ocean-white moon and castles of cloud.

Founding Year: 16; two High Gates.
Ruling House: Dallanar (Dorómy).
Color and Sigil: Acasius's Star in ice white on a field of dark blue.

Nod

A world of black, wet jungles and weird, moaning cliffs; undoubtedly haunted.

Founding Year: 29; one High Gate.
Ruling House: None (Contested).
Color and Sigil: None. At least three "high houses" currently claim dominion of Nod.

Sodemar

A world of decayed cityscapes and skeletal, dark castles long since destroyed.

Founding Year: 26; one High Gate.
Ruling House: Sode.
Color and Sigil: A black tower against a split field *(party per pale)* of grey and red.

Selánon

A world of dread ice; deadly blue-grey glaciers and giant war-bears.

Founding Year: 14; two High Gates.
Ruling House: Jellenyr.
Color and Sigil: A giant silver bear *(rampant)* on a field of ice blue.

Weron

A world with high towers of air, color, grace, and clarity.

Founding Year: 30; one High Gate.

Ruling House: Weron.

Color and Sigil: A blue spear on a split field *(party per pale)* of high yellow and high white.

The Fifth Great Sister, Margot the Gentle

5 worlds recovered

Baleen

A world of dusty plateaus, faded trees, and leeched soil; all but barren.
Founding Year: 45; one High Gate.
Ruling House: Jomónoz.
Color and Sigil: A barren, lifeless tree in black on a field of dead grey.

Dayáden

A bountiful world with honey farms, cheerful winds, and sweet clover.
Founding Year: 16; three High Gates.
Ruling House: Dayon.
Color and Sigil: Acasius's Star over a field of sweet green.

Escena

The land of eternal night; inhabitable only at the northern-most pole.
Founding Year: 27; one High Gate.
Ruling House: None (Contested).
Color and Sigil: None. At least three "high houses" currently claim dominion of Escena.

Jenysyn

A rainy world; blue-grey; high cliffs; home of the best horse cavalry in the Realm.
Founding Year: 33; one High Gate.
Ruling House: Tworn.
Color and Sigil: A silver horse *(rampant)* against a rain cloud of grey on a field of high blue.

Targus

A world with nine quick, golden moons; skillful and sharp; home of the Guild of Assassins.
Founding Year: 19; one High Gate.
Ruling House: Targon.
Color and Sigil: A crescent of deep gold on a field of dead white.

Appendix 2

The Canon of Tarn and the Dallanar Monarchs

The Canon of Tarn—also called The Tarn's Canon and, less commonly, The Silver Book—is an epic prose work begun by the Third Great Sister, Aaryn Dallanar ("The Chronicler") during the Second Year of Alea the First (F.Y. 29). The descendants of Aaryn, and many others, continue the composition of the Canon to the present day.

The original copy of the Silver Book is located on the world of Kon, in the central library of the Tarn. It has been protected there (with two brief interruptions) since its inception. There are five other "primary copies" of the Canon—all endowed with unique properties. Three thousand and twelve other "official manuscript copies" of the Canon are known. Many of these copies are housed on the worlds of Kon, Genonea, Itáteos, and Paráden. Countless other printed copies, of various quality, are available throughout the Kingdom. At present, the Canon consists of 128 main entries (one for every Dallanar monarch) and well over ten thousand appendices that treat various heroes, villains, mercenaries, warlords, merchant-princes, healers, adepts, explorers, brigands, poets, and scholars. Also included in the appendices are stories that pertain to notable events in which otherwise unknown characters play prominent, if brief, roles.

The Canon is the founding literary monument of the Silver Kingdom. It has been considered a work of history, an epic poem, and a historiographic treatise. It is all of these and more. Throughout the Realm, the Canon is regarded as the foundation of a liberal education in both the practical and scholarly sense. To "know one's Canon" is a mark not only of basic literacy but also of cultural and historical fluency.

At its core, the Canon is a history of the Kingdom of Remain, beginning with the creation of the Realm by Acasius Dallanar and his five Great Sisters and continuing to the present moment. The Silver Book is constantly being updated, copied, and transcribed. It is a living, breathing document. The work is not precisely chronological (especially when the magical "primary copies" are "consulted") but, even in those instances, there is a clear sense of movement through time. While the organization of the work is bound to the reigns of the Dallanar monarchs, the Canon's sustaining theme is that of the Silver Kingdom itself. This is important to remember, since some scholars continue to claim that the Canon is nothing more than Dallanar propaganda. This debate need not be treated with much seriousness here. (Indeed, the Canon's accounts of Christopher I "The War Bringer," Christopher II "The Cursed," Simon I "The Silver-Hand," Michael I "The Peacemaker," and—above all—Hakon I "The Terrible," are so unflattering as to make any notion of royal interference in the Silver Book's composition near impossible.) The Canon does include accounts of the Dallanar monarchs, but those are hardly the full measure of its contents. Indeed, if there must be one, then the true protagonist of the Tarn's Canon is not the Dallanar family, but rather the Eternal Kingdom itself.

The Canon is divided into three parts: the heroic, the historical, and the contemporary ages. I have treated the debates regarding the nature and origins of these divisions at length in my *Introduction to the Study of the Canon of Tarn*. Although some controversy remains, it is almost certain that these divisions were created in the second year of Hakon I, by Hakon's Chief Librarian, Kator Xu. Academic opinion is divided on the reasons for Xu's move, but most scholars now believe (as do

I) that it was an attempt to mark Hakon's reign as the end of an era. In at least one sense, then, the Canon's organization is entirely arbitrary.

Two final notes on the List of Dallanar Monarchs, below:

First, Founding Year designations are given here for convenience only. In educated parlance, the dates in question are known exclusively by the names of the ruling monarch. Thus, Founding Year 10,315 (F.Y. 10,315) would be called "The Third Year of Michael I." This convention was dictated by the practice of Great Sister Aaryn; it has been adhered to here.

Second, following the murder of the Fifth Great Sister, Margot I, in the Third Year of Her Reign (Founding Year 45), all Dallanar rulers until Hakon the Terrible belonged to the House of Alea. Following Hakon's Purge, all Dallanar rulers belonged to the House of Aaryn. Since all ruling families, on all one hundred and four of the Kingdom's worlds, are of "Dallanar" descent, only those High Dallanar belonging to the ruling House of Aaryn now employ the Dallanar family name.

— Nordo Ness, Chief Librarian of the Tarn
Third Year of Dorómy III, F.Y. 12,040

The Dallanar Monarchs

The Heroic Age

The Founding — The Founding Monarchs

      Acasius I "The Great" or "The Great One" (01-27)
      Alea I "The Cruel" (27-42)
      Margot I "The Generous" (42-55)
      Garen I (55-67)
      Julia I (67-79/80)
      Adara I "The Kind" (79/80-101)

The Founding War — The Warrior Monarchs

      Christopher I "The War Bringer" (101-102)
      Poder I "Poder Jarlen" also "The Invincible" (102-109)
      Bellános I (109-110)
      Katherine I (110-112)
      Terence I (112-113/4)
      Dorómy I (113/4-120)
      James I (120-129)
      Jessica I "The Trickster" (129-131)
      Samuel I (131-133)
      Diégan I (133-167)
          — The First Peace —
      Emily I (167)
      Jordun I (167-169)
      Kelian I (169)
      Julia II (169-171/2)
      Korlen I (171/2-173)
      Katherine II "The Scholar Queen" (173-191)
          — The Second Peace —
      Jon I (191-192)

Derek I (192-193)

Margot II "The Strong" (193-195)

Samuel II (195)

Christopher II "The Cursed" also "The Blight" (196)

— Dawn of the Plague Years —

The Plague Years (196 - 10,211)

Also known as the "10,000 Year War."

The Restoration — The Avenging Monarchs

Marden I (10,211)

Jason I (10,211)

Peter I (10,211)

Heath I (10,212-10,213)

Samuel III (10,213-10,216)

Kelian I (10,216-10,218/19)

William I (10,118/19-10,222)

Jane I (10,222)

Daniel I (10,222-10,217)

Simon I "The Silver Hand" (10,217-10,245)

Jon II (10,245-10,266/7)

Peter II (10,266/7-10,278)

Margaret I (10,278-10,282)

Derek II (10,282-10,284)

Kendal I (10,284-10,289)

Jeremy I (10,289-10,298)

Hugo I (10,298)

— The Siege of Paráden —

George I (10,298)

Korlen II (10,298)

Gregg I (10,298)

Richard I (10,298)

Karen I (10,298)

Julia III "The Siegebreaker" (10,298-10,300)

Falmon I (10,300-10,301)

Susan I "The Silver Whore" (10,301-10,312/13)

Michael I "The Peacemaker" (10,312/13-10,349)

   — The Final Peace —

Peter III (10,349-10,367)

Katherine III (10,367-10,401)

Hugo II (10,401-10,433)

George II (10,433-10,458/9)

Doldon I "The Eternal" (10,458/9-10,519)

The Historical Age

Délen I (10,519-10,522)

Délen II (10,522-10,568)

Fen I "The Silver Dog" (10,568-10,590)

Samuel IV (10,590-10,604)

Susan II (10,604-10,616/7)

Filip I (10,616/7-10,643)

Peter IV "The Just" (10,643-10,699)

David I (10,699-10,717)

James II (10,717-10,726)

Marden II (10,726-10,744)

David II (10,744-10,825)

Alea II "The Virgin Queen" (10,825-10,868)

Terence II (10,868-10,874)

Roger I (10,874-10,901)

Kendal II (10,901-10,916)

Mikal I (10,916-10,924)

Xavier I (10,924-10,943)

Órtha I "The Explorer" (10,943-10,975/6)

James III (10,975/6-11,003)

Fen II (11,003-11,012)

Vymon I (11,012-11,045)

Tomas I (11,045-11,046)

Marcus I (11,046-11,058)

Peter V (11,058-11,069)

Deborah I (11,069-11,081)

Heather I (11,081-11,085)

Acasius II (11,085-11,110)

The Contemporary Age

Hakon I "The Terrible" (11,100-11,132)
— Hakon's Purge —

Michael II (11,132-11,146)

Dorómy II (11,146-11,158)

Jessica II (11,158-11,190)

Roger II (11,190-11,208)

Elizabeth I (11,208-11,222)

Kyla I "The Pale" (11,222-11,270)

Króan I (11,270-11,271)

David II (11,271-11,301)

Charles I (11,301-11,345)

Filip II "The Wandering King"(11,345-11,402)

Roger III (11,402-11,431)

Andrew I (11,431-11,467)

Peter IV (11,467-11,489)

Xavier II (11,489-11,520)

Hakon II "The Beast" (11,520)

James IV (11,520-11,534)

Délen III (11,534-11,572)

Sophia II (11,572-11,604)

Derek III (11,604-11,616)

Marcus II (11,616-11,660)

Marcus III (11,660-11,663)

Hugo III (11,663-11,687)

Susan III (11,687-11,706)

Tarlen I "The Finder" (11,706-11,770)

Garen II (11,770-11,794)

Orlen I (11,794-11,809)

Hana I (11,809-11,832/33)

Sophia III "The Deceiver" (11,832/33-11,840)

Sabella I (11,840-11,845)

Michael III (11,845-11,867)

Susan IV (11,867-11,884)

Filip III (11,884-11,905)

David IV "The Lonesome" (11,905-11,910)

Marden III "The Silver Shield" (11,910-11,913)

Timothy I (11,913-11,923)

Poder II (11,923)

Peter V (11,923-11,925)

Dana I "The Caregiver" (11,925-11,948)

Adara II (11,948-11,972)

Tomas II (11,972-11,996)

Balmás I "The Frail" (11,996-12,012)

Bellános III "The Silver Fox" (12,014-12,034)

Dorómy III "The Iron Lion" (12,034 – present [12,040])

Acknowledgments

Deepest thanks are due Cari J., Erika J., Erin M., Heidi G., Jaiman W., Jen K., Kari M., Kelsey D., Matt C., Nikoli F., Patty D., Robert K., Robert R., Ron P., Shell S., and Tamara W., for their generosity, criticism, support, encouragement, and faith. High Ladies and Lords of Remain, the Kingdom and its peoples salute you.

Extra special thanks are also owed to a tough squadron of young Legionnaires who reviewed this book at an early stage: Archer G., Gentry N., Lisa X., Thomas W., and Trygve R.. Let it be known throughout the Realm: The next generation of the Remain's elite fighting force is blessed with warriors of the highest quality—smart, dedicated, and fierce.

Finally, the Kingdom of Remain would not exist without the love and friendship of the following warriors and poets: Anna S., Aurora M., Cady R., Christina J., Darcie D., Eugene L., Jesse H., Kan L., Kelsey, D., Liz N., Elizabeth P., Mari H., Mark E., Olga P., Roger S., Ruth S., Tianhua X., Tom M., Travis K., William S., Vanessa H., and Zach F. I have not the words—so these, I borrowed: Πᾶς γοῦν ποιητής γίγνεται οὗ ἂν ἀγάπη ἅψηται.

ABOUT THE AUTHOR

Peter Valerianos Fane served in the Silver Legion's artillery corps for over forty years, rising to the rank of Peer Colonel under High Lords Bellános and Dorómy Dallanar. His most well-known actions took place on Colodóx, Batládea, and Ebum—all in the service of the High House of Remain. In retirement, Colonel Fane spends the majority of his time on the great library world of Genonea, where he lectures on military theory, ancient Davan-órian war poetry, and moral philosophy. He winters at his clan's hereditary estate on Egáton with his wife, his family, and a small flock of messenger dragons.

The Silver Kingdom awaits your thoughts regarding the latest tale from the Canon of Tarn. Indeed, Colonel Fane dispatches messenger dragons weekly to retrieve the latest reviews from Amazon and Goodreads, which he then archives along with other material from the Canon. So don't be shy—let your voice be heard. For the Remain!